The Hornbrook Prophecy

By Robert Wickes

First Edition

Oshawa, Ontario

The Hornbrook Prophecy
by Robert V. Wickes

Managing Editor:	Kevin Aguanno
Copy Editing:	Susan Andres
Typesetting:	Peggy LeTrent
Cover Design:	David Cortner
Photographs:	Holly Gardner
eBook Conversion:	Agustina Baid

Published by: Crystal Dreams Publishing
(a division of Multi-Media Publications Inc.)
Box 58043, Rosslynn RPO, Oshawa, Ontario, Canada, L1J 8L6.

http://www.crystaldreamspublishing.com/

All rights reserved. No part of this book may be reproduced or transmitted in any form or by any means, electronic or mechanical, including photocopying, recording or by any information storage and retrieval system, without written permission from the publisher, except for the inclusion of brief quotations in a review.

This is a work of fiction. Any resemblance of real persons or organizations to those depicted in this novel are purely coincidental.

Copyright © 2010 by Crystal Dreams Publishing

Paperback	ISBN-10: 1591463424	ISBN-13: 9781591463429
Adobe PDF ebook	ISBN-10: 1591463432	ISBN-13: 9781591463436

Published in Canada and printed simultaneously in the United States of America and in the United Kingdom.

CIP data available from the publisher.

To My Children

The Founding Fathers of the United States stated in the Preamble that one of their principal purposes in crafting the Constitution was to *"secure the Blessings of Liberty to ourselves and our Posterity..."* I believe, however, that recent years have rendered the *"blessings of Liberty"* for posterity very much *un*-secure. For my own, therefore, I was inspired to create this work:

For Adam,
a self-guided missile who has met
every challenge in life with excellence;

And

For Keith,
who has proven that the true measure of a person
is not so much defined by what they do
as by what they overcome.

Robert Wickes

PROLOGUE

Their Glorious Fling

> *"Do not the idler and the spendthrift know,*
> *even in the midst of their glorious fling,*
> *that they are heading for a future of debt and poverty?"*
> —Henry Hazlitt, *Economics in One Lesson*, 1946

September, 43 B.C.

The day was going to end poorly. Probably bloodily. For someone.

Summer was refusing to yield and as the afternoon sun beat down mercilessly the streets of Rome, with few exceptions, were devoid of life. The same could not be said of the steps of the opulent marble buildings of the Temple of Concord, although the scores of armed, helmeted centurions were barely more animated than the sculptures inside. Only the soldiers' eyes moved as they scanned their surroundings for signs of threat, while their ears were alert for sounds from inside, as it was from within that their services would most likely be summoned.

The rising of temperatures inside the building had little to do with the weather. The robed figures were speaking to, more often shouting at, each other as a debate raged back and forth over Rome's fate. Titus Pomponius Atticus stood quietly next to a slender fluted column near the entrance to an annex at the rear of the circular room. Although a Roman of the respected equestrian class, he was not a Senator, and his presence today was only due to the influence of his close friend who wished him to understand his growing frustrations with recent developments. Rome was the center of a great and powerful nation, but many concerned citizens like Atticus could see that discontent was again being sown by the aspirations of the ambitious and fueled by the politics of envy.

A small man strode to the center of the floor, and the Senators fell silent. To Atticus, his friend was anything but an imposing figure, as his high forehead, large nose, and small mouth were draped with an expression of perpetual worry. His formidable reputation as an orator, however, made his presence commanding. Marcus Tullius Cicero had for many years railed against the corruption of rapacious officials and the erosion of constitutional principles. He had seen his lands confiscated, had narrowly escaped death, and had been forced into exile all because of his opposition to those who would erode the freedoms of the citizens of Rome.

Atticus turned to look over at a small group sitting apart from the rest. The frown that furrowed the brow of Marcus Antonius, Cicero's most frequent rhetorical target of late, almost made Atticus smile. For Antonius, Cicero was naught but a festering sore.

"*O tempora! O mores!*" began Cicero, stridently. "Yes, what terrible times we live in! The Republic has exacted too much from her citizens and it leaves them poor. The people are reduced to begging for a share in the riches they see around them. Our politics have become merely a way to make ourselves rich; our votes are bought and sold."

As the senators girded themselves for another of Cicero's famous verbal onslaughts, he plunged forward. "A nation can survive its fools, and even the ambitious, but it cannot survive treason from within! Were we supposed to enjoy the highest position that the state is able to confer, and yet remain entirely oblivious of the national interests? Curse it! Do you have to be voluntary slaves?

"And the people? Duped, I tell you! They were made fat and happy with those ridiculously expensive *panem et circenses*. Yes, as long as they had their bread and spectacles in the circus they easily traded their votes and their vigilance, along with their liberties and rights! For *panem et circenses!* Caesar's actions were an affront to a free people! And while we may have survived him, you still will not learn. So I ask you again, O conscript fathers, will you rise up from your offices and tell the people the inevitable fate of Rome unless they return to virtue and thrift and drive from the Senate the evil men who have corrupted them for the power they have to bestow?"

Cicero paused for effect but a corpulent, balding senator, who had close ties to many wealthy merchants as well as to the new plebian landowners, interrupted. "Do not disturb us with your lamentations of disaster. Caesar was over-zealous. He unwisely took advantage."

Cicero summoned even more indignation. "Do not blame Caesar! Blame the people who hailed him when he spoke of the 'new, wonderful good society' which shall be Rome's, with more money, more ease, more security, and more living fatly at the expense of the industrious."

"As you said," offered another senator, "Caesar is gone, the danger past."

"We have only cut down the tree," said Cicero, "not rooted it up!"

Marcus Antonius had had enough. He jumped to his feet and strode forward to the podium where Cicero stood. An unnoticed lieutenant at the rear of the Temple stiffened as he saw the movement of his general. "Sit down, you bloated fool!" cried Antonius to Cicero. "This is the Senate. The law is what we make it!"

Cicero was outraged. "Do not advertise your ignorance, Marcus Antonius! Government is morally obliged to protect human life and private property, or else the people must expel the tyrant! To other men, the Republic may seem well established, but I am afraid of every sort of shipwreck so long as you are at the helm!"

Antonius was fuming. "Is it conceivable, O Cicero, that you remain so entirely unaware of how fragile is the hold on life for any person who opposes and obstructs the will of Rome?"

"I defended the Republic as a young man, and I will not abandon it now that I am old. I scorned the sword of Catiline; I will not quail before yours!"

"Your perceptions must be diminished for you to pursue so reckless a path."

Cicero merely turned and addressed the other senators, spreading his arms wide. "Perceptions? Perceptions, indeed! Do you not see that we are convened within the sight of drawn swords? Do you not wonder why the Senate has been surrounded with a belt of armed men?"

He paused, demanding by his look alone a return to sensibility by the Senate. "I implore you to be reasonable. The public debt must be reduced. The arrogance of the authorities must be controlled. People must again learn to work, instead of living on public assistance. Only you have the power to cure Rome of this disease. I only pray for this: That upon dying I may leave the Roman people free."

"Save your prayers for yourself," said Antonius who turned away, effectively ending the debate. Atticus grew fearful. Antonius had climbed over many bodies in his rise to power.

Bidden by an unseen signal, centurions flung open the doors and swept into the Temple of Concord, seizing Cicero and taking him from the building, his fate sealed by his own words. The centurion Herennius, acting on the explicit instructions of Antonius, cut off the head and hands of Cicero, and nailed them to the Forum Rostra. In the throes of the ensuing tumult, probably Atticus alone of those present remembered Cicero's last shouted question:

"O conscript fathers, is there no end to our folly?"

More than two thousand years later, his question was answered.

No.

Part One

The Effects of the Preceding

"The sober people of America…have seen that one legislative interference is but the first link of a long chain of repetitions, every subsequent interference being naturally produced by the effects of the preceding."
—James Madison, 1787

The Hornbrook Prophecy

CHAPTER 1

> *"Do we not see that noble cities are erected*
> *by the people and destroyed by princes?*
> *That a state grows rich by the industry of its citizens*
> *and is plundered by the rapacity of its rulers?"*
> —Desiderius Erasmus, 1500

All things considered, the end would come quickly. It would be shocking, but not surprising. It had been predicted more than two hundred years before. Analysts had seen it coming for decades. By the beginning of the new millennium, major national newspapers were trumpeting it in their front page headlines. And still no one did anything to prevent it…

Tuesday – January 12

The morning sun was as intensely bright as the air was clear and frigid on a January day a week after Congress resumed conducting (or complicating, some would say) the nation's business after the holiday recesses. A stiff breeze stood the flag straight out atop the Capitol Rotunda, and made the young woman pull up the collar of her overcoat and tighten the scarf about her neck as she finished a hurried note to herself. She hoped the tip was correct because she really, really didn't like standing here in the cold.

Superficially, it seemed like just another wintry day. But even the reporter, not so very long out of school, was astute enough to know that the entire character of politics in the capital was changing. All the rules, all the constraints, all the common sense had seemed to go right out the window at the end of 2008, when first one party and then another desperately tried to keep the nation's economic house of cards from collapsing. But their solutions had been political, not economic. Both parties found it more advantageous to point fingers than to admit they were equally culpable for the entire mess. Both parties seemed hell bent on spending the country into bankruptcy.

The Hornbrook Prophecy

So it had hardly mattered to her that the liberals were nominally put back in control after riding the 2008 wave of their extraordinarily shallow, but immensely popular presidential nominee, Winston Dillard, the Governor of New York. Although nearly every day there were arguments in her station's newsroom concerning the growing federal control over society and the economy through increasing taxation, regulation, and virtual nationalization of entire industries, she sensed an undercurrent of concern even by the station managers who were long inured to political mischief. Government budgets were exploding; deficits were astronomical; soaring debts seemed ready to buckle the knees of every level of government. The burden was onerous, the practice suicidal. And the mood in the capital reflected the rest of the nation. The people were not happy. The politicians were not happy. Something *had* to be done.

A large black sedan pulled up in front of the east steps of the Capitol building where the reporter was standing, and she held her breath. If she could get even a short interview with a major player her editor might reward her initiative. The door opened and two men stepped out onto the sidewalk. *Yes!* The woman forgot the cold in her excitement. She was finally in the right place at the right time. She watched them as they talked for a moment as the car pulled away. The two men were a study in contrasts. Senator Henley Hornbrook appeared still very much the former history teacher neatly, but not expensively, attired and looking average in all other physical attributes—average height, average weight, average mid-50s waist, wire-rimmed spectacles, and salt-and-pepper hair thinning in back but worn in more or less the same regular barber cut he had sported since grade school. The other man was his Chief of Staff, Lewiston Weiser, although she thought he looked more like a yacht salesman than a former international commerce attorney. Weiser, in an Armani suit, was an inch or two taller than his boss, but more slender; he favored vividly-tinted contact lenses which almost glowed from a face well-tanned from frequent tennis and framed by his neatly-styled shock of perfectly, if prematurely, white hair.

As the pair began to climb toward the building entrance, the reporter descended the steps to meet them, pulling her digital recorder out of her purse. "Good morning, Senator," she greeted them as they closed to about ten feet. But so deep in conversation were the men that they appeared not to have heard her.

"Senator Hornbrook!" she repeated more strongly.

Again there was no reaction.

"Senator Hornbrook!" she said in a particularly strident voice this time as she reversed her direction to fall in step with them. This time it penetrated. The men looked up, apparently somewhat surprised to see they weren't alone. She swallowed and took advantage. "Linn Benton, Senator Hornbrook. With WTOP NewsRadio. You've really been taking Senator Halsey Brownsville and even President Dillard to task recently. Do you have any comments on the Senator's new bill?"

"Why would you care what I have to say? Not just Democrats but many Republicans are supporting this bill. I am but a voice in the wilderness."

"That may be true, Senator Hornbrook, but your voice commands a lot of attention across the country. And people are more concerned than ever about the economy. Senator Brownsville claims that the legislation he is about to introduce will provide full employment and financial security for all, and that defeating it could mean financial ruin for the poor and the elderly. So again, Senator, do you have any comment?" She kept the recorder in view, but not obtrusively.

Hornbrook broke his ascent and slowly turned to face the reporter, one of the myriad clones of the modern, stereotypical journalist—young, pretty, sharply dressed, overly made-up, and, above all else, obnoxious. Choosing his words carefully so as not to betray his quickly rising emotions, Hornbrook replied, "I would most urgently suggest to the Honorable Majority Leader that he either defecate or arise from the commode."

Benton said nothing, sensing more sure-fire quotables for the noon news report.

"If he's got something that will do what you say, I surely haven't seen it yet. What I *have* seen is a joke." He took a breath, and gave her what she wanted. "For eighty years we have been unswervingly careening down the big government road to disaster. The wheels are damn near to coming off entirely while we pretend that make-believe paper money will fix everything. All those trillions we've spent and promised to spend so far have only bought a little time—and we're nearly out of *that* now. Unless we take immediate and comprehensive steps to reverse our direction, then while we *may* win a few more temporary moments of respite for a few small groups of citizens, in the end the larger war for our rights, for our collective financial well-being, and for the true security of our future will be regrettably, inevitably, and irreversibly lost."

"But Senator," the reporter persisted, "President Dillard himself is going to address the Senate on Thursday because he insists that the polls show that the American people not only expect, but demand that Congress enact this tax bill because, and I quote—" she said reading from her notes, "'—*in spite of our massive efforts to this point, it is unfair that they suffer unemployment and loss of benefits and services while business and the wealthy continue to enjoy windfall profits.'*"

Hornbrook snorted. "A definition of insanity is doing the same thing over and over and expecting different results. The President's proposals are indeed propitious. Right now the American people are being slowly strangled to death by the current levels of oppressive taxation and regulation. This legislation will be much more merciful—like a bullet between the eyes."

And with that, Hornbrook stepped past the woman and continued up the steps with Weiser, leaving her last question unheard. When they reached the door to the Capitol Building, Weiser remarked, "We should have detoured back to the office and taken the shuttle." They had attended a breakfast meeting over in Arlington with members of the U.S. Chamber of Commerce and had decided to forego the quick trip on the underground tram which enabled Senators to commute, out of the weather and in relative privacy, between the Capitol and their offices in the Russell, Dirksen, and Hart Senate Office Buildings.

"I can't imagine what that reporter was even doing there. It's not a regular haunt. Actually, as reporters go, she's pretty fair. Maybe she just hasn't been around long enough to be jaded. But I do know she'll be nothing compared to the flak we're going to get after Brownsville brings his bill to the floor," said a determined Hornbrook.

"Yeah, no kidding. That's why Dillard is going to introduce it himself," Weiser rejoined. "HB pushed it through committee in record time with Milt Freewater's help. They finished yesterday, and now they want to get it up for a vote on the floor as quickly as possible, and with as much public support as possible. There's virtually an identical version that they're gonna shove through the House, in spite of Sunny's best efforts," he added, referring to their friend and neighbor-Congresswoman, "but this is where they expect the fight."

"You're right," agreed Hornbrook. "Sunny said the House is virtually a done deal, and Veradale isn't about to let it get sidetracked. I expect it will be passed before the end of the week."

They entered the stately Capitol building via the northeast entrance and went straight down the hall past the Cloakroom into the Senate Chamber for some morning business.

Two hours later, they returned to their third floor offices in the Hart, this time via the convenient Capitol subway. No sooner had Hornbrook taken his coat off and settled in behind his desk in front of the tall, west-facing window, than his long-time secretary, Elma McCleary, whom Hornbrook had never seen in anything other than a dress and who changed her short brown hairstyle no more frequently than did her boss, came in with a fistful of messages and, without waiting for acknowledgment, pushed her horn-rimmed glasses up her nose and started right in.

"Senator Packwood called to confirm the meeting with you, here, at five. Oswego called and wants 'a few minutes of your time,' and suggested 12:15 at 1600."

"I'd like to give that son-of-a-bitch more than mere minutes," chortled Hornbrook. Stafford Oswego was President Dillard's Chief of Staff, and while everyone respected his savvy use of White House power, his overbearing manner and insufferable arrogance won him few friends.

"You also have the Eagle Scout group at 11:30 and —"

"You'll have to take them, Lew, since we ran long on the floor this morning."

"My pleasure."

"—the students from the National Young Leader's Conference coming by at two. Tomorrow night's the White House reception for the Japanese, and the President hopes you'll be able to attend, of course."

"Of course."

"Also, don't forget your speech at CPAC Friday. Reception at six-thirty, dinner at seven-thirty. It's at the Crystal City Marriott in Arlington. That's it for now," she concluded.

"Okay, thanks, Elma. Extend Oswego my most abject apologies, but if he wants to see me today, it'll have to be here, maybe about three. Oh, and call Brooks Gervais and ask him if he would like to join Loren, Mort, and me this evening."

"Will do," his secretary answered in her usual, efficient manner. She spun on her heel and went back out into the outer office, pulling the door closed behind her.

"Oswego's such an ass, and he thinks everyone salivates just at the thought of a White House summons, but screw it. If he wants to talk to me, he's got my address. As for this bill, HB expects to run right over us and, since the House version is essentially the same, they won't even have to go to Conference. Dillard will have it on his desk the same day it passes here," said Hornbrook.

The Hornbrook Prophecy

"But maybe lightning will strike and we can seriously deflate it or derail it before we're done. Lew, have you put the finishing touches on our amendments yet?"

Weiser plopped a thick sheaf of papers down on the desk, and handed an overview sheet to Hornbrook. "They just don't get it. We're drowning in red ink. You'd think it would have begun to sink in, after the last few years especially, that we're only in this mess today, needing something drastic to be done, because stuff just like this has been the rule, not the exception, for so long. A hundred different social welfare programs that have been eroding the economy for decades without really helping the poor at all. Worse still have been the billions of dollars that annually go to imaginative varieties of private and corporate business welfare arrangements. Except that now we've graduated to trillions. Good grief, Webster Dictionary even made 'bailout' the word of the year in 2008. The sorry thing is that even all those trillions were riddled with pork…and stupidity." He shook his head. "Anyway, here are the amendments, and this is the summary of the salient points our group has been discussing—tax and spending cuts, business credits, the Social Security option idea, and savings stimulus—along with the projections and comparisons of costs and benefits."

Weiser continued, "I've got to be honest with you, Henley. Brownsville *is* going to run right over us, and these counter proposals don't stand the chance of a donut at the Policemen's Ball. We're way out in right field on this one. Even many of the Republicans are supporting this, mostly because they think they'll get beat up in the next election if they don't look like they're trying to help. That stupid reporter hit it right on the head—the people *do* expect Congress to pass this, precisely because that's what been happening for the last five, or six, or eight decades, and precisely because they've completely bought into the idea that there's only so much wealth out there, and if Joe Sixpack is going to get any more of it, then Joe Champagne is going to have to give it up to him."

"I know, Lew. This bill is even crazier than all that 2009 crap. All that did was flood us with monopoly money. This is going to cut the legs right from under the very foundation of our system."

They went over several points that had arisen that they thought they might get some mileage out of during their rebuttal and attempts to amend the upcoming legislation. Hornbrook paged and spoke to one of his young staffers, who materialized a few minutes later with a tray from the small office kitchenette. He produced a small fruit bowl and some cheese for the Senator, and a ham sandwich for the Chief-of-Staff, along with a couple of cans of chilled soda.

They ate and talked, going over the notes Weiser had prepared, as well as posing some ideas for their evening strategy session with their colleagues. Promptly at two, Mrs. McCleary buzzed her boss and announced that the Washington state representatives to the NYLC had arrived for their introduction and short meeting.

After the NYLC students had departed, Stafford Oswego was ushered into the Senator's private office. Hornbrook was aware the short, squat, half-bald Chief of Staff for President Dillard only rarely ventured over to the Hill. So he knew the game was afoot. He was willing to bet Oswego had quietly alerted some of the press that an overture was going to be made today.

"Good afternoon, Senator," said Oswego, as he swept into the room and approached Hornbrook for the perfunctory handshake between two adversaries, nodding to Weiser who was exiting to his own office.

"Hello, Stafford," replied Hornbrook with an equal lack of enthusiasm. "Sorry I couldn't get over your way today, but…"

"Hey, no problem," the Chief of Staff lied with ease. He took a seat without invitation and waited for the door to close before he began. As Hornbrook resumed his seat behind his desk, Oswego continued, "The President asked me to talk with you before he addresses the Senate on Thursday."

"Of course he did. Not that he cares. You're not here just because you respect me ignoring your summons to the West Wing."

"Certainly not," the man said simply. "I'm here because it's a signal to all observers, especially the media, that the President is going to make every effort to enlist full support for the new legislation."

"Why bother? He has no intention of groveling whatsoever before an essentially party-less Senator who doesn't have enough votes to derail a toy train, let alone what will be another wildly popular screw-the-rich legislative juggernaut!"

"He knows you have supporters across the nation and he respects that. He also knows you will, of course, have some misgivings about the bill, but feels that the people are demanding that something be done to help them and that they want that something done now. This bill is the something, the President is putting a lot of personal stock in it and, yes, he knows he can get the votes to pass it. But to avoid divisive debates, negativity in the media, endless parliamentary procedural delays, and to defuse corporate resistance, he is prepared to make some concessions if you will let this reach its inevitable passage without undue pain."

"Such as?"

"The Columbia River/Snake River dam removal bill disappears. The National Marine Fisheries Services' shoreline management guidelines which you have been fighting because of the violations of the takings provisions will be withdrawn indefinitely 'for review and revision.' The transportation budget will see to it that the Sea-Tac Airport gets all the funding it needs for expansion, and the Puget Sound Light Rail system will get full backing. And, within limits, additional tracts will be made available for sustainable-harvest logging on federal lands."

"I see," was all Hornbrook said, as he leaned back in his chair, elbows on the armrests and fingers steepled at his lips.

"Senator, if I can be frank?"

"How refreshing."

"S.100 is going to pass no matter how much kicking and screaming you do. It'll be over before you can say 'laissez-faire.' Done deal. The President will get his way. But he feels the country will suffer if this gets all dragged through the mud, and he'd like to do what he can to prevent that."

"So if I understand this correctly," said Hornbrook, "all I have to do is be a good boy and keep my yap shut, and the President will give me plenty of re-election pork paid for with federal dollars he doesn't have now and isn't going to have even if he gets his way. Is that about right?"

"The President sees it differently," said Oswego sternly, his lips tightening for a moment, before relaxing again. "But he thought that would be your reaction. So he would like you to stop by the Oval Office tomorrow evening before the dinner to discuss this with you himself. Say about six-fifteen?"

Hornbrook knew he could get away with making the Chief of Staff come to him, but there was no way he could blow off a Presidential summons. It just wasn't done without getting castrated by the press. "Very well, I'd be delighted."

Oswego rose. "I'd suggest you listen to him, Senator. No reason to go away empty-handed, is there? Think about it."

He turned and walked out without further ceremony, filed past the maze of staffer cubicles and through the reception lobby of Hornbrook's front office, took the elevator down to the ground floor and walked out into the spacious atrium, where he found a small group of reporters waiting for him as expected.

The reporters, alerted to Oswego's visit to Hornbrook, were ready for him as he emerged. Several questions were fired at him simultaneously, to which he answered, "The President asked me to personally meet with Senator Hornbrook to gain first hand insight into the concerns he might have with the pending bill, *The American Employment and Financial Freedom Act of 2010*. As you reporters well know," Oswego said like he was their oldest friend, "lots of political maneuvering and speeches are just posturing for the TV news and the folks back home, so the individual can score a few points and gain some minor concessions to make himself look good. But in most cases, there's a lot of room for real negotiation and cooperation which will ultimately insure the success of an important bill such as S.100."

"Excuse me, Mr. Oswego," asked one reporter, almost as if on cue. "Isn't it a bit unusual for the President's Chief of Staff to visit Capitol Hill for such a meeting, especially since Hornbrook is kind of a maverick?"

"It certainly has become unusual in recent years, yes," said Oswego, agreeably. "But I'm here because Winston Dillard is a President who doesn't want to dictate from afar. He felt it was much more important to really understand the fundamental feelings and positions involved than it was to stand behind some petty personal protocol. He doesn't want to conduct business as usual, just because that's the way it's always been done. He wants to help the country."

"What was Senator Hornbrook's response to your visit?" asked another reporter.

"Well, you have to understand that I would not want to speak for the Senator, but he is an earnest and diligent leader, and I'm sure he wants what's best for the country. I guess I can say that he is taking the next step and has accepted an invitation to meet personally and privately with the President prior to tomorrow night's state dinner for the Japanese Prime Minister. I'm sure it will be a meaningful and productive discussion. Thank you all, but I'm afraid I must get back to the White House." And amidst a mild barrage of further questions, Oswego made his exit out of the building and to a waiting car.

After the President's Chief-of-Staff had left, Hornbrook shoved his glasses up on his head and rubbed his hands up and down a few times on his face. Lew Weiser poked his head through the door and said with a smirk, "Do you need the air freshener, Henley?"

"I wish that was all it would take. I'm afraid it's not over. Dillard wants to meet with me."

"He's got all the votes he needs, for crying out loud," complained Weiser. "Is he just putting on a show?"

"Probably. I should send McCall over to knock some sense into him." The thought made Hornbrook smile. Then, abruptly, "Where the hell is McCall, anyway?"

"He and Sunny are still out west," Weiser offered. "They're due back before the House vote. They worked on her House presentations all through the Christmas break."

"Life's tough all over," growled Hornbrook. "Vacation's over, too. Get him back."

CHAPTER 2

"Bring me men to match my mountains/Bring me men to match my plains/Men with empires in their purpose/and new eras in their brains."
—Sam Walter Foss (1894)

reezing to death is just not all it's cracked up to be, thought McCall. *Damn, it's cold!* He didn't much care that his discomfort was born of changes in the jet stream amidst yet another freakish fluctuation in meteorological patterns. It only mattered that the weather front had dropped down suddenly from the Canadian wilderness, causing the bottoms to fall out of thermometers in these snow-clad Montana Rockies. The air was so cold that the night's foggy mist had been turned into microscopic floating ice crystals which, he knew, would almost sparkle in the sunlight when the new day was old enough for the weak winter sun to rise above the distant crags to the east.

McCall spent no more time reflecting upon climatic mysteries as he stood as still as an ice sculpture because he realized that he must move soon before the metaphor became the reality.

The huge bull elk, head low as it searched for greenery, was now a mere forty-five yards away as it slowly high-stepped through the thick wintry shroud of snow. It would have been point blank range for McCall to fell the elk were he hunting with his customary old, but reliable Weatherby Mark V .30-06 bolt-action rifle, but this year he had been determined to spend his few stolen vacation days bow hunting as in his youth. Clutching his Realtree camo-colored Mathews Drenalin compound bow, arrow nocked, he silently urged the huge animal to keep moving, past the thicket of young saplings, into the clear.

Forty-five yards wouldn't be a challenge, but he knew that limited practice kept him from being comfortable at longer distances.. The demands on his time had turned previously inviolable hunting seasons into the rarest of luxuries. It was a bit of stretch, of course, to describe as a "luxury" the body-abusing, nearly life-threatening practice of standing stock still in sub-zero temperatures. But it would definitely be a luxury to have elk on the dinner menu again.

Patiently waiting as the elk slowly crunched through the snow, McCall tried to summon his rusty knack for ignoring the elements. The elk lowered its head again as it found a small treasure of surviving bunchgrass just outside the thicket. McCall slowly raised the bow as he simultaneously pulled back the string until his right thumb just grazed his ear lobe. Willing his teeth, knees, and heart to stillness he aimed carefully.

At that precise moment there was a loud buzzing noise from the right front breast pocket of McCall's parka. In a flash the elk bolted off through the thicket without looking. McCall didn't flinch and nary a muscle twitched for almost three full seconds, before he finally sighed and slowly let the bow string pull back to its resting position.

***

Sunny knew it was getting late. Looking up from the pile of papers scattered across the table and glancing out the window she could see the shadows of the trees extending forever, it seemed, toward the advancing dusk. She couldn't believe how cold it was outside, and she had spent some time after lunch bringing a new pile of seasoned firewood from the porch to stack inside. Brushing back a disobedient lock of her shoulder-length hair, she looked away from the window.

Her eyes scanned the interior of the cabin, taking in its rustic charm. She had no idea how old it was, but in spite of its rough features, the cabin had a comforting sense of strength and durability. The main living room was dominated by a huge, floor-to-ceiling rock-faced fireplace with an incredible, hand carved mantle jutting out above the fire pit and the raised hearth. There were the usual adornments on the walls—mounted deer and elk horns, a few fur pelts, and the like—but also a remarkable collection of local Native American art, tapestries, and fine crafts which lent the cabin a more refined atmosphere than she had expected when she and McCall had first driven up several days ago.

She stood up to stretch out the fatigue in her joints from sitting too long, and walked softly in her boot-socked feet the length of the room to the wood stove that provided the heat for the cabin more efficiently than the open fireplace. After pouring a cup of hot water from the pot on the stove, she sat on the deeply padded cushion on the handmade rocking chair, and let a tea bag slowly drift around her spoon. The lazily rising steam was nearly hypnotic, and she leaned her head back, eyes closing gently as she allowed her mind to slip back, embracing memories. Even now, after the years, the pain could still easily be felt. The pain of love. The pain of loss. She welcomed the tear at the corner of her closed eye—it was important to remember. Then, another memory. A better one. She smiled slightly.

The wood door of the cabin crashed in unexpectedly and noisily, startling Sunny out of her thoughts, and almost making her drop her tea. "*McCall!* Is it your life's ambition to see that my heart doesn't reach old age?" she shouted in anger, as McCall grinned widely at her surprise.

"Oh, Lucy, I'm hoooome," he pronounced in his best Ricky Ricardo accent, holding his arms out wide, and then ducking as a small pillow sailed harmlessly over his head.

"Geez, McCall, I'm serious. One of these days you're going to wake up and find that I poked your eyes out while you dozed with that dopey, smug grin on your face."

He walked over to her. "I *knew* you'd miss me." He took her hand, raised it up, and bent over it with great flair. "I beg your forgiveness, fair maiden."

Sunny whapped him on the back of the head with her other hand, then he straightened, and they embraced. After a few moments, she said, "Yes, you big goof, I missed you. How did it go?"

"I spotted a big bull late yesterday afternoon, but he was too far away to get to him before dark, so I made camp and picked up the trail early this morning. I liked to freeze my grits trying to get into position to get a shot, but I wasn't going to lose him. Unfortunately, I managed to catch up to him at probably the only place in the whole freakin' mountain range where I could get a cell signal. Just as I got set, my cell phone rang, the elk spooked, and I lost my shot. And after all that, the cell signal was so weak it dropped the call. It was Lew. Oh well, I'm sure he'll try again. The reception actually isn't too bad here at the cabin. Unfortunately, he knows that."

"Too bad. I like the peace and quiet for a change. We were lucky to escape for a couple of days even if I did have work I had to get done. But I'm sorry about your elk."

"It's okay. Tracking's the most fun anyway, although my elk sausage is absolutely *primo*." He kissed his finger tips with dramatic flair.

After retreating to the porch to shed his hunting apparel, McCall followed Sunny into the kitchen. He pulled out a bottle of Paraduxx, opened it, and grabbed a couple of wine glasses. "I'm sure you had tons of fun while I was gone. But here's the most important question."

"What's that?"

"When's dinner?"

"Maybe after you stop smelling like Tarzan after a hard day in the jungle."

"Yes, Jane." McCall took another swallow of the deep red wine, put the glass on the counter, and left the kitchen.

When he returned, clean-shaven and dressed in blue jeans and a tan chamois shirt, he walked up behind Sunny and put his arms around her waist. He nosed aside her reddish-brown hair and planted a soft kiss just behind her right ear. She giggled softly, and said, "MUCH better, Tarzan." Turning, she handed him another glass of wine.

He took the glass and said, "More? I'm not that easy, you know."

"Yeah, right. Actually, the alcohol will numb your palate and you won't notice how bad of a cook I am."

McCall inhaled deeply. "It hasn't numbed my nose, and from the smell of things, my palate's in for a treat."

They enjoyed a quiet dinner of spinach salad and beef bourguignon over noodles, as George Winston's *December* played softly in the background. After they finished off the wine and cleaned up the kitchen, Sunny switched off the light over the sink and the cabin was bathed only in the glow coming through the sooty glass door of the wood stove. McCall went over to the sideboard behind the old rocker, poured a couple of small glasses of Havensight, handed one to Sunny and went over to put more wood in the stove.

"Good idea, it's getting cold in here," Sunny said, looking up at McCall.

"Well, I'm always glad to be of service." He sat down on the sofa beside her. She turned toward him and pulled one foot up under her other leg. Sipping his drink and savoring the liqueur's sharp, tangy citrus flavor, he put an arm across the back of the couch and rested his hand lightly on her shoulders, mildly toying with her hair. Even in the near darkness, he was transfixed by her brilliant green eyes. She leaned into him and they kissed. For the second time that day, as if on cue, there began an insistent, repetitive buzzing sound from across the room.

"Dang!" said McCall. "You've been saved by the bell, my dear!"

"Shut up, McCall," she said, playfully whapping his head again as he got up and crossed the floor.

"*Fear not!*" he proclaimed melodramatically. "I'll get to the bottom of this!"

Crossing the room, he collided with a footstool hidden in the dancing shadows from the fire and exclaimed, "Damn!" He located his cellular phone on the kitchen counter, flipped it open, held it up to his ear and said, "McCall." He listened for a minute then said, "Okay, thanks." He closed the phone, and looked over at Sunny, disappointment on his face just visible in the flickering light.

"Sorry, Sunny, things are heating up. I've got to get back. That was Lew. They have a reservation for me out of Kalispell tonight, and—"

Just then, there was yet another buzzing noise, slightly different in pitch than the last. "Oops," said Sunny, leaning over to find her bag on a chair. She fumbled around in it, and pulled out her own cell phone. "Want to bet my vacation is over, too?" She answered the phone, listened and said, "Right."

Hanging up, she heard McCall call to her, "Going my way, good looking?"

"Yes," she sighed.

Sunny climbed up to the loft to get her things together and McCall disappeared into the small bedroom next to the kitchen. He was disappointed, not because of losing the elk and the quiet evening, but because he sensed that this trip might be the last for some time. He knew the country was in deep trouble. His last several years in the nation's capital had been like watching a combination of the Super Bowl and a horror film. There was a weird feeling that something big was about to break loose, but there was an equal sensation that it wouldn't be good. It was sad, really. The President and Congress both knew what the problem was. The President and Congress both had the ability to fix it. But they just couldn't. They just couldn't let go. They just couldn't give it up. It was all they lived for.

Power.

Chapter 3

> *"I am sure there was no man born marked of God above another, for non comes into the world with a saddle upon his back, neither any booted and spurred to ride him."*
> —Richard Rumbold, 1679, in his scaffold speech

Wednesday – January 13

Winston Dillard sat behind the huge desk in the Oval Office, as the First Lady helped him go over his remarks before the reception for the Japanese Prime Minister. Dillard was a politician because, as he had often thought to himself, *it was the easiest, most powerful, goddamned best job on the face of the planet.* There was simply no other way to put it. And it didn't matter to which office you had been elected. He had learned at an early age that it was way more fun to tell other people what to do than either to do it yourself, or, God forbid, to be the one being *told* what to do. You didn't have to be brilliant, you didn't have to have any great fundamental philosophical convictions, and you didn't really have to do much work—at least *he* didn't, once he learned how to work the angles. All you had to do was get one more voter to like *you* than liked the other guy, and you were in! And getting people to like Winston Dillard was easier than getting people to like chocolate. It just didn't take any effort at all.

He recalled clearly the day in high school in Rochester, New York, when it had first started. He had wanted to impress one of the cheerleaders so he could get her to go out on a date with him. He hadn't worked hard enough to have great grades, and he hated sports, so he ran for student body president. The other candidate had a real, honest-to-goodness platform, with lots of ideas about student activities, class schedules, extracurricular events, community service, and more; Dillard simply smiled a lot, studied the yearbook so he could call everyone he met by their first name, acted like he was everybody's best friend, and promised to improve the food in the cafeteria. His got his first political victory and it wasn't even close.

He'd loved the feel of it, all of it, even then—being in charge over the other students, waving at the crowd at assemblies, the deferential attitudes of the teachers, even a reserved spot at the football games (which he would never have bothered to attend if it were not for his new cheerleader girlfriend) all served to stimulate him. He knew before he graduated that he wanted to be a politician forever. He didn't have any particular manifesto; there were no particular ills of the world he wanted to cure; he actually didn't much even care about the people who might elect him. It was just that he couldn't imagine any other way to get such a rush out of life. And so he pursued it with zeal.

He went to college mostly because it was a necessary credential to have. It wasn't as though college would make someone a good leader, it was just that most people expected their elected representatives to be college grads. He had gone to Syracuse University where he studied psychology (naturally) and then, again because of the credentials it bestowed, to Yale for law school. He graduated near the bottom of his class, but mostly because he only studied enough to get by. He knew that on the campaign trail no one was going to ask to see his GPA.

"Best idea I ever had, Flo," said Dillard.

"What was?" said his wife without looking up from her notes.

"Going to Yale wasn't just a good career move. No Yale would have meant no Florence."

She just smiled. "I didn't realize the President of the United States was so sentimental." But she liked his words. Although he had successfully entertained an endless parade of attractive co-eds at Syracuse, he became fascinated with Florence when he met her in a Yale contract law class. It certainly was not because of her rather plain looks, but because he had never met anyone who was so passionate about her beliefs. Sure, she had a lot of crazy ideas about Karl Marx and the evils of businesses, but her fervor was contagious. To some extent she filled a void in his psyche. He had never adopted any particular political ideology, and he often found himself being swept along by the strength of her emotions.

"We've helped each other, Win," she added, knowing he always enjoyed the stroking. Her own dream had been to one day transform her beliefs into action, but she had never considered herself personally very, well, electable. She annoyed people too easily. Neither of them had known early in their relationship that he would someday actually be able to help her overcome her perceived personal shortcoming.

Dillard had wasted no time after graduation from Yale. He had barely joined a mid-sized New York law firm when he threw his hat in the ring for one of the ten seats representing the Manhattan borough on the New York city council. He soon discovered, however, that he needed more than a smile and a promise to convince New Yorkers to vote for him, and he lost the race by a wide margin. Utterly dejected and depressed after his failure to achieve even the relatively modest first step of a ladder which he had for so long aspired to climb, he eventually called Florence, who was working in a Boston firm, looking for sympathy. She drove down to New York the following weekend, and they talked for two days. At least *she* talked for two days. When she left, his confidence and his determination had returned.

A year later, a repackaged, aggressive Dillard candidacy emerged and swept an election for one of the fourteen Queens borough seats, representing the region he and Florence had found to have the best demographics for the type of campaign he'd wished to run. It was basic math: There were more voters in that district who had *little* than there were voters who had *a lot*, so he went after the numbers, mostly by asking every voter he talked to what they needed most and then promising them that he was the one who could give it to them.

He was almost surprised by how easily he was elected. During his term, any time he was asked about the things he had promised but had failed to deliver, he would merely blame the opposition on the council. *I tried my hardest, but others on the council just didn't care as much as I did*, he would tell them. His constituents simply didn't have the time or the inclination to check his story.

His marriage to Florence a year later might have seemed an unusual union to outside observers, but they had become perfect complements for each other.

He patiently served five years on the city council before running for Mayor of New York and, by winning, becoming the youngest mayor ever in the Big Apple. He had barely passed the mid point of his term as mayor when he cast an eye toward the governorship. With the help of a few of his closest friends who were part of his mayoral administration, he began to selectively seek wider opportunities to be seen and heard about the state. Invitations were garnered to speak at conventions, holiday events, and commencement exercises that took place in all parts of upstate New York. Leaders of other New York cities were pleasantly surprised to have the mayor of the largest city willing to hold meetings in *their* cities to discuss issues of mutual interest, such as transportation, crime and police policy, education, infrastructure, public health, and the like. Each occasion was orchestrated to permit "spontaneous" additional opportunities to learn about the problems and challenges facing the other municipalities, and he made countless visits to schools, hospitals, service clubs, and union meetings where those present were left with the undeniable impression that here was a man who, in spite of all the problems he faced in one of the most complicated urban areas in the world, was willing, even eager, to listen to their own difficulties and concerns.

The press, well aware of the implications of a state-traveling city leader, covered the events with glowing reviews as if in partnership with an obviously ambitious mayor. And their eagerness to please was rewarded by an unprecedented open-door policy for the press at City Hall.

When the actual gubernatorial election season rolled around, it had become a forgone conclusion that he would carry the banner for his party, and pity the poor fellow that was put on the chopping block to oppose him. He had done his homework carefully, under the constant direction of Florence, and the rest was simple. All he had to do was just follow a variation on an old technique—smile a lot, be everybody's best friend and, in one form or another, promise to "improve the food in the cafeteria."

Dillard actually found that being Governor of New York was easier than being mayor of New York City, where there were very few good things that happened to provide relief from the constant onslaught of problems faced by more than eight million people all living in the same cage. One thing was certainly true—he still loved to be loved. Unlike many others who sought to change the world, and who saw political office as a means to that end, for Dillard being elected *was* the end. "Who cares," he once remarked privately to Florence, "if the rats are winning the rat race." His wife had just smiled; she had her own agenda.

Toward the end of his second year as governor, Florence sat down at the breakfast table one morning and, without preliminary, said, "Win, the national convention is in Boston next year, and we need to get you to be the keynoter."

"Pray tell, why?" he asked, as he looked up from the morning's *New York Times*, which he was scanning without great interest as he held it over his bowl of frosted flakes, a meal seemingly out of place in the stately Governor's mansion perched above the Hudson River in Albany.

"God, isn't it obvious?" She often acted more like his stern mother than a loving spouse when they were alone. "Our party lost the White House in 2000, because Clinton left too much baggage behind and Gore was about as dynamic as a tree stump. Those damn terrorists will probably make it impossible to beat George W. this time even though he's clearly incompetent. But we'll never get back on top with the has-beens who are running the party right now. What our party's going to need *five* years from now is a fresh, new, exciting, dynamite candidate."

"Me?" he asked, somewhat disbelievingly.

"Of course! What the hell else do you think I've, I mean *we've*, been working toward all these years?" Florence sat down in the bow-back chair next to him, forcing him to abandon both his paper and his cereal for the moment. She looked him squarely in the eye and began to tick off, for the first time for him, the outline of her ultimate plans. "You'll be the answer to the party's dreams—young, attractive, popular, good demographics, a good resume with lots of experience, no obvious flaws—at least none that have gotten out. Plus, you start with 33 electoral votes in your hand and the press in your pocket. What more could the party—and the contributors—want? All you need is a little more national exposure between now and then, and what better place to start than as one of the focal points of the national convention? Who cares if they lose the election? It'll be better if they do—then we don't have an incumbent from our own party in our way the next time around.

"Now," she continued in a business-like manner, "you've got a tremendous relationship with Biggs Wasco's national longshoremen's union and all we need to do is use him to put a bug in Stafford Oswego's ear, since he's the new national party chair. I happen to know Wasco'll be in the city tomorrow, taking care of the last of the negotiations on a new city contract. I'll give him a call today before he leaves Montgomery, and set up a time." She grabbed the small note pad and pen which were always on the table and wrote herself a short note.

"Fine," said Dillard, already fully accepting the new scenario. He had unquestioningly accepted his wife's guidance for the last twelve years, and had known nothing but success. So if she thought he was ready to be the Big Crapola, then he was. Simple as that. *God*, he thought fleetingly, allowing a small smile to cross his face, *the whole world kisses ass to the President of the United States.*

"In that case," he suggested, "I think it might be time to give Dumb-Ass a call over at BSN."

"Absolutely!" exclaimed Florence. The real name of the weekend anchor for Broadcast Systems Network, the nation's newest TV news network, was Garrison Dumfries, but his name and personality had led easily to the nickname Dillard often used for him behind his back. Helped in large part by some inside information Dillard had leaked to him as New York mayor (and not bothering to ask how Dillard knew) Dumfries had broken a story about one of Dillard's council opponents' alleged involvement in a drug deal, and then ridden the journalistic fame to become a rising star for a new network that itself had adopted such a sensationalistic style that it was frequently referred to not as *BSN, the Nation's Network*, but as *The BS Network*. "Definitely give him a call. He's such a lap dog, I can't believe he's gotten this far in broadcasting. But, it's a good idea. He'll probably be on the phone to Oswego as soon as you hang up."

The next five years played out almost exactly as they planned. The only unexpected development was the accidental death of New York's junior U.S. Senator, which opened an unanticipated door for Florence's suppressed political aspirations. Disregarding the objections of the other party, her popular Governor-husband appointed Florence to fill the Senate vacancy and she suddenly found herself on the inside of the nation's power circle instead of having to be satisfied solely with the vicarious role of devoted spouse. Dillard gave a rousing keynote address at the 2004 convention, while the party's nominee, John Kerry, could not inspire enough voters in November to overcome even a war-wearied Bush. Four years later, with the added benefit of his wife's skillful lobbying, Dillard himself wrested the presidential nomination away from more established candidates because his party was desperate for an apparently centrist candidate who could radiate confidence and instill hopefulness. He then won the ensuing election and swept into office with his own party still strongly controlling both houses in Congress. It had been easy to promise peace to voters tired of military news and to cast blame on the lame duck administration saddled with an economy that had been kept afloat with massive borrowing and deficit spending.

On his first night as President, returning from a long evening of inaugural balls and uncountable numbers of congratulatory handshakes, he entered the private quarters of the First Family, strode out onto the balcony overlooking the Washington Monument, and took in the magnificent Capitol panorama. He then proclaimed out loud to no one, *"This is going to be the easiest, most powerful, goddamned best job on the face of the planet!"*

After nearly a full year in office, Winston Dillard no longer spent any time wandering around relishing his own presence in the impressive, historic center of the Free World, as he had after he was first elected. But he still savored the respect he commanded and the deference others gave him, so when his secretary buzzed and announced the arrival of his next visitors, he smiled. He summoned, and they came. Anyone. Including his political enemies. "Well, Flo, I guess it's time to play President."

The First Lady/Senator snorted and stood up. "Have fun, Win. Especially with HIM."

"I'm looking forward to it. See you later." Dillard watched the door close behind her just as another opened. Stafford Oswego came in with Henley Hornbrook close behind. The President rose and smiled. "Good evening, Senator. I'm glad you could come." *As if he had a choice,* thought the President of the United States, as Henley Hornbrook entered the room.

"No problem. It was on my way," replied Hornbrook evenly. "What can I do for you?"

Goddammit! thought the President. *I hate this condescending know-it-all.* But Dillard just rose, offered a handshake and said, "Well, Senator, please sit down with me for a moment." They took chairs opposite each other, while Oswego dropped onto the settee on the left side of the President. "Stafford was telling me earlier that he had spoken with you, and he reminded me of how many concerns you had about our bill, and of all the valid points you raised. And it struck me that although we hardly see eye-to-eye in many areas, we both have the same goals. Namely, we both want the country to be the best that it can. Am I right?"

"Certainly," said Hornbrook, eyeing the President suspiciously. "But?"

"Oh yes, I know what you're going to say. Philosophically we're direct opposites. Of course. I know that. But we can both also agree that the country's in a bit of trouble. And my feeling is that it's just too big a problem—and too important—not to be involving the very best minds in fixing it. Other administrations may have given lip service to bipartisanship, but talk is cheap. I don't think we have the time to be arguing about it. If somebody like you has some good ideas, then we want to hear them."

Dillard was enjoying this. He knew Hornbrook had no idea where this was heading. He was probably thinking this was 100 percent pure Dillard bullshit. He would have been right. It was bullshit. Dillard almost chuckled, but kept his manner serious.

"Senator Hornbrook, the current Secretary of Commerce has developed some personal health problems and will be resigning as soon as I can find the right person for the job. I think that person is *you.*"

Hornbrook looked stunned. The President could read his thoughts. *Join Dillard's Cabinet? Is he serious? Why on God's green Earth would he think I'd consider this?* His stupefaction was obvious, and Dillard continued once again.

"Don't be so surprised. Why not be part of a new approach? It's a hellava lot easier to get your way when you're on the inside, instead of the outside. And you'd have to admit, as an independent, you don't always get much say in things. Now, let's just use this bill as an example. Like I said, we admit the country's in a bit of a bind, because a lot of problems first were neglected for too long and then were addressed with only half measures. But we think this legislation is going to fix the problem. You know the major provisions. How would you make it better?" And with that, he leaned back in his chair and just smiled across the table.

"Well, Mr. President, we hardly have the time tonight for me to detail everything I think is wrong about this bill. But in a nutshell, it's this: You're selling this bill as middle-of-the-road common sense. I think it's economic suicide! You want to raise taxes and make more people give more money to the government at a time when virtually every segment of the economy is reeling. Plus, you want to manipulate prices and wages and labor, and you want to manage even more of the economy. Every administration has the same problem. You just can't let people take care of themselves. And you refuse to even look at what has happened even in our own lifetimes. Super inflation and interest rates over 20 percent at the beginning of Reagan's first term. He cut taxes, and the economy started to take off. Congress, of course, didn't behave, and Reagan didn't pay close enough attention, so deficits ballooned and the debt soared, . They tried to stop inflating the money supply, and boom, recession. Eventually, the economy started to bounce back, and if they had brought federal spending under control it would have been okay, but Bush and his stupid 'Read my lips' double-cross kowtowed to Congress and raised taxes. The economy funked again. And that got your buddy Clinton elected. But he was such an idiot that the voters put the Republicans in charge in Congress for a change. So they cut taxes again, and the economy took off again. Long and hard. Of course, they were idiots, too, so the inevitable happened. The government kept spending too much, and they started screwing with the interest rates again and credit and the money supply. The economy took a nose dive. Then Bush II gets elected. They tinkered some more. More spending. More government programs. More regulations. A make-believe tax cut mostly back-loaded and based on suddenly-discovered surpluses kept a lot of people happy, but it didn't last. More spending. An explosion of deficits. Still more programs. Then the big meltdown. Fannie. Freddie. And half of Wall Street, aided and abetted by crooks in Congress looking for fat campaign funds and free beach houses. They look the other way while the government is demanding banks give home loans to people who don't make enough to afford the mailbox, let alone six- or seven-digit mortgages. Now you've picked up the baton and fill up your Administration with another bunch of crooks who think they shouldn't 'waste a good crisis' and run left faster than Karl, Uncle Joe, or even good old Lenin himself could have ever hoped. So POW! Here we are. In a 'bit of a bind,' as you put it. The whole country's about to fall on its

The Hornbrook Prophecy

nose because of the taxes and enormous spending at all levels. Your bill will do nothing but make it worse."

Dillard leaned forward again, ignoring the slurs. "So what's your answer to it?"

"Cut taxes. Cut spending. Cut programs. If the budget gets bigger every single year, no matter if the Democrats or the Republicans write it, the result is the same. That money to pay for it has to come out of the economy somehow. Tax *cuts* usually turn out just to be tax *shifts*. The burden just gets moved onto some other, more hidden, or less vocal group. And cutting spending is just baloney, too, if you're only merely reducing the rate of budget *increases*. It has to be fewer *real* dollars. Period. Make the cuts across the board. The people can far more easily decide themselves what to do with their money. And let's not forget that. It IS their money."

Dillard rose abruptly. "Well, I tell you what, Henley," he said, acting like his best friend and escorting Hornbrook toward the door to the outer office, "you don't have to give me an answer right away. Let's go have a good time with our Japanese buddies, and you think about my suggestion. You just never know how things'll turn out." And Hornbrook left, obviously appearing to not quite know what the entire meeting had been all about.

As soon as the door closed, Dillard turned to his Chief of Staff and said, "You were right, my friend. He's absolutely insufferable. I wouldn't let him mow the White House lawn, let alone sit on my cabinet. And he's probably fully aware of that. But it was worth it to confirm your idea."

"I'll call Brownsville and tell him to get cracking.

Robert Wickes

CHAPTER 4

*"To let oneself be bound by a duty from the moment
you see it approaching is part of the integrity
that alone justifies responsibility."*
—Dag Hammarskjold (1905-1961), U.N. Secretary General

The Voice. He heard it, but he didn't believe it. After all these years, it really hadn't changed. It was still The Voice.

The tall, lean man leaned casually against the side of the run-down, old brick apartment building with his arms folded nonchalantly across his chest as he listened to the old preacher across the street mesmerize his few listeners in the neighborhood park. Well, at least it was *called* a park, and it may have actually *been* a park at one time, but frankly, with the mostly-dead grass, litter-strewn sidewalks, broken down playground equipment and graffiti-obscured ball-field wood backstop, it bore little resemblance to an actual park. Then again, neither did the leathery, bald, wrinkled figure, standing straight and still wearing a clerical collar to go with the battered hat, rumpled pants, and well-scuffed shoes, bear much resemblance to the Reverend Ukiah Hilgard of old.

But it *was* the Voice he remembered, thought the man, excitedly, behind his wire-rimmed glasses. *That* hasn't changed. It was a voice that was hard to describe to someone who had not heard it. Were he asked to characterize it, the younger man would probably have likened it to a hybrid of towering Black actor Michael Clarke Duncan and the professorial James Earl Jones. It was still captivating, still powerful, and still as capable of commanding attention as it had decades ago in the days of marching with Martin Luther King, Jr. The old man hadn't been so old then, but after King's assassination he had fallen *out* of favor with the main line Black leadership, and fallen *into* favor with the bottle. For a long time he ceased being able to command any attention at all, save for the odd gathering at the park or an occasional group of other bottle-fed derelicts.

The Voice. What a fabulous tool it had been, building the passions of the poor, and instilling in them previously unknown feelings of pride, of hope, and

The Hornbrook Prophecy

even of history. For many, it had helped build the beginnings of even a little self-respect in people who had never known or felt it before.

The bespectacled, well-dressed African-American man hadn't come to park this day to hear what the old preacher had to say to the small crowd, most of whom, if they listened at all, listened only because it was a diversion, a break to the monotony of another dreary day in a life that offered little beyond the subsistence level existence made possible with their monthly assistance checks. The younger man looked across at the people and felt his heart ache and his anger rise. Slavery had been legislated away nearly one hundred and fifty years earlier, and yet these poor souls—and millions like them around the country—were still enslaved, in substance if not in fact, this time as wards of the politicians instead of the plantation owners.

He glanced at his watch, turned away from the park, and reluctantly headed back to his car. An idea was swimming around inside his head that bore some consideration.

Chapter 5

> *"I observed in different countries, that the more public provisions were made for the poor, the less they provided for themselves, and of course became poorer. And, on the contrary, the less was done for them, the more they id for themselves, and became richer."*
> —Benjamin Franklin, 1766

Thursday – January 14

"Thank you, Mr. President." President Winston Dillard nodded graciously to the Vice President of the United States who was serving, as specified in Article I, Section 3 of the Constitution, as the presiding officer of the U.S. Senate.

"Honorable Senators," he began pompously after he turned back to face the semi-circular rows of desks in the so-called *upper* chamber of the Congress, "I am honored to have been invited here today to speak to you at this critical time. I know how unusual it is for the President to be asked to be involved at this juncture in the legislative process. But the legislation before you today is NOT just another tax bill. It is NOT just another meaningless band-aid on the gaping wound of tragic poverty and injustice in our country. It is NOT just another sleight-of-hand to rob Peter to pay Paul as you will, no doubt, soon hear some claim in this august Chamber."

Henley Hornbrook leaned toward Lew Weiser and whispered, "He's right! This time Peter and Paul are both being mugged!" Weiser smiled and nodded, without taking his eyes off his legislative summary and notes.

"No, guardians of America. Not this time!" Dillard bellowed, looking directly into the lens of the BSN camera, and knowing that along with the feeds by the other networks as well as CSPAN, there would be very few voters who would not see enough soundbites on the evening news to guarantee overwhelming popular support, as well as ample pressure on the opposition.

The Hornbrook Prophecy

"We are now well into not just a new millennium, but a whole new epoch of expectations waiting to be realized! The progress—and, yes, the mistakes—of the last century have given us wisdom, shown us our faults, and taught us that only at our peril can we any further ignore the suffering of many in favor of those few who have created a modern day feudal system which exploits the labor of hardworking Americans and deprives them of opportunity much the same as did barons and warlords a thousand years ago!"

There was thunderous applause from nearly two-thirds of the Senators present, as well as from the packed gallery above. The administration had also made the usual effort to see that the gallery was significantly populated with sympathetic supporters. The President, enjoying the moment, but not wishing to appear as anything but humble, gently gestured with his palms out to subdue the response. When silence fell again, he resumed.

"Our nation has suffered greatly over the past three years because of the greed and mismanagement of the financial/industrial complex. In spite of the trillions of dollars we were forced to throw at banks and other industries to keep them afloat, our working and poor citizens benefited virtually not at all. As if foreclosures and job losses weren't enough, they had to watch as their retirement plans were sacrificed on the altar of executive bonuses. Now, it is time to turn the tables!" There was another eruption of applause and cheering from the gallery in particular, and Dillard waited for it to quiet down.

"It is my great honor, today, to present for your approval—and I do pray that such approval is readily forthcoming—Senate Bill 100, *The American Employment and Financial Freedom Act of 2010*. This bill rights the wrongs, raises the lowly, and humbles the arrogant!" Again, the ovation was widespread, loud, and lasting. When it subsided, he continued.

"There are three main parts: First, wage and price relief for those who need it most; second, tax reform so that those who can least afford it will find their burden lightened by those who can more easily manage it; and third, the re-opening of job opportunity for all those who need it. Now, let's get down to work and examine this more closely before the cries of the downtrodden rich are lost in the wakes of their yachts as they head for their offshore tax havens." Laughter echoed throughout the immense room.

"The first section includes some very basic steps for financial fairness. The minimum wage would immediately be raised to $12 an hour, with automatic annual increases, over the next 5 years, of 2.5 times the Consumer Price Index. This will allow these workers—the bottom of the labor pyramid upon whose backs the corporate pharaohs build their gleaming glass temples—to gradually regain the ability to feed and house themselves and their suffering families with some degree of the respect which we historically have failed to accord them!" Applause again rang out.

"At the same time, we call for an immediate, albeit temporary, freeze on the prices of goods and services across the board, to keep those same greedy charioteers from simply restructuring their books to maintain their obscene profits." The cheers from the gallery far exceeded those from the floor this time, as Senators remembered how well they had personally benefited from those "obscenities" in their own campaign fundraising efforts.

"Next, corporate income tax rates will be raised to 50 percent and individual tax brackets will be adjusted to reflect the ability of the well-to-do to act more responsibly with the rewards this country has made available to them. The top bracket will be increased to 60 percent on incomes over $200,000. Let's be realistic, people! The divisions in our country are deepening and widening, and we cannot keep expecting the middle class and the working poor to keep their broken down picket fences repaired while the wealthy hide behind their country club gates!" By now, the gallery was nearly falling over itself to cheer on their Robin Hood.

"Our tax reform measures in this bill will also eliminate a bundle of loopholes the rich currently fill with their loot. Capital gains tax rates will gradually be rebuilt, over the next several years, to 45 percent—it's just plain senseless to claim that you should only pay tax a single time on money that keeps growing and earning and growing and earning over and over and over. The millions of taxpayers who cannot afford the American dream of owning even a single home will no longer bear the burden of tax deductible country estates and vacation retreats for the rich. No more business entertaining and travel for tycoons, or exotic vacations for so-called 'continuing education' for rich doctors, all paid for by their taxpaying office staffs. And while we don't want to see mom and dad's little candle shop, or the family farm, sold off just to pay taxes when the owners die, neither should billions of dollars in real estate and capital assets built up with the sweat of the employee or farm hand be hidden from at least some measure of reasonable taxation, which would then benefit those whose real labors made it possible.

"Our tax reform measures will also close another huge loophole. You know, even drug lords and billionaires SPEND money, don't they? So under the direct supervision of Secretary Stanfield Heppner, a new Department of Retail Revenue will be established within the Department of the Treasury to collect a new national sales tax, at such rates to be established by Congress, on all net annual purchases above an exempted level initially established at $25,000 per person or $50,000 per household. This will include all goods and services other than food and medical services, and will include all electronic commerce over the Internet—it's not fair to give a loophole to someone just because they are rich enough to afford a computer, is it?"

The gallery thundered, "NO!" and renewed their clamor. Hornbrook was convinced they could not realize the full implications of the proposals the President was outlining. Again, Dillard gestured for quiet.

"OK. Enough of the bad news for the rich." A voice or two above yelled out, "No!" or "More!" before falling silent. "No, really. I told you this legislation addresses past problems on many levels. And we don't want to ignore the rest, just because it's so easy to point fingers at tax rates and numbers. This bill is also about saving money and creating jobs. We want be the first to agree that tax burdens for ALL can be lightened if we cut wasteful government spending. And I'm not talking about reductions in proposed increases. I'm talking about reductions in real dollars!"

A quick glance at his colleagues told Hornbrook that the collective Senators were largely startled by this last announcement. Dillards's party was hardly noted for cutting spending; indeed, it seldom met a government program it didn't like. Weiser immediately sat bolt upright and turned to Hornbrook, whispering, "There was NOTHING about spending cuts in either the House bill or the bill that came out of committee! What is this?"

Hornbrook nodded knowingly, glancing over at Senator Brownsville, and replied, "It's my fault. Dillard tried to sucker-punch me last night at the White House. I knew it, but I wasn't sure just what his motive was. Now I know. I gift-wrapped that idea myself by talking to him about cutting spending instead of raising taxes. He's going to undermine our arguments before we can even bring them up."

Brownsville, as if feeling Hornbrook's stare, turned and nodded right back to him and smiled, as the President continued, "Oh, yes, I know this may come as somewhat of a surprise to some of you. But, as I said before, we have learned from our past mistakes. Now, naturally, much of the federal budget is protected for important and necessary entitlement programs that have been created in response to changes in our country over the years. But other areas of the budget haven't always reflected change. The leadership came to this admittedly late realization after the bill passed out of committee yesterday, so they called an extraordinary session last night and the quorum present unanimously added a few additional considerations."

Hornbrook, without breaking his gaze at Brownsville, remarked to Weiser, "Yep, I'm sure of it. He probably was on the phone to Brownsville before the door closed behind me, and they conjured up this little addition just so they'll look like they're trying to take a balanced approach. He has enough votes to make anything work, so he just conveniently forgot to let us in on their secret and kept us from crying 'foul' to the press. And this way he undercuts us completely."

Hornbrook could see that Dillard was enjoying himself by now. "Take our immense and ponderous military establishment, for example. We've now brought all but a handful of our troops home from most all of the world, including the Middle East. The cold war fizzled out decades ago, and except for a few tin pot dictators around the world, our defensive needs have lessened considerably. Therefore, we are calling for an immediate reduction in the Department of Defense budget by THIRTY-FIVE PERCENT—" his voice rising above the increased noise in the chamber—"leaving us more than a still excessive force to help the international community keep peace in the world. Our opponents may claim we already took a 'peace dividend' years ago, but reductions in the rate of increases in military spending are not the same as absolute cuts in real dollars spent!"

"Boy, where have I heard that argument fall on deaf ears before?" said Weiser.

"Finally, my fellow Americans," said Dillard, without skipping a beat, "while we are pledged to continue to protect the young and the old, the weak and the infirm, the poor and the helpless, we are also going to insure that every able-bodied person in this country who needs a job will have one!" He paused only briefly for the hearty response, before gathering himself for his finale. "The final step in this great Freedom Act is government at its best—the re-establishment of a New Deal-like Works Progress Administration-style agency to create jobs for everyone who needs one. A new cabinet level office for the Secretary of the Department of Human Resources will be formed, and given the responsibility to see that each and every decent American who has been denied employment by CORPORATE America will have the opportunity to have their dignity restored with the promise of a paycheck from PUBLIC America!"

Most of the Senators, and all of the gallery, jumped to their feet applauding and cheering the President. The ovation carried on for several minutes, and the President was of no mind to temper it this time. He raised both hands in the air like a televangelist channeling a message from above, and let the commotion run its course. Finally, he lowered his arms as the noise fell off, took a long look up at the gallery, and then gazed directly into the television camera lens. In his most righteous voice he said, "All that has to happen, my fellow good Americans, is for each and every one of you to let your Senators and Representatives know just how important YOU think this bill is!"

And then, raising his voice to be heard over the response from the gallery, he waved his arm back and forth pointing his finger at the rows of desks in front of him, and added, "And for Congress to listen to you! THANK YOU!" A final time the ovation burst forth, as Dillard waved to the gallery and to the camera, then turned and shook hands with the Vice President and the President Pro Tempore, and made his way up the aisle greeting the Senators as he left.

Watching the President leave, Lew Weiser leaned over again and said to Hornbrook, "*Panem et circenses*, Henley. The emperor still likes to give bread and circuses to the little people. Because it still works."

"Yeah, but who the hell's gonna be able to afford to make the bread?"

"Not I, said the duck."

"Not I, said the goose," lamented Hornbrook. "Lew, I'm afraid you're right. We're going to get steamrollered on this one, big time. I don't think a traditional approach to amendments is even going to create a ripple. We might as well just chuck 'em out the window. The best we'll be able to do is to just jump in and make some waves and hope that it creates some trouble. This is going to be disastrous when this passes, but we'll never muster enough votes to prevent it. Well, let's grab Loren, and Mort, and maybe Brooks, and get some lunch."

***

Sunny Turner also had lunch on her mind when she poked her head through the doorway into the small room that McCall used in Hornbrook's Hart Building office. McCall had his back to the door, leaning over the credenza behind his desk obviously engrossed in something he was reading. Hoping to reverse the tables and surprise him for a change, Sunny walked quietly up behind him and announced herself in a sharper and louder than normal tone. "MCCALL!"

Not a muscle moved. It was as if he had not even heard her. Then he quietly replied without turning around, "Hi, Sunny. What's new?"

"Geez, McCall," she pouted, "you're no fun at all. Doesn't anything startle you?"

"Not when the anything's high heels clickety-click their way like a hyperactive typist all across the tile in the outer lobby. Better than a telegraph." He straightened up and turned around, flashing a wide smile. He sat down in his chair, leaned back with his hands behind his neck and put his feet up on the desk. "So what can I do for you this fine day, beautiful?"

Occasionally, just occasionally, she wanted to smack him right in the middle of his smug mug. The moment passed, and she simply replied, "I've decided to let you take me to lunch."

He jumped to his feet and bowed. "At your service, m'lady."

"Just get your coat," she said, shaking her head. "I'm hungry."

"What are you hungry for?"

"I'm done for the day," she said with a bit of relief in her voice. "Let's head over to Cap City."

"Sounds good to me." McCall grabbed his long knitted scarf and wrapped it around his neck before sliding into his overcoat, and holding out his elbow. Sunny took it familiarly and they headed out.

It wasn't raining when they exited the Capitol building, so they just rolled up their collars against the breeze and enjoyed the walk across Capitol Plaza, past the fountain and small reflecting pool. The gardens, so green and colorful in the spring and summer, were quiet in their winter hibernation, and the big trees lining the Plaza were bare of leaves. Still, there was the promise of rebirth in the carefully pruned shrubs and roses, and Sunny looked at them thinking that if the country could just get through the economic winter it was in then maybe things could get better. She had serious misgivings, though, about whether the proposed new legislation would do what it was supposed to do. She had plenty of firsthand experience with life not going according to plan.

"I'm starved, Eagle," said Sunny as they walked, "but I think I want to walk a bit first."

"As you wish," McCall replied noncommittally.

Sunny had her left arm hooked under his right and she leaned her head on his shoulder and brought her right hand over to hold his upper arm. "You've been very good for me, Eagle."

"Aw, that's what all the women say," he said, deflecting the praise.

"No, I mean it. You let me have my space and haven't made any demands upon me. And you've never acted like you wanted to pry into my past."

McCall allowed his tone to match her own. "I knew that you'd tell me someday what you wanted me to know."

"Today's that someday," she said. "I need to talk with you."

He kept silent, letting her set the pace.

"I had lots of plans when I graduated from high school," she began. "I moved from Ridgefield first to go to school in Wenatchee. I had a small softball scholarship."

"Really?"

"Yes. I didn't always just clickety-click my heels across the tile. I was actually pretty good. I played second. And I was able to move on later to Portland State, which was barely a half hour from home." She was quiet for a while. They continued walking, oblivious of the chill. "I started going out with the lab instructor for the "Physics for Poets" class for non-majors I had been taking to satisfy a graduation requirement. He wasn't like the jocks I'd often gone out with before. He was gentle and charming and funny. We fell in love. And we got married."

McCall remained quiet as she opened up her past for him.

"I got my degree in Communications and I was intent on getting into broadcasting, but I found out I was pregnant. Having a child was the most incredible experience of my life. My daughter became my life. And then my life ended." The quiet utterance became a sob, and they stopped as Eagle turned to envelop her in his arms. "It was so sudden. And so final." She cried into his shoulder.

After a few minutes she composed herself, determined to share the whole story. "My birthday was coming up, so Luke took Beth to go shopping in Portland. It was a pretty quiet Sunday afternoon. And then some…some…crazed…" she stammered, having difficulty getting the words out, "*lunatic* came aboard their MAX light rail car. People said later he just started shooting. A couple of other people were wounded before an off-duty cop shot him. And killed him. But it was too late. Luke and Beth didn't even make it to the hospital."

Sunny looked up at Eagle, his forehead furrowed and lips tightened. Then she turned, took his arm again, and continued walking. "The following year was a kaleidoscope of exploding emotions for me. I was lost. I started on a roller coaster in and out of depression. I alternated between despair and loneliness, and then fear and anger and confusion. I couldn't get out of it. I honestly don't know how long it went on. It was like a horrible dream that I couldn't wake up from. It was debilitating. Gradually, I guess, with the help of my folks and a few close friends, the shadows receded and I found that I could set aside my memories for short periods, by overwhelming myself with other activities. I interviewed for a research job at KGW-TV, the Portland NBC affiliate, and was pretty surprised when I was hired. By the time I learned, much later, that I got the job less because of my resume and more because station management valued the human interest possibilities, I didn't care. Work became the most effective therapy for me."

Their pace picked up as she told her story. "I began to spend my extra time investigating the problems of violent crime in America. I guess I was looking for some kind of closure. When my producer found out about my extracurricular project, he couldn't have been happier. He gave me the chance to present the story on camera myself."

"Nothing like a little human interest opportunism to help the old ratings. Not to mention that you're a hot tottie, too!"

"Shut UP, McCall!" But she had to turn her face to keep him from seeing her smile. He always helped lighten her mood. "Aaaanyway, I think the biggest surprise for them was the conclusion I came to on air. It was true, the ratings were pretty good, but I know I caught a bunch of people off guard when I didn't come out in favor of more gun control laws."

"I think I remember. It sparked a bit of debate, didn't it?"

"I guess. I said something to the effect that the answer to violent crime in America might not lay in banning firearms for all, but instead to simply enforce the many laws we already have, increasing punishment for violations, and even—and this was the part that got them the most upset—encouraging more law-abiding citizens to arm themselves. After all, if that cop hadn't been on the MAX a lot more people would have died for certain. Coming from me, however, after all I'd personally suffered, it was like blasphemy to say that."

"So then what?"

"Well, mostly I scored more points than I lost, so the station did okay. I got to do more stories. Later, I got a weekend anchor slot. And I guess some other people took notice, too. About a year later, I was asked to run for the 3rd district congressional seat in my home county in Washington. The incumbent was an aging liberal who had actually been a prime sponsor of some federal gun control legislation, and some people thought my TV exposure and personal story—"

"And hot tottie looks!"

"—would be enough to unseat him." She threw Eagle a disgusted look, but went on. "It was. Barely."

"And the rest is history." McCall proclaimed loudly.

"Yeah, except for having to suffer you!" she retorted.

***

The Hornbrook Prophecy

But ultimately that had turned out to be the best part for her. By the time she was thirty-four, she was already in her third term in Congress, and found herself much in demand by a variety of organizations and interest groups. But she was disillusioned with the way the political system worked—the deal-making, the legalized bribery called lobbying, the constant need to keep an eye on the next election. She had almost decided to just finish out her term and go home when she received an invitation to attend a barbeque at the Washington state home of her senior senator, Henley Hornbrook, during the off year August recess. Not wanting to offend, but dreading the thought of attending yet another of the countless demeaning fundraisers that are the lifeblood of office holders, she called the Senator's office to make her excuses. She was asked to hold for a moment, before a new voice came on the line.

"Good afternoon, Sunny. This is Lew Weiser."

"I'm sorry, Lew. They didn't really need to disturb the Senator's Chief-of-Staff for this."

"I let them know that when you called I was to be notified, because I had a feeling you would be declining. Sunny, this is not any official function. The Senator is simply inviting a few people over for dinner and conversation. Mort Packwood and Loren McClintock will be there. They have been very impressed with the work you did on the House side of that logging bill Senator Hornbrook sponsored. He likes the way you dig in your heels, if you'll excuse the sexist expression, and would like you to join them, if you can give up a day or two of your much deserved vacation."

"Tell him I'm very flattered, and I'll see if it looks good, but I won't make any promises right now. I'll let you know before the end of the week."

In the end, she went. Back room scheming was one of the aspects of politics she liked least, but all three of the Senators had sterling reputations on the Hill. To her surprise, it was a delightful weekend. It took her only about an hour and a half to drive her Cherokee from Ridgefield up to Hornbrook's small ranch on the site of a former game farm in rolling, timbered hills west of the state capital in Olympia. Everyone was extremely casual, and Sunny enjoyed how the conversation became increasingly spirited as they played mental ping-pong with ideas, and verbal demolition derby over their political opponents.

Sunny had also been intrigued by another person who, while frequently called upon for opinions and insight into certain subjects, had generally stayed in the background. She had not previously met Senator Hornbrook's Special Assistant, Eagle McCall, but liked his obvious self-assuredness, easy-going manner, and sense of humor. He projected a carefully-controlled combination of power and energy, and she was sure he was the type of person who would seldom fail to master a challenge. There was something about him that seemed familiar, but she couldn't place it. After dinner, she accepted the Senator's offer of the guest house, unable to suppress a quick, almost involuntary glance in McCall's direction.

The following day she had arisen early and dressed for her customary morning run. There was a low cloud cover and a light mist, hardly unusual for Western Washington, even in the summer. She put on a pair of light gray warm-up pants and a nylon windbreaker that perfectly matched the green of her eyes, slipped into her running shoes, quickly fixed her hair into a short ponytail, and stepped out of the cottage into the chilled morning air. She glanced down the hill and saw the barn and riding arena on the other side of the main house, then turned and ran up the dirt road that led up toward the tree-covered hills to the north. She had probably gone about a half mile when the road was barred by a tall gate in a six-foot high wire fence that ran along the edge of the forest. The thick rust on the six-inch square mesh, and the state of the large wooden posts which held it, gave her a hint of its age. She stood for a moment wondering about it, and what it could possibly be for. Then she looked up the road beyond the fence. The mist and quiet stillness of the morning seemed to create a sense of mysteriousness in the darkened woods. She strained her vision, half expecting to see shrouded eyes staring back.

"Elk."

Sunny nearly leaped over the fence she was so startled, and she whirled around to locate the source of her fright. Eagle McCall stood there in navy blue sweats and a plain white tee shirt stretched tight across his broad chest and shoulders, with his hands on his hips and a wide smile on his face. She had not heard him come up behind her.

"The fence," he explained, pointing at it. "There used to be a huge herd of elk on the game farm way back, and they could easily jump anything shorter than that."

"You ever scare me like that again," she glowered at him, "and I'll poke your eyes out!"

"But they're such nice eyes," he protested innocently.

"I don't care! I only come with one heart, and if it stops too many more times like that, I'll be in big trouble!"

"Come on," he said, ignoring her irritation, and walking up to the gate. He unlatched it, and swung it partially open. "It's a good run up this way." And he headed up the road at a comfortable pace.

Sunny paused, pursing her lips, before starting after him. She caught him after about fifty yards and, without any further words, they settled into stride together. After they had gone another mile along the twisting, rolling road, the morning mist thickened and it began to rain, lightly at first, then quite heavily.

"Nothing like summer in Washington!" McCall shouted. "Come on!"

He picked up the pace and she was forced to chase after him. Thirty seconds later McCall veered off the road down a narrow path through a thick underbrush of sword ferns and blackberry vines. When Sunny caught up to him he was standing easily in the doorway of a ramshackle, moss-covered wood hut.

"There's no place like home," he said.

"This is yours?" she said in disbelief.

"Nah, but to the game wardens years ago, it made a damn fine winter shelter."

"Are you from around here?" she asked.

"My place is on the other side of that ridge," he said, pointing at the hill beyond the road, "up the east fork of the Postas River."

"Place?" asked Sunny.

"Well, I've got six or seven acres with the house. I don't grow anything so it's not a farm and it's too small to call it a ranch. So I just call it my 'place.' I found it after I went to work for the Senator. It's convenient. Actually I'm from Montana originally. I'm kind of a curious mix of bloodlines. My dad's ancestors had a bad case of wanderlust. They came over from Ireland not too long after the Mayflower, but Massachusetts was too tame, I guess. Or maybe they couldn't stand all the liberals! Who knows? Anyway, over a few generations they worked their way all the way to the Rockies before they dug in. Mom's a Blackfoot Indian—oops! I forgot we're Native Americans now. She's cool. She had to be to put up with all my and my sister's shenanigans growing up. Dad's gone now, but my mother still lives in Missoula, and I have an old cabin up near Flathead Lake. I don't get back there as often as I should."

"Why'd you leave?"

"Ancestral wanderlust, I guess. I had a scholarship to play football at UM. I liked busting heads. When I graduated, I let Uncle Sam teach me a few new ways."

She looked at him quizzically, but only said, "Have you lived here in Washington very long?"

"Oh, maybe about seven years," he replied. "Ever since I went to work for the Senator after I got out of the Army."

"That's it!" she exclaimed, snapping her fingers as recollection finally surfaced. She pointed her finger at him. "The Army! I remember you. You testified before Congress a number of years ago. During all the hoopla over the War on Terror and—." She stopped suddenly, recalling yet another memory. "Oh my gosh, you were that Army guy who saved all those people in Afghanistan!"

McCall shook his head and tried to correct her. "Nah, it was my team that pulled it off. I just happened to be there."

"No, I remember it now. There were a bunch of geologists and their families trapped up near the Russian border after 9-11 and they were captured by al Qaeda forces. You led a Special Forces unit that rescued them. Something about a night parachute drop from way up." She appraised him in a new light. "It was quite the big deal at the time."

"Ahh, it was pretty routine, except for the circumstances. We call it a HALO drop—high altitude, low opening. Makes it pretty tough for anyone to know you're coming. Kinda fun, actually. It's sorta like flying, except you go straight down. The low opening part can be a little hairy sometimes."

"Kinda fun?" she said, astonished at the way he made light of it. "I get petrified on a ladder. I can't imagine…" She let the words tail off. Then she shifted her inquiry again. "How'd you end up working for the Senator?"

His expression darkened, only for an instant, but she caught it. She expected a reply to match his face, but he resumed his light tone, masking the fleeting feeling, whatever it was. "Well, he was on the committee I was hauled in front of while Congress was doing one of its famous investigations into the whole campaign. I guess he liked me." He snickered, then looked away. "I think I'd have to say that he's the only politician I know that I'd ever consent to work for."

Sunny looked at him sharply. "I'm a politician," she snapped, a little too quickly.

"Hold your horses! I said, 'that I *know*.' I don't know you well enough." His smile broadened. "Yet."

The rain stopped as abruptly as it had begun, and they moved out from the shack and continued their run for another thirty minutes before ending back at the game farm property. Later, after breakfast, Senator Hornbrook and

Sunny talked for a couple of hours, and Sunny then got her things together before saying goodbye. As she thanked her host, she glanced around.

"I keep a lot of irons in the fire for McCall," Hornbrook said, reading her mind.

Sunny blushed a little. "Please tell him I enjoyed our run."

Once back in the nation's capital, Sunny found frequent reasons to visit the Senator's office, and she and McCall began to see a lot of each other.

***

Sunny and McCall continued walking and Sunny found that her emotional catharsis had fueled her hunger. They crossed Massachusetts Avenue near Union Station and ducked through the doors of the Capitol City Brewing Company just as it started to rain. Once inside, they were overwhelmed with the warmth, aromas, and noise of the crowded restaurant/bar. The barstools, booths, and high cocktail tables in the center of the room were all packed with a variety of bodies. It was off-season for tourists, and the locals knew it, so there were more business types and government workers than in the spring and summer months. McCall pulled Sunny to the side, and they were escorted up the stairs to a booth in the loft area overlooking the main floor and its centerpiece giant copper-clad fermenting tanks. Shedding their outerwear, they accepted menus from the black-skirted young hostess.

When the waiter appeared, Sunny handed him the menu. "I'll have the Capitol City Hummus," she said, remembering that she had previously enjoyed the classic Mediterranean spread, which was served with fresh baked pita bread, along with cucumbers, tomatoes, and Kalamata olives. "And a Lady Liberty Lager."

McCall snorted. "I thought you said you were hungry," he teased. "That's hardly fit for a growing young girl."

"I've done all the growing I want to do," she sighed. "Especially sideways."

"Whatever." He looked down at the menu again, then announced, "I'll have the Hofbrau Bratwurst Sandwich, a Bier Garden Salad with the roasted garlic balsamic vinaigrette, and a St. Adrian's Alt." He handed the menu with anticipatory satisfaction to the smiling waiter, while Sunny wrinkled her nose.

"That's so you," she said, with feigned disgust.

"Whaaat?" he cried in surprise. "Salad's good for me."

"Yeah, right. Okay, now. Fair's fair. I told you about me. Now I want to know something."

"Uh, oh. This can't be good."

"Can't you ever be serious?"

"Do I have to?"

"I don't know what I see in you."

"You mean beyond my steely good looks?"

Sunny rolled her eyes. "I just wanted to know why you left the army and started working for the Senator."

"Oh, that. No big deal. The army was good for a while, but it ran out of challenges for me."

"Oh, yeah. Like jumping out in the dark and free-falling twenty thousand feet over enemy territory isn't enough of a challenge?"

"Well, you know. I bore easily."

"Right. Come on. Out with it."

"All right, all right." McCall paused. When he spoke again, his voice was flat. "It was the whole phony *'We support our troops'* rah-rah crap the Administration was feeding the public at the time." It was just so much BS."

"What are you talking about?"

"Okay, look. We had a problem with the mission. You know, the rescue mission in Afghanistan."

"What kind of problem? I didn't hear about any problem at the time."

"It didn't happen *on* the mission. It was afterwards. They tried to court-martial one of my men for shooting an Afghan civilian."

"I never heard anything about it," Sunny repeated.

"It was typical two-faced politics," said McCall. "Look, the Constitution says the president is commander-in-chief of the military. That's a good thing. Too many other countries have been undone by feuds between politicians and generals. So it's good to have checks and balances like we have. But the politicians can't seem to understand how different war is from other life. It's not pretty. Ever. Fatigue, stress, pain, injury, death. That's the life of a soldier. Every day in war is one you don't want to live again. Every day can be a life-and-death situation where judgments have to be instantaneous, made without the luxury of Monday morning evaluation. Politicians want political correctness. Politicians want war with rules, so they can sleep at night. And we had rules all right. Plenty of them. We even had like a seven-step list we had to go through before we were supposed to pull a trigger, just to make sure we weren't committing a war crime."

"It sounds kinda cumbersome in an emergency."

"It was insane. One of my guys only got to maybe step six when he pulled his trigger. And somebody died. But if the soldier had counted through seven, *he* most likely would have been the dead one. Was he hasty? Could he have restrained himself? Who knows? Maybe. But under the circumstances only he could make the call. It was his butt on the line. Not someone ten thousand miles away in an air-conditioned office."

"So what happened to the soldier?"

"Well, like I said, the rules said the Army should court-martial him. And the *'We support the troops'* President/Commander-in-Chief wasn't going to stop it. But the public loved the rescue, so dumping on the soldier would have been bad at the polls. Ultimately, they swept it under the rug."

"That's how you left the Army?"

"Well, that's the why. The how is a little more involved. The first time I laid eyes on Senator Hornbrook was when the Senate Armed Services Committee summoned me after that deal in Afghanistan. The media kinda made a big thing out of it, so the politicians wanted to get in on the action, I think. War crimes aren't as important as vote-getting opportunities, evidently. The Senator, to his credit, seemed a lot more reasonable than most of them, but he did ask me one question that got me a bit hot."

"I can't imagine that. What was it?"

"You've got to realize civilian leadership was wearing a little thin on me by this time, so perhaps I wasn't as charming as I would normally be."

Sunny rolled her eyes again, but waited for him to finish. McCall puffed himself up, and tried to imitate his boss' voice. "Major McCall, in your opinion, why does it take the military so long to take care of business in operations like Bosnia and Afghanistan?"

"Oh, boy. I'll bet a guy like you just loved that! What did you say?"

"I simply said that I objected to the implication that the military takes its time fulfilling its missions. I said that the collective Army, Navy, Marine, and Air forces of the United States have *always* accomplished their missions successfully, IF they are given well-defined missions, and IF they are given specific goals and objectives, and IF they are given the means and authority to carry them out." McCall was getting a little animated now. "The thing is, Sunny, that when the mission is ill-defined, or when the goals are poorly established, the military cannot proficiently determine its course. Powder-puff political policy is the bane of any military application. Will Rogers once said that when Congress makes a law it's a joke, and when it makes a joke it's a law." He looked at her. "With all due respect, when you guys in Congress act, whether it's a joke or not, you only risk your own standing in the polls. But when you send the armed forces around the world, you are risking lives. I hate to be blunt, Sunny, but the military is trained to kill people and break things. They can do it efficiently and they can do it effectively. But you can't say 'we support the troops' if you don't even let them defend themselves. And when you send them into harm's way, and fail to permit them to be either efficient or effective, then bad things happen."

"I'll bet that all went over pretty well. Was that all you said?"

"I did get off one last salvo. I told the Committee to remind their colleagues that the military has never undertaken a mission or fought a battle that was not ordered by *civilian* leaders. That makes it the responsibility of the entire population to make sure that they elect leaders who are *good* leaders and if the people don't like what the military does, it is their own fault for putting fools in office!"

"Wow! What happened then?"

"Well, I don't think they were quite sure what to make of me. Senator Hornbrook thanked me for, uh, oh yeah, my candor. And then I left. It wasn't too long after that that I decided that ten years in the Army had exhausted its attractiveness. So I returned to Montana to spend some time with my mother. Then, out of the blue, I got a call from Lew Weiser. Two weeks after that, I was on my way back east again to work for them. I suppose I thought it was a chance to help influence things somehow. You know, help keep some other poor grunt from being dumped on. The Senator's a pretty straight-shooter. I like that. Besides, he said he could introduce me to some hotties," he said, grinning at Sunny.

"Oh, for Pete's sake! You just can't be serious, can you?"

"Where's the fun in that? Anyway, I don't think Mom was too happy when I left again, but she liked that at least I was only flying on airplanes and not jumping out of them anymore."

McCall looked at the crowd below. There was a small, sharply-dressed blonde sitting at the bar with an open briefcase in front of her. She had a cigarette in one hand, a cell phone held to her ear with the other, and an untouched salad next to the briefcase. "Look at them all," he said. "Everybody's so hyper in this town."

"It's an affliction," Sunny responded. "You get caught up in it. Job security is only one election term long, so it makes everyone edgy all the time. This new bill is going to cause some more headaches, I fear. There are only so many times you can go to the well before it dries up."

The waitress arrived to divert their attention to more earthly needs and they fell upon their lunches with enthusiasm.

Chapter 6

*"I cannot say whether things will get better if we change;
what I can say is they must change if they are to get better."*
—G. C. Lichtenberg, 1789

Monday – January 18

Don Quixote enjoyed far greater success than *he* had, Elgin LaGrande felt. He needed some allies; he at least needed his own Sancho Panza. But what he found was far different, and far better. He was attending a workshop at the Workforce Training Conference, part of the annual Alabama Training Exchange, being held this year in Huntsville. One of the speakers was a striking African-American woman, in her mid 30s, Elgin guessed, who was participating in a panel discussion on something called *"Business Reengineering and Technology Integration."*

The topic was mostly just administrative gibberish, but Elgin was captivated by the young woman. What attracted Elgin was not merely her looks, but her quiet confidence and adherence to what were obviously strong opinions. She was well-composed in front of the audience, although it was readily apparent that she was clearly outnumbered on the panel by those who advocated quick changes utilizing the recruitment of out-of-state talent and job-shopping, instead of her own position which urged the slower, but more economically-rewarding practice of developing in-state labor pools via expanded government-sponsored training programs.

Elgin glanced down at his program and flipped through the pages until he found the listing for this seminar. After reading the name of the moderator, he ran his finger down the list of names on the panel until he came upon *Athena Weston, Assistant Director, Alabama Industrial Development Training*. AIDT was a state agency under the Department of Post-Secondary Education. "Good grief, she works practically across the street from me!" he said out loud, then pretended to ignore the loudly-whispered "*Shhhss*" from some of the few in the audience near him who weren't dozing off.

He suffered impatiently through the next forty-five minutes, astride a padded but uncomfortable stackable steel chair, until the moderator called the discussion to a conclusion, and attendees either started to drift off through the double doors of the hotel conference center meeting room or try to corner a panel member with one more question before they departed. The woman, finding her presence no longer in demand, quietly gathered her papers, and started to leave. In the hallway just outside the room, Elgin walked up to her and began to introduce himself.

"Excuse me, Ms. Weston, I'm—"

"Elgin LaGrande," the woman finished for him, shaking his outstretched hand. "Athena Weston. I'm very pleased to meet you. Actually, I even voted for you, although I might not have if I'd known you were going to waste your time and the taxpayer's money attending worthless, boring meetings like this one." Her smile robbed her words of any offense.

"I hate to disagree with you with in my first sentence, but I found your ideas to be full of merit, and worth listening to."

"Well, don't feel you have to rush to get in line, Mr. LaGrande. As you can see, it's not too long."

"Believe me, I know just how you feel. I've spent my entire adult life confronting problems and finding ways to overcome them, but the last three years have been incredible. Nobody wants to change anything; nobody wants to try anything new, because if it actually solved a problem, heaven forbid, their budget might get cut." He paused. "Ms. Weston—"

"It's *Miss* Weston, if you want to be technical," she said, cutting him off again. "But it's Athena if you want to be nice…Elgin."

He felt his skin flush. "Athena, I'm looking for some people to help me make some headway in areas I talked about in my campaign. Areas that currently aren't finding great favor in Montgomery, but which I think are absolutely vital to the future of Alabama in general, and the poor in particular. I think it is absolutely imperative—"

"Elgin, have you had lunch, yet?"

***

"My, my, Mr. LaGrande," said Athena, "you sure do know how to show a girl a fine time." They had left the Von Braun Community Center, driven past the grounds of NASA's Space Camp facility marveling at the full-scale space shuttle that dominated the surroundings in front of the entrance, and stopped at the first restaurant they came upon.

Elgin looked around the interior of the Wendy's and peered sheepishly over his single-patty cheeseburger which he held with two hands as it dripped onto the yellow paper wrapping on the table. "Well, I might manage to do better if I get another chance," he said hopefully. "But I mostly wanted someplace away from the meetings where I could talk with you in private."

"My, my," she said again, "are we starting a conspiracy?"

He chuckled, put down his burger, and wiped his mouth with a yellow napkin. "I hardly think it would qualify as that," he began, "but that might be just how it ends up. When do you have to be back?"

"I don't. That was my grand finale. I'm driving home this afternoon."

"Me, too. My mother lives in Birmingham and she'd kill me if I didn't stop in."

"I doubt it takes much persuasion," Athena remarked. "I seem to recall that the Birmingham Skills Center was one of your pet projects."

"It still is. I try to never miss an opportunity to see how it's doing. Since I moved to the Capitol I haven't been able to as much as I'd like."

"Tell me about the Center."

"Well, it started not long after I went back to work for Southern Office Supply, before I ever ran for any office."

"Wait a minute. Pardon me for asking, but I've always wondered. How on earth did you go from sorting paper clips to being Lieutenant Governor of Alabama? That's a bit of a leap, especially in this state."

"It's kind of a long story."

She looked down momentarily. "Looks like I still have some fries left. Go ahead." Her smile was persuasive.

"Well, after high school, I took a couple of jobs, including one with S.O.S. doing deliveries around downtown Birmingham. The other was a job as a janitor at night in a little office building. I gave half the money I made to my mother, who was working in the housekeeping department of the Marriott Hotel."

He saw Athena looking at him oddly.

"My father left when I was about six. It was hard for her." He shrugged. "After three years, I quit the delivery job, bought an old car and enrolled in the local community college. I got my AA, which I thought was pretty darn good at the time, but one of my teachers encouraged me to apply to the University of Alabama campus in town. Two years later I got to drive my mother to my graduation ceremony. I felt pretty cool. It was the first time in years she'd crossed town without taking the bus."

"I'd be willing to bet your mother was a lot happier about your degree than your car."

"Yeah, she was. And I was tempted to enter the job market immediately, but one thing I learned working those early jobs was that if I wanted to rise much above entry-level positions I'd need to have the same credentials as the Whites who seemed to dominate the business world. So I got myself an MBA. My first job after school was with an auto maker. But what I found was that they didn't care as much about my knowledge and capabilities as they cared that my skin color looked good on management's side of the negotiating table. I didn't stay there very long."

"What did you do then?"

"I got an offer of a real management position back with Southern Office Supply. They needed someone and they knew me. I jumped at it. Even though it paid less at first, it was only a mile and a half from Mom's. Plus it gave me the chance to get involved in helping my old neighborhood. S.O.S. managed to grow. I got them to try some new approaches toward inventory tracking and delivery methods, and we built a reputation for efficiency that large businesses liked. Eventually, I became Vice-President in charge of Operations, supervised the expansion of S.O.S. to Mobile, Montgomery, and Huntsville, and when the founder retired I was given an opportunity to be CEO as we guided it into its interstate phase."

"So what about the Skills Center?"

"Oh, yeah. Actually, I can't really claim much credit for the inspiration. It was the owner of a McDonald's I had once read about. He used to get frustrated trying to get kids to work for him and then having them stay for only a month or two before they'd quit. Granted, it's not glamorous work, and there's no tips—just straight minimum wage stuff. They'd get tired of it, and couldn't see it leading to anything."

"You can't really blame them."

"No, you can't. No one was making much effort to show them it *could* lead somewhere."

"So what did he do?" Athena asked.

"He made a deal with each one of them. As long as they would keep on working there, at least 10-15 hours a week, finish high school, and keep at least a C average, he would pay their expenses to go to college."

"Wow!" she exclaimed. "That's quite a deal. How could he afford it?"

"Well, it was only Community College, but even that was more than most of those kids had even thought of, let alone could afford, and they could still get a two-year degree. And some of them went on to four-year schools afterwards. The neat part, actually, was that he wasn't really rich at all. Having to train new employees all the time, and coordinate constantly changing shifts and crews was costing him a small fortune. Each time somebody quit, it cost him money. First, he had to pay new trainees who are not very productive while they're learning. Then, whoever is training the new guy is also less productive than when just doing his regular job. He figured each time he didn't have to hire someone new, he saved at least one full set of wages.

"So he wasn't doing it because he was a saint. He was just being a good business man. In exchange for the deal he offered, he got dedicated, hard-working employees that melded together into efficient, highly productive teams. Job positions became very hard to come by there, both because he didn't need as many at any one time to do the same amount of work, and also because attrition was very low. As the word got around it motivated a lot of kids in school to work hard in the hope of getting hired."

"It seems so simple. It's a lot like what is really at the center of what I've been trying to do. You know, the industry-based training programs. Why can't more businesses see the advantages?"

"Who knows? But we found that working one-on-one we were able to convince some other businessmen that it made sense to invest in their own futures. The idea of the Skills Center was to get them to think of spending some money now to develop the labor skills and talent they would need eventually to cover growth and attrition."

"Sounds like a baseball farm system," Athena said.

"That's exactly what we told them!" Elgin said with enthusiasm. "And it can work for all kinds of jobs in all kinds of industries. It might be a different arrangement with a building contractor than an accounting firm or a chain of grocery stores, but the principles are the same. The key is getting the kids into the program while they're still in high school, even as early as 9th grade. It creates motivation early enough that they still have time to learn the basic reading, writing, and math skills they need—did you know that in the last fifteen years, over 10 million kids in America have reached the 12th grade without having learned to read at a basic level? Over 20 million reach their senior year unable to do basic math. The average Black and Hispanic 17-year-old child has NAEP scores in math, science, reading and writing that are equivalent to average White 13-year-old's.

"Our belief with the Skills Center was that many, maybe most, of these kids don't learn because they have no reason to. So we hook up with companies that give them a reason. They earn some money while they perform entry-level tasks and learn basic trade or business skills, then after graduation they can move right into full-time jobs. And, depending on the company, some manage to arrange work/study college opportunities. We are pretty small scale, and it's been pretty tough during the recession the last few years. It's hard for companies to plan ahead when taxes, regulation, and employee relation rules are changing almost daily. But it's been working okay."

"Aren't there other existing programs just like this already? What about the School 2 Career program in the capital?"

"That's a fairly common mentor/internship-type program. But it doesn't involve higher education like I want. I mean, college isn't for everybody, but in many cases those who could really profit from it can't afford to go. But our program makes that a key issue, and for those who are college material, they still get the benefit of a head start on making their way in the world. It's been a rewarding project but a tough one. I admit I was pretty lucky in how my life turned out, but the better I did the more vividly I could see even in my own neighborhood that too many others weren't doing so well. And it was almost like they had been talked out of helping themselves. The more I tried to show kids that their lives could be different the more problems I ran into in dealing with some of the well-entrenched bureaucracies."

"Government?"

"Yes, but not entirely. I seemed to be spending as much time fighting with some of our own leaders. I swear they think the route to personal success and self-empowerment is simply to blame the Whites. A lot of other minorities embraced the free market system and did well. But instead of building commercial power to help ourselves out of our social and economic chasm, we've built greater dependence on government intervention as the major remedy to our problems. By allowing ourselves to be at the mercy of welfare and other entitlement programs—for the middle class as well as the poor—we are effectively saying we are inferior to every other population group."

"But you don't believe that, do you?"

"Of course not!" said Elgin, his voice rising. He saw other people in the restaurant glance over at him. He lowered his voice. "But perpetual dependency upon others eliminates any chance of encouraging and building Black self-reliance and economic independence."

"So what's the answer?" challenged Athena.

"I don't have all the answers. But I think I know *some* of the answers. That's why I decided to get into politics. I felt I had to get on the inside. I was lucky, at least at first. I won a seat on the Birmingham City Council, thanks in large part to a lot of leg work and enthusiasm by some teenagers I'd had some luck getting through to. Three years later, I was elected Mayor, and five years and one re-election later I decided to try for LG. We had done pretty well with the Skills Center, so I figured it was time to expand the concept."

"That was a pretty nasty election."

"It sure turned out to be. The issues almost never even came up, at least not on his part. Biggs Wasco had managed to muscle and buy his way up through the state party thanks to his control of the longshoremen union. He had never before run for elective office, but his personal bankroll and his influence with the regional media gave him a lot of exposure. I'd done okay with the people of Birmingham. Probably too well. We didn't have many problems we couldn't deal with, so we didn't make many statewide headlines. I tried to run a clean campaign and talk about the issues but, oddly enough, I got my biggest bump from the *negative* press generated by the Wasco camp. He let the race become increasingly racial in tone, re-polarizing the state which had been, until that point, slowly overcoming generations of interracial ill-will."

"Your reputation was wider that you think. And the voters liked your honesty and your track record of proactive problem solving with the Skills Center."

"I'd like to think so. At any rate, I think a lot of voters were suspicious of Wasco and the way he was throwing money around during the campaign."

Athena leaned back in her chair. "No one ever pays any attention to a race for Lieutenant Governor, but I think your race even overshadowed Scio's reelection. That was a lot closer than it was expected to be. He probably lost a lot of votes because of his support for Wasco. Okay, you ran for office as a way to gain support for the Skills Center. Now you're Lieutenant Governor. What's the problem with expanding the program on a statewide level?"

"There were some early objections based on child-labor, but we got local school cooperation to develop it as externship and work-credit programs." He sighed. "No, the biggest problem is that the bigger the arena the more numerous the gladiators. And the stronger they are. Governor Scio not only doesn't support my efforts, but ties me up with time-consuming and utterly worthless unrelated endeavors. Most state agencies and departments dealing with social assistance programs are constrained by federal guidelines. The term "stonewall" has taken on new meaning for me. And maybe worst of all, I'm just amazed at how much resistance there is among our own prominent Black leaders, elected or otherwise, to any efforts which would change the status quo and improve the lives of the people mostly, I suspect, just because such change might diminish the prominent standing they themselves enjoy. It's been a triple-whammy for the last three years."

"So all you're up against is the Governor, the state, and ourselves. What's the big deal?"

Elgin laughed. "Well, don't forget the unions. They don't want to be cut out of the picture by having potential members beholden and loyal to employers, for obvious reasons."

"Any union in particular?" she said evenly.

"It's hardly any secret that Governor Scio and Biggs Wasco are as thick as thieves, if you'll pardon the expression. And rumor has it that Scio is going to appoint Wasco head of the new Labor Commission."

"Oh, God. I heard about that. The Commission is supposed to be the state version of the NLRB."

"Except that with Wasco in charge there won't be any pretense of balance at all. True, the National Labor Relations Board is hardly there to coddle the employers, but the ALC will be even more biased. They'll sink places like the Skills Center right off the bat, for any one of a number of reasons which will probably include words like 'justice' and 'fairness' sprinkled throughout."

"But wouldn't such a program help more people get into the work force?"

Elgin could feel himself getting worked up. "Established workers will do fine, but it'll be really hard for new workers trying to get started or move up. There'll be a great show of creating new jobs, but their goal will be quantity, not quality. The problem is that as it becomes tougher to make a profit, such as when their labor costs go up and productivity goes down, then companies simply won't have the capital to invest in expansion, or new equipment, or new facilities. And people who *do* have jobs will find their wages stagnant. So, even though some jobs may be created in the beginning, over the long haul, the opposite is true."

"So? You planning on doing something about it?" Athena inquired, raising her eyebrows.

He snorted. "Not alone. I've spent three years trying. I'm outmanned and outgunned. They've got the money, they've got the mike, and they've got the media."

"So what do you have?"

"Damn little. But I think I can convince the people. I feel I was elected because they liked my ideas."

"Governor Scio got elected, too," she argued.

"But he had no real opponent. At least the open LG seat gave me a level playing field. Well, sort of."

"Wasco sure tried to up-end it though."

"He almost succeeded," Elgin stated. "But the fact he didn't gives me some hope. I just need more firepower. I need a better way of attracting attention, getting my message out, and neutralizing the press."

"Oh, oh," Athena said with a smile. "Why do I think I'm about to get conned?"

"Your agency is the logical one to take a lead on this, but the Governor isn't going to permit any intramural sparring. But you have great personal credentials, great ideas—I know, I just suffered through an hour of hearing them beaten to a pulp—and—"

"—and I have a good, well-paying job with lots of great benefits."

"I know. You're right, of course. You'd have to be crazy to risk all that."

"I'd have to be crazy to let the Lieutenant Governor of Alabama get away with taking me to Wendy's on our first date!"

"I'm glad to hear this got promoted from a meeting between state employees to a date," Elgin grinned. "But let me tell you about what I've got in mind."

"Hmmm. Okay," she said cautiously, not entirely disarmed by his smile. "But remember, I already *went* to college."

He chuckled at the reference to his McDonald's story. "How much do you know about the Reverend Ukiah Hilgard?"

Athena Weston sat back in her chair and pondered the ceiling. "Not much, really. I mean, at least not much lately. I know he used to be with

Martin Luther King, Jr. But after the assassination, he became a drunk. I think. That was a bit before my time," she said coyly and pretending to fluff her hair.

"Yeah, yeah," he smirked. "I was a mere child myself. But the story is a bit more complicated than that." He took a deep breath before continuing. "Ukiah Hilgard was not as fiery a preacher as King was, but he spoke with an amazing voice that drew people's attention just because it was so compelling."

"Oh, that's right. Wasn't he actually *called* the Voice, or something like that?"

"Right, although that was really in his early days before he joined King. After that, they tried to downplay other personalities in order to keep a single focus. But I remember once when I was a small boy, he came and spoke at our church. I don't remember what he said, of course, but I always remember thinking he was God himself." He smiled at the memory. "I'll bet my eyes were as big as saucers."

"What happened to him? Why didn't he move into the forefront after King died?"

"He stayed with the movement for a while, but he disagreed with the direction it began to take. And as the others began to get comfortable with the bones they got from the government, he got eased out. His wife passed away, he began to drink, and eventually dropped out of sight."

"Is he still around?" Athena asked.

"Yes. A lot of years went by, but somehow he managed to stop drinking. He was broke, not many remembered him, and eventually he ended up at a small church outside Tuscaloosa that was too poor to hire much of a pastor. He took over, got some of his passion back, and built a small but dedicated congregation. And when he's not at the church, he's out on the sidewalk or in the park, or any other place he can find a few people, and he's still trying to make a difference."

"How do you know all this?"

"I saw him not too long ago. Actually, somebody in my office said they knew somebody who had a relative or somebody who belonged to the church. It took some doing, but eventually I found out where it was, and drove over to see if it was true. It wasn't a Sunday, but I lucked out, and spotted him in a park as I drove by."

"Huh. Did you talk to him?"

"No, I got out, and listened for a while. I could actually hear him from across the street. He didn't look like much, but he still had the Voice."

"So what's your interest in him?"

"Well, it was just curiosity at first. But as I stood there listening to him, I realized that a lot of what he was saying was similar to a lot of what *I* believed, too. That's when I started to think about developing a new approach. That's when I realized that I needed more groups and more key people to join together and create a demand for new ideas.

"Do you really think Rev. Hilgard can help?"

"You'll agree the very first time you hear him."

Chapter 7

"Some say this; some say that; some say just the opposite"
—Father David Linehan (1999)

Tuesday – January 19

Henley Hornbrook watched as the Senators were gathering on the floor of the Senate chamber, some chatting informally with colleagues, others already at their desks gathered in semi-circular rows facing the rostrum on the north wall. Rules had varied over the years regarding the admittance of outsiders to the Senate floor. During the historic debates on the Missouri Compromise in 1820, Vice President Daniel Tompkins had at one point invited so many ladies into the chamber that there were not enough seats left for the senators themselves. In modern times, access became rigidly restricted.

Hornbrook disagreed on virtually every issue with the Majority Leader, but he respected him and admired the facility with which he orchestrated the symphony of the Senate. There had been nothing haphazard about the timing and scheduling of the President's speech before the Senate the previous week. That Thursday date had been selected by Brownsville so that there would be no serious voice heard in opposition to the bill until the following week, when debate would start in earnest. And sure enough, by the time the talking heads and weekend pundits had finished with it, the groundswell of support was overwhelming. Polls by CNN/Gallup/USA Today, and ABC News/Washington Post were conducted early Monday, and the evening news anchors delighted in showing the enormous backing the bill enjoyed across the nation. Brownsville would know that every Senator would read those polls and, regardless of their party affiliation, they would have to give them serious consideration before daring to vote against such an obviously popular bill. As the Senate was gaveled to order this morning, Brownsville also would know that S.100 would be as good as passed.

So Hornbrook was not surprised to see Senator Brownsville rise with satisfaction on his face as he was recognized by the presiding officer of the

Senate. "Mr. President, fellow Senators, distinguished guests, and citizens across the country," Brownsville began, with his eye on the camera, "it would not be possible to more eloquently outline the case for helping people better attain financial certainty in their lives than did President Dillard in this very chamber last week. And if there was any question before, the outpouring of support I have personally received in my office in the last few days, as well as the results of every poll that has come out recently, leaves no doubt in my mind that it is imperative that we take action, and take action now! The swiftness and decisiveness with which the House passed their version of this bill underscores the need for the Senate to act in concert. Therefore, Mr. President, I do hereby submit Senate Bill 100, *The American Employment and Financial Freedom Act of 2010*, for consideration by the full membership of the Senate, and move for immediate passage."

"I second the motion," cried out Senator Milt Freewater of New York.

The Vice-President was again presiding over the Senate. Sheldon Osborne Branford had represented Michigan for three terms in the House and two terms in the Senate, and in that time had learned to become a real political killer, easily earning the nickname his initials suggested. His place on the ticket with Dillard had been a political payoff. "It has been moved and seconded to pass S.100," he began. Then, with anticipatory reluctance, he added, "Is there any discussion?"

There was a general undertone of quiet conversation mixed with numerous more excited voices while the members of the Senate prepared to sink their legislative teeth into this massive new bill. After a few moments, the Minority Leader stood and called for recognition, officially launching the opposition to the Act. A number of senators from both sides offered their opinions, but for the most part it was a very mild debate considering its scope.

Finally, Hornbrook could no longer keep his peace.

"Mr. President!"

"The Chair recognizes the senior Senator from Washington."

"Thank you, Mr. President." Hornbrook turned back toward the seat of the Senate Majority Leader. "And I would also like to extend my personal congratulations to the esteemed Senator from Pennsylvania, a great gentleman who, with this bill, has once again successfully demonstrated the total conviction with which he holds his beliefs." He waved his arm in a backhand motion and extended his palm in an elegantly-gracious gesture.

Senator Brownsville nodded his acknowledgment, but looked wary.

Hornbrook continued. "As I studied this legislation over the past week, I have found myself to be in total awe of the logic and principles which are the underpinnings of these measures. So caught up in them did I become that I soon found myself trying not, as I would have anticipated, to swim against the current but, instead, being enthusiastically-swept along by its compelling arguments."

"Would the Senator yield for a question?" asked Senator Milton Freewater, peering over his half-eye reading glasses, his hair, as always, defying gravity.

"Of course, Senator Freewater."

"At the bottom of this honey pot the Senator is emptying, is their some kind of point that needs to be made?"

"Why, Senator Freewater! I am truly wounded. But please, surely you misunderstand me. I am on *your* side," Hornbrook pleaded. "I am here to help you make this legislation even stronger. Would the Senator grant me his indulgence for a few moments? You'll soon see what I mean."

"Very well."

"Thank you. With the ever-profound concern of the Senator from New York for the precious time we have here in the forefront of my thoughts about the economy, let me waste none further." He picked up the first paper on the pile on his otherwise uncluttered desk. "Let me begin by addressing the provisions for changes in the federal minimum wage."

There was a subdued murmuring in the gallery and an accompanying quiet rustling of papers on the floor, as everyone sensed the real debate was about to commence.

"The bill calls for an immediate increase in the federal minimum wage to a hearty $12 an hour. And, as the President so eloquently stated, this is only fair because it is, after all, nigh on impossible to raise a cat on minimum wage, let alone a family. Now, let us, at least for the moment, ignore the fact that the unemployed will not be hired and existing employees will be laid off when wage rates are artificially set above the level of their productivity. And let us ignore the fact that minimum wage earners are the least productive, least skilled cogs of the economic wheel, and that if wage rates prevent their entry into the labor market they will lose the opportunity to gain the experience necessary to move up to more productive levels. And let us ignore the fact that even where employers are able to retain their workers at these new rates, they will be forced to raise the prices of their products, thus again widening the very gap between labor and consumer that you were supposedly attempting to narrow. Let's instead just concede that all you have stated, and all that the President outlined is absolutely true!

"In that spirit, therefore, I offer the following amendment. This would be on page 4, Section 3, paragraph one." The intensity of paper rustling grew markedly. "Where it says, '*The federal minimum wage will be increased to Twelve dollars per hour*,' et cetera, just strike out '*Twelve*' and insert the number '*Twenty-four*.'"

Freewater was on his feet. "What sort of nonsense is this?" he demanded, forgetting the Rules of Order.

"I would think it was obvious," replied Hornbrook calmly. "If a raise to twelve dollars an hour is helpful to these people, then think how much better off they'd be with a raise to *twenty-four*!"

"This is preposterous!" snarled Freewater. "You know damn well business would never go for that!"

The Vice President banged his gavel a few times. "I would like to remind the Senators that, especially in light of the importance of this bill, the Senate rules for debate are to be adhered to. Rebuttals will be allowed during normal discussions if the amendment is seconded. Senator Hornbrook has the floor."

"Thank you, Mr. President. Now, since the good Senator brought it up, am I not correct in understanding that businesses should be ignored since, as President Dillard said if I'm quoting him correctly, they are nothing more than '*corporate pharaohs*' in '*their gleaming glass temples*'? So once again, I offer this amendment, to change the federal minimum wage to twenty-four dollars instead of twelve."

"Is there a second?" the President of the Senate inquired sourly.

Loren McClintock stood and spoke into the microphone. "For the sake of discussion, I second the motion. I've just *got* to hear this."

"The motion to amend Page 4, Section 3, paragraph one to read 'twenty-four' instead of 'twelve' has been made and seconded. Would you care to open the discussion Senator Hornbrook?"

Hornbrook said, "Actually, Mr. President, I'm tempted to amend my amendment to make it fifty bucks an hour, but as I see Senator Brownsville stirring, perhaps I'll just leave it alone for now and let him help me make our colleagues understand the wisdom of this amendment as is."

"Would the Senator yield?" inquired Brownsville.

"Does the Majority Leader have a question?" asked Hornbrook.

The Hornbrook Prophecy

"I'm sorry the Senator from Washington has chosen to make light of this landmark legislation at this critical time. He knows very well, as Senator Freewater stated, that twenty-four dollars an hour would bankrupt small businesses across the board. I urge Senator Hornbrook to withdraw his motion and let us get on with the serious consideration of this legislation."

"Okay, Senator," stated Hornbrook intently. "Before I consider that, let me ask you a question. Would you imagine that somewhere in the country, in some state, in some industry, there's a business—maybe a lot of them—which will close this year because it cannot make enough to cover its existing payroll liabilities?"

"Unfortunately, yes. Businesses fail all the time."

"Since that is so, would you suppose that there are even more businesses that might fail if their payrolls were artificially inflated due to a mandated increase in the minimum wage to twenty-four dollars an hour, as I just proposed?"

"Again, yes, and again, unfortunately."

"And probably some that would fail if the minimum wage were increased to fifteen?"

"It's likely."

"And maybe even if it were raised to thirteen?"

"Yes, probably," said Brownsville somewhat angrily. "And before you bother, yes, I'll admit that some will fail even though our legislation asks for only twelve. But those are inefficient, barely-productive businesses that we are probably better off without."

"The employees in those businesses might disagree with you but, okay. One last question before I consider withdrawing my motion. Senator Brownsville, do you know what the overhead, production, operation costs, and profit margins are for all of the businesses and all of the industries in the country?"

"No, of course not."

"Most of them?"

"No. How could I?"

"Any of them?"

Brownsville hesitated, then said, "No."

"So how on earth can you propose ANY legislation whatsoever that tells ANY business what they have to pay someone regardless of their level of productivity?"

"I don't have to know," replied Brownsville, stubbornly. "All I need to know is that the hardest working men and women in this country can't live on eight bucks an hour, so we have to help them."

Brownsville sat down and his supporters on the floor and in the gallery rewarded him with sustained applause.

Hornbrook glanced over at Lewiston Weiser and murmured, "In for a penny, in for a pound."

Weiser grinned and said, "Nothing to lose, Henley. Have some fun."

Hornbrook looked over at the Majority Leader, then rose again. "Mr. President," he began again.

Vice President Branford, who had made sure he would be acting in his official role in the Senate until this legislation was passed, sighed reluctantly, but said, "Go ahead Mr. Hornbrook, you still have the floor."

"Thank you very much, Mr. President. Senator Brownsville's brilliant analysis is unassailable. I withdraw my amendment."

"I'll withdraw my second," said Senator McClintock.

Hornbrook continued, but this time without the tongue-in-cheek manner he had been using. "I admit that my amendment was not submitted with any great sincerity, but I did it for a reason. This legislation, in my opinion, is the *capstone* of three-quarters of a century of misguided, misleading, and just plain mischievous efforts which have cut a swath through the individual rights of all Americans as subtly and as effectively as the Grand Canyon was eroded by the Colorado River. I can only pray that it not be the *tombstone* as well!"

There was an uproar in the gallery, and Brownsville and several members of both parties jumped to their feet in protest. Senator Brownsville, looking imperiously indignant, spoke out strongly. "Mr. President, the *Honorable* Senator from Washington just insulted every effort of every man and every woman who have sacrificed their private lives to serve their country as Representatives, Senators, and even Presidents, making this the most successful country in the history of the world! I demand that he be reprimanded for this outrageous breach of professionalism!"

The Hornbrook Prophecy

Vice President Branford banged his gavel to restore order. Just as he was about to open his mouth and join the fray, Hornbrook calmly, but forcefully, spoke into the microphone.

"Put a cork in it for a change, Senator Brownsville. Your inference that being a Senator is a *sacrifice* is a real affront to those patriots who have paid with their fortunes, their properties, or even their lives. Good God, Senators, have you no shame? You all come to Washington and make laws for everyone else to live under, while you make yourself exempt from most of them, and instead craft your own benefits of fat salaries, fat per diems, fat housing allowances, fat travel perks, fat health care benefits, and fat retirements. So don't let's hear any more about your sacrifices, Mr. Brownsville!" He looked back at the Vice President and offered, "I will, however, apologize, Mr. President."

Branford, not sure how to proceed, merely shrugged. "Get on with it, Senator."

"Thank you. We would not be considering this legislation if there were not serious problems in the country today. And we've already spent magic trillions of dollars we don't have for so-called stimulus and bailout plans over the last two years, trying to avert disaster. I think *this* bill will assure it. Government debt is soaring at every level. Some say it's because spending is too high. Others say it's because too many aren't paying enough. But any way you look at it, we are perilously close to a financial train wreck and, as I said, this will assure one. Our collective government debt is close to eighty trillion dollars, and—"

"Mr. President!" came the expected objection from Senator Brownsville. "Would you remind the esteemed Senator from Washington that the serious proceedings of the United States Senate is no place for such fanciful fiction. *Eighty* trillion dollars, indeed! That's six or seven times what we all know is the actual national debt. Please, Senator," he directed toward Hornbrook, "let's at least play with the same deck."

"Now, don't get your knickers in a knot, Senator Brownsville," smiled Hornbrook calmly. "Yes, we have as of today a current official debt of better than twelve trillion dollars. Anyone can go to the government's own website at w-w-w-dot-publicdebt-dot-something-or-other, and read the up-to-the-minute, to-the-penny official national debt. Every day it's just a little bit bigger number. We just can't help ourselves. We just keep finding new programs and new causes and new crises that we just *have* to cure. And it's way past time to admit that there are two *other* major pillars of federal debt lurking just around the corner waiting to collapse upon us."

"Oh, do enlighten us, Senator," said Brownsville, convinced that his opponent was persuading no one.

"Happy to oblige. In the real world, if you manage a private pension plan and you mess with it—even for normal business expenses—you go to jail. But the Congress of the United States thinks it can do things private pension managers cannot. Like stealing."

"MR. PRESIDENT!"

The Vice President banged his gavel repeatedly to quiet the latest uproar. The staid Senate Chamber was beginning to resemble a rancorous British Parliament debate, and Hornbrook could see that Branford was not going to have any of that. As the din died down, Branford looked at Hornbrook, but as he opened his mouth to chastise the Senator, he hesitated momentarily. And then it was too late. Hornbrook plowed on.

"I cannot be chided for speaking the truth, Mr. President. Congresses have, for decades, been taking the surpluses from the Social Security Trust Fund, replacing them with worthless IOUs, called special-issue treasury bonds, and spending the money elsewhere to make the deficits look smaller. And if you look in the Trust Fund right now, you know how much real money you'd actually find? Absolutely nothing! It's time to come clean, fellow Senators: We've been stealing from the American worker!"

Pausing only briefly for the renewed wave of outrage to sweep across the room, he kept going. "We have a shrinking work force, and an expanding population of recipients. That's bad. You didn't save the surpluses when you had them. That's bad. You didn't invest them like any other pension plan would. That's bad. You not only didn't invest them, you spent them on other things. That's bad. And now you need them, and you don't have them. And that's really, really, REALLY bad!

"How bad? I sincerely hope the people of America are sitting down, because this is going to be a bit of a surprise. This is not just a *'Honey, I'm sorry, but I took the money out of your jar above the refrigerator and spent it on new bowling shoes'* kind of surprise. You see, my friends," Hornbrook said, staring at the C-Span camera, "while you may think you *know* about being in hock for the twelve trillion dollars of official debt—and another ten or twelve trillion we've already promised over the past two years to spend on more misguided bailout baloney—nobody ever tells you about your hidden debt. It's called *contingent liabilities*. It's the money we've promised to spend on Social Security and Medicare over the next several decades. That is, it's the piles of money we would need to put away right now in order to generate a large enough revenue stream to fill in the growing gap between the revenues brought in and the benefits paid out. If this was your household budget, it would be like spending all your paycheck before your credit card bill arrives. You gotta pay it, but you don't have it. And that's us—WE DON'T HAVE IT! Why? Because we are on a 'pay-as-you-go' system, and we don't save a dime. Not one dime. We aren't even CLOSE to having it. The liability for Medicare alone is easily FIFTEEN TRILLION DOLLARS. That's right, my friends, just for that one program it's more than entire *official* national debt. And even ignoring the estimates of some reliable sources that the amounts could be three times that, the GAO just last year said Medicare is going to be unable to function within seven years. And you guys think you can run healthcare for the entire country and not have the same results? Remember what I said about insanity.

"And what about Social Security? Well, get the paddles ready, doctor, because this is pure heart failure. Estimates of our contingent liability for Social Security at this point range from THIRTY to FIFTY TRILLION DOLLARS! And, again, we don't have a single penny of it saved! In addition, and while it may only be pocket change by comparison, hard-working Americans are also on the hook for collective state and local government debts of another two and a half trillion bucks. So, all together—national debt, bailout promises, unfunded contingent liabilities, federal pensions, the whole ball of wax— you've got as much as EIGHTY trillion dollars of debt. And those, of course, are just the conservative estimates.

"The cameras are on, dear colleagues. So tell me again—and your fellow citizens out there—just how you plan on paying for all that? Or do you figure, as you always have, that the voters will just forget all about it, as *they* always have, before the next election?"

The Senate was quiet, as if someone had told a dirty little secret without permission, and they were all a part of it.

Hornbrook sought to drive home the point. "Do you think it's an accident that we got in this mess? Hell, no. It's been a deliberate, ongoing effort. By the end of the Clinton's second term, 40 million adults were receiving Social Security payments; 5 million Americans got Supplemental Security Income; 8 million benefited from Temporary Assistance to Needy Families; 20 million got food stamps; 5 million received subsidized heating and air conditioning; 26 million kids ate subsidized school lunches daily; 30 million people received free medical treatment; 10 million benefited from public housing or housing subsidies; 20 million households shared $26 billion annually in Earned Income Tax Credits; 2.5 million received veteran's benefits, 1.7 million enjoyed federal civil service retirement, plus another 1.1 million military pensioners and 3 million retirees from state and local government. Frankly, there are so many separate—and often overlapping—federal welfare programs alone, it's hard to determine just how many total recipients of the public largesse there really are. Government is also now the biggest single employer in the country. Good grief, people, we have more people working for the government than in all manufacturing industries combined! More Americans now receive government checks of one kind or another than there are full-time private employees. And as every penny paid out in government benefits or wages has to be extracted as taxes out of the private economy, it means that each private worker has to support not just his own family but, in effect, some other government dependent or employee simultaneously. And this was true even *before* we started throwing umpteen trillions at banks and insurance companies and auto manufacturers and states and cities and lots of others who were just as fiscally irresponsible and poorly managed as Congress obviously is. Do you really think this can go on indefinitely?"

Hornbrook's incredulity was obvious. The Senate stayed silent. Hornbrook finally exhaled in an exaggerated sigh. "Well, I have some good news for you. I'm going to sit down."

"You have no idea how I welcome this announcement," growled Branford.

"I'm sure. But before everyone gets their hopes up, I am instead going to yield to my friend and colleague, the senator from the great state of Oregon, my neighbor to the south, Loren McClintock."

"Very well," intoned Branford, with obvious disappointment. "The chair recognizes Senator McClintock."

Loren McClintock, the senior senator from Oregon, stood and approached the speaker's podium. She was dressed in a simple navy blue business suit and white blouse, with a red and yellow scarf loosely tied around her neck under the collar of the jacket. She spoke in a clipped, no-nonsense style, and with her impressive grasp of issues she was always either a sought-after ally or an opponent to be reckoned with. Now, as she stood before the Senate podium, Hornbrook knew his colleagues were going to get another dose of in-your-face argument. "Thank you, Mr. President. This won't take long. My honored colleagues, I swear there is more ignorance about economics than anything else we discuss, even after all these years of obvious successes and failures of basic approaches. In this case, it's patently simple: Price freezes never work. They never accomplish their stated goal. There are lots of variations, but they're all the same in the end. Minimum wages, rent control, maximum prices, minimum prices. It doesn't matter. Time after time after time it's been proven around the world that they are doomed to failure—or else they backfire, which can be even worse. It never varies—fixing *maximum* prices below what the market would dictate creates shortages; fixing *minimum* prices creates surpluses.

"Let's start with rent control." And she was off, zinging from one point to another as she illustrated the fallacies associated with the issues. Presently, she concluded by saying, "It is through the market system of prices that the indispensable information about demand is conveyed between producers and consumers. Many of you would condemn the market economy for being an evil 'profit' system. But it is not a profit system. It is a profit and *loss* system. And losses convey just as important a message as do profits—together they tell manufacturers what to produce, and in what quantities. Break up the flow of that information, and you destroy the system that ensures the smooth functioning of the entire economy. Set prices outside the market and the entire framework collapses. Mr. President!" said Senator McClintock, abruptly ending her discourse, and catching Vice President Branford almost napping.

"Yes, Senator?"

"I intended be short and sweet. I was neither. However, I've had my say. Any questions?"

"Senator McClintock!"

"Yes, Senator Gervais?"

"Would the Senator yield?"

"Mr. President," said the short woman, "I yield the floor to my colleague from the great state of Wisconsin."

"The chair recognizes Mr. Gervais," intoned an already weary Branford.

Senator Brooks Gervais strode forward to replace Loren McClintock at the same podium. There was another shifting of the unobtrusive, nearly clone-like recording staffers who rotated on and off the floor, seldom being noticed by the Senators, even though these blazer-clad minions were responsible for documenting every word uttered within the Senate for the Congressional Record. "Thank you, Mr. President. And thank you, Senator McClintock, for trying to pound understanding into solid rock."

Brooks Gervais was generally a steadfast party man in only his second year in the upper house, but he was known to have an open mind. Hornbrook liked his perspective and his knack for seeing through most of the political nonsense and calling it like it was, to the delight (mostly) of his constituents.

"Mr. President," Senator Gervais began, giving no sign of being intimidated by the arena or the circumstances. "I would like to discuss these new tax rates for a moment. Let's see," he said, consulting some papers in his hand. "Looks like we're jacking up rates pretty good again. Now, stop me if I'm wrong, but I do think you're going to stir up some of our beloved 'unintended consequences' if we do that. May I ask our esteemed Majority Leader a question?"

"I'm all ears," Brownsville snidely replied.

"If you are poor and out of a job, to whom will you turn for help? To your poor friends at the soup kitchen?"

"Of course not."

"Of course not," repeated the younger man. "It's the rich people who invest the capital that creates new jobs. So why do we want to shoot our collective self in our collective foot by penalizing the very people who provide the lifeblood of our economy and provide the majority of the jobs? Do you really think that if you ask them to pay even more that they are going to sit still for it? This may come as a shock, but most rich people aren't stupid! Do you really think they are going to leave all their money hanging on the clothesline for you to pick off as you please with higher taxes? Do you really think that they are going to keep on investing their money in expanding their businesses or creating new ones, when you've taken away all of the incentives, but none of the risk?"

"Only those who can afford it can help those who cannot," retorted Brownsville.

"Okay, let me see if I've got this right. The government wants to spend more money. So it has to raise more money. So the obvious answer is to tax more heavily those who have more money. Right?"

"That's very simplistic, but yes."

"Simplistic is right! And I do believe you'd have to be a simpleton to believe that it will work. Even if we overlook the fact that more than one half of the entire population pays virtually no income taxes at all—"

"You are distorting reality, sir!"

"Baloney. The bottom fifty percent of wage earners pays less than five lousy percent of all income taxes the government gets. That's right. Half the population pays hardly a dime! That's no distortion. But let me finish, and I'll give you another dose of reality. First, raising taxes will not raise revenues collected. I really don't know how many more times that you will have to try that before you'll get the picture. Raising the top marginal rate in 1916 from 7 percent to 77 percent resulted in a lousy *four* percent increase in revenues.

The Hornbrook Prophecy

Is that too long ago even for you? How about 1990? When the tax rate was increased from 28 to 31 percent? Yep. Tax revenues from the rich ended up *falling* by five percent. On the other hand, when Congress cut taxes by a third in 1964, revenues doubled over the next eight years. In the 80s, the same thing happened: Tax rate cuts actually *increased* revenues to the government. See a correlation?"

"Thirty or fifty or even a hundred years ago isn't the same as today," said Brownsville, determined to throw this whippersnapper out on his ear. "All you have to do is look at the plight of so many hard-working Americans today to realize that history lessons aren't going to put bread on the table for them. It's as plain as the fuzz on your face that we simply haven't done enough, or these poor people—the very people who are the heart of the economy—wouldn't be in the mess they're in right now."

"The only thing that's plain is that no matter how much money the government taxes out of the economy it can't solve the problems. And to give you both an income AND a sales tax to play with? Well, I think you're too old for it."

"What are you talking about?" demanded Brownsville.

"Well, I believe you'd get 10-14 years for raping the taxpayer, and another 25 years to life for murdering the economy!" Brownsville had bounced to his feet again, but before he could say anything, Senator Gervais said, "Don't bother, Senator. I'm done. I urge, as strongly as I can, a NO vote on S.100." And having concluded his remarks, he returned to his seat.

Henley Hornbrook and Lewiston Weiser began a quiet discussion in the interlude, but Brownsville was on his feet first. "Mr. President."

"The Chair recognizes the Majority Leader."

"Thank you, Mr. President. I, and I'm sure many of my colleagues, need relief from this diatribe. As such, I am calling for a recess until tomorrow."

"Very well, we will continue with debate at 10 a.m. tomorrow. We stand in recess."

Chapter 8

> *"There are two methods, or means, and only two, whereby man's needs and desires can be satisfied. One is the production and exchange of wealth; this is the <u>economic</u> means. The other is the uncompensated appropriation of wealth produced by others; this is the <u>political</u> means."*
> —Albert Jay Nock (1873-1945)

Thursday – January 21

So far, so good, thought the Majority Leader, as he entered the Senate Chamber. *Two days worth of debate and nothing of consequence to worry about. They scored a few points, but no big deal.* He saw Milt Freewater talking with Florence Dillard and went over to them.

"Hi, Halsey," greeted his Majority Whip. "What do you think?"

"No sweat, Milt. They'll never be able to turn this around. I expect that we'll be calling the vote by three or four at the latest. Well in time for the evening news." This would be a crowning achievement for his stewardship of the Senate and he was finding it difficult to contain his pleasure. Having such a prominent role in the crafting and passing of such crucial legislation at such a precarious moment in the nation's history would make the heads of lesser men spin. History books would forever link his name to the era when the country was successfully pulled back from the brink of calamity.

"Hornbrook hasn't put up much of a fuss, has he?" said the nation's first simultaneous First Lady/Senator.

"No," said Brownsville, warily. "But you never know."

"Win has the utmost confidence in you. It appears you made good use of the information he gave you about his meeting with Hornbrook."

"We probably didn't need bother," said Freewater. "But before a big game you need to study the other team's game films. Besides, it was a good change, throwing in that defense spending cut. The Pentagon is bloated anyway and we get to finally chip away at it without even needing another excuse."

"Sort of a two-fer," added Dillard.

Brownsville let his friends banter while he turned his attention back to business. The Chamber floor became increasingly active as the members flowed in. The gallery was nearly full also. About ten minutes later, Vice President Branford strolled in, talked with several of the senators in the front, and then climbed the rostrum. The session was brought to order, some housekeeping chores dispensed with, and then the attention once more was focused on the major business of the day. Those senators arguing points and expressing support in favor of the bill had been, by and large, heard from the previous day. As Majority Leader, Brownsville would be the last act, and it would be his job to settle the nervous, sway the fence-sitters, and deliver the votes. But before he could do that, there would undoubtedly be a few more salvos fired by opponents. He glanced in the direction of the desk of the senior senator from Washington, but Hornbrook was sitting back in his chair, apparently chatting idly with his chief of staff.

He resented Hornbrook's belittling of the bill, because he really did consider the AEFFA to be a capstone, as Hornbrook had called it, not of decades of "misguided, misleading, and mischievous efforts" but of his own life. Today might even help Brownsville balance the books of his heritage. The enormous wealth of the Brownsville Freight Company had embarrassed him all his life, if only because people knew that his political career had been bought and paid for by his father and his connections—at least in the early days. He frowned. Most people did not know that the family business—and its subsequent prosperity—began with a single truck delivering bootleg liquor near Bewleyille, Kentucky back in the late 1920s. Even the family name had shady roots, invented and painted on the first truck in an attempt to avoid scrutiny by the police. It hadn't worked. His grandfather had spent several months in jail for what he later described as "tampering with temperance." It was only after the 21st Amendment ended the profitability of Prohibition that the growing fleet turned to more legitimate transportation efforts.

The AEFFA could also erase the last of the guilt Brownsville had quietly felt during much of his political career. His father's Depression-bred ambition and toughness expanded the company into air cargo and maritime shipping. He made too many enemies to gain political power for himself, but he bought a lot of friends in high places. And his money paved the way for his son to enter politics so he could get the family inside the power game.

Brownsville laughed ruefully to himself as he thought of his father. He knew he would not have been successful in politics without his father's money, but he wasn't as certain his father would have liked what he bought. Instead of the contempt for "the masses" his father had held, Halsey had, over the years, developed a real compassion for the people he served, convinced they were often incapable of managing their own lives only because of what he liked to characterize as a *"discriminatory denial of opportunity."* With the passing of every year, he had become more widely recognized as the standard-bearer for the little guy. Even today, as Majority Leader of the Senate, Brownsville was most proud that women, elderly, children, immigrants, minorities, and countless other groups of the oppressed, whether real or imagined, came to him to lead their fights.

Now, finally, this legislation would be justification for their trust. Deep in the recesses of his psyche he knew there lingered a tiny portion of doubt, the barest hint of a feeling that, on top of the excessive spending of the last few years, this might be too much for the framework of society and the economy to bear, as that damnable Hornbrook was bound to declare. But that twinge was insufficient to overcome a career's worth of ideological and practical witness to the benefits of government stewardship of the public trust.

"Okay, HB, let's get this done," said Freewater.

Embarrassed to have been lost in his thoughts, Halsey Brownsville looked around quickly and saw the chamber was relatively full. He nodded, rose and approached the microphone. Gaining recognition, he began, "We have heard a number of interesting comments, criticisms, and, of course, a lot of support for this legislation over the past few days. I'm sure that most all of us have reached our decision by now, and are ready to get on with the vote. Just to be proper, I will ask again, is there any other discussion?" He paused for a count of three, then just as he was about to speak again, the voice he knew would be waiting for him rang out.

"Mr. President!" said Henley Hornbrook.

Shit, thought Brownsville.

"The Chair recognizes Senator Hornbrook," said Branford, with obvious impatience.

"There's just one other area I'd like to explore concerning this so-called 'Financial Freedom Act,' began Henley Hornbrook. "No matter how much Americans pay in taxes, it is *never* enough for you. So you keep asking for more. And it isn't enough. So you print up more money. And it isn't enough. So you borrow more money. And it isn't enough. So now we're all desperately

The Hornbrook Prophecy

in debt—perilously so—and here you are again, asking for more! And you expect the American taxpayer to believe you one more time when you tell them that this will fix the problems, and we'll all live happily ever after. But you know what? It's not going to work! You know why? It's because you've knocked the legs out from under people. What made this country great is that people had an *incentive* to work hard, and take risks. With the punitive tax rates and regulations that you've crafted here, you're destroying that incentive. And I'm warning you all right now. If you pass this bill, these tax rates and price freezes and wage mandates and benefit guarantees are going to be so burdensome that people will stop trying!"

Brownsville smiled inwardly for having anticipated his opponent's opening remarks and he leaned again toward the microphone. "I find it unfortunate, maybe even surprising, that the Senator from Washington has so little faith and confidence in the American people. Indeed, I would encourage the Senator to look at the polls. The American people *want* this bill. Overwhelmingly, this legislation represents the *will* of the people themselves. That's what makes a democracy great. We can respond to their needs."

"There is no will of the people! There are only individuals, trying to keep their boats from being swamped by an ever-expanding government leviathan which then steps in so it can save them from drowning."

"Bull-pucky. I repeat, the people want this bill passed. Sixty-eight percent of them, according to yesterday's polls."

"Senator, if sixty-eight percent of the people voted to, say, confiscate the property of African-American people, would that be just the 'will of the people'?"

"Don't be ridiculous."

"It's not ridiculous. You say it's just the 'will of the people'—you know, *democracy*. But an unrestrained democracy is just another word for mob rule. That's why we have laws: The Constitution and the Bill of Rights—laws that are supposed to protect everyone, from either dictators *or* mobs. The *will of the people* cannot—must not—be allowed to supercede the protection of the inherent rights of *individuals*. And a law that confiscates the property of rich people is no different from a law that confiscates the property of Black people."

"You're comparing apples to oranges."

"You should have said 'peanuts to pecans,' because anyway you look at it, to pass this law would be nuts. What you propose it not going to make things equal. Some people will still have way more than others. So why stop short of true fairness? Wouldn't it be even more fair if we just took the entire gross domestic product—the national income, if you will—divide it by the total population and give an equal share to all people, no matter who they are or what they do, or don't do?"

"Don't be ridiculous," Brownsville said for the second time.

"It's not ridiculous at all. It's the very same idea as you're proposing, only more comprehensive. Actually, why stop there? If you're truly interested in fairness, shouldn't we really talk about fairness for all people no matter on which continent they live?"

"The United States Congress can hardly solve all the problems for every nation."

"Well, that's certainly a welcome admission. In my book, we can't even fix the problems in *this* nation. All we do is cause more of them. But indulge me for a moment, again. Have you ever heard of the Theory of Logical Extension?"

"I'm afraid not."

"That's probably because I just made it up. Let's extend that noble sense of fairness to *all mankind*, not just the poor in our country. After all, are not the *poor* in our country actually RICH compared to the average income and standard of living of the *world* population? Most of the poor in America have cars, televisions, microwave ovens, cell phones, and a good roof over their heads, but certainly the same cannot be said of the poor in Central and South America, Africa, India, or Asia, many of whom don't even have electricity. So let's be really fair. If you extrapolate your arguments about taxes, fairness, ability-to-pay, and redistribution of wealth to their logical extension, should we not simply divide the sum total of *global* income by its total population to arrive at a truly equitable world? You could get by on three or four thousand dollars a year, couldn't you, Senator?"

"Don't be ridiculous!" exclaimed Brownsville.

"You're starting to repeat yourself. But why is it ridiculous? That's what you've been advocating all your life: From those with the greatest ability to those with the greatest need. So all I'm saying is, let's not pussyfoot around anymore. If it's good enough for Americans, as you propose, it should be good enough for the entire world!"

"You're comparing—"

"Peanuts to pecans?"

"It doesn't—"

"Make any sense?"

The Hornbrook Prophecy

"It would—"

"Destroy our lives? You've just discovered the meaning of the *Theory of Logical Extension*, which is this: Liberal policies applied globally would create a world in which not even a liberal would wish to live." Hornbrook didn't let up. "You don't mind telling hard-working Americans that they should give up half of what they earn so that you can keep enough people indebted to you that you are assured of reelection, but God forbid you yourself would have to live the kind of life to which you want to condemn them. Like most liberals, you would fall apart if your cherished policies adversely affected you personally."

Brownsville had, by this time, recovered enough from the unexpected table-turning to realize he had to derail his opponent's arguments. "This is *LUNACY*! The people of America are not going to be duped by your extreme exaggerations. Of course we all care about the poor around the world. That's why we are so generous as a nation. But you're making common sense seem like extremism!"

"Oh, please! Congress has the patent on exaggeration. We have made class warfare an absolute art form by declaring every problem to be a 'crisis' and drumming up enough sob stories and outrage to justify letting the government interfere in our lives more and more every year. If you enact this bill, jobs will be lost, business will fail, there will be shortages, and you know what else? The tax revenues you are trying to increase will not only *not* increase, they will *fall*. And then watch the deficits take off!"

Hornbrook paused, took a long look around the large room which was in total silence, and said, "Senators, please think about this carefully. Vote with your heads. Think about the future of the country for a change, not just your chances in the next election. I urge you, emphatically, to vote 'NO' on S.100."

Senator Brownsville, immediately jumped to his feet and said, "Mr. President!" He did not want a recess to allow the other senators to reflect on Hornbrook's words.

"The Chair recognizes the Majority Leader," said Vice President Branford, gratefully.

"No…No…No…" began Brownsville, emphasizing each word slowly. The elderly senator was the consummate floor leader, and phrased his words for maximum effect. "That's the best the Senator from Washington has to offer. No suggestions, no constructive amendments, no alternatives. Just 'no.' First he jokes about the minimum wage, a subject of vital and immediate concern to millions of low-income workers. Then he scoffs at a necessary measure to prevent erosion of workers' buying power. Then he belittles the hopes of the unemployed to make their own way in the world. And now, finally, he laughs at the very idea of leveling the economic playing field so that less fortunate people can gain the financial foothold they need to climb out of the depths of their plight. Well, I can assure all Americans that we here in Washington are listening to you, and we know that this is no laughing matter."

He waved a dismissive hand toward Hornbrook as he addressed his colleagues. "Mr. Hornbrook here would have us believe that more than two and a quarter centuries of benevolent rule by democratically-elected representatives, a period during which this nation has reached unprecedented pinnacles of achievement, progress, and world-wide acclaim, has led us to a point where we have suddenly awakened to discover that we are driving off some cliff! *MADNESS!* Shame on you, Mr. Hornbrook! Shame on you for threatening to tear out the very foundation of our constitutionally-framed government, a government which created a revolutionary system of checks and balances ensuring that the rights of all citizens would be protected, and in which every voice can be heard. A government where the will of the people can be reflected in its legislative bodies and ratified with every new election." He had his feet under himself now, and continued with vigor. "Fellow Senators, Mr. Hornbrook would have us believe that the greatest Presidents, the finest statesmen, the most dedicated public servants in our history did nothing more than trample Americans under their feet in their quest for personal fame and glory. Every wise and experienced father, every nurturing and loving mother throughout the long and difficult development of our country has taught their children that the key to success in life is to work hard, and they will be rewarded. But Mr. Hornbrook tells us that happiness lies only in having the government do nothing while corporations ride roughshod over their workers. There has not been a civilization in the history of mankind that has had its government sit back, stop working, and still raise their standard of living. Why is that? I'll tell you why. BECAUSE IT CAN'T BE DONE! I was right before. This is indeed *INSANITY!* It is time to reverse the constant and continuous disregard for the homeless, the jobless, the helpless, and the hopeless. Mr. President, it has been moved and seconded to pass Senate Bill 100, The American Employment and Financial Freedom Act of 2010. I call for an immediate vote."

"Very well," said Vice President Branford, with much relief. "The Clerk will please call the roll."

The Senate Clerk began working her way through the alphabetical listing of the Senate membership, votes being cast now electronically from each Senator's desk. *"Mr. Albrecht. Mr. Albrecht, 'Yes.' Mrs. ApRoberts. Mrs.*

The Hornbrook Prophecy

ApRoberts, 'Yes.' Mr. Banbury. Mr. Banbury, 'No.' Mr. Butterworth. Mr. Butterworth, 'Yes'..."

As the roll call proceeded, Senators began milling about, talking quietly with their friends and colleagues. No one left the floor. For most of them, this would be the most important legislation they had ever been involved with.

"Mr. Gandolfo. Mr. Gandolfo, 'Yes.' Mrs. Grady. Mrs. Grady, 'Yes.' Mr. Hathaway. Mr. Hathaway, 'Yes.' Mr. Hedges. Mr. Hedges, 'No.' Mr. Hornbrook. Mr. Hornbrook, 'No'..."

Henley Hornbrook was talking with Brooks Gervais and Morton Packwood, not paying close attention to the tally, but understanding the general sense of it. He was making some notes to himself, and nodding somewhat absentmindedly at the conversation.

"Mr. Marting. Mr. Marting, 'Yes.' Mrs. Masters. Mrs. Masters, 'Yes.' Mrs. Misbach. Mrs. Misbach, 'Yes.' Mr. Monroe. Mr. Monroe, 'No.'..."

A larger throng was gathering around Halsey Brownsville. It was obvious to everyone that his rebuttal had stemmed the bleeding and his patient/bill had recovered nicely. Handshakes were plentiful.

"Mr. Wells. Mr. Wells, 'Yes.' Mr. Winkleblack. Mr. Winkleblack, 'Yes.' Mrs. Woodrich. Mrs. Woodrich, 'Yes.' Ms. Zurcher. Ms. Zurcher, 'No.'"

There was a noticeable quieting of the chamber when the last name was called, as people on the floor and in the gallery, while already knowing the outcome, nonetheless waited to hear it officially certified. They didn't have to wait long.

"In the voting on Senate Bill 100, The American Employment and Financial Freedom Act of 2010, the Ayes are 73, and the Nays are 26. The motion is carried."

In the uproar and commotion that followed, few paid any attention to the Vice President who gleefully announced, "WE ARE AJOURNED!" even though no one made any motion to do so.

CHAPTER 9

> *"Taxes on the very necessaries of life enable an endless tribe of idle princes and princesses to pass with stupid pomp before a gaping crowd, who almost worship the very parade which costs them so dear."*
> —Mary Wollstonecraft, in
> "A Vindication of the Rights of Woman," 1792

Friday – January 22

There was no shortage of Senators, Congressmen, Cabinet members, and other dignitaries in the President's Room of the Capitol, all jockeying for position for the photo-opportunity as President Winston Dillard entered and shook hands all around. It was a historic room, where Lincoln had defied his own Senate leaders over the Wade-Davis reconstruction bill, and where Chief Executives and other important figures had often gathered for dramatic bill-signing ceremonies. The décor featured elaborate Brumidi frescoes, a portrait of George Washington's War Secretary Henry Knox, and Madonna-like figures in the ceiling medallions representing both religion and executive authority.

Dillard settled behind the ornate desk to sign the newly-passed American Employment and Financial Freedom Act of 2010. The President, in accordance with custom, used numerous different pens to sign the bill with as much ceremony as could be afforded such a simple act.

"There is a great sound being heard across the land," he began with the proper blend of dignity and gloating. "It is the sound of relief. It is the sound of a people who have been holding their breath waiting for us to help them. It is the sound of gratitude from those who will now enjoy new opportunity, new jobs, and new financial freedom."

"It is the sound of gagging," said Lewiston Weiser, watching the television across the room in Henley Hornbrook's inner office.

The Hornbrook Prophecy

"It's the sound of people gasping at the sight of their empty wallets," said Hornbrook. He was realistic enough to have gone into this battle with no significant expectation of winning, but the extreme lopsidedness of the vote was more disappointing and disheartening than even he anticipated.

"So much for the two-party system, Henley."

"It ended a long time ago, Lew, but this was truly brutal. Well," he said, putting his feet up on the desk and leaning back in his chair, "I said that I wanted to make some noise, and I guess we managed that all right. It was almost worth it just to see Brownsville almost go ballistic." He laughed.

"I thought for sure he was going to have a stroke!" Weiser said, joining the private laughter. "*LUNACY! MADNESS! INSANITY!*" he mimicked. "I hope I can get a copy of that from the CSPAN archives someday." Then he lost his smile. "I wonder how long the honeymoon will last?"

"Good question. Most of the provisions are retroactive to January One. Monday's polls will probably give Dillard eighty or ninety percent approval numbers. But if they're half that by the end of the quarter, I'll be amazed. Well, onward and upward. We'll just have to see what unfolds. In the meantime, what's next on the horizon?"

"There's the Pacific Rim Trade Conference in LA starting two weeks from Sunday."

"That's great. Southern California is not a bad place at all to be in the winter. I just hope I'm wrong about this whole thing. It's not because I hate to think about being in a 26-vote minority for the rest of my term. I fought it because I was convinced—I *am* convinced—that it will be a disaster."

"So, do we continue the fight?" said Weiser.

"Nothing left to fight, Lew. It's law. But if the problems are going to be as bad as we suspect, maybe we can help people develop some kind of strategy to cope with it. First we need to get a better idea of what specific developments we might expect."

Weiser thought for a moment, then slapped his thigh. "Sebastian Fellsmere!"

"Come again?"

"Sebastian Fellsmere. He's a friend of mine. A Brit. We met a long time ago, back when there was so much craziness before the Chinese took over control of Hong Kong. One of our clients had huge contracts with a manufacturing firm there, and wanted to survive through the transition.

Sebastian was a financial officer for the British outfit which managed the operations of the firm. Anyway, he proved to be a remarkable prognosticator of how events would ultimately unfold. Now he's got his own financial management and consulting group. In New York. Their record is enviable by any standards for turning around problem companies and positioning clients advantageously. I haven't talked with him for a while, but I just know he'll have a handle on this already."

"Great! Give him a call. I'd love to talk with him."

Lew Weiser pulled his cell phone out of his coat pocket, punched up his address book, and found the number for SFG. Hitting the call button, he was soon connected to his friend's private secretary, who responded to Lew's inquiry, "I'm sorry, Mr. Weiser, but Mr. Fellsmere is not here. As a matter of fact, he's in Washington himself right now. Let me get you his number." A few moments later, Weiser was speaking with the analyst himself.

"Hi Sebastian. It's Lew Weiser."

"Lewiston! Splendid to hear from you. I won't ask you how you are, because this silliness your boy Dillard just signed is bound to have made you and your boss a little hot under the collar."

"You have hit the nail on the head, Sebastian. As a matter of fact, the Senator would like to talk with you a bit about what you think might happen next."

"Well that's really no mystery, but I'd be happy to bat it around a bit if he'd like. I'm going back to New York tomorrow, but I've got a little time this evening if that's convenient. Say about seven?"

Weiser mouthed *"Seven?"* and Hornbrook nodded his agreement. "Seven's just fine," Lew said into the phone.

"I hate to be a bother, but I'm working on some matters which are probably related to your sticky wicket, so would it be at all possible for you to drop by my apartment here in the Watergate?"

"Sure, that's fine," agreed Weiser. He got the apartment number, expressed his thanks, and said good-bye. He folded his phone to cut the connection, and slipped the phone back in his coat. "It's all set, but we have to meet him at his place. It'll be worth it."

"That's okay," said Hornbrook. "I need a break from this place."

***

The Hornbrook Prophecy

Lew Weiser rested his glass on his crossed leg. They were sitting in the spacious living room of the Watergate apartment. It was expensively, but tastefully furnished, and decorated with original oils by mostly obscure artists. There were a multitude of small, exquisite porcelain and crystal figurines placed upon the mantel, on wall units, and all over an ornate glass étagère in one corner. Sebastian Fellsmere, upon seeing the reaction to the extensive figurine collection by his entering guests, had explained, "My wife is an absolute fanatic about these things. There's nary a city in the world where we've visited that she's failed to find something new and unique that she's simply *got* to have. It's frightful, really. Our home in Manhattan is absolutely overrun with them, so she's put this bunch here and the rest in our little cottage in Wales." Weiser took in the surroundings and decided the Welsh abode would likely be considerably more than a "little cottage." And yet the fineness and beauty of the pieces gave the apartment an atmosphere of serenity that seemed unnatural, albeit welcome, in the midst of an otherwise frenzied city. Fellsmere might work in the frantic and often chaotic world of international finance, but it was obvious that he knew how to retain or regain the tranquility of a peaceful soul.

After he had served small snifters of cognac to his guests now settled on the delicate brocade sofa, Fellsmere settled into a high-backed Queen Anne chair, and prompted his old acquaintance, "I'm pleased, Lew, to have a chance to talk to you and the Senator. I was never quite sure, for one thing, why you left Seattle for this place."

"I've wondered the same thing many times," Weiser replied with a smile, looking at his boss.

"Lew does keep threatening to return to his firm," said Hornbrook.

"Well, small wonder. Weiser, Rincover, and Nagle was one of the most aggressive young law offices in the Pacific Northwest and, what with their expertise in Pacific Rim trade agreements and multinational contract law, it's easy to see why they were so busy with all kinds of corporations who had to cross swords with the nightmarish bureaucratic alphabet soups which pour forth from their own state capital there, let alone D.C. Of course, the USG isn't the only government engaged in seemingly endless attempts to ensnarl private domestic and foreign commerce."

"Henley's a persuasive guy," Weiser chimed in. "Besides it's not a huge switch from law to politics. You know what they say: 'Rope. Tree. Politician. Some assembly required.' I think they said that about lawyers first."

"Lew had first hand experience seeing how difficult government could make things. I think he liked the idea of trying to do something about that more directly," said Hornbrook.

"You should talk," scoffed Weiser. "Henley was a lowly Congressman until the party wanted him to run for the Senate. His wife had died the year before and I think he might have gotten out then if the Senate seat hadn't tempted him to play with the big kids."

"True, true. But I nearly missed the chance altogether."

Weiser explained, "Henley had been unhappy about his own party, even before they approached him about the Senate seat. He thought it had strayed too far from its own avowed beliefs."

"I was fortunate to get elected as an Independent, but I had to live with myself, too. You can't campaign one way, legislate completely the opposite and still look yourself in the mirror."

"You see, Sebastian, the fact is that Henley's too much of an idealist. In the Senate, his lack of party affiliation and his unwillingness to compromise his basic philosophies certainly reduces his effectiveness as a legislator, but he's nothing if not a man of reason and common sense—two traits in extremely short supply on Capitol Hill. Both parties frequently court his favors and both parties often turn to him as a mediator of sorts in a Congress more sharply divided over the reins of power than because of their seemingly merging ideologies. Of course, I don't know how he got along in Congress without me, to tell the truth. He was a history professor, for crying out loud! Loves it, as a matter of fact. And he still thinks the first few thousand years of mankind's history was just a warm-up for the exploration and settlement of the New World."

"Too bad not enough people studied their history," said Fellsmere. "They might have learned something from it."

Hornbrook shook his head with apparent disgust. "You're absolutely right. Lincoln said this was the 'last, best hope of mankind' because it was such a new and unique experiment in government. And this is it! There's simply no place else left to go and start over. If we screw it up here, we'll never get another chance."

"Well, I'm afraid this bill the President's just signed is not going to help much. I read summaries of your debate with great interest. I must say you, and some of your fellows, seemed to have won on the battlefield of common sense, but evidently lost the war of ideology."

"I don't know about the former, but the latter, certainly. Now, the question is, what will the price be?"

"We're mostly interested," added Weiser, "about your feelings for how events may unfold from this point."

"Well, that is the question, is it not?" replied the Brit. "First of all, your basic economic assumptions were dead on. This new legislation will undoubtedly have the opposite effect of what is desired. They simply will not raise the revenues they hope by raising taxes, but I've never known your Congress to have the willpower to stay within its means, so the result will be new debt. As you stated, you have three main pillars of existing debt—the official debt from outspending your pocketbook, and the twin, unfunded, but mandated liabilities of Social Security and Medicare. The numbers are nearly impossible to calculate exactly, but I have no trouble with the additional trillions you suggested in your debate. They are probably even higher."

"I'd almost rather you hadn't agreed. It seems like no one else wants to admit it," said Hornbrook.

"Naturally. These pillars are driven by demographics, and with your so-called baby boomers retiring, the dependency ratio of retirees-to-workers is accelerating also. More and more retired people will need to be supported by fewer and fewer workers, since the system does not actually put money from each worker into savings to be used for that worker later on but rather tries to pay as it goes. That's the basic flaw of the plan, and why it is unquestionably doomed to failure. However, the really bad news is that I doubt that the whole house of cards will stand up long enough for Social Security to meet its own end."

"What do you mean?"

"Simple, sir. The Social Security system right now is still in the black—barely, mind you, but still on the plus side. Those are the funds your Congress raids every year to keep your budget afloat. But if we're right about expecting tax revenues to fall, then soon even those Social Security surpluses will be gobbled up and the debt will balloon without control."

"How fast, do you think?" asked Weiser.

"Very, I suspect. The market was closed by the time the vote was in yesterday but it fell today. I suspect that will continue on Monday; maybe even worse. And it could easily continue. Capital markets "vote" instantly, like you said, all day, every day, on government behavior. Every time the government makes a "mistake" that hurts the market, the 'voters'—the bond and stock traders—punish it by sending their capital elsewhere. And this will be seen as a huge mistake. Whenever a government tries to confiscate wealth, capital runs for its life, and in today's electronic world, a 100-foot high 'Berlin wall' could not prevent it. In the late 90s, when Russia was flirting with a return to Communism, their major capital exited the country *within a day!* When the threat retreated, the money returned, although slowly and cautiously, and not without having caused great hardship by its even temporary absence. Global capital is truly democratic; it flows to wherever it is treated most kindly."

"And then?"

"Intuitively obvious, if you don't mind me saying so. Capital leaves, companies wither, jobs are lost, tax revenues fall, and the debt goes positively ballistic. A debt spiral is created."

"What on earth is a debt spiral?" asked Hornbrook.

"Simply put, as the total debt increases, so does the total *interest* on the debt, which further adds to the debt, which then further increases the interest on the debt, which again increases the debt, and so on. But that's not the worst of it."

"God, I knew you were going to say something like that. So what then?"

"There are other international considerations. Much of your debt is 'owned' by foreign governments, businesses, and investors. That's not as bad as many people think. Actually, it has always been a sign of the strength of the economy, not a weakness. Everybody wants to own dollars, so they buy dollar-denominated assets, like Treasury bonds, which are simply dollars plus interest. When other foreign economies have gone in the tank, as with the Asian markets in the early-to-mid 90s, then there is a rush to buy even more T-bills which have been seen as a safe haven. In 2008, however, you began to dramatically inflate your money supply via the 'print more' approach. Inflating the money supply ultimately debases the value of the dollar so, for the first time, the 'full faith and credit' of the United States of America was starting to look pretty shaky. It became tougher to sell Treasury notes, because foreign lenders, like China, were starting to look for more tangible guarantees. If the U.S. economy goes any further south now, then such dollar-denominated assets will become even more of a hazard, and there would be a big move to sell bonds and T-bills. The government cannot afford to have that happen on a large scale, so in order to attract buyers, it would have to make such assets more attractive, which it could only do by increasing the return on investment they yield—that is, it raises the interest rate paid to buyers."

"Which raises the costs of borrowing."

"Exactly! And then we're off to the races again with *another* spiral: If there's no confidence in the U.S. economy, investors will sell T-bills and bonds to buy Asian or Euro-bonds. As the demand for dollar-denominated assets falls, interest rates have to be increased. That increases the costs to the U.S. government, which increases debt, which increases the percentage of the budget spent on debt, which worsens the economy, which makes those dollar-denominated assets even harder to sell—"

"Which increases interest rates again, which creates more debt…"

"And so on, and so on," said Fellsmere, completing the picture. "I'll give you an example. At the end of WWII, Argentina was one of the wealthiest countries in the world but, because of debt and inflation-via-devaluation, it went to the near-bottom in only a single generation—and the wheels came off completely just a few years later."

"Sounds like it'll be worse than even I thought," said a gloomy Hornbrook.

"Sorry, but it actually gets worse. The global economy is not a zero-sum game. If it was, then if the U.S. went *down*, all the other countries' economies would go *up*. But actually, economic problems spread like a virus. And since the U.S. is the world economic leader, when you blokes catch a *cold* then the rest of the world gets *pneumonia*. Your decline could set off a world-wide depression. And since most countries operate on deficit spending, this exacerbates the debt spiral. Again, for example, let's say the European economy goes down. Then no one is going to want to own Euro bonds. So they increase *their* interest rates to attract buyers, but that forces us to increase *our* rates to compete with them, which increases *both* our debt loads, which worsens both our economies, which makes our respective assets even harder to sell, which, again, forces us to raise the rates paid, which increases costs, et cetera, et cetera, et cetera."

"Yes, well, thank you," said Hornbrook. "I just feel SO much better now. I should have put *you* in front of Congress."

"Sorry again. The place gives me the willies."

"Me, too, I'm afraid. Is that it?"

"Well, not completely. Sometimes governments will deal with debt by inflating it away. If they can't repay interest and expenses fast enough with tax revenues, they simply print more money. Unlike private or corporate borrowing, the government never has any limits on its ability to borrow money. No one turns down the opportunity to lend to the government—after all, it *is* backed by that hitherto famous 'full faith and credit' of the United States Government. The advantage of simply printing more money is that if you inflate the currency enough it will erode the real value of the debt that is outstanding. Theoretically, you can inflate it enough to erode the debt all the way to zero. The problem is it also erodes the value of money, and therefore the real living standard."

"Which creates its own problems."

"Precisely. Either the country makes a 'correction' such as when Ronald Reagan was elected in 1980, or it shifts further to the left. In the latter case, the government, taking action to supposedly fix the problems—but never acknowledging or admitting that it created them in the first place—moves even faster to a more socialized structure. It rides a new wave of class warfare—a hallmark of socialized governments—shifting the blame to 'the rich,' making them the target of its remedies."

"Which is exactly what we just did," said Lew. "Blame the rich. Tax the rich. Eat the rich."

"Quite so, my friend," concluded Fellsmere.

***

On the network news that evening, most of the talking heads of the television news outlets reported that the Dow Jones Industrial Average of the New York Stock Exchange had moved "sharply lower." Some labeled it as a "correction."

CHAPTER 10

> *"What kind of man would live where there is no daring?*
> *I don't believe in taking foolish chances, but nothing can*
> *be accomplished without taking any chance at all."*
> —Charles Augustus Lindbergh (1902-1974)

Sunday – January 31

Two weeks after their initial meeting, Elgin and Athena strolled out of the Good Lord Baptist Church in Remus, Alabama, and patiently waited for the rest of the congregation to emerge, give their Sunday greetings to the old pastor and to each other, and gradually dissipate. Athena held Elgin's left arm in a comfortable manner, and remarked on what she had just heard.

"Wow, Elgin!" she exclaimed. "You were right. He's absolutely inspiring. Almost hypnotic. And I just loved his message, you know, working hard, not blaming others for your problems, and all that."

"Personally, I think it's tragic that he's telling it to fifty people and not fifty thousand."

"Isn't that where you come in?" smiled Athena questioningly.

"I hope so. We seem to have an awful lot of the same basic feelings." Elgin looked over and saw that Reverend Hilgard was bidding good day to the last of his flock. "Let's find out for sure."

The two moved together across the walk and Elgin held out his hand to the elderly clergyman. "Good morning, Reverend Hilgard," he began. "I'm—"

"Good morning, Lieutenant Governor LaGrande," broke in Hilgard in his distinctive baritone.

"Reverend, I'm flattered you would recognize me," responded a surprised LaGrande.

"Mr. LaGrande, I may not march in the streets as in my more youthful days, but I'm not exactly pushing up daisies yet. You are one of very few of our people who have risen to executive positions in the governments of our nation. Shame on me if I were unable to recognize a rising star from a mere three feet away." He turned toward Athena, saying, "I will permit you, however, to introduce me to this beautiful young lady."

"Oh, forgive me. This is Athena Weston, Assistant Director of the Alabama Industrial Development Training." Athena beamed as she took the proffered hand, very dark and wrinkled, but with a surprisingly firm grip.

LaGrande smiled. "Reverend, when I was a boy, the pictures of you and Rev. King and the others were really an inspiration to so many of us."

"Mr. LaGrande, the one thing I learned during those very active days back then was that there were never enough hours in the day to do everything that we wanted to do. So if you are as good a lieutenant governor and as important to our people as you ought to be striving to be, then I doubt very much that you are here merely to reminisce about your boyhood memories. But I'd appreciate if you'd just a-wander next door with me to my humble lodgings where we can sit and talk a might more comfortably."

Reverend Hilgard gallantly extended his elbow toward Athena. She took it while Elgin fell in stride next to her, and the trio walked down the sidewalk and up the steps of the old, weary, but clean home on the grounds of the church. LaGrande held the creaky screen door open while Hilgard stepped inside with Athena. The old man invited them to sit in the parlor while he disappeared into what served as a kitchen, clinked around out of sight for a few moments, then reappeared with a pitcher of ice water and three glasses.

"I apologize for the limited beverage selection, but the Bible tells us that water is more precious than gold to a thirsty man," Hilgard said.

"We really didn't wish to impose, Reverend," said Athena.

Elgin waited until the glasses were filled, then began. "Reverend Hilgard, I did in fact come here to see you today not to talk about my childhood, as you say, but to seek your advice, and perhaps your help. I'm not sure how much you know about my background, but the motivating reason that I sought office was to try and see if it was possible to create for other poor boys and girls the type of opportunity that I had as a young man to make something of myself. I'll be honest with you, Reverend—I'm nothing special. I'm no genius; I'm not gifted with special talents. The only reason I'm not still in my old neighborhood scratching to feed my kids is because I was just lucky—lucky enough to find a job, save a little money, and get some experience and training that I was able to build on as I went."

"And I'll be honest with you, young man," said Hilgard. "These days that *does* make you special."

"But it *shouldn't*," countered LaGrande. "That's my point! Getting a job shouldn't be like hitting the lottery. And we shouldn't be sitting around waiting for the next wagon to toss us a bone. I want to forge a partnership between education, business, and the government. I want to be able to show business the human resources we have right under our noses in cities all across the state, and the profitability of creating a reliable, skilled work force that not only increases productivity but even pays for itself by becoming an important new group of consumers of their own products in the marketplace. I want government to recognize that it can provide a better service to its citizens, not by continuing the drain on our collective wealth through the perpetuation of and reliance upon assistance programs, but rather by encouraging and enhancing the ability of the private sector to create more taxpayers—after all, more taxpayers mean more tax revenues." He paused only briefly before continuing, "Finally, we have to go into the schools and homes of our young people, and convince them that change *is* possible, that they can break the cycle of dependence they're in and have a real chance to improve their lives. I don't believe that the way things are is the way things have to be. I do believe, though, that we have to help ourselves and stop relying on misguided philanthropy. But they need real hope that there are real opportunities and real jobs."

Elgin stopped, and found that he was on his feet and had paced across the room. The old preacher smiled and said, "You better take a breath, Mr. LaGrande. I do believe you might explode." He chuckled. "I don't have to ask you if you really believe what you say. Your conviction pours out of you. I honestly haven't seen that kind of passion in some time." He turned to Athena and said, "Is he that way all the time?"

Athena laughed, and replied, "It kinda grows on you."

Hilgard looked back at Elgin, losing his smile, and said, "Well, Mr. LaGrande, that was a fine speech. Now just why in the Good Lord's name did you come all the way out here just to impress a wrinkly old coot like me?"

"Very simple, Reverend," stated LaGrande. "I need you to help me."

"Oh my," sighed Hilgard. "I was just starting to like you."

"Hear me out, sir." Elgin stopped again, recalling some of the things he had explained to Athena on their drive to Remus. "I am truly appreciative of the blessings life has bestowed upon me. I am honored to have been trusted by the voters to serve as this state's second-highest official. But I also know my shortcomings—I'm a relatively new kid on the block, and Lieutenant Governor or not, I still have no real power of my own. And I also know what I'm up against. Without Scio's permission, I can do nothing—and we don't exactly see eye to eye. He worked very hard for Biggs Wasco, so he barely tolerates me. Plus, I have no pull within the traditional Black leadership—they greet me, and talk with me, and lament with me over the dire plight of our brothers and sisters, but I think they only see me as a threat to their own power in the status quo. And since they've been on the stage a lot longer than I have, they always command a bigger audience."

Hilgard listened, saying nothing.

"Frankly, I need a bigger voice. I need a more important voice. I need a more compelling voice." Elgin looked at him. "I need THE Voice."

The old Black man visibly winced, and bowed his head slightly. "I haven't been called that in a long, long time," he said slowly, and with a hint of melancholy. "But I think you vastly overestimate my value. I am like an old Halloween jack-o-lantern. I might have been a bright and useful light at one time, but they put out my flame and tossed me on the compost heap to get moldy and be forgotten. Nobody wants to see an old moldy jack-o-lantern, Mr. LaGrande."

"I think you're wrong, Reverend Hilgard," stated LaGrande firmly. "I'd say you're more like a wonderful Christmas story, one that we all used to listen to as children and find in it the meaning of hope and joy and purpose to our lives. Yes, we stopped telling the story for many years because we thought it was no longer relevant and we didn't need it. But we've all grown up now, and we want our children to know the true meaning of Christmas as we once did."

Elgin walked across the room again, sat down facing the pastor, and leaned toward him. "We need to hear that story again."

"It's my turn to be flattered, Mr. LaGrande," said the preacher, gently wiping a tear from the corner of his eye. "I just don't know."

"Reverend," said LaGrande. "I *do* know. People still listen to you. Several weeks ago I watched people in a park gather around you. I could see it in their faces. They *listened*. I saw it today in the faces of your congregation. They *hear* you, and they like what they hear."

He looked at Athena, who nodded, so he continued. "Reverend, you represent the very best of those who have struggled for the cause of the Black people. You've spent your whole life telling us that we need only to try and we can succeed. That we need only to believe we *can*, and we *will* make things better. But the obstacles have been overwhelming. Now, let me ask you: Do you believe what you've been saying?"

The old man straightened, and looked at Elgin. "Yes."

"Do you believe it is possible to create opportunities that help poor people help themselves?"

"Yes."

"Do you believe our people need only to have the opportunity and they will seize it?"

"Yes."

"Do you believe that if they take it they can succeed?"

"Yes."

"Do you believe that the ideas I outlined to you today could be the beginning of that opportunity."

"Yes."

"Do you want to help me?"

Hilgard paused for only a moment.

"Yes."

***

Elgin and Athena drove along US Highway 82, cutting diagonally across the heart of Alabama heading back to Montgomery, alternately offering suggestions or playing devil's advocate about their basic plans, and considering what steps they needed to be taking next. Both were enthused about their meeting with the once-famous Reverend Hilgard, and his agreement to join their cause. For the first time, Elgin felt that perhaps, just perhaps, he might actually have a chance to leave the arena of rhetoric and justify his election with real action. There were enormous hurdles—and hazards—ahead, but he felt good for having passed an important test.

Now it was nearly dark, and both had fallen silent for a while. Presently, Athena nodded, more or less as to herself, took a breath, and turned to Elgin. "A little while ago, we talked about other people or personalities we might enlist to help get behind our little crusade."

"Right."

"You know, besides the obvious clout we could use with businesses and, of course, Scio and company, ultimately we are going to have to sell it to the neighborhoods."

"No question. More than anywhere else, actually."

"I've been thinking about that a bit," she said. "And I think I know someone who might be really helpful."

"Great! Who is it?"

She hesitated, then said, "Perry Robbs."

LaGrande sighed. He glanced in the rearview mirror as he changed lanes to pass a semi. After he had settled back in his original lane, he thought about Athena's suggestion.

"Why on earth would you think that Perry Robbs would abandon a lifetime of publicity-seeking and come down off his high horse to get involved with a boring job training venture?" he said, somewhat sarcastically.

"First of all, I don't think it's fair to characterize his career as self-aggrandizing. He's got a pretty solid resume of getting his hands dirty and his knuckles scraped in pretty good causes," Athena bristled. "And I think you'd be pretty surprised to find out that he'd probably be pretty sympathetic to your ideas."

"Whoa!" said Elgin. "Don't get your dander up! I didn't know you were such a big fan of his."

"I didn't say I was a fan. I just said that he's worked hard, too. Just like you. And he's generally fought for poor Blacks. Just like you. I also know that he's had doubts as to whether his legal battles are really accomplishing any real permanent changes. And that he has agonized over the continued problems that many Blacks seem unable to escape."

Elgin shot her a questioning glance. "And how is it you have such an insight into his less-public image and personality?"

Athena looked out the window. "Well, I used to know him."

"Really. And what does that actually mean?"

"We sort of used to, you know, see each other for a while."

"Ah."

"No, it wasn't all that serious. It was some time ago. While I was still in college. We met on campus. He was visiting as a guest of some campus group and I was young, and impressed, and, I guess got a little infatuated."

"How interesting. I had no idea you collected us famous Black guys."

"Oh Elgin, don't get—" Athena broke off as she looked at Elgin and realized he was grinning in the darkness, feigning his indignation.

CHAPTER 11

"You can no more win a war than win an earthquake."
—Jeannette Rankin (First female member of Congress, 1916)

Wednesday – February 10

Eagle McCall was a patient man, but the rush hour traffic on the Hollywood Freeway was sorely testing him. He had spent the last four days in Los Angeles while Senator Hornbrook was attending the annual Pacific Rim Economic Conference. Economics was hardly McCall's area of expertise, but the head of Japan's security team for this Conference was a former military colonel with whom McCall had become acquainted when he had been stationed with the Army in Japan years before. Hornbrook had suggested that McCall seek him out and try and get an additional inside feel for Japan's current perception of how US domestic economic issues and problems might unsettle the Far East. McCall found his foreign friend pleased to reestablish their relationship and full of interesting insight. Japan in general, and the military especially, were concerned that if the US economy fell off significantly it would not only affect their own, but the Chinese as well, since the US was their largest trading partner. If China's emerging financial markets were adversely affected, then there was no telling how its leaders might be tempted to react. It was too early to know if there was a problem looming but, for the Japanese and Chinese, a thousand years of mutual antagonism made it easy to find new excuses for new problems.

McCall had relayed the Japanese concerns to the Senator earlier today, and then hopped in his rental car to make a quick trip up the freeway to the San Fernando Valley to visit his sister, Laurel, and her husband, his old college roommate, Tom Warner. The trip was proving to be not so quick. He drummed his fingers on the steering wheel. He couldn't even remember the last time he'd seen them. And their kids. *Hmmmm*, he thought. *Let's see. Ellie graduated last June so she must be eighteen or nineteen by now, which probably makes Kate seventeen. Maggie's three years younger, so fourteen, and Tommy's probably only 11. And Emily can't be more than, ah, eight, no nine. Okay, got that straight. I think.*

Eventually, after he crossed the Ventura Freeway, the congestion eased and he began to pick up speed. Within a few minutes he transitioned to the 118, was able to exit the LA freeway system with relief moments later, and a few stop lights later finally pulled into the Warner driveway.

"Uncle Eagle's here!" yelled young Emily when she opened the door to his knock.

The entire clan was home and welcomed him in with great enthusiasm. Dinner was a boisterous collection of stories and smiles. Laurel sat between Tom and her brother and the kids jammed in around the table which was wedged into a corner between the kitchen and the living room.

As the plates were being cleared, Maggie complained, "Gosh, Uncle Eagle, how come you don't come see us more often?"

"Well, freckle-face," her uncle began, "it's not that I don't want to. But it's hard to get here very much since I work back east and live up north. And tell me, Maggie, would you like it if you couldn't see your mom?"

"No."

"Well, sometimes, when I DO get some time off I want to go see MY mother. And she lives in Montana."

"Hey, Dad," asked Tommy, "isn't that where you went to school?"

"Yep. I got to go to college up there. In Missoula. That's where I met your mom."

"Oh, I know. I just wasn't positive."

Emily chimed in, if for no other reason than to make sure her young siblings knew how smart she was. "Dad and Uncle Eagle were roommates in the dorms."

"Was that fun?" asked Maggie?

"Not as much fun as being roommates with Mom!" answered Kate. Everyone laughed.

"We had a good time," said Tom. "It was a neat place to live. Uncle Eagle could get a little crazy sometimes, but he did get me to go out with his sister."

"Look, I'm really sorry about that," said Eagle. "OW!" he then cried as Laurel punched his arm.

"So why didn't you stay up there?" asked Kate.

"Well," Tom began, "I sure wanted to. But I got interested in microbiology while I was working part-time in the community hospital lab, and I decided to change my major. The problem was that the school didn't have the classes I needed. And your grandpa didn't want to pay out-of-state tuition if I wasn't going to stay in the major I went up there for."

"Was Mom mad when you left?"

"She wasn't Mom yet but, yes, she wasn't very happy when I told her." Tom looked over at Laurel. "Somehow we managed to stay interested. I got to go back up in the summers to work at the hospital and I was pretty sure I was going to get a job when I graduated, but the guy I worked for, the supervisor, well, he died and the hospital filled the job I wanted with somebody else."

"So then what?" Kate was old enough to be interested in romance, even if it was her parents.

"I got a job here at Valley Memorial."

"That must have really made Mom mad."

"Not just Mom!" said Tom. "I thought Uncle Eagle was going to beat me up for leaving his sister."

"So you proposed!" said Kate, triumphantly.

"It was easier than getting beat up!" This time it was Tom who cried, "OW!" as Laurel punched him just as she had her brother.

"So how come we never moved up to Montana?" asked Ellie.

"Not so easy," lamented Tom. "First, your Uncle Eagle decided to go play GI Joe, so he wasn't even going to be there. Then you popped into the world. And then Kate."

"And me," said Maggie.

"And me!" Tommy shouted.

"And ME!" cried Emily.

"Yeah, yeah," said Tom. "And you ALL wanted to eat and have clothes and wear shoes and live in a house. So somehow we just never managed it."

"Maybe, someday," Laurel dreamed out loud.

"Yeah," agreed Tom. "Someday."

"Hey, Uncle Eagle!" interjected Tommy. "Wanna go shooting with us on Saturday?"

Eagle knew Tom was a semi-serious gun collector, and even did his own ammunition reloading. While they seldom hunted, the whole family now shared his passion for target shooting and often drove up into the high desert area to have fun plinking at random targets. Along they way Tom had taught them gun safety and responsibility—and defensive gun use.

"Yeah!" said Ellie. "Mom and I are making fried chicken and potato salad."

"Oh, boy, I do love your Mom's potato salad," Eagle drooled. "But I'm afraid I'm flying back to D.C. tomorrow afternoon."

"OHHHHH!" lamented several voices at once.

"I'm glad to hear you're still going out to the desert from time to time."

"Well," said Tom, "we have fun. And if nothing else, it's cheap entertainment."

"And it doesn't hurt to know how," said Eagle, looking at Tom. "It's a tough world out there."

"Boy, howdy."

Later, the children drifted off to bed or to finish homework assignments regrettably due the following morning. Tom, Laurel, and Eagle settled into comfortably worn chairs in the family room and spent some time catching up before the conversation finally turned toward recent political events.

"I can't say as I'm too excited over having my tax rates increased," Tom began. "God knows it's tough enough sometimes making ends meet. And I don't believe for one second that price freezes are going to help me; somehow I'll get screwed, no matter what."

"Eagle," said Laurel, "the Senator came off as being pretty worried about what this law might do. Is he really that concerned, or was that just the usual political posturing?"

"Well, I'll tell you, sis," answered her brother. "He's genuinely convinced that there's going to be serious fallout from this. Look at what the stock market's done so far—it dropped a lot the first day and has dropped more every day in the two weeks since. It's a bad trend. Senator Hornbrook thinks that in a couple of months, the economy will have slowed down so much that we'll be in big trouble."

"How big?" said a frowning Tom.

"Big big. Look, he hates the doom-and-gloom act, but I'm pretty sure the Senator thinks we're going to have a really big crisis. He's not saying much, but he did invite me in on one discussion he had with his chief of staff, and we talked about civil unrest issues. Pretty non-specific, mind you, but I got the distinct impression that he thinks the government's going to get itself into real financial trouble and if that happens then the first ones hit will be those who get the most benefits from it—like the poor. So it could get kinda nasty, especially in the cities, if there are any delays or whatever in sending checks out to people."

"Would that happen?" asked Laurel. "I mean, delays like that?"

"It's happened before when they've shut down parts of the government for political reasons, but those were very short term. Theoretically, I guess it could happen. I doubt it, because Congress would just borrow more."

"Yeah, it's not like they've never spent more than they had," lamented Tom.

Eagle added, "And if they couldn't borrow it, they'd probably just print some more."

"Government-issue rubber checks?" asked Laurel.

"Sure, why not?" said Tom. "Who's not going to accept a check from the richest country on earth?"

"Well, I can't believe they'd let anything happen," pronounced Eagle. "They'll borrow it, or print it, or something."

The conversation turned to other, lighter topics, mostly about the kids and their most recent antics. Finally, Laurel announced that she had to call it a night, since she would be working at the kids' school in the morning. They said their farewells, and Eagle picked up his jacket and headed for the front door. Tom walked out with him to the car.

"Look, Tom," said Eagle, "I didn't want to worry Laurel, but it doesn't take much to upset people anymore. Remember the Rodney King riots?"

"Of course."

"People don't react rationally when emotions are involved. I don't know, it's just crazy out there."

"That's for sure."

Eagle shook Tom's hand, opened the car door, then paused and turned back to face his brother-in-law. "If for some reason I find out something that I think might cause real problems, I'll try and give you a heads-up. If things are really hopping, I might not have too much time to give a lot of details." He hesitated. "Remember that book you gave me once about a comet hitting the earth?"

"Yeah. *Lucifer's Hammer*. Great book; it was one of my favorites. Everybody went nuts. And the whackos tried to take over."

"That's the one. If I remember correctly, the comet was named after a guy named Hammer—"

"No, it was *Ham-NER*, but the religious weirdos started calling the comet the *Hammer* of Lucifer and it stuck."

"That's right," remembered Eagle. "Anyway, after it hit the earth, they began to refer to that day as *Hammerfall*."

"The end of civilization as they knew it."

"Right. So if I call or get word to you somehow that a worst case scenario is unfolding, I'll use the word *Hammerfall*."

"The end of civilization as *we* know it?"

"Well, probably not quite like that. But today's *Hammerfall* would probably result in serious civil unrest."

"Riots?"

"Probably. And the cities would be the worst. And since you're in the middle of one of the biggest, it could be big trouble for you."

"I'll be ready."

"No, I mean BIG trouble. You won't want to be a part of it. Get out. It would probably happen pretty fast, so if I tell you, '*Hammerfall*,' get the hell out of here. At least get up to your folks' place out of the Valley. And if it gets that bad, it won't be over as fast as it begins. You might want to even think about coming up to Washington. I've got nothing but room, and the kids would think they were on vacation."

"That'd be a pretty extreme situation," protested Tom.

"Yeah, but I won't be saying *Hammerfall* unless it's pretty extreme. Think about it. And take this," he said, handing Tom an envelope. "This is a letter from the Senator, which says you're sort of on assignment for him. It basically asks that you be given consideration in travel. I thought it might help if you needed to, say, scoot on up my way. Keep it in the van. One way or another, a little preparation might be real handy."

"I suppose. Thanks." He took the letter. "I guess we'll see what happens."

"Okay." They shook hands a final time, and Eagle settled into the driver's seat and closed the car door. Rolling down the window, he said earnestly, "Take care."

"Later."

Chapter 12

> *"Education makes a people easy to lead, but difficult to drive; easy to govern, but impossible to enslave."*
> —Henry Peter, Lord Brougham (1778-1868)

Saturday – February 13

"Good morning, Lieutenant Governor LaGrande," said the impeccably-dressed Black man, wearing a pin-striped Armani suit and carrying a camel overcoat on his arm. With him, standing to one side and just behind him, was a very dark complexioned, sullen-faced Black man.

"Good morning, Mr. Robbs," said Elgin. Stepping back from the doorway of his downtown Montgomery condominium while he mentally tried to recall the face of the second man, he added, "Please come on in." He took their coats and hung them in the closet off the small terrazzo-tiled foyer. As they crossed into the living room, he said, "I believe you know Miss Weston?"

"I am truly thrilled to see you again, Athena. I must admit to having been very surprised when my secretary told me you were on the line last week. Surprised, but pleased." He took her extended arm, grasped it with both hands, then pulled her closer and gave her a light peck on the cheek. Then he released her and turned toward the other figure in the room, standing next to the deeply-cushioned arm chair from which he had just risen.

"Reverend Hilgard," said Robbs, crossing toward the pastor. "Other than the delightful opportunity to reminisce about grand times with Miss Weston here, I might not have been overly interested in what she outlined to me had she not informed me that the Right Reverend Ukiah Hilgard was already a part of the project. Your work with Dr. King broke barriers for all the rest of us."

"You are kind to say so, Mr. Robbs," rumbled Rev. Hilgard. "But I doubt we ever generated as many headlines as you have yourself."

Robbs raised an eyebrow at that remark, and then laughed. "Well, I won't apologize for it. Racial discrimination, police brutality, slum lords, dilapidated schools, and a whole host of other things are worth fighting against. Yes, it got me in some trouble. But if I hadn't been arrested in South Central LA following the Rodney King verdict in 1992, I never would have ended up studying the law and never would have seen just how good a tool it can be. For us."

"Which is why you got yourself into law school after you argued your own appeal so successfully?"

"Hey, let's hear it for prison libraries! But I think I've justified myself. Sure, I made a lot of money, and I've managed to piss off a lot of private groups, corporations, governmental agencies, and even Black organizations. But that's what activism is all about. Upsetting the apple cart. Somebody's got to be the asshole."

"Yes, I've followed your efforts with the National Poverty Law Council, particularly in cases involving hate crimes against our people."

"Perry, I don't think we know your friend," said Athena, gesturing toward Robb's companion.

The darker man smoothly slid forward a couple of steps, and as the poker-face broke into a sly grin, he announced quietly, "Rufus Pendleton, Miss Weston." He then turned and shook the hands of Elgin and Rev. Hilgard, before retreating to the background without further elaboration.

Recollection finally struck Elgin as he gazed at the man. Rufus Pendleton. Alleged former leader of the Black Guard. More militant than the more widely-known Black Panthers, the Black Guard had risen to its own level of notoriety following a series of gangland-type assassinations of several members of the Ku Klux Klan who had been arrested and tried for, but acquitted of, Black church burnings, rapes, and a murder. One week to the day after the not-guilty verdict was handed down in each of the four separate jury cases, the former defendants were found dead, three of them in bed and one in his car in his own garage. All had been shot behind the left ear with a .22-caliber bullet, in an unmistakable message that these murders were not only methodically systematic, but perpetrated by the same person or organization. However, unlike the pattern and behavior of many terrorist actions around the world, those responsible for these "rebound" attacks had left no evidence of their identity—no marks or symbols or signs left at the crime scene, no anonymous phone calls made to claim credit, no manifesto ever sent to newspapers.

After months of investigations, the FBI quietly concluded they were never going to solve the murders. Only later, after many other actions against White supremacist groups, was there rumored to be a new player in the game, known as the Black Guard. But rumors notwithstanding, the authorities were never able to pin any substantial charges on the group, mostly because they had such difficulty in identifying individual members. The only successful conviction was a weapons charge against a hitherto unknown man named Rufus Pendleton. He refused to enter into a plea bargain. As a matter of fact, during his entire incarceration from arrest, trial, and imprisonment, he refused to say so much as a single word to prosecutors, even in his own defense.

The only person Pendleton talked to was his attorney, Perry Robbs. Robbs did plenty of talking for the both of them, attacking the White criminal justice system, the "racist" media, the government, the White-dominated corporate world, and everything else that came into his sights.

Rufus Pendleton was widely assumed to be ruthless and vindictive. He was not widely considered to be brilliant. Many in the White community speculated, quietly and generally among only themselves, that Perry Robbs had really been the principal organizer and conspirator of the Black Guard.

"This is beginning to look like a meeting of the Biggs Wasco Admiration Society," observed Elgin, to lighten the tone of his memories.

"HA!" laughed Robbs. "We are probably the top two on his personal hit list." Robbs had very publicly dealt the longshoremen union leader a humiliating setback some years ago, when Wasco had nearly engineered a purely racially-motivated attempt to limit the admission of Blacks to the union.

"When I saw the TV coverage of your appearance at that union meeting, it looked like Wasco was going to go postal."

"Yeah, too bad he remembered the cameras. It would have been even more fun if he hadn't. But we not only derailed his plan, we forced them to create a minority recruitment office and initiate federally-monitored affirmative action practices. It really undermined his power. I loved deflating that fat bigot!" Robbs smiled with the memory. "Of course that ended up dumping him in your lap for the election, didn't it?"

"I should say so," replied Elgin.

"I guess he and his pals figured that they needed to enhance their influence. I know Scio played a big part in his decision to run against you."

"Yes, our esteemed Governor is not my biggest fan. I was particularly fond of how Wasco tried to pretend the union practices you forced on him were his own idea."

"Well, the voters didn't buy that anymore than they believed that story his campaign planted about alleged fiscal mismanagement at your Southern Office Supply business."

"Or the one about the prostitute," laughed Athena.

"Yeah, that was cute," Elgin agreed. "Except I did have to do some explaining to my mother."

With the conclusion of the introductions, Robbs lay his coat across the back of a chair, then circled around and sat in it. In the only manner he knew, he took the initiative to begin. "Mr. Lieutenant Governor, I spoke at length with Athena last week, and…no, wait, that's not quite accurate. I *listened* at length last week, as she explained some of your ideas and objectives. And I must say I was interested for two reasons. First, the Governor and his buddies, especially Wasco, will absolutely *hate* this, and any time somebody wants to kick them in the shins, I want to help."

Elgin was still dubious of the value of including Robbs in his plans, or even the motives the latter might have for being involved. And the presence of Rufus Pendleton, a certain felon and probable killer, was most unsettling. This wasn't a public meeting, and he didn't want to burn any bridges until he learned more about both Robbs and Pendleton, but he still spoke out. "Forgive me for interrupting," said Elgin, "but we're not going to be able to sell this on the strength of merely making Governor Scio look bad."

"Then please let me finish. I did say I was interested for two reasons. And the second is that I actually feel like your ideas have some merit. Perhaps even a great deal of merit. But you also have some huge obstacles to overcome."

"No kidding," replied Elgin.

"But good ideas are strong tools when it comes to building a new foundation," continued Robbs. "You just need to sell them."

"Then we are indeed on the same page, Mr. Robbs."

"Please call me Perry. I suspect we are in for some long days or nights, and I prefer spending long hours with friends."

The Lieutenant Governor considered his words. "Thank you, Perry. And just make it Elgin. I'm not really comfortable with titles."

"If you don't mind, since Athena's shared your ideas with me already, I'd like to cut right to it and give you some of mine."

"Please."

"First, what's our biggest obstacle?"

Elgin noticed the use of the possessive "our" but decided to accept it as a good sign. "The establishment."

"I agree. In all its forms. They'll all hate this, the bureaucracies, the unions, probably even the media, since they often dance to the tune of the others. So what are our odds of persuading them to embrace these ideas?"

"Slim to none."

"Again, I agree. So who's left to be on our side?"

"The people."

"Assuming that we can sell it to them. But, you see, we don't have to sell it to all of them. After all, this is a program that will primarily benefit our brothers and sisters in the inner city and poorer towns, right?"

"That's the whole point, all right," agreed Elgin.

"So it merely depends on your salesmen." Robbs sat back in his chair as though he had just scored a satisfying point in the courtroom. "Just send the right people to the right places and the brothers and sisters are going to react just like I started out a few minutes ago. Namely, if Scio and Wasco hate it then it *must* be good!"

Elgin looked over at Athena, who returned his glance. This was just what they had talked about, and Elgin's look was to acknowledge that she was correct to suggest bringing Perry Robbs in as an ally.

"Now, I'll be the first to admit," Robbs continued, "that some of my cases have done more to raise awareness of an issue than actually solve it. And in that respect I'm just as irresponsible as some of our other so-called leaders. Like Jackson, that hypocritical son-of-a-bitch. He gives preachers a bad name." He looked over at Rev. Hilgard.

"No comment," the elderly man said, with a slight smile.

"We all know that the only way our people are going to get out of their own ghettos—actual or psychological—is by gaining power of their own. Financial power. Education. Jobs. Independence. No more tossed bones. Okay. We have *two* sales jobs. You have to sell the idea to business—small business and big business alike—in a big, comprehensive, state- or even nationwide way. And Elgin, I see that as best being *your* job."

Elgin nodded, but said nothing. His lips were pursed as he anticipated the second part of Robb's summary.

"And you have to sell it in the ghettos and cities. And that's *my* job. More correctly, that's my job with the absolutely indispensable assistance of Mr. Pendleton."

Elgin sighed to himself. He had for several minutes seen it coming, but he still had his doubts. "I mean no offense, Mr. Pendleton, but if I don't raise the issue amongst ourselves, you know damn well everyone else will. They will anyway, so we might as well hash it out now. Namely, I have to be concerned that our message, our objectives, and our efforts might be, probably will be, completely ignored in the controversy that is sure to be raised over the involvement of the program—and the Lieutenant Governor, I might add—with Rufus Pendleton and the Black Guard."

Pendleton smiled, but remained silent, letting his advocate carry the argument. Robbs replied, "Yes, you're right, but you fail to realize that that very controversy is apt to make the effort ultimately successful!" He looked at Athena, who suddenly grasped his point.

"Perry's right," she said. "Those who are opposed to our ideas are not going to be won over until the program is already undeniably working. But your job selling it to business will be easier because of the street credibility you'll have with Perry and Mr. Pendleton involved."

"Oh, baby, you're brain is sooo sexy," smiled Robbs.

"Too late, Perry."

"My loss is Elgin's enviable gain. But you've got it. Elgin, what factors most keep old businesses from growing or new ones from coming into this state?"

"Mostly lack of a suitable workforce. That's the whole idea."

"But you're still missing the point."

"Which is?"

"Fear!"

"Fear?"

"Of course! Fear. Forget all the political correctness and liberal speechmaking. It's crap. Deep down in their guts, Whites are still afraid of Blacks. They always have been. They still have a plantation owner's mindset. You know, Blacks are too lazy to work, Blacks are too stupid to learn, Blacks are too irresponsible to keep their dicks in their pants long enough to be productive. But underneath it all is *fear*. They're afraid that if they make one small mistake, there'll be a riot. They're afraid if they fire a Black who's not doing their job they'll be accused of being racist, and some hot shot legal beagle like me will storm into their office with a court order. They're afraid of seeing their entire investment go up in smoke when some White cop beats up some ghetto kid."

Elgin considered the attorney's remarks. "I know. You're right. I used to see it when I was first trying to make business deals. I still see it as LG. Even the so-called 'open-minded, politically-correct' types who think it makes them look good by working with us. So how the hell is involving a bunch of Black militants going to ease their minds?"

"Because we can show them that the brothers *want* this. That they are hungry for this. And that if they're given the chance they'll protect it like their own. They won't have to be afraid of us because we'll finally be working together in the best possible arrangement—we'll each offer what the other side needs. They won't have to be afraid of the Black Panthers or the Black Guard or Perry Robbs crying 'Racist!' and starting a riot because *we* will finally have something to lose. The Black Guard—not that it ever was more than an *alleged* group—would actually be working in the cities recruiting teens, and getting the unemployed in line—not for a check, but for a chance to regain their own souls. Business will be able to look at us as an ally to side with them against the immovable bureaucracy or the stifling regulation or anything else. Can you imagine it? Business and labor teaming up to fight together! The only fear that will be created will be by those businesses who don't get involved, and by those who work in the welfare offices and soup kitchens, and by the Toms who suddenly find that they speak for no one but their own greed. Can you imagine it?" he animatedly repeated.

"Actually, yes," said Elgin with a broad smile. "I can imagine it. It's been my passion for years." He rose. "Can I get anyone something to drink?"

The meeting went on for four hours. Each one alternately talked and listened. Sometimes they explored generalities, and sometimes they strayed into specifics. Elgin took an opportunity to corner Pendleton for a quiet talk, in which he could sense a strong undercurrent of racism. *How is it*, thought LaGrande, *that only Whites are talked about as being racist?* He gradually steered the conversation in that direction, out of hearing of the others. "I get the feeling, Mr. Pendleton, that you have some reservations about this whole idea."

"No disrespect to your intentions, Mr. LaGrande, but I ain't never seen no White businessman hug no nigger. And I ain't about to turn my back to them. But, Perry says we can't win the war in the jungle, that it's time to try something else. So I guess I ain't gonna walk away from the table, either, if it means there's a real chance. I ain't the smartest dude on the street, Mr.

LaGrande, and I've done some things in my life that most people wouldn't like. And I'd do them again. They were necessary. But if there's a better way, then I'll listen to options. Just so you'll know where I'm comin' from, though, I'm keeping all my options open."

LaGrande studied the dark face across from him. He would not want to be the reason Pendleton ever exercised one of his other "options." "I appreciate your frankness, Mr. Pendleton, but in that same vein, let me remind you that even a hint of violence could derail the program before it even gets started. And there won't be a second chance. We hope to persuade everyone that this is a real solution to a lot of racial history, but if we blow it, we'll never be trusted again. They'll shut us down, and make us beg for the bones again. And not only will those of our people who are poor and uneducated still be poor and uneducated, but they'll be worse off than before. And all the rioting and late night bedroom assassinations in the world won't make a dent in changing that!"

"I hear you, LaGrande," said Pendleton with equal emotion. Then he took a sip of his drink, before continuing, "I'm just keeping my options open. But I'm also willing to do what I can to help this happen."

"Then that's all I can ask." He stuck out his hand which the other man accepted, in a gesture not lost on the other three who had been speaking together across the room.

CHAPTER 13

> *"The extraordinary progress of the world since the Middle Ages has not been due to the mere expenditure of human energy, nor even to the flights of human genius. No, it has been due to the accumulation of capital. It provided the machinery that gradually diminished human drudgery and liberated the spirit of the worker, who had formerly been almost indistinguishable from a mule."*
> —H. L. Mencken (1880-1956)

Thursday – February 25

"I understand your objections, Mr. Anderson," said Elgin LaGrande. He, Athena Weston, Perry Robbs, and Rufus Pendleton had been in the meeting with the CEOs of Southern Steel, Mercedes-Benz, the Taco Tom restaurant chain, and decision-makers from a dozen other local and regional corporations and industries for over an hour, attempting to outline their proposals. Only two of the group were Black. The group had mostly offered only skepticism and reluctance, and Elgin had more than once questioned Robbs' insistence to include Pendleton in their initial talks with business leaders.

"The idea is simple enough," he continued, "but it's natural to be hesitant over such a radical, untried, concept. It's not just another federal jobs program. There's no government money involved here at all. This is a straight private venture between the corporate world and high school students."

"I suppose it's not all that radical," said a tire company executive. "Internship programs are common all over the country. But you're asking us to hire a bunch of poor Black—mostly Black, I guess—high school kids with no experience and no skills, and who are probably only about ten minutes away from dropping out anyway, and expect them to make us money? And pay for their college education to boot! Come on. Let's get real!"

Robbs broke in. "Look, Mr. Anderson, let's put it on the table. On the surface, this is just another classic Catch-22 runaround: You can't get a job unless you have experience, and you can't get experience unless you have a job. But this goes way beyond that. This is a race issue, whether you want to admit it in public or not. Us Blacks are lazy and ain't got no ambition, right?" he said, using his on-call street accent.

"I didn't—"

"Hey, don't sweat it. I'm not offended. You know why? Because you're absolutely right! The average Black kid on the street feels like he's in quicksand and can't break free. And there's plenty of people on both sides who tell him it's just plain hopeless. So after a while he stops trying. And then there's nothing to do but *be* lazy."

Elgin picked up the ball again. "All these kids need is a chance. You all spend a fortune on training, another fortune trying to improve productivity, another fortune trying to eliminate wasted effort and inefficient inventory management to make up for the first two, and another fortune fighting labor problems. What we're trying to show you is that you have the means available to you—all of you," he said, looking around the table, "to erase all these headaches and money pits. And the key is a skilled and educated workforce. Better workers means greater productivity per worker, which actually translates into *fewer* employees, and therefore a smaller payroll. Saving money here—big money—means making money—big money. That keeps your stockholders happy, and that keeps you happy. The money that is saved can be better used for capital expenses, modernization, and expansion. And that, ultimately, means more jobs, better paying jobs, in the long run. And that makes *us* happy. Both sides benefit. *All you have to do is start by giving the kids a reason to stay in school and become better educated!* You start them in any sort of entry level, minimum wage kind of position—even less, probably, since we can use work-study credit approaches to modify the normal regulations—and dangle the college or trade school carrots out in front of them. You save tons of money on these jobs that you currently spend much higher wages on while still losing the employees anyway because these are usually dead-end jobs. The kids stay with you because they know they'll not only get paid, but will get a better education out of it—an education that will actually lead somewhere."

He paused, sensing that he might actually be making some headway. "It's no accident that we have come to you, particularly. Many of your companies are non-union, but in spite of the apparent savings you gain with non-union labor, you still end up with labor problems. We feel this will help you as well as them. After they get out of school, there are no further formal obligations for either party. No *quid pro quo* for indentured service. You saved money;

The Hornbrook Prophecy

they got their schooling. Even Steven. But, now they need a real job, and you need trained, knowledgeable, motivated employees. Seems like a good fit to me. They know the company, they know the business, they understand the problems, and they're ready to go. They quickly become more efficient, and production increases. You also will find that they have probably developed a growing sense of loyalty and responsibility, meaning fewer sick days or other absences. The rest is up to you. Make it worth their while—good pay, good benefits, maybe some stock purchase capability—and they'll more than make it back for you."

The room was mostly silent when Elgin finally stopped. He saw a few heads nodding in general agreement (*I hope,* he thought), and some contemplative expressions. Finally, the tire executive spoke. "We can certainly see the logic of your ideas, Mr. LaGrande. *If* it actually worked that way." His voice trailed off.

Robbs stepped in again. "I think I can offer a final thought for you. The Lieutenant Governor has proved himself in education and business, as well as government, gentlemen. I'm sure you hold him in as high regard as do I. I'm equally sure that Mr. Pendleton and I represent all that you feel uneasy about. No, no, that's okay," he said waving off the polite objections. "The track record of cooperation between Blacks and corporate America is nearly non-existent. Segregation, civil rights marches, the KKK, riots, protests, busing, and the Black Panthers—or Black Guard—are much more likely to come to mind. You're right to think of them now. You're right to fear," he glanced at Elgin, who was keeping his face expressionless, "that your investments would be at risk. But Mr. Pendleton and I are here today, because Mr. LaGrande has absolutely convinced us that this is a road to a better future. We have lived in the cities and on the streets. We know that *your* skepticism is mirrored there. But while the Blacks in these neighborhoods are proud of their Lieutenant Governor, they have almost as much trouble relating to him as to you! But not to us. They know us. They listen to us.

"We can deliver the cities to you," he concluded quietly. No one thought it was idle boasting. "Play fair with us—and with them—and they'll be all that you hoped for. We can sell it, we can bring you the best, and we can keep the *problems* away."

No one really knew what he meant by "problems," but they accepted the statement.

"So where would you propose to go from here, Mr. LaGrande?" said the executive.

Elgin was elated. He felt at long last that he was close to realizing his dream, and he didn't hesitate. "I feel the best approach would be to initiate a pilot program in each of your companies. You could start with a specific, but limited, number of internship positions for an initial five-year trial. We could bring to you a pre-selected pool of high school applicants from which you could choose the best available for your needs." He nodded at Athena, who stood and began to pass out personalized binders to each of the company representatives.

Elgin continued, "These are some preliminary suggestions and ideas we have put together on how we think this program might be incorporated into each of your individual companies. I would recommend you study them and come back to us with your own comments and changes. Progress and performance would be followed and reviewed by a partnership committee all the way through the completion of their formal college, trade school, or even on-the-job training. The entire program could be reviewed and revised—and hopefully quickly expanded—as often as necessary. There are no rules, gentlemen. This is not your typical government pile of manure operation. We can set this up any way you want to make it work right."

"You're right, Mr. LaGrande. That's not typical at all. Maybe that's what will actually make the difference. I can't speak for the others, but I'm willing to give this a look." The man stood, and extended his hand. Elgin shook it with feeling.

"Thank you, sir. We'll contact you again shortly to arrange another meeting to discuss the details and your suggestions. If you want to send your personnel directors or someone else to handle it, that's no problem. We'll make sure you stay apprised of the developments. Please call me anytime if you have any questions. Thank you all for your time and consideration." The two groups did a general round robin of hand shaking and mutual well-wishing as the meeting broke up. When the business leaders had departed, Athena gave Elgin a brief congratulatory hug. Perry Robbs came up to him and said, "Well, nothing ventured, nothing gained, Elgin. I think you did a fine job." Rufus Pendleton solemnly nodded his agreement.

None of them were aware of how national developments would soon dramatically alter all their lives.

Chapter 14

> *"The greedy hand of government...watches prosperity as ts prey and permits none to escape without tribute."*
> —Thomas Paine, The Rights of Man, 1791

Monday – March 15

Henley Hornbrook leaned back in the executive style chair behind his desk as Lew Weiser came in and sat down in the armchair at the corner of the desk. "Desperate times often lead to desperate measures, Lew, but the desperate measure called the American Employment and Financial Freedom Act of 2010 was destined to be a disaster. And this time I really hate being right."

"It's been pretty predictable," agreed the Chief-of-Staff. "Congress really ramped up its love of spending in the last decade, even though much of that time the Republicans were in control. The War on Terror created not just unanticipated costs, it reinvigorated the growth of government as both Congress and the White House felt action—and spending—would keep the nation happy."

"The problem, of course, is that the nation ISN'T happy. The average American working family is reeling, and it's sure not from the 'benefits' being showered upon it. It's costing them more of each workday to support the tax burden. That cuts their incentive to work as well. Plus there are other financial strains on the country. Baby boomers are beginning to retire, so not only are demands on Social Security increasing, but since the highest-earning taxpayers are leaving the workforce, tax revenues will sharply decline. There has also been a steady loss of property tax revenues to states and counties as more and more land is removed from private ownership or productive use and entered into environmental trusts. Home building, commercial interests, manufacturing, farming, and lumber industries are declining or becoming enormously more expensive because of the twin economic impacts of taxation and regulation.

"I tell you, Lew, if we were going to interfere in the economy it should have been to keep people from taking all of the equity out of their homes to pay off their other debts." Hornbrook shook his head in disgust. "No one saves enough. And what little they do get into the bank gets sucked up by government borrowing. It's worse than ever now, I fear."

"Well, Henley, if the economy had not already been teetering, there would have been no demand for something like the AEFFA. So many features of the bill were retroactive to the first of the year, the effects of the bill were beginning to be felt almost before the President's signature was dry. The costs and projections by the Congressional and White House budget and economic advisors were, as always, gross underestimates. Almost every aspect of the bill is producing less of the positive effects and more of the negative effects than predicted."

"Surprise, surprise!"

"Yep. Wage guarantees simply raise the costs of production, but since they froze prices on so many things, businesses are taking a beating. Shortages are developing for many products."

"How's unemployment?"

"Growing. Plus, as small and large businesses alike begin to adapt to the effects of new tax rates, earnings estimates are beginning to shrink, giving shareholders reasons to sell. So the market continues to fall."

"No news there, either. Go on."

"The new federal sales tax, while relatively small, became effective the first of March and has had a frighteningly-quick effect reducing consumer spending on everything from Dad's new car to Junior's new soccer shoes. Corporate profits are affected correspondingly."

Hornbrook rubbed his eyes. "Is that it?"

"I wish. But no. As the economy is slowing, tax revenues are falling—more and more. The government doesn't have enough money to inaugurate all the new jobs and other spending programs it so glowingly promised, and financing its old programs is seriously jeopardized." Lew looked up from his papers. "Henley, you know there are limited ways a government can raise the funds necessary to satisfy its budget. It can raise taxes, borrow money, or print more of it. Raising taxes is backfiring badly. The market is reacting quickly, and in order to attract lenders the interest rates are climbing, along with the government's debt load, just as Sebastian predicted. The credit rating of the United States government, such as it is, is being seriously eroded."

"Good news all around."

"Do you think Dillard will react?"

"I shudder to think what he might want next. But he'll never admit the AEFFA is a failure."

"Yet."

"No. Never. If it really hits the fan, he'll just find a way to blame someone else."

***

"Scio!" Biggs Wasco nearly yelled into the phone after he was put through to the Governor.

"Biggs, what can I do for you?" replied the Chief Executive of Alabama evenly.

"My people tell me that your boy, LaGrande, is about to stir up a whole heap of trouble for all of us."

"He ain't my 'boy,' and would have me castrated in the press if I said so. Now just what the hell are you all worked up about? What trouble?"

"It seems he's cooking up some plan to get companies to hire high school kids for their labor force. They're gonna call it some kinda bullshit training program, but it sounds to me like child labor or somethin'."

"Now, simmer down," said Scio, trying to calm his labor ally. "I'm sure there's some simple explanation. Besides, LaGrande can't do anything by himself—he's got no power or authority for it."

"Are you brain dead, Scio? That's the whole point. He's bypassing the government—and the unions, not so incidentally! He's coordinating the whole thing privately, for god's sake!"

"Get a hold of yourself, for cryin' out loud. Hiring a couple of kids ain't like the end of the world," said the Governor.

"You idiot! You don't get it, do you? Well, let me spell it out to you so even you can read it. Every time they hire a kid it means they ain't hiring a union guy. No union guys means no union. No union means no union contributions to political campaigns. No union contributions means Jefferson Scio don't get elected to nothing! Does that get your attention better now?"

"All right, all right. I'll do some checking and see what this amounts to. Don't sweat it. We'll dismantle this before it amounts to anything."

"I'll give you a week and then my boys'll be bound to take an interest."

"Don't be stupid. I'm telling you, we'll manage this just fine. Just don't blow it up where the press is against us."

"Fine. But you still only get a week. The further this goes, the worse it'll be."

"I know. I'll call you soon." Scio hung up the phone. He sighed. This was way worse than union contributions. But Wasco was pretty one-dimensional. The real issue here was LaGrande. He had gotten elected because he appealed to the hordes of poor and middle class Black voters—and in Alabama that was a huge piece of the electoral pie. LaGrande had also attracted a significant percentage of middle and upper class White voters who didn't like the rough, abrasive Wasco. Scio couldn't afford to let the Lieutenant Governor gain even more popularity. If Wasco was right about this, he'd have to find a way to derail it. Quietly, if possible.

Wednesday – March 24

Elgin LaGrande had no way of knowing whether Jefferson Scio and Biggs Wasco were aware of his plans, let alone what action they might be contemplating. But Perry Robbs had not only anticipated it, but planned on it. He had seen to it that their initial presentation to the various company executives had been followed up closely, and as soon as the CEOs had given their go-ahead for a trial run, Robbs had leaked the deal to the press.

The media found it appealing, to say the least. Inner-city kids, mired in poverty and lacking vision for a better life, would be given jobs with significant companies in or near their communities, and be promised at least two years of college education or trade school as long as they stayed on the job and graduated high school with at least a 2.0 GPA. Local television news shows, radio talk show hosts, and newspaper columnists all portrayed the experiment in glowing terms, interviewing student applicants and company officials. Elgin LaGrande preferred keeping a low profile, saying that the program would be measured over the years by its successes, which would be up to the schools and industries involved. He deliberately downplayed his own role in the matter, not wanting to create a political sidebar to the story. Perry Robbs was also interviewed frequently, but he was not at all reluctant to go on at length about his views. To be fair, he did give major credit to LaGrande for his formulation of the plan, and the organization of its founders, but he also managed to find the opportunity too good to pass up to share his perception of the future of Black Americans. Rufus Pendleton was never mentioned nor interviewed.

The Hornbrook Prophecy

The Reverend Ukiah Hilgard, dressed in a new but modest off-the-rack suit, did double duty. He made the talk show rounds routinely in the first two weeks, his moving descriptions of poverty and inner-city life softening the viewers and listeners in a way that made even more persuasive the view of opportunity the newly-christened *"High Schools – High Hopes"* program could offer. And he was tireless in traveling from neighborhood to neighborhood talking to kids, to parents, and to school officials. He went to the churches and spoke from the pulpit about joining the new march, *"the march from poverty to prosperity, the march from gangs to goals, the march from the pool room to the board room."*

As the *Hopes* program, as it became known, began to draw attention and interest, not just to itself, but to its personalities, the Governor grew more and more angry. After one news conference featuring Robbs, Scio punched his intercom and told his secretary, "If it's not too much trouble for the Lieutenant Governor, would you please have him get his butt in here!"

Elgin appeared in the outer office about ten minutes later, and was let in to see Scio right away. "Good morning, Mr. Governor," he began.

"Good morning, my butt!" said Scio. "Where the hell do you get off starting up a new job program on your own! You can't do that!"

"I beg your pardon, Mr. Governor, but you're wrong. The *Hopes* program isn't a state program. There's no state money involved, no state employees involved, and no state resources or facilities involved."

"*You're* involved! Your girlfriend from AIDT is involved!"

"Even state employees and elected officials have hours during the day when they are on their own time, as are we whenever we pursue private interests."

"Don't give me that shit! You are always on the clock when you're Lieutenant Governor. This is nothing more than a transparent publicity stunt designed to win you enough points with the bleeding hearts so you can run for *my* job in November. Don't pretend you aren't. Well, forget it. And forget this stupid charade. When it falls flat, you'll look like a fool." He paused, then added, "And I guarantee, it *will* fall flat."

"Governor, you have taken every opportunity you could to keep me boxed in and ignore ideas that might actually help the people of Alabama. Well, I'm telling you, the people are getting tired of you and your pet thug, Wasco. You barely squeaked by in the last election even though you were running against an old drunk with mistress problems. If you demonstrate to the people your obvious disregard for their well-being, then even the old drunk would win the next election. Or maybe I *will* run, now that you mention it. Either way, I really don't think you want to mess with this. There's simply no reason to." He adopted a more reasonable tone. "This can be good for the students and their futures, and therefore it can be good for the state."

"Bullshit! Helping a handful of ghetto kids will win you some votes, but when the public realizes you're just helping some greedy corporations get cheap labor they'll chuck you out on your ass."

"I've *so* enjoyed our conversation this morning, Governor," said LaGrande. "I guess you're right. We can just let the public decide. Good day." And he turned his back on Scio and strolled comfortably out of the office.

Two weeks later, Elgin decided not to run for reelection as Lieutenant Governor. Instead, he filed to run for Governor. Scio was to be unopposed by his party in the primary, so with a little luck the voters could decide the future of the *Hopes* program.

***

In mid-March, the first of the high school kids had been selected for the *Hopes* internship programs and began their job training in afternoon and alternate weekend sessions. There had been a huge pool of interested applicants to choose from. The successful ones were not necessarily those with the best grades or other accomplishments with which to impress the employers, although many of those were included. With Elgin's encouragement, the companies also selected a lot of more at-risk kids, who even surprised themselves by the ease with which their own initial distrust and reluctance was overcome once they were treated with respect and introduced to the concepts of responsibility and accountability. The selection of these kids might have been construed to be a form of affirmative action, but in actuality it was part of the overall evaluation process for the entire program.

It would take years to see if the program would work as envisioned, but the early reports from students and industry officials alike were very encouraging. Other companies began to contact the new *Hopes* office, which had been set up with grant money from the tire company and Southern Steel. Athena Weston had left her job with the state to become the one-woman office staff, and she found herself rapidly putting in longer and longer days.

Perry Robbs kept the media spotlight shining. Pendleton stayed out of it, but was a tireless force in the inner cities and poorer neighborhoods, constantly on the streets where quiet conversations led first to skepticism, then to questions, then ideas. His efforts led to the first negotiations between LaGrande and a small, struggling, regional soft drink bottling company to consider relocating to a low-income, high crime area in Montgomery. With safety guaranteed, they could have access to an unskilled labor force they could pay minimal wages but provide the economic stability so badly needed in the area.

In June, Elgin LaGrande easily won the right to oppose Jefferson Scio for Governor in the November election.

Chapter 15

"If Patrick Henry thought that taxation without representation was bad, he should see how bad it is with representation."
—The Old Farmer's Almanac

Thursday – June 24

Henley Hornbrook had had his fill. It was killing him to be proved right in so dramatic a fashion. He called Sebastian Fellsmere in New York. When the Brit came on the line, the greeting reflected his own thoughts. "Henley, my friend! Are you as worked up as you were during the debate five months ago?"

"That's a wonderful understatement, Sebastian. The only good news is that it must finally be dawning on even the most stubborn fuzzy-head that we've managed to shoot ourselves in the foot. I can't help but think that we'll be lucky if we only lose the leg."

"I hate to say it, but your analogy may be right on."

"So how do you see things at this point? I'd appreciate your view."

"Pretty straightforward, I'd say," Fellsmere began. "In mid-April, first quarter earnings reports were almost universally demonstrating a sagging economy. Virtually no sector was spared. The stock market zagged down as almost-daily corporate reports disappointed investors. Many of their normal safe havens—the corporate and municipal bond markets and treasury bills—were no longer attractive either. For several weeks I noticed that foreign market segments were enjoying a bounce. International mutual funds—large, small, and mid-cap; growth and value; equities and bonds—all benefited. Money is oozing out of your American economy in search of friendlier environs. Many foreign banks, which hold much of the U.S. debt, are now declining to renew notes in order to help their own economies, further burdening the now cash-poor U.S. federal government."

"I remember when we talked about that before. And about how hard it becomes to keep those investors."

"Right you are. And it's getting tougher. Now, at almost the end of the second quarter, the picture is even gloomier. Businesses are failing at record rates and unemployment rates are showing increases in new claims each month. In countries with fixed-rate monetary units, governments might resort to currency devaluation. But in a floating-rate system like the U.S. dollar, there is no choice but to deal with plummeting revenue shortfalls and soaring debt by simply printing more money with which the government could pay its bills. So the money supply is being inflated."

"And prices are rising in spite of the economic controls imposed, along with the emotions of consumers and taxpayers."

"Quite so."

"I'm going to be meeting with the Majority Leader soon, after the holiday weekend. He's a die-hard, but over the years he's at least been well-intentioned. It's not impossible that he may be having the light dawn on him finally. If so, I'd need him to lead a fight to reverse the bill."

"Good luck!"

"Yes, I know. It's a tough one. Frustrating. What ideas can you give me? Where can we go from here?"

"You already said it—dump that idiotic legislation, cut taxes like crazy, cut spending, and then hope like hell that businesses recover. And you've got to do it now. It's like I said before—your virus is spreading. The European and Asian markets enjoyed your investors' capital infusion but let's face it: American consumption is the engine for the global economic vehicle, and the engine is dying. Fast."

Chapter 16

I'm proud to be paying taxes in the United States. The only thing is—I could be just as proud for half the money."
—Arthur Godfrey (1903-1983)

Sunday – July 4

The Fourth of July is always one of the most popular holidays of the year for Americans. The weather is hot, the barbeques everywhere, and the fireworks spectacular. Lip service is usually paid by legislators and newscasters to the philosophical importance of the date in the nation's history, but few people actually give it much deep thought.

This year, however, Independence Day was different. A single businessman made it so. His name was Richmond Shadwell, CEO of the Shadwell Mining Corporation, one of West Virginia's oldest continuously operating coal mining concerns. He had always been proud of his heritage as a descendent of the founders of Shadwell, Virginia, the birthplace of Thomas Jefferson, but had no idea of the effect he personally was about to have in shaping the course of the nation.

For years, he had been in quiet consultation with his board of directors and with union leaders for the past three weeks, concerned over the economic decline and the eroding value of their workers' paychecks. Encouraged by these discussions, he then began to have additional meetings, first with other mining companies, then, widening his circle, with other corporate acquaintances. His ideas were often met with initial resistance, but gradually more and more companies began to consider them with interest. As those involved grew more numerous, it became harder to keep the lid on it, and the cat was out of the bag when someone made an offhand comment to a television network executive at a holiday weekend party on July 2. The executive slipped away from the party, and used his cell phone to have his network track down Shadwell that very evening. Shadwell agreed to an interview, as long as it was live, and the next thing he knew he was in New York for one of the Sunday morning news shows.

"Good morning. I'm Garrison Dumfries, and this is News Talk Sunday," began the lightly-respected, but popular anchor for BSN. "I sincerely hope you are all enjoying your Fourth of July celebrations today. Our country has a rich heritage, and also a strong record of overcoming tough times. We have fought wars, depressions, and invisible enemies of terror. Today, many people are feeling we are engaged in our toughest struggle, trying to overcome serious fiscal difficulties and keep the economy chugging. Our first guest this morning is Mr. Richmond Shadwell, the Chief Executive Officer of Shadwell Mining Corporation. BSN has learned that Mr. Shadwell and several other prominent companies are forming a new political party, the details of which he has offered to share with us today. Mr. Shadwell?"

"Thank you, Mr. Dumfries. Under other circumstances I would consider it an honor to be here. But many of us in the business and labor world are deeply upset by current trends, and we feel it incumbent upon us to take some action. My employees do some of the toughest work in the country, and yet their paychecks are becoming worthless. I've talked with our labor representatives, and I've talked with other leaders with other industries, and they've talked with their companies. It's a measure of the direness of the circumstances that both labor and business are in agreement for a change. So we've decided to take some action to gain mutual relief."

"And that's where the new political party comes in?" asked the news anchor, trying his hardest to look concerned and interested.

"That's right. I am proud to announce the formation of the *Tax Equality for America Party*, dedicated to relieving the tax burden on hard working Americans everywhere. We are going to force Congress to rewrite and simplify the 25000 pages of tax codes and regulations and replace it with a simple, flat rate system that eliminates the exemption and loopholes that do nothing but invite corruption by special interests—including by us, I might add."

"That's kind of an awkward name for a political party, isn't it, Mr. Shadwell?"

"It's an awkward time, Mr. Dumfries. But it makes a great acronym, don't you think?"

"An acronym? Ah...I don't—"

"Initials, Mr. Dumfries, initials!"

"I'm sorry, I—"

"Sheesh! Have you ever run for office, Mr. Dumfries. I think you're qualified. Oh well, never mind. As I was saying, we were inspired by the acronym for Tax Equality for America. T-E-A."

"T-E-A. Hmmm. Oh, yes. I get it. The TEA Party. Ha ha," said the somewhat slow-witted news anchor. "Yes, of course. Like the Boston Tea Party? Wasn't that a tax protest?"

"Gee, no kidding! You know your history well," said Shadwell facetiously.

"Thank you," said the commentator, unaware of the implied derision. "But how will we characterize your new party?"

"Well, I'm not so sure you're going to think it's a party. Like those Tea Party rallies last year and like our Boston brethren two hundred and some years ago, we've also had it up to here," said the CEO, holding his hand flat across his neck. "Like that news guy in the movie, we're saying, *'We're as mad as hell and we're not going to take it anymore.'* But unlike the recent Tea parties, we have a definite agenda and a definite plan."

"What do you mean by that?"

"Like I said, we're as mad as hell and we're not going to take it anymore. Only we're not just going to stick our heads out the window and yell to the neighbors, like in the movie. We're going to do something about it."

"And we're all going to hear about it next. But first, this message." And the talk program broke for commercial messages, just as Shadwell was primed. Years at the negotiating table, however, had taught him how to mask his emotions. He took a drink of water from a glass on the table next to him, and waited for Dumb-Ass to return to the set.

Finally, the show was set to resume, and when the director's finger pointed at him, Garrison Dumfries picked up where he left off. "All right, ladies and gentlemen. We're talking to Richmond Shadwell about a new political party he says he's forming with other business, industry, and even labor leaders. Okay, Mr. Shadwell, you're mad as hell. Tell us what this means."

God, what an imbecile, thought Shadwell. "Connect the dots, Mr. Dumfries. The Boston Tea Party was a tax protest, as you said. The Tax Equality for America Party is also a tax protest movement. But unlike a normal political party that talks now about doing something later, we're going to do something now and talk about it later. Tax reform is the 'talk later' part. But the 'do something' part comes first."

"And that is," said Dumfries, a bit impatiently.

The Hornbrook Prophecy

"We're not going to pay taxes anymore. None. Not one red cent."

"Excuse me?" said the amused anchorman. "You can't *not* pay taxes. That's ridiculous. Everybody has to pay taxes. Don't be silly."

"It's not silly anymore." Shadwell was now dead serious. "Taxes are part of the contract between a government and its citizens. We pay taxes and are supposed to get certain services in return. Those services are spelled out in the Constitution. Well, the services being delivered are not the ones we ordered. Only a fraction of the budget has to do with those things the Constitution says Congress is supposed to do. The rest of our taxes are paying for a whole lotta crap we think Congress is NOT supposed to be doing. So we're not paying anymore. The Shadwell Mining Corporation and those others who are joining with us will no longer pay corporate income taxes. We will also no longer withhold taxes of any kind from our employees' paychecks. We're giving them all that money, including the employer's share of normal payroll taxes and letting them make their own choices. But ninety-seven percent of them indicated they're not going to pay either."

Dumfries was dumbfounded. It took him several moments to recover, and then he decided that he and his network had just been played for fools by a nut case. "If you don't mind me saying so, Mr. Shadwell, you almost had me there for a moment. I almost thought you were serious. It's not often that our guests pull a fast one on us."

"I can't believe it's much of a chore! But let me tell you, this ain't no fast one, pal. This *is* happening. And by the time this TV show is over, I'll bet we'll get a thousand other companies and a million other workers to go along with it. We'll set a record for the fastest-growing political movement ever! We're mad as hell, all right. Fighting mad. *Shooting* mad, if we have to. It's Independence Day, Mr. Dumfries. And we're going independent!" And with that, he stood up and walked off the set, leaving the broadcaster completely bewildered.

Overnight, the media reported that the phenomenon was, indeed, spreading fast. Aside from some of the big corporations that did not want to upset a Congress that so routinely rewarded their contributions, there was a huge groundswell of support for Shadwell's new TEA Party. Small businesses and the self-employed, especially, jumped all over the idea. It was an unprecedented repudiation of Congressional legislation.

And the effects were dramatic. Form 941 deposits of payroll taxes decreased by 72 percent. Second quarter tax reports, due by the end of July, were ignored in equal proportion. In a show of support for their customers, a huge percentage of small retailers stopped assessing and collecting the new national sales tax.

The United States Treasury reported to the White House Office of Budget and Management, and to the Congressional Budget Office, that total tax revenue collections in July were only 54 percent of normal levels. For a government long reduced to living from month-to-month it was a startling development. It would take time for new Treasury bonds to be auctioned, if they could be, or even to print new money. Some non-essential government services—non-essential even in the eyes of the government—were suspended, offices shut down "temporarily."

The government was suddenly—and seriously—running out of cash.

Chapter 17

> *"The rule of law is preferable to that of any individual...*
> *For he who bids the law rule may be deemed to bid God*
> *and Reason alone rule, but he who bids man rule adds an*
> *element of the beast; for desire is a wild beast, and passion*
> *perverts the minds of rulers, even when they are the best*
> *of men. The law is reason unaffected by desire."*
> —Aristotle (384-322 BC)

By July, the *Hopes* experiment was winning early and widespread acclaim for its innovative approach. Widespread, but not universal. There were many others besides Jefferson Scio and Biggs Wasco who resented the attention it had received. And certain influential opponents were highly receptive when the pair approached them with a plan to derail the program. A popular newspaper investigative reporter in Montgomery was fed false documents and computer-doctored photographs purported to show Rufus Pendleton, alleged mastermind of the famous Black Guard assassinations, taking payoffs from the tire company executive in order to buy both protection from Black gang leaders for company operations, and also to guarantee that union protests would be disrupted. Other documents detailed meetings between Pendleton, Robbs, and the state's Lieutenant Governor, Elgin LaGrande. The reporter, Jordan Stowell, responsibly attempted to verify the information he was given, and was eventually led down a false trail to some "eyewitnesses" who claimed to have been present at the restaurant in Birmingham or the Montgomery sports bar where the meetings were alleged to have been held.

Tuesday – July 27

Jordan Stowell went to his city desk editor at the *Montgomery Advertiser* with his preliminary findings and found his boss very interested because the *Hopes* program was a hot issue right now, and readers were interested in it. But the reporter had not achieved his degree of stature in journalism without having developed certain instincts. And there was something about this story that just didn't feel right. He expressed his reservations to his editor who told him that it seemed he'd done his homework and that it looked clean. Stowell argued and managed to get her to promise to hold the story for twenty-four hours while he checked a few other details.

Wednesday – July 28

The next morning the story was splashed across the bottom of page one of the *Advertiser*. Stowell found out when he woke to the first of many rapid fire phone calls. The first was from Perry Robbs, and then in quick succession he got an earful from three different corporate attorneys. He rolled out of bed, ran downstairs and threw open the front door of the townhouse where he grabbed the morning paper, opened it, and read his by-lined story at the bottom of the front page. He groaned, then turned and retreated to the kitchen where he snatched up the phone and called his editor. The woman explained that at yesterday's editor's conference, the managing editor had personally asked to review the file. She had explained to him the 24-hour hold and had had no idea the story would be run anyway.

The success of an investigative reporter is closely tied to their professionalism and their integrity. Jordan Stowell knew that his name, reputation, and entire career could be in jeopardy, and he silently prayed that just this once his instincts were wrong. Still in his shorts and tee shirt, he went in the second bedroom he used as his office, grabbed the file marked "Hopes" and pored through it, trying to discover a reason for his earlier misgivings. If there was a problem with the story, as loudly indicated by the previous phone calls, he would have to find it and put it right himself—before deadline tonight—or he might as well start looking for a whole new line of work.

It took but an hour, and he was surprised that it was both so easy, and so obvious. It was in the transcript from the patron at the sports bar. The man had stated that he "just happened" to stop in the tavern on the way home from work one evening, and was just watching a few minutes of a blowout Braves game when he recognized the fast food taco restaurant chain owner who'd become semi-famous by doing his own commercials. The witness had said the restaurateur was arguing about something with a scowling, very dark faced Black man he didn't recognize at first. The witness said he wouldn't

The Hornbrook Prophecy

have paid too much attention, but at one point the White man had slammed his hand down on the table and said, *"That's too damn much money!"* The witness thought it seemed kind of strange, but later saw the Black man in the background of a news conference about some new kind of program for poor kids, and a policeman friend who was with him had identified him as a suspected killer, and suggested he go down to the station to report what he'd seen. But the informant had thought that if it was important he might make some money at it, and had instead made a call to the newspaper.

There were too many coincidences here, thought Stowell. He picked up the phone and dialed his paper's sports desk. When he was put through to one of the sportswriters, he asked him, "Stan have there been any recent, one-sided Braves games on television?"

"Nearly every Braves game is on TV, what with Turner's superstation and whatnot," replied the sportswriter. "But they're having a rotten season for a change, and they haven't had many blowouts all season. The last one was, like, ten-zip, and I think it was about ten days or two weeks ago. Why?"

"Might help me with a story."

"Okay. Hang on a sec."

Stowell could hear papers rustling over the phone, then his friend came back on the line. "Yeah, here it is. Ten-nothing over the Reds on Tuesday the thirteenth. Actually, there was also a 9-1 game the Saturday before that, too, and some people thought maybe the Braves were going to finally get something going, but they went right back in the ditch."

"The thirteenth, and the, ah, twelve, eleven, tenth, right?"

"Right."

"Okay, thanks, Stan."

"Do I get a co-byline?"

"No. But thanks." Stowell hung up. He shuffled through his file and verified that the sports bar witness worked a Monday through Friday shift as a laborer. So if he was coming home from work, it must have been the Tuesday night game. Six more calls revealed that it was highly unlikely that anyone would be able to verify Rufus Pendleton's whereabouts on Tuesday the thirteenth, but he hit pay dirt on Taco Tom. On Tuesday the thirteenth he had been in the middle of a three-day tour of New York, New Jersey, and Massachusetts, attending the grand openings of the newest franchises in the Taco Tom world. Two more calls confirmed his presence in the northeast all day on the Tuesday in question. There was no way he could have been present at the Montgomery sports bar on that day, no matter what the meeting was about. The entire thing was a fabrication.

Three emotions hit Stowell in a row. First, he was relieved that his instincts were still accurate. Then he was worried because his reputation had been jeopardized. And finally he was really and truly pissed, because someone had gone to a great deal of trouble to make him look bad. *Why?* And then he realized it wasn't him. He was just a tool—that pissed him off even more. No, the real reason behind all this probably had something to do with the *Hopes* program itself, a seemingly very popular idea getting a lot of media attention lately. Somebody was trying to screw it up.

He called Perry Robbs back and talked with him for fifteen minutes, telling him what he had learned. Robbs then gave him a bagful of information about Scio, Wasco, and those others who stood to benefit the most if the *Hopes* program went under, or who just couldn't stand to see it succeed.

Then, using the number given him by Robbs, Stowell called Elgin LaGrande and talked with him for another twenty minutes. The Lieutenant Governor had been understanding, even apologetic to *him* for being caught up in the politics of it all, and had, off the record, shared the nature of his last conversation with Jefferson Scio.

Stowell had worked feverishly, making phone call after phone call, talking with many of his contacts and sources in government, in the unions, and on the streets. Five hours later, after pinning down all the details and putting it together, Jordan Stowell walked into the office of his publisher, where he had arranged to have the managing editor in attendance. He addressed the publisher, saying "Thank you for seeing me, sir. I assure you that by the end of today, either I or your illustrious editor here will no longer be in your employ." He dropped a sheaf of papers on the desk. "*This* is the real story that should have been printed today, instead of the one shit-for-brains here ran before I was finished. If the paper desires to retain my services, it will need to run this version in tomorrow's paper—complete and unedited. In addition, you have to print this," he said, dropping a single page on top of the stack, "which is the explanation of how you *inadvertently* came to run the story, and an apology to me for damaging my integrity, for the inaccuracies of the story, for misleading the reader, and for casting aspersions on both the founders of the *Hopes* program and the companies who are working with them to help these kids." Then he dropped another single page on top of the others, and turned to face the managing editor. "And this one is another story explaining how *you* knowingly ran the story in conjunction with the fabricated facts and phony eyewitnesses provided by Biggs Wasco and his cronies. Here's the documentation on *that*. For now, I will leave the treatment of it up to our publisher here." He turned back to the publisher. "However, if the paper fails to run these first two on page one of tomorrow's edition, then I will take all three and see if our journalistic brethren across town might be interested in them. I'm sure they'd love to get the drop on y'all."

To his point neither of the other men in the room had said a word. Stowell made to leave, then paused and looked at the elderly publisher. "I have appreciated the opportunity to write for you, sir. Thank you for helping me with my career."

The publisher stood and walked over to Stowell. He put his left hand on the younger man's shoulder and shook his right hand. "Don't go packing your desk just yet, son," he drawled, looking past him at the editor. "I expect that just may not be necessary. Thanks for coming by. I always enjoy an entertaining chat."

Stowell left and heard the door close behind him. He smiled.

Thursday – July 29

The next day all *three* articles occupied the attention of readers of the *Advertiser* in Montgomery—except for the omission of the kindly use of the word "inadvertent," but including the full narrative of the managing editor's complicity—and the entire affair became a news item across the state, receiving even some national attention. The ripple effect spread quickly, creating an unexpected backlash. In a state where there was a relatively low average income, and a high percentage of families living below the poverty level, the *Hopes* program had been viewed as more than another welfare program. It had offered some real answers to some real problems, and, like the adopted name, some real *hope* for the future. The newspaper stories had been like a one-two punch. The first article had scandalized the whole affair, crushing those people's new hopes and creating feelings of betrayal. The second article, Stowell's ultimatum story, had turned those feelings to anger—readers felt like they had been personally attacked, as Governor Scio and Biggs Wasco had lied to them and tried to steal something valuable from them for which they had waited so long. And they told their friends.

The anger soon grew to unrest, and in most cities across the state, including Montgomery, Mobile, Birmingham, Tuscaloosa, and Huntsville, there were escalating incidents of civil disorder. The entire state tensed and authorities feared it could get out of control quickly. Within two days, the uneasiness had spread clear across the deep south, as word of the phony story played into the hands of those more militant Black advocates who portrayed this as another attempt by the establishment to keep their foot upon the backs of Blacks everywhere. Every time the story was told it was more extreme. It didn't matter that the *Hopes* program itself was so early in its infancy that it was impossible to predict if it was actually going to help poor Blacks at all. It was only important that Blacks had wanted it and Whites had tried to deny it to them.

Governor Scio released a statement denying any involvement in the affair, denounced Elgin LaGrande and Perry Robbs as troublemakers attempting to undermine civil authority, and put the Alabama National Guard on alert, stating he would not allow a few individuals to incite the entire state into conflagration. Biggs Wasco held a televised news conference to announce that he and his union were filing a libel lawsuit against Jordan Stowell, his newspaper, and Elgin LaGrande.

The *Hopes* group met at their office to discuss the implications of the developments for them. Perry Robbs laughed and said he'd relish taking on Wasco in court. The Reverend Hilgard said a prayer and promised to visit the cities to try and assuage their anger. Elgin more or less sighed that he couldn't believe there would be such repercussions from their efforts, but said he would contact the liaisons of their corporate partners and make sure there were no lingering problems or doubts. Rufus Pendleton said nothing.

Chapter 18

> *"The politicians are a-swarming, and if'n there's any worst pest than grasshoppers it surely is politicians."*
> —Rose Wilder Lane (1886-1968)

Thursday – July 29

Winston Dillard, his Senator-wife Florence, and Vice President Branford were in the Oval Office early in the morning, quizzing Secretary Heppner on the current status of the Treasury. Heppner finished his assessment, and said, "Tomorrow's the end of the month and a lot of checks have to go out. But tax revenues have almost completely evaporated. The budget is fantasy. The till is essentially empty at this point, so I need your emergency authorization to print the checks anyway."

"That's normal procedure, isn't it?" asked the President. "I mean, that's the nature of deficit spending, isn't it? Just get the Fed to inflate the money supply and authorize a transfer to the Treasury?"

"Yes, although normally Congress would make it happen. But this time it's a bit out of the ordinary." The Secretary was very concerned, and looked it. "We're facing an unprecedented and indeterminate shortfall of revenue."

The room was silent for a while. Then Florence Dillard lifted her head and proclaimed, "Marie Antoinette was right. Let them eat cake!"

"What?" responded her confused husband, belying his position as the most powerful man on the planet.

"Don't print a single penny's worth of checks!" exclaimed his Senator-wife, triumphantly. "Tell the people it's their own fault, and blame Shadwell and the others. No one understands the Federal Reserve system anyway. But they need to be taught a lesson. As soon as they fall flat on their faces, they'll beg us to make things right!"

"She's right!" echoed Branford.

Secretary Heppner was shocked. "You can't do that. There'll be enormous problems!" he said, understating the obvious.

"So what!" growled the Veep.

"They'll all come running, Win," said Florence, standing at the President's side as First Lady, not Senator. For the moment.

Dillard was quiet. Then he simply said, "Yes. Of course. You're right. Of course."

Friday – July 30

A call came to Senator Hornbrook's home in the early evening. He was having dinner with Lewiston Weiser and Eagle McCall, when the phone rang. "Damn," said McCall. "How is it the phone always knows just when you sit down to eat? Fear not, I'll get to the bottom of this!" Hornbrook and Weiser exchanged grins, then lost them when they saw the expression on McCall's face. The latter said, "Hold on, please. Senator?" and handed Hornbrook the phone.

The legislator listened quietly for a few moments, then said "Thanks," and hung up the receiver. He looked at Weiser and said, "That was Mort Packwood. He's had his people keeping tight watch on developments over at Treasury, and he's also got a contact in the White House. Both sources are telling him that Shadwell's tax revolt is twisting the tail but good. He says there seems to be a consensus that some of the interest payments that are due will require restructuring, and this month's benefit and pension checks weren't sent out."

"Default," said a grim Weiser. "Good grief. It's one thing when they just play politics and won't pass a budget, like in '95, but this time it's really going to hurt. A default on the bonds is technically the worst case development financially but delaying the checks is going to wreak havoc, especially among seniors and the poor. Most welfare monies are channeled through state agencies, so there won't necessarily be any benefits lost right away, but the block grant transfers probably will be delayed also. The problem, however, is that too many won't understand how that all works. There's going to be a lot of unhappy people out there when the word gets out."

"And large groups of unhappy people tend to behave in socially-unacceptable ways. What do you think?"

"Oh hell, who knows? Could be anything from protesting in front of government buildings, all the way up to full-blown, nationwide strikes, or even rioting."

"I'm afraid I have to agree with you. I'd bet on the serious stuff. I don't think I'd want to be anywhere near a big city for a while." Hornbrook paused, and looked at McCall. "Sorry, Eagle, I know your sister and her family are in LA. You might tell them it could be a nice time for a vacation."

McCall nodded, and left the room, pulling out his own cellular phone. He punched a few buttons, then waited while the connection was made. To his relief, Tom Warner answered the call. "Tom, it's Eagle," said McCall.

"Hey, Beret," replied Tom, using the rhyming greeting he had used ever since his former roommate had joined the Army. "What's new?"

"Hammerfall, Tom."

"Come again?" said his brother-in-law, hearing the word, but not wanting to comprehend.

"Hammerfall," repeated McCall. "I'm sure you've been following the news the last few months, and especially the last few weeks, what with the tax revolt and everything. Well, the Senator just received word that the Treasury may have to default on some payments and delay check disbursements and probably the block grants to states."

"Not good."

"Not good. He's convinced that there will be repercussions as soon as the word gets out. Remember what we talked about?"

"Yeah."

"So I think you oughta get outta Dodge, pardner. The temperature's about to go up."

"Shit. Are you sure?"

"No," conceded McCall. "But I'd probably bet on it."

"Yeah," repeated Tom. "I know. How long do you think we have?"

"Good question," McCall answered. "But if the cannon's loaded, it doesn't take long to burn a short fuse. People could go crazy in a hurry. I'd get out tonight. Don't screw around. As Neil Diamond would say, pack up the babies and grab the old lady."

"Do you think my folks' place will be safe enough?"

"Maybe. Maybe not. It's not that far from the city. You want to gamble on it?"

"No." Tom fell silent. Finally, he said, "Are you sure? *Hammerfall?*"

"It looks that way."

"Okay." He paused again, then said, "If it's that bad, we'll head up your way."

"I may not be there at first, but I'll make sure you're expected. You have my cell number. Keep me posted."

"Okay." He hesitated. "Thanks for the heads up, Eagle."

"See you soon. Take care of my gang."

"Okay."

The Hornbrook Prophecy

Part Two

From Want of Foresight…

"It happens then as it does to physicians in the treatment of consumption, which in the commencement is easy to cure and difficult to understand; but when it has neither been discovered in due time nor treated upon a proper principle, it becomes easy to understand and difficult to cure. The same thing happens in state affairs; by foreseeing them at a distance…the evils which might arise from them are soon cured; but when, from want of foresight, they are suffered to increase to such a height that they are perceptible to everyone, there is no longer any remedy."
—Niccolo Machiavelli, The Prince, 1513

The Hornbrook Prophecy

CHAPTER 19

"No society is more than three meals from a revolution."
—Unknown

Friday – July 30

With his left hand, Tom quietly replaced the cordless handset onto the telephone cradle on the wall above the desk next to the window in the kitchen as he ran his right hand through his relatively short-cropped light red hair. He shoved his gold-rimmed glasses up on his head, closed his eyes for a moment, placing the heels of his hands against his temples, and grimaced as he assimilated the conversation he had just ended. Just as with any problem that had arisen suddenly at the hospital over the years, his first move was reflexive—a quick, but systematic mental digestion of every possible option. The only difference this time was the enormity of the problem, and the simultaneous twin realizations that not only was this one a HUGE problem, but that virtually all his other problems just evaporated. *Silver lining*, he thought, incongruously.

He paused for a quiet moment or two more, as if realizing that such moments were about to become few and far between. And then with a single exclamation of, "CRAP!" he slammed the flat of his hand down on the desk, rattling the juice can full of pens and pencils, pulled his glasses back down onto his nose, and jumped to his feet, sending a flurry of loose papers cascading onto the linoleum.

He ran through the kitchen and flung open the screen door.

"Laurel!"

"Yeah, Tom. What?" Eagle's sister, dark hair springing from side to side as she moved, was helping young Emily pick up toys and other kid droppings in the backyard, and her husband's loud and unusually-demanding tone didn't help her mood.

"That was Eagle on the phone. It's bad! He says the government's all coming unglued, and as soon as people realize what's going on it's going to get ugly. Especially in the cities. Especially here. He says we oughta get out. Now!"

"What about the—"

"Sorry. No time for 'what abouts.' He's serious. This is what we talked about when he was here. And he thinks that if it does get bad the President could take extreme steps to deal with it, including declaring martial law. Travel could be prohibited. And we'd be trapped here while it gets *really* bad. We gotta go. Get the kids together in the living room and tell them to grab their quake packs, and anything else they'll want. You, too. I'll get the van ready."

She hesitated. She had managed pretty well through nearly twenty years of marriage, job ups and downs, five children, dozens of her children's illnesses and injuries, roughhousing, quarrels, teachers, homework, history projects, five rounds of often-painful piano lessons, countless trips to the park, cooking, cleaning, budgeting on a shoestring, summer camps, boyfriends, the birds and the bees, coupons, car problems, a gazillion headaches—and two big earthquakes. Somehow, she'd met every challenge and still had her sanity. Or at least most of it.

She and Tom had talked at length, together and also with Eagle, about where the ongoing national problems might lead, and how they might personally be affected. Although they had never succeeded in leaving the LA area for dreamed-of greener pastures of a less-crowded, less-hectic, less-dangerous place to live, they had done what they could to cope with the unexpected. Aware, if not fearful, of the dangers of living in an area known not just for movie stars and "California girls," but also for earthquakes, wild fires, drugs, gangs, and race riots, they had long ago prepared for the possible need for a hasty evacuation away from their home, in case of a sudden natural or social disaster. For some reason, however, Tom's words stunned her in a new, unimagined way. She instantly knew what she had to do, but felt paralyzed, and couldn't keep from being bombarded by truly irrational thoughts.

"But the PTA meeting's tonight!"

"CRAP!" muttered Tom, turning on his heel to make for the garage. But he stopped himself, and ran over to his wife, and kissed her forehead. "Laurel, my sweet, you are a real piece of work. Now, MOVE!" He smacked her on the bottom, and went careening through the screen door again.

Laurel was jarred back to reality, dismissed the brief but unwanted mental misstep without further thought, and dashed into the house. Two seconds later, the door sprang back open and Laurel leapt out, grabbed Emily, and disappeared back into the house. *This is not a good start*, she thought to herself.

After pushing Emily into the pink-curtained, teddy bear-adorned bedroom she shared with Maggie, and instructing her to grab some toys and books, Laurel dashed down the hall to her own room. In a few minutes, she heard Tom come in the front door, and she whirled around to ask him about the other kids.

Tom answered, "Tommy's getting his stuff, Maggie's putting hers in the van, and I sent Kate on her bike down to Angel's to find Ellie. I called her cell phone, but she didn't answer. You need to grab our stuff and Emily."

"OK. Is the van ready?"

"Not quite. We're going to take the truck, too. This isn't going to be easy. Even if we get out of the city, we don't stand a prayer unless we find a safe place to hole up for the long haul. I know it's a risk, but I think we've got to try to get to Eagle's place."

"All the way to *Washington*?" Laurel was incredulous.

"Yeah. It's the only thing that makes sense. Remember? We talked about it when he was here back in February."

"I know, but I always just figured your folks' place up in Canyon Country would be good enough."

"Maybe for your run-of-the-mill disaster. But, if this is going to be as bad as he thinks, it could take forever to calm down, let alone recover from it. And it won't be any better at Dad's; I'm glad they're in Canada right now, but I can't even reach him where he is. Look, this is probably going to blow over quickly, 'cause I don't think the government's stupid enough to let it get out of hand. So this will just end up being a nice little vacation. But if it is bad, Eagle's got resources up there that could mean the difference between making it and not, or at least simply being safe. Besides, if we take both vehicles, we can take more stuff—and we'd have an extra means of transport if something happens to the van."

"Like what?"

Tom was exasperated as well as hurried. "I don't know what! But I doubt that Pep Boys will be open at two AM if I need a new engine."

Laurel looked at the wall, thinking as she shifted mental gears. "Okay, then. We all need to get some winter stuff—coats, boots, gloves, sweaters. And underwear! And more food. Tell Maggie to get a couple of boxes from the garage and bring them into the pantry."

"All right. But we really need to hurry. People may not understand right away, but if they start to panic like I think they will, their first reaction will be to flee, and that means the freeways will jam up fast. I don't want to be sitting here when the whole city gets pissed."

The phone rang. Laurel ran over to the nightstand and picked it up.

"Hello?"

"Mom! It's Ellie. Kate's over here telling me some story about the end of the world. What's *really* going on?"

"Don't argue. We have to leave the city. Dad thinks there's going to be trouble. He's packing the van and we're going to Uncle Eagle's."

Tom was halfway to the front door, heard Laurel's words, and ran back into the bedroom. "Tell her to come home immediately, but stop and fill the truck at Ernie's." Then he ran out.

"Ellie, Dad said come quickly, but stop and get gas first. Ernie's is right down the end of the street from where you are. Please hurry, OK?"

"OK." The phone went dead.

Out in the garage, Tom made sure all seven quake packs were in the back of the van. First prepared several years ago, after the last big earthquake, each pack held emergency gear for a member of the family—clothing, water bottles, a flashlight, a sleeping bag, matches, a space blanket, a pair of shoes, personal items, and some non-perishable food. Kept in the garage to be grabbed in a hurry while fleeing the house, and updated periodically as bodies grew, they were intended to provide enough basics for someone who conceivably might be chased out of the house in the middle of the night in their pajamas, and who might not be able to return for a couple of days.

As Tom's suspicions grew over the years that a social—not geological—catastrophe might be more likely, he also prepared other boxes of emergency gear, telling the kids that it made packing for camping trips easier. Now, his fears realized, he gave hurried thanks to his one great instance of foresight.

He backed the van out of the garage, got out, and disappeared back inside the garage. Reemerging with a strap-on, enclosed rooftop cargo carrier, he spent a few minutes securing it on top of the van. Boxes of tents, lanterns, camp stove, propane bottles, and other equipment were rapidly pulled off the shelves and loaded into it. Then, moving aside some carefully arranged garage clutter, he opened the gun safe hidden in the back corner and pulled out his entire collection—the Ruger 10-22 rifle; a Remington 870 pump-action 12-gauge shotgun; his .223-caliber Colt AR-15 semi-automatic—a so-called "assault" rifle (*thank God I didn't get rid of this when they passed that stupid ban*, he thought savagely). "I'll bet those asshole legislators will wish *they* had one before the week is out," he added out loud. He also put in a venerable, well-worn and well-oiled Colt-.45 semi-automatic handgun, and his favorite plinker—a semi-automatic Calico M-950 pistol, complete with a cylindrical beehive magazine clipped on top that held 50-rounds of 9mm, and a second, longer, 100-round magazine that went with it. Nine millimeter might not be considered a "stopping" round, but Tom always felt being able to fire 150 rounds at someone would at least make them think twice. He'd kept all the guns loaded while they were locked away in the safe, but he checked each one quickly to make sure, then put them next to the van. They'd go in last.

He also found and retrieved several metal "ammo" cans each full of reloaded ammunition of various calibers. He pulled out an empty handgun holster, slapped his forehead, and ran inside again. A few moments later he came out with a cloth-wrapped 9mm Sig-Sauer P220 semi-automatic handgun he kept in the bedroom. Gun control advocates had lots of fine things to say about stopping violence, but Tom had made sure he would have more than slogans at hand if his family ever faced an immediate deadly threat. He thought for a moment, then clipped the holster to his belt and slid the Sig smoothly into place.

Okay, he thought. *What else? Oh, yeah. Gas! We won't make it to Washington on good intentions alone.* He had just filled the van the day before, and had only driven maybe ten or fifteen miles since. *Let's say one gallon gone out of a 36-gallon tank*, he thought. *It's about 1100 miles to Eagle's place. At 18 miles per gallon on the highway, we can go about 600 miles on one tank. Halfway. No, more.* In addition, he had four, five-gallon red polyethylene cans of unleaded gas in the garage. *Another 20 times 18 is…is…uh, another 360 miles Okay, that's almost enough. But not quite. Oh crap! If we take two vehicles, that's twice as much gas. Duh!*

Then another thought struck him. The cities! The most direct route to Eagle's was a bee-line shot up I-5. But even if they got out of L.A., they'd still have to contend with possible—no, likely—traffic jams (or worse) coming out of the Bay Area, Sacramento, and Portland at the very least. If there was any trouble at all, it was over. A single accident or incident of road rage could shut down the interstate easily and indefinitely.

No, he thought, *maybe we ought to go the back way. Up 395 through the desert and Owens Valley, then up the back side of the Sierras and into eastern*

Oregon. He'd been up that way before, on vacations to Idaho and Montana. The routes are almost parallel, but 395, and the other, lesser highways they'd be on, are often only a single lane in each direction. Slower. Longer. Maybe two- or two hundred fifty miles longer, he guessed. More time. More gas.

So, what'll it be, genius? Drive like a bat out of hell up I-5 and pray that you get past Portland before people really panic? Or, be sneaky, take the scenic route, and hope like hell that the hillbillies don't shoot you for target practice?

"CRAP!" he said again. "I don't know. But what I *do* know is that no matter what, I'm still gonna need more gas sooner or later." So he grabbed about an eight-foot length of half-inch clear vinyl tubing probably left over from some forgotten 6th grade science project, coiled it up and put it in the box with the camp stove.

Just then the small Toyota pickup truck that they'd had since Ellie was a toddler came lurching into the driveway. Ellie and Kate piled out of the passenger door. Ellie had the long, straight dark hair and smooth complexion of her mother, while Kate had the fair skin of generations of Warners and short, sandy blonde hair that was as unruly as her independent spirit. A young Hispanic man climbed out from behind the wheel. He was pleasantly good-looking, with a moderate cleft in his chin and dense black hair cut to a style somewhere between a biker and a stockbroker, Dressed in a sleeveless sweatshirt, jeans, and sneakers, he stepped forward next to Ellie.

"Dad," Ellie said, speaking quickly, "Angel's folks are in San Diego at his Grandma's house. He wants to come with us."

Tom started to open his mouth, then caught himself. Angel St. Paul was a year or so older than Ellie's eighteen. They had sort of grown up playing together in the neighborhood, and were now commuting together daily to classes at Cal State Northridge. Their relationship had always resembled one like close siblings, but Tom often wondered if it had been deepening over the past year or so. A great fan of cheesy horror movies, and creator of his own tongue-in-cheek video versions, Angel loved role-playing of all kinds. He could easily slip into the slang and mannerisms of the local gang leader, but could just as readily switch it off and begin discussing current music trends. He played a lively bass guitar in his own rock band, but was attending college with a goal of getting a teaching credential for elementary school.

Tom liked Angel a lot, but wasn't sure what to say. Before he could reach a decision, Angel walked over to him and turned him toward the garage so he could speak quietly. "Mr. Warner, I read the papers, and I know pretty much why you're leaving. I agree with you. It's not going to be safe here. But it's not going to safe along the way, either. Now, your wife is great, and Ellie and Kate are pretty mature, and they can probably put up with a lot. But I'm not sure any of them are ready for what might happen when this all gets heated up. I think I could be a lot of help to you. If there's any trouble at all, I think you're gonna need me."

Tom didn't hesitate this time. "You need to get some gear together, Angel. You three will drive the truck and follow behind the van."

"Dad," Ellie spoke up again. "Angel's already got his stuff in. And he had two gas cans at home, so we filled them and brought 'em along, too!"

"You're right, Angel," Tom said. "I *am* going to need you. Good thinking. Now, Ellie and Kate: Since we're headed to the northwest, you need to grab winter coats and footwear, plus as much other clothes and underwear as you can get in one bag, 'cause I don't know how long we're going to be there. Then help your Mom get whatever else she needs. And, for heaven's sake, go to the bathroom. You've got five minutes! Angel, check the oil and water in the truck."

In the distance, sirens could be heard.

***

Their short caravan climbed the freeway on-ramp with trepidation, afraid of what they might find. It had taken less than an hour, from the time Tom hung up from talking with Eagle, to get the vehicles loaded and moving out the driveway. The intense activity and commotion at the house forestalled any serious or prolonged contemplation of the hours or days ahead of them. Tom and Laurel sat up front in the white, five year old Dodge Ram Van, with Maggie, Tommy, and Emily sitting quietly, for a change, in the middle seat. Behind them were the quake packs, and duffels full of other clothes and shoes. The firearms and ammunition were carefully packed out of sight, but close at hand. Tools, motor oil, and everything else Tom could think of to grab out of the garage also went into a box under the seat. He had decided to leave the rear seat in the van, in case they were forced to abandon the truck. At the last minute, Laurel had emerged from the house carrying a box of photo albums and home videos which she had placed under a seat after a wordless but knowing nod from her husband.

The last item Tom had thrown in was a roll of duct tape—he just couldn't fathom facing the end of the world without a roll of duct tape.

Tommy had been declared the first hero of the day when he pulled two walkie-talkies out of his duffel just as they were backing out of the driveway. Tom slammed on the brakes, grabbed one, jumped out of the van and ran back

The Hornbrook Prophecy

to hand one through the truck's driver window to Angel. "Keep it on for now, we'll work out signals as we go," Tom instructed him.

Angel was driving the old blue Toyota, with Ellie and Kate crammed into the small seat next to him. Before they had departed, Tom had given Angel the .45 Colt which he placed under the seat along with an extra clip, and the shotgun which he propped up behind the seat, covered with a towel. In the back, under the boxy camper shell, they had placed all six spare gas containers, the rest of the camping gear, and the supplies they had gathered from the pantry.

After leaving the house, they'd made a quick detour to their bank, where Tom got to the drive-up window just before the 6 pm evening closing time and withdrew all but one hundred dollars from his checking account. With what they'd had on hand at home, they now had just under $3000 in cash. "Thank God those bills we paid the other day hadn't cleared yet," he said. "They're gonna bounce a mile high if the banks are still in business when they come in. I wish we could've gotten to the credit union, too, but I'm not waiting until tomorrow. I hope to hell that in a few days I feel really stupid for doing this, but…" He didn't finish the sentence.

So off they drove. *Ready or not, here we come*, Tom thought.

As they reached the top of the freeway on-ramp, other cars and trucks were screaming by at better than 80 miles per hour. "Hell," commented Tom to Laurel, "they always drive like this here. The traffic's heavy, but not unusual for a Friday evening. Turn on the radio."

Laurel punched the knob on the radio and switched the tuner to AM. She jumped from one station to the next, listening to each just long enough to see what they were talking about. She finally found a station just starting to break the story of the federal government's decision to "*delay the meeting of certain financial obligations pending the imminent restructuring of its short-term economic strategy. Treasury Secretary Stanfield Heppner issued the following statement moments ago at the White House…*"

After a brief pause, a new voice said, "*A few minutes ago, President Dillard instructed me to implement a contingency plan to cope with an unexpected shortfall in domestic spending capability. This will include some delays in the issuing of certain payments to private citizens as well as to current holders of specific federal liabilities. The President will have a full statement tomorrow morning.*"

The first radio voice came back on, saying "*The Secretary immediately left the press briefing room after the statement, ignoring the uproar and barrage of questions from reporters which followed hard upon his heels. It is not known at this time what the full implications are of this statement, but we will keep you advised as we learn more details."*

"Wait a minute," said another voice. *"Do this mean that my sainted mother's Social Security check will NOT be in the mail as expected this week? And what about—"*

"I don't know, Charles," said the first voice. *"But I suspect that gobbledygook we just heard from Secretary Heppner is just the tip of the iceberg. We've been following the…"*

Tom leaned over and turned the radio down. "The word is just getting out, but no one really knows just what to make of it yet. That explains why the freeway's not any crazier than usual. Let's see, it's about 9 pm back in D.C. If the Secretary's right, there probably won't be anything other than media speculation until the President's news conference in the morning. But you can tell that this is really serious."

He thought for a moment as he maneuvered around traffic. As he made the turn transitioning from the 405 onto the I-5 Golden State Freeway, he said, "No way they'll keep the lid on this one, but it's possible the entire government will be in a state of shock. If that were true, then no one would be doing much before the President speaks, which would give us about twelve hours before people start to wise up. We could be clear past Sacramento and out of the Central Valley by then. STUPID ASS!!" A heavily-loaded minivan came speeding by in the fast lane and swerved sharply in front of them on his way to changing two lanes at a time while weaving his way around slower cars.

"He may just be a moron, but by the look of him he's try to clear out, too. I'll bet within another hour or two it's gonna get real crazy. I really hate the idea of going up 395, but I'm sure if we stay on I-5, we'll be sorry."

Laurel responded, "Do you think gas will be a problem?"

"I don't know," Tom said. "But either way we'll still need some. It should take some time before stations run out, even if things really get shut down and they don't get any deliveries for a while. People in the rural areas probably keep some on hand anyway, and they aren't apt to be running off either, so they won't be as likely to create a run on the gas stations. I hope. But just to be safe, we can top off the tanks every couple of hours or so as long as stations are open."

"You're probably right," said Laurel, trying to encourage herself as much as Tom.

Tom picked up the walkie-talkie, and pressed the call button. "Angel, Ellie, are you there?"

"We're here, Dad!" It was Ellie's voice, anxious, but steady.

"We're going to head out to Mojave and up through Bishop. So we'll take the Antelope Valley Freeway exit in about three miles."

"Okay, Dad."

Tom put the walkie-talkie back on the engine console. They made the change off I-5 onto Highway 14 with no trouble, and Laurel checked the map. "It looks like we stay on 14 for a little over 120 miles. It's about 40 minutes to Palmdale, another half hour to Mojave, and then maybe 50 miles to where we intersect Highway 395," she said. "Call it two hours."

"OK. That's about 8 pm. It looks like we've got the jump on the LA crowd," Tom ventured, "so if we can get to 395 ahead of the San Bernardino traffic, we should be in the clear. Thank God we were home when Eagle called. He's given us a *huge* advantage." He applied more pressure to the accelerator pedal, watching both the speedometer needle climb to 70 and the rearview mirror to make sure the Toyota was still with them. He had to consciously keep from trying to go faster. The old truck wouldn't manage more very easily. Besides, it was going to be a long drive.

They were less than fifteen miles from home, but he felt good about their efforts so far. They cleared out in good time, the extra ten gallons of gas Angel brought would give them a lot more flexibility later on, and so far they appeared to have a lead on most everyone else. At this rate, we'll be there in no time, he thought to himself. If, if, if…

***

Molallo Estacada had been making bad decisions all his life. As a young boy growing up in the farm fields around Modesto, California, he'd seldom listened to his migrant worker parents, when they had time to pay attention to him at all. Facial scars from an accident involving an open fire pit became the subject of merciless taunts and teasing by other children, but the young Estacada learned early that his fists could make the teasing stop. The tears he caused gave him some sense of satisfaction. The next fifteen years did little to improve his attitude or his decision-making skills, and, although fairly intelligent, he often found himself in trouble at school, on the streets, and even in the fields. The juvenile authorities grew tired of dealing with him, and were actually pleased when, at sixteen, he was arrested for armed robbery at a 7-11 and was tried and convicted as an adult. His time in jail served to teach him everything he needed, except how to make good decisions.

The only bright spot in Estacada's life was his younger brother, Sandolfo. Sandy was not as quick-tempered as his older brother, but neither was he as quick-witted, and he was frequently the butt of jokes about his dimness much the same as Molallo had been because of his scars. When the older brother was taken away for two years, Sandolfo felt lost.

After his release, Molallo, now eighteen, took a job working in an auto salvage yard. Here he met a talented mechanic, Ramon Montesano, who took a liking to him. His employers were expanding their automotive restoration business into the Sacramento area and Ramon offered to get them a job. Molallo insisted that Sandy be allowed to come along as well, and they left Stockton without even saying good-bye to their mother.

Working out of warehouse space near the former Mather Air Force Base in Rancho Cordova, the auto "restoration" business certainly caught Molallo's fancy. Expensive, usually foreign, late model cars were stolen and brought to the warehouse, where they were stripped to the chassis. The bare frames then were taken away and abandoned, to be found and impounded by the police. Written off by the insurance companies, the frames were bought back by intermediaries of Molallo's employers for mere pennies at auctions, where the buyers were given clear, legal title. Returned to the warehouse, the autos were reassembled back to their completely functional—and valuable—state and sold at nearly full value. The idea of ripping off rich people and then legally selling their own cars back to them really appealed to Molallo. It was revenge, justice, and a paycheck all in one.

Molallo and Sandy Estacada were just finishing shining up the paint of a newly-reassembled silver 2009 BMW 760i when Ramon revved into the shop in a nearly new Mercedes SL600 Roadster and screeched to a quick stop. As Sandy lowered the overhead roller door, Ramon jumped out, ran over to Molallo, and told him the news.

"Things are going *crazy*, man," Ramon said excitedly. "The radio said the government fell apart and can't pay its bills, and people are going to starve, and they'll be no police or fire, or army, or nothin'!"

"No way, Ramon," said Molallo, resuming his polishing. "There's always gonna be cops, just so they can beat the shit out of *us*."

"No, is true," insisted Ramon. "They said people are shootin' at each other, and there's lootin' and burnin', because everyone thinks they are gettin' screwed again by the Man."

"Well, I don't give a shit. I got nothin' to burn." Molallo thought for a moment. "Hey, you remember that place where we lifted that black Ferrari last month?" he said conversationally, as if ignoring what he had just heard. "They had a place tha' look like Disneyland, man."

"So?"

"So I don't wanna be a grease monkey all my life. So I bet there's a lot more toys inside that place that they don't need. Maybe we should pay 'em a visit. You know, do a little 'shopping.' Like you said, no cops, right?"

"I don't know, 'Lallo," said Ramon.

"Well, I do," proclaimed Molallo. "Sandy, you wanna go for a ride and find some nice things to play with?"

"Okay, Molallo," his brother said simply.

Molallo went to his locker in the corner of the warehouse, opened it, pulled a Taurus .38 Special 5-shot revolver off the shelf, and stuck it in his belt. Then he went over to the locked door of the small room that was used as an office, smashed the window with his elbow, and reached in to unlock the door.

"Hey, shit, 'Lallo!" cried Ramon. "They gonna kill us."

"Leave 'em a nice note. Tell 'em to take it out of my severance pay."

Once inside he found a sawed-off 12-gauge shotgun leaning against the back corner in the closet, and three 25-shell boxes of Winchester double-O buckshot, which he shoved in his jacket pockets. Searching around, he found a real prize up on the shelf under a pair of dirty overalls—a loaded TEC-DC9 auto pistol, with two spare 32-round magazines. He gathered them all up in his arms. He saw a small safe in the corner, but knew it defied his skills, so he shrugged and left the room.

He threw the shotgun on the back seat of the BMW, lay the auto pistol next to the driver's seat as he jumped in, and smiled with satisfaction as the engine caught and quickly settled into a throaty purr. Sandy hopped in the front seat. Jamming it into gear, Molallo drove up alongside Ramon and looked up at him with a raised eyebrow. Ramon paused, looked around, then climbed in the rear, and Molallo gunned it out of the warehouse.

***

Two hours after leaving Los Angeles, the Warners were moving steadily up U.S. Highway 395, having encountered no delays or congestion at all. Barely believing their good luck, but not wanting to take anything for granted, they had stopped in Mojave, barely more than an hour from home. While

Laurel ran across the street and loaded up on burgers, McNuggets, fries and drinks at a McDonald's, Tom topped off both vehicles with gas at a Circle K convenience store. They only needed a few gallons, but it gave them maximum range again. It would be dark in another hour, and fewer places would be open. With full tanks, however, and another 30 gallons in cans, they could manage about 700 miles. *Oregon easily*, Tom thought. *About 10 hours of driving time.* He checked his watch. *That's almost dawn.*

Now, bouncing along 395 north of Ridgecrest, Tom caught the announcement of a news bulletin on the fading reception of the LA radio station they'd been monitoring. Turning the volume up, they heard the news reporter saying, *"…and while the reports of violence and looting in South Central Los Angeles may not be too surprising, Mayor Townsend and Chief Barrows seemed to have been caught completely off guard by the reports of riots in Santa Monica, Pomona, Westwood, and in many parts of the San Fernando Valley…"*

"I guess we did the right thing getting out when we did," said Laurel quietly.

"Yeah, Eagle was right about the cities," Tom remarked. "Wait, listen!" He held up his hand.

"…along with reports that major fires have broken out in San Francisco, San Jose, and on the east side of the Bay Area. And while many people are attempting to get out of the area, complicating a normally heavy Friday evening commute, a 40-car pileup on eastbound Interstate 80 at the Carquinez Straits Bridge south of Vallejo has shut down the freeway in both directions.

"Our sister station KFBK in Sacramento has reported that at present there does not seem to be any major civil breakdowns, but people evidently fearful of violence are flooding the highways creating massive slowdowns. The California Highway Patrol reports rapidly escalating incidents of road rage, as well as increasing numbers of people who are completely disregarding normal traffic laws in their attempts to get around the tie-ups.

"All this violence and panic-type behavior by the populace appears to be the result of the announcement just after 9 o'clock Eastern Daylight Time by Secretary of the Treasury Stanfield Heppner of an apparent potential major financial disaster facing the federal government and the resulting eruptions of rumors flashing laser-like from coast to coast of everything from national bankruptcy to a crash of the stock market.

"It sounds like it's more than laser-like rumors that are erupting," Tom said.

"Shh!" said Laurel, leaning closer to the radio.

"We will continue to follow very closely the news out of Washington, across the country, and throughout the state. At the present we have no indication that President Dillard has changed his intention to address the nation in the morning, or to advance his timetable in response to the current early unrest we are learning more about almost by the minute.

"To summarize events to this point…"

Tom turned the radio back down again. "Well, the stock market isn't even open so it can hardly crash, but geez, it's happening so fast! I mean, Eagle said it would, but …*man*! I just still can't believe it."

"Well, if you had any doubts at all about cruising up I-5, I guess you shouldn't have."

"Yeah, I know, Laurel, but I'm beginning to think *this* isn't going to be a cakewalk for much longer either."

"Do you want me to drive?"

"Not yet. I'm still too wound up to relax, so I might as well keep going."

Forty minutes later, Tom keyed the walkie-talkie and raised Ellie again. "There's a rest stop a couple of miles ahead. I think we'll pull off, stretch, and change drivers. OK?"

"Okay, Daddy-O," said an upbeat-sounding Ellie.

They pulled off at the rest stop south of Owens Lake (a "lake" mostly in name only after decades of water diversion via aqueducts to Los Angeles), but the buildings were unlit, and the solitary car in the parking lot had its hood up and was being attended by two men who looked as if they were glad to see the two new vehicles pull in.

"Angel!" Tom said over the walkie-talkie.

"Yeah, Tom?" Angel answered while Ellie held up the mouthpiece in front of him.

"Change of plans. I don't like the looks of this, so just keep moving. And keep your eyes open."

"Gotcha."

The van had slowed as it entered the rest stop and cruised by the parked car as the men looked at them. Then Laurel screamed, "Tom, he's got a gun!"

"*ANGEL! GUN! HIT IT!*" Tom yelled into the mike in his hand. Then he stomped on the gas pedal and looked in the side mirror to see if Angel had heard him. The truck was lurching forward and picking up speed when they heard a gunshot. Laurel screamed again, but after the truck swerved suddenly to one side, Tom could see it straighten out and close on the van.

Laurel grabbed the walkie-talkie from Tom and yelled into it. "Ellie, Kate! Are you all right?"

"Mom? We're okay, I think. I think they hit the canopy window, but we're fine. Angel's really pissed and Kate's scared. Why did those men shoot at us?"

"A lot of people are starting to panic because of this trouble that's going on, Sweetie. Dad thinks those men probably wanted to steal one of our cars if they could, because something seemed to be wrong with theirs. Hold on, Dad wants to talk with Angel again."

"Okay, here he is."

"Angel?" Tom asked.

"Yes, Mr. Warner?" Tom could hear the extra apprehension in Angel's voice, and noted the change in address.

"I think we just encountered our first taste of fallout from this thing, and while we were lucky this time, we are really going to have to be on the alert. Make sure at least one of the girls is awake with you all the time, and acting like a lookout. You done good, Angel. But let's be *real* careful. Keep a little extra distance behind us, so you have plenty of reaction time, but be prepared to close up quick if necessary. OK?"

"I'm with ya," Angel replied.

"Oh, and Angel?"

"Yo!"

"Perhaps you might make sure Mr. Colt isn't too cramped," Tom said quietly.

"Roger. I will." Angel clicked off the walkie-talkie.

The past three or four hours had started to take on a kind of feeling of adventure, at least so it had seemed to the three of them in the truck. Now as Angel reached under the seat for the pistol, he looked at Ellie. The adventure was over. And reality didn't seem too fun. Angel grabbed the wheel more firmly, Ellie now stared intently out the windshield and Kate, while shaken, was quiet.

The two vehicles drove on in the darkness.

The Hornbrook Prophecy

***

Ramon Montesano and the Estacada brothers cruised up Sunrise Boulevard until they came to Highway 50, where they pulled smoothly around the on-ramp and headed east. Just a few miles up the road they exited at Folsom Blvd, turned left under the freeway and drove toward the former rough-and-ready town of Folsom, which had become a Sacramento commuter community of million dollar homes beginning in the 1980s. At the doorstep of the California gold rush foothills, Folsom offered a quaint old-fashioned main street full of trendy boutiques and cafes, and nearby beautiful neighborhoods overlooking the American River and Folsom Lake.

Ignoring the irony of being within a stone's throw of the notorious Folsom Prison, the trio found the street they were seeking and slowly drove along looking for "Disneyland." "There it is," said Molallo quietly, pulling into the driveway of a magnificent but darkened home like he belonged there—after all, who was going to question the presence of an expensive BMW in front of such a mansion? "Looks like nobody home," he added. They got out quietly and went around the garage to the side gate.

"I don't see many lights on," offered Ramon, warming up to the circumstances. He hefted the shotgun. "I think we gonna have some fun."

Once around in back, they eyed the lush landscaping and grotto-like swimming pool. "See, Sandy, like Disneyland," said Molallo. His brother just stared. They looked at the doors and windows on the rear side of the house, then ignored the alarm warning signs and heaved a potted plant through one of the double 10-lite glass French doors that led into the kitchen area. As they entered, a steady buzz sounded from near the front door, signaling that the alarm had been triggered. Ramon found the wall console and smashed it with the butt of the shotgun. The noise stopped. Then he ran up the stairs.

Molallo quickly went through the main floor looking for inhabitants and, finding none, headed back to the living room, where Sandy was looking at some silver and gold figurines on the mantle. Ramon clumped down the stairs.

"We're alone," he said, triumphantly. "I found some jewelry in the bedroom, but it's not much. They must have a safe somewhere down here, 'cause there's no sign of one up there."

"There's a room with a lot of books through there," said Molallo, pointing across the living room. "Try that." He continued to look casually around the living room, in no particular hurry, picking up the delicate or unusual ornaments, sculptures, and other decorations that were so foreign to him. The oil paintings and Chinese silks on the wall looked expensive, but they didn't appeal to him.

"Hey, 'Lallo!" cried Ramon. "I found it."

Molallo came into the library. Ramon said, "Just like in the movies, man. It was behind the picture," he said, showing how a painting swung out on hinges away from the wall, revealing a small wall safe with an illuminated electronic display and numeric keypad instead of a combination lock dial. "But how in hell do you open it?"

"Shit, I don't know," protested Molallo. "But it's not even steel, man. Try a 12-gauge combination."

Ramon smiled, then retrieved the shotgun from the desk where he'd laid it. He walked up to the safe, pointed the gun at it and pulled both triggers. The roar was deafening, and a cloud of smoke filled the room.

"Molallo?" they heard a call from the living room.

"No sweat, Sandy," yelled Molallo. "It's cool."

Ramon went up to the safe and found that the handle on the door turned without resistance, and he pulled open the safe. "So much for electronic wizardry," he said with a grin. "Why build a million dollar crib and put in a hunerd dollar safe? Probably from Wal-Mart, man. They just don't build them like they used to. Wow!" Inside he found a small stack of cash, several folders with papers in them, and some velvet boxes. Molallo took the boxes from him and set them down on the desk. Opening one he found a diamond and pearl necklace, with matching earrings. Others yielded varieties of bracelets, rings, and watches, each of which were adorned with gold, diamonds, or other stones.

"We hit the lottery, man!" he exclaimed. "Disneyland! I definitely ain't being no mechanic no more."

They took the jewelry out of the boxes, and stuffed it into their pockets, along with the cash. Just then they heard a loud command from the living room.

"FREEZE!" said a scratchy voice.

Ramon held up his forefinger to his lips, and gestured to Molallo to follow him. Peering through the hallway opening into the living room, they saw an elderly uniformed man holding a pistol on Molallo's brother, both looking terrified. Just then the man noticed the movement from the hall and he spun around to bring the gun to bear on the direction of the distraction. His eyes started to widen as he found himself looking at the double-barreled shotgun in Ramon's hands. Ramon pulled the trigger. *Click.* He had forgotten to reload after blasting the safe.

The guard saw Ramon suddenly lurch into the room and he fired his pistol before realizing that there was a second man behind Ramon who had just pushed him out of the way. Molallo dropped to one knee, pulled the trigger of the TEC-9 and let loose a six-round burst of 9-mm hollow-point, three of which stitched the man across the chest and sent him reeling back falling across the recliner.

At that same moment another uniformed man rushed in through the kitchen. Molallo whirled and fired again, this time a longer burst as the gun swept horizontally across the room. Bullets ricocheted off the kitchen appliances and hanging pans, sending up a shower of splinters as they tore into the cabinets, and caught the new man in the upper chest and neck, dropping him on the marble tile floor.

After he checked the two men, Molallo called to Sandy. "You OK?"

"Yeah, I'm OK."

"'Lallo," said a soft voice from the corner. Ramon was slumped on the floor, holding his side just above his belt. Blood covered his fingers.

"Shit," said Molallo, running over to his friend. He moved Ramon's hand and pulled up his shirt. He yanked a white armrest cover off the chair next to him and wiped at Ramon's side. There was a two-inch long gash that was bleeding steadily, but not profusely. "You dumb shit! It barely scratched you."

He went down the hall to a bathroom he had seen earlier, found some clean towels and ran one of them under the hot water. Pulling open more drawers, he finally found a first-aid kit, and went back to where Ramon was now sitting in the arm chair. Molallo cleaned up the wound, poured some iodine over it, stuck a wad of gauze on it and taped it securely into place. He went over to the body of the first man and looked down at it.

"I thought you said there were no more cops."

"He ain't no cop. Wrong uniform. I think he must be private. Maybe he already got paid, so he's still on the job. Did you see his face? He was more scared than Sandy. I'll bet he's never had a call before." Ramon laughed, as he got up. "Well, he ain't gonna get any more practice."

"We better get outta here, anyway. There may be more. Come on Sandy, get your things and let's go."

The three went out through the front door and got into their car. As they drove off, Sandy, sitting in back, said grumpily, "I don't like Disneyland."

Just before ten o'clock, the Warners slowed as they drove into Lone Pine, the truck now up close behind the van as if trying to huddle together in a strange place. In the daylight, Lone Pine was dwarfed by Mount Whitney, looming above it to the west on the eastern boundary of Sequoia National Park. Lone Pine, in a curious topographical coincidence, lay between Whitney, which at 14,495 feet was the *highest* peak in the continental United States, and Death Valley, just 60 miles to the east where you could stand in the *lowest* elevation in the US, 282 feet below sea level.

They were somewhat surprised to find things calm, and several stores still open for business. When Tom spotted a Texaco mini-mart station with lights on, he quickly pulled in and they again refilled the gas tanks. Laurel went inside with him and grabbed some orange juice, milk, Corn Pops, and donuts for the morning. *This is no time to worry about nutrition,* she thought. She also picked up some 9-volt batteries for the walkie-talkies and extra D-cells for the flashlights they had in the quake packs. A tall, slender gray-haired man wearing a green and black flannel shirt, jeans and cowboy boots, and sporting a huge, bushy mustache, greeted them with a smile.

"Howdy."

"Hi, how are you," Tom replied cordially.

"You folks from down south ways?"

"Yeah, we're going up to visit some relatives in Washington."

"Well, I 'spect that's a good idea. Hear tell things aren't so good in L.A."

"We lost our radio station about an hour ago. What's the latest?" Laurel asked

"A giant gang war going on, I reckon. The Mexicans are going at it with the Blacks. The Vietnamese are whomping on the Koreans and the Mexicans. The Japanese and the Chinese are whaling away at each other. And damn near everyone is beating up on the Whites."

"Holy shit!" exclaimed Tom. "Last we heard it wasn't nearly that bad."

"I guess they figger the cops don't got no money, so time's awastin'."

"But the police are city and county, not federal."

"Probably don't matter to them. They just figger either way the law's too busy to mess with 'em. So it's kinda like one giant game of 'King of the Hill.'"

"Thanks," said Tom as he picked up his change and left.

"Have a nice day, folks."

As they neared the freeway after leaving Folsom, Molallo said, "Where to?"

"I say we head up to Tahoe,'" answered Ramon. "More fun now we got some spending money."

"How much did we get?"

"There's a stack of fifties and a stack of hunerds. Could be twenty grand."

"I'll bet it wasn't the grocery money."

They reached the freeway, and Molallo paused for a few moments, then went through the underpass and climbed the on-ramp onto eastbound Highway 50. Traffic was extremely heavy, often barely moving. They merged into the slow lane and Molallo, never long on patience, exclaimed, "This is shit! What's with these people?"

"Everybody's bailin', man," said Ramon.

"Well, I ain't everybody." Molallo pulled off onto the right shoulder and accelerated up along past the near parking lot-like freeway lanes. He was frequently frustrated in his efforts by others who had the same idea at times, and at one point his temper got the better of him when someone pulled out onto the shoulder in front of him. He roared up behind them, then let loose a couple of shots from his revolver through the rear window of the offender, who immediately swerved wildly and disappeared over the side of the freeway embankment.

After they passed Cameron Park, and then Placerville, the traffic progressively thinned out, and Molallo was able to maintain a good pace just by weaving around slower vehicles, at least until the highway narrowed to two lanes. An hour or so later they were over Echo Summit and descending down into the Lake Tahoe basin.

"I don't know about you, but I'm starved," said Molallo.

"Big time," Ramon replied. "There's a McDonald's"

"Screw that, man. I wanna steak!"

They pulled into a parking lot in Stateline, stashed their things in the trunk, and wandered into Harvey's, a long-time favorite of the gambling crowd. Molallo had never before even been outside the California Central Valley area, and the noise and commotion of a casino floor in full action was amazing to him. They walked by the rows of slot machines, by the craps and roulette tables, through another maze of one-armed bandits, the blackjack tables and even more slots, then finally emerged on the other side near a restaurant. Molallo just shook his head.

"I guess some people don't care that the government's broke."

"They probably just figure the more, the merrier," said Ramon. "Half of them end up broke, too."

"Who cares? Let's eat."

After they finished dinner, they went outside onto the busy street, and Ramon stretched his arms up in the air and said, "I need some beer, man. There's a liquor store." They went into the store and grabbed a 12-pack of Coors. When they went up to the counter to pay, the store clerk said, "How 'bout some ID, boys?"

"How 'bout you shut up and take the money?" said Ramon.

"Sorry, I just can't sell it to you unless you show me some ID."

"Here's all the ID you need, dumb shit," said Molallo, pulling out his revolver.

"Whoa, boys, don't be stupid, just get on out of here and I—"

They left, so he turned to the counter behind him and picked up the phone. As he punched in 9-1-1, he did not hear or see the figure come up behind him. He was just about to speak into the mouthpiece when Molallo brought the butt of the revolver smashing down on the back of his head.

The phone dangled on its cord as it announced, *"911. What is your emergency? ...Hello?"*

As Molallo came outside to join the other two, he said, "Time to go. I think Nevada."

"How 'bout Vegas, man?" said Ramon.

"Las Vegas is too far."

"I think Reno's pretty close. Carson City's probably only an hour."

"Carson City's for cowboys. I don't want to go there. Reno's okay, I guess."

They went back to the BMW, and Molallo said, "Sandy, you drive. I'm tired, and Ramon's thirsty."

"But where?"

"Just stay on this road, going that way," he said pointing, "and follow the signs that say Highway 50. Just don't go too fast; we don't need any attention."

Sandy tentatively pulled the BMW out onto the road and turned east. Within a few minutes they were out of the bright lights and headed down along the shore of the lake, black in the darkness except for a few reflections. Ramon and Molallo were enjoying the beer in the back seat, but lapsed into silence not long after the road rose up over Spooner Summit and then started to twist its way down toward the high desert floor.

Sandy was tired, too, but didn't want to wake Molallo. When he came to the intersection with Highway 395, he stopped, uncertain as to which way to turn. One sign included "Carson City, 3 miles," with an arrow pointing left. He knew Molallo had definitely said he did not want to go to Carson City. So he turned right and headed south.

***

Laurel relieved Tom at the wheel of the van after they stashed their purchases in the cooler. Ellie took over from Angel in the pickup, with Kate opting for the center seat for a while. Tom wasn't tired, but their mad rush north the last four hours had created knots in his neck and shoulders from holding the wheel so resolutely. It hadn't been their average vacation trip. But traffic was still fairly light, and he figured that it would be safe enough for "the girls" to drive.

About an hour north of Lone Pine they pulled into Bishop, figuring to repeat their adopted practice of keeping the gas tanks full while the going was good. Nary a single station in the town displayed lights, however, so when they hit the far side city limits they just climbed back to highway speed and kept going.

Tom switched on the console light and pulled out the map. It was roughly 200 miles to Reno. *Maybe four hours over this stretch of road since it involved a more twisting, hilly terrain,* he thought, glancing at his watch: *Almost dead-on eleven o'clock. Reno by 3 AM?*

"Okay, Laurel, just keep it going, but don't push it too hard. Everything between here and Reno's probably closed, but if you see a gas station open, stop. Keep an eye on the kids back there. I told Ellie to keep close, so if she drifts back on the hills, slow up some for her."

"Yes, Master," answered Laurel with a grin.

"Wench!"

***

Thirty minutes after turning south on Highway 395, after passing through Gardnerville, Sandy Estacada lost the battle to keep his eyes open, and as his head dropped forward the BMW slowly drifted to the side until the right wheels hit the soft shoulder and made the car veer abruptly to the side. The right front fender smashed sharply against a boulder extending out from the hillside, and sent the car careening back across the highway at an angle, jarring the occupants awake.

"Sandy!" screamed Molallo, jerking awake.

It took a moment for his brother to comprehend what was happening, and that was a moment too many. Unable to regain control, Sandy threw his hands up in front of his face as the car slammed almost headfirst into the hillside, flipping onto its right side before skidding to a stop.

Molallo found himself lying on the desert soil. He climbed to his feet and lurched over toward the BMW, where Ramon was standing up, his head and shoulders visible above the open door sill. "'Lallo, what the hell happened? What are you doin' way the hell over there? Your brother can't drive worth shit, man!"

"Shut up!" Molallo shouted back. "I think he fell asleep, so shut up! Can you see him? Is he OK?"

Ramon ducked down inside the rear seat compartment again. Sandy was collapsed in a heap against the side window on the passenger's front seat, his head bloodied, and not moving. Ramon stood up again.

"He looks hurt, 'Lallo. Bad, I think."

Molallo had reached the driver's door and opened it upward. He peered over the side and saw Sandy on the opposite side.

"Help me get him out," he said urgently to Ramon.

Ramon straddled the center seat console and kicked out the badly fractured front windshield. Then he and Molallo pulled and lifted the limp figure out of the car and stretched him out on the shoulder of the road.

"Shit!" said Molallo mournfully, shaking his brother. "Come on, Sandy, wake up!"

As his body was being moved, Sandy's head turned awkwardly to one side and lay at an unnatural angle. "God damn it," screamed Molallo. "Why didn't he wake me up? I never should have let him drive at all. Shit! Shit! Shit!"

He fell over onto his side and held his head between his hands as he moaned and cursed. Ramon then noticed the matted hair, wet with blood, on Molallo's head. He climbed back into the car, found an unopened can of beer and emerged with it and his sweatshirt. He told Molallo, "You're bleeding, man. So hold still while I clean it up. He pulled the tab on the can of beer, held it to one side as it foamed over, then poured it over the side of his friend's head.

"Yow! Shit, man," protested Molallo.

"Hold still."

Ramon continued pouring the beer until it washed away some of the blood and he could see the wound.

"It's not bad," announced Ramon. He fetched a first aid kit out of the trunk, and returned to bandage the wound.

"We're gonna need wheels, man," said Ramon.

"Well I don't see no car lot, do you?"

"Shut up. We'll have to borrow one." Ramon stood up and looked up and down the road. "Shit, man. I don't even know where the hell we are. But I see some lights coming. Get the guns. When they get near, you stand in the road and wave your arms. They'll see the car wrecked, and Sandy lying there, so they'll probably stop. Then I'll come out from behind *our* car and we'll get them to agree to let us 'borrow' *their* car. Simple."

"Yeah, right."

Ramon grabbed both the shotgun and the machine pistol—he was not going to be out-gunned like he had been at the house in Folsom. He stood behind the BMW as they waited for the approaching vehicle to get closer. Molallo shoved the revolver inside his belt behind his back and went to stand near his dead brother's body. When he saw the beams of the headlights sweep around the last curve before them, he motioned to Ramon to get down, turned back toward the car, and starting waving his arms frantically over his head just as the headlights found him.

Rather than slowing down or stopping as they had hoped, they heard instead the increased whine of the engine as the driver stepped hard upon the accelerator, and swung the car into the opposite lane, roaring past the two would-be carjackers before they could react.

"God damn it!" yelled Molallo at the receding taillights.

"Shit!" said Ramon angrily.

"No way they didn't see us! They even went clear around us to keep away. They didn't care what had happened to us. They weren't gonna stop for nothin'."

"Okay, okay. We gotta be better prepared for the next one."

"You got that right, Ramon. The next one gonna have the car blasted right out from under him."

"We gotta drive it after we get it, man. So we can't destroy it!"

"I know, I know. Okay, then, we'll blast them with the shotgun if we have to. That should be enough."

They talked and plotted for another fifteen minutes but couldn't figure out any better way to commandeer a car, except for a roadblock. They tried to right the BMW so they could roll it out into the middle of the road, but they couldn't get enough leverage or momentum by rocking it to get it turned back onto its wheels.

"Someone's coming!" Ramon shouted.

"We gotta move up closer to the curve so they don't have enough time to react or stop and turn back when they see us." Molallo grabbed the TEC-9 and started running up the road. Ramon cursed at losing possession of the high capacity auto-pistol, but followed quickly behind, checking the chambers of the shotgun again to make sure they were loaded, and patting his pockets to make sure he had extra shells.

They stood in the middle of the road, about six feet apart, with their guns held chest high in front of them like sentries. When the big white van came around the corner, they were almost blinded by the high beam halogen headlights. Ramon fired both barrels of the shotgun, and the headlight on the left side shattered instantly, but they had to leap out of the way as the van bore down on them. As they rolled to opposite sides of the road, they saw that another, smaller vehicle was just coming around the same curve. Ramon had just enough time to break open the shotgun, reload, and snap it shut before the vehicle came roaring into view. Again he loosed both barrels, then grinned like a demon when the dark colored import pickup truck veered off the road and smashed at an angle into the embankment, staying upright, but coming to a sudden stop.

The Hornbrook Prophecy

They jumped up and approached the truck cautiously from behind, Ramon slightly in front of Molallo, who was walking on the shoulder. Just before they reached the back of the camper shell, Ramon suddenly was thrown backwards, his chest erupting in red. His head hit hard upon the asphalt, but he was already beyond any capacity for sensation. Molallo, half in shock, immediately jumped to the side and then scrambled up and over the low roadside hill and into the darkness.

As he jumped over and crouched down behind a large desert laurel, he looked back just in time to see a dark figure run up clutching a black military-style rifle, and kneel down briefly beside Ramon's body, before turning and rushing up to the truck's cab. He could hear voices, and crying, and some moaning, as three occupants got out of the truck and lay or sat down beside it. Just then, a single headlight illuminated the area, and the white van drove up quickly and stopped. A woman got out, yelled something back at someone else inside, slammed the door, and rushed up to the man with the rifle kneeling by the three figures on the ground. One of the three then rose, and staggered off somewhere in front of the truck, where he lost sight of them in the darkness.

Molallo, from his hiding place in the shadows, realized that the two vehicles must have been traveling together, and Ramon was dead only because they chose the wrong set of headlights. He was filled with rage at the thought of both Ramon and Sandy, the only two people in the world who had meant anything to him, now lying dead on a desert road. He moved out quietly from behind the shrub, felt his way back to the edge of the hillside, and looked over the group gathered in the beam of the single light not fifteen feet away. No way he was going to let them live, he thought, and now was his chance. He quietly removed the ammunition clip from the auto pistol and fitted a full magazine back into its place.

Molallo jumped up, pulled the slide on the side of the barrel to chamber the first round, and yelled, "God damn you all!" He leveled the gun at the group, enjoying the look of terror on some of their faces. But before his finger found the trigger, his head snapped violently over onto his shoulder and he toppled over and half-cartwheeled down the slope until he pitched into the fender of the truck with a thud and lay silent.

***

"TOM!" screamed Laurel.

She had been driving along uneventfully, passing the occasional car going the opposite direction, but almost lulled into complacency by the surprising lack of traffic and the relative monotony of driving through the darkness. Tom had fallen asleep in the seat opposite, and the three young kids were sprawled in the back. She had known from the moment she looked at Tom while she was loading the box of family photo albums that it was unlikely that they would be returning to their home in the near future. His silent nod had confirmed for her the seriousness of the circumstances. There would have been many more things she would have packed and included had she had more time, but nothing she couldn't do without, she had told herself honestly. She had the six things she valued most in her life, in the van and the truck.

Laurel had grown up in the boisterous McCall family, and had never considered that her own family someday would be anything else as well. She had liked Tom the first time Eagle had brought him home to dinner from college. She earned her own Bachelor's degree in Recreation, but marriage and a family followed so soon after graduation that she had never actually used her credentials. Three daughters in a row might have caused some couples to question their family planning efforts, but when Tommy came along they were ecstatic. Emily was a bit of a surprise and almost did them in; her petulant nature was a challenge to both parents.

As she drove along, Laurel thought about their early struggles making ends meet. She was smiling to herself as she cruised around yet another bend in the road. The headlights swept across the landscape as the van rounded the curve and then suddenly right in front of her were two armed men swinging their guns up to point at her.

"TOM!" She had no sooner yelled her husband's name than she saw the flash of gunfire from the left figure. One headlight went dark and something hit the windshield, but then the gunmen had leapt out of the way and the van sped by them. Tom, startled by Laurel's shout and the sudden movement of the vehicle, had instantly come awake in time to see the figure on the road in front of him jump sideways out of the way.

"WHAT WAS THAT?" cried Tom

"I don't know! They were just there all of a sudden and then they fired at us."

"THE GIRLS!" Tom shouted again, abruptly remembering their daughters and Angel in the truck behind them. "QUICK! PULL OVER!" He reached behind the driver's seat, and grabbed the AR-15, chambered the first round and jumped out of the van just as Laurel brought it to halt around the corner from the near ambush.

Tom ran back and saw the truck smashed into the small slope by the road, and then he saw the two dark forms walking carefully up behind it, barely illuminated by the truck lights reflecting off the embankment. He crouched down instantly and rested his left elbow on his raised knee. He brought the rifle sights into alignment on the man in front and pulled the trigger twice, quickly. The man fell backwards onto the road, but the other figure disappeared into the desert.

Tom ran up to the still form, and knelt down beside it, holding his rifle in readiness. He prodded the body and felt the wetness on the shirt. Then he rose, looked into the black desert, and rushed back to the truck. Just as he arrived the driver's door opened and Ellie stumbled out, crying and holding her arms around herself, and immediately lying down on the ground. Right behind her Angel emerged, holding his left shoulder awkwardly, and sat down beside her. Kate crawled out, apparently unhurt, but holding the .45 in one hand, as if having sensed if not fully comprehended the sudden danger that had been sprung on them. When she saw her father standing there with the rifle, she started sobbing, and stepped quickly to him hugging him hard, before dropping down beside her sister. Tom turned as he heard a vehicle approaching fast, and then the van came into view, lighting up the scene with a single bright headlight.

Laurel opened the door and paused briefly, leaning back into the interior. "Stay quiet, and keep flat on the floor! Don't move until I come back and get you!" Then she slammed the door and ran up to Tom and the others.

"Ellie, are you hurt?" she asked, kneeling beside her eldest daughter.

"It hurts a lot when I take a deep breath."

"The seatbelt probably bruised your ribs or made you pull some cartilage. Just stay down for a minute. Angel, are you OK?"

"My…my shoulder…hurts real bad," moaned Angel. "I had my belt on, but tried to brace myself on the dash."

"Can you move your fingers or bend your elbow."

"I don't know." Angel was on his knees. There was no problem moving his fingers, but he seemed unable to move the arm at the shoulder in any normal way. He was attempting to find some position that would lessen the intense pain, when suddenly he felt a tremendous *pop* as the ball of the humerus bone slid back into the socket.

"Unhhh," he grunted forcefully. There was an immediate huge reduction in the pain sensation, and arm movement was largely restored. "God, it just popped back into place. It must have been totally dislocated. Man, that felt *sick*. But at least it moves again."

"This is too much," cried Kate, and she got up and stumbled off into the darkness.

"Kate! Get back here!" said Tom in an exaggerated stage whisper. But she didn't hear him and disappeared out of sight.

"CRAP!" muttered Tom. "There's still another guy out there. I gotta get her back here quick. Laurel, stay down 'til I get back."

Before he could take a step, they heard a metallic clunk, and a voice cried out of the darkness, "*God damn you all!*"

They looked up quickly and saw a man with a bandage wrapped around his head and wearing a bloody tee-shirt standing, holding a machine pistol in his hands, up on the embankment on the other side of the truck. He raised the gun, pointing it at them as they stood frozen by the unexpected, frightening appearance of this horrible apparition.

Suddenly, there was a bright flash and a loud report from the desert darkness, and the man's head seemed to jerk abruptly to the side and he fell over, tumbling down the slope with the gun still in his hands, until he rolled into the side of the truck.

Laurel and Ellie both screamed in fright. They looked in the direction of the flash and just on the edge of the light was Kate, the Colt handgun still pointed in a classic two-handed Weaver grip, wisps of smoke coming from the barrel. Tom ran over to the body, took one look at the bloodied mass that used to be the side of the man's head, and knew there was nothing more to fear from him.

Kate tottered over to them, her arms now hanging limply at her sides. Then her knees buckled and she dropped to the ground, and vomited. Laurel and Tom both rushed over to her, Laurel putting her arms around her daughter's shoulders and Tom carefully taking the pistol from her hand.

"I'm sorry, Dad," Kate sobbed. "I don't really know what happened. I was in the shadow over there when I heard this guy scream at you. I didn't know where he came from or who he was. And then I saw him cock his gun. I almost panicked. And…and…and then I shot him." She broke down and the tears flowed as she trembled

"Don't worry, Kate," said Tom quietly. "You had to do it. You saved our lives." Then he added, "He just made a bad decision."

Laurel went over to check on the injuries to Ellie and Angel. Ellie's side was very sore, but as long as she didn't inhale too deeply or move too quickly, she felt all right. Laurel decided there were no broken bones. She pulled a wide stretch Ace bandage out of the first aid kit and gave it to her daughter. "If it gets to hurting too much, wrap it snuggly but not too tight. It will give you extra support, especially against sudden movements while we're driving."

Angel was on his feet, and had gone over to be with Kate.

Laurel said, "Angel, what about your shoulder?"

"It's okay, Mrs. Warner. I can move it some, just not too high. Short of tying it to my side, there's not much you can do for a dislocated shoulder once it's back where it belongs. It aches a lot, but I can live with it. Don't worry about me."

Meanwhile, Tom was assessing the damage to the vehicles. The right front fender and bumper of the pickup was crumpled and pushing in on the tire. The truck couldn't be moved an inch until that was fixed. He walked over to the van. The right headlight was shattered and there were several cracks on the windshield, but it seemed intact. He opened the driver's door, reached in, grabbed a flashlight, and pulled the hood release. Walking back around in front of the grille, he lifted the stubby hood and shone the light around underneath. He could see no signs of radiator or other leaks, so he closed the hood again.

"Laurel, get in the van, back it up and angle in with the headlight pointing at the front of the truck." Then he walked over to Angel, held out the .45 and said, "Can you still handle this?" Angel nodded. "Okay, go over across the road where it's dark and just keep an eye out. I only saw two, but I have absolutely no idea if there are any more."

"Gotcha," answered Angel. Then he trotted away.

Laurel moved the van, then got out and went to look after Ellie and Kate. Tom got a tire iron out of the back of the van and went over to the truck. He shoved the bar between the tire and the fender, prying up as hard as he could. The end of the bar slipped off the tire and he fell back hard on his butt. *"CRAP!"*

He positioned the bar again, made sure the angles were correct, and pulled more carefully. This time the leverage worked, and the fender bent back part way from the tire. He repeated the procedure until there was sufficient clearance to turn the wheel freely without hitting anything. Then he got in the truck and backed it out onto the road. Slipping it into first, he rolled forward slowly, then shifted into second and drove a hundred yards down the road. Feeling and hearing nothing out of the ordinary, he turned around and drove back to the van.

"Okay," he said, getting out. "I think it's drivable. Angel and Kate, get in the truck. Laurel, help me get Ellie in the van."

When everyone was loaded in, he said to Laurel, "Follow me. I'm going to find some place to turn off and stay for a while, at least until it gets light. I think we've had enough fun for one night. I wanted to drive straight through, but we've all gotta calm down some. We'll just have to take our chances tomorrow."

He got in the truck, and led the way, slowly gaining speed. He kept it at about thirty miles an hour, peering beyond the reach of the headlights, until he finally spotted a dirt road leading west toward the mountains. Signaling with his turn indicator, he slowed down and turned off the highway, the Toyota right behind.

The dirt road was bumpy but serviceable, and they drove about a mile and a half before they entered a forested area. He slowed to a crawl, and pulled off the dirt road when he saw a small clearing. The van drove up alongside the truck, headlights were switched off, and engines cut. Tom got out alone, closed the door to avoid the cab light, and looked around, listening as he turned. Then he went over to Laurel in the van. She rolled down the window.

"This looks like as good a spot as any. I don't see any other lights around. We'll stay here until dawn and get some rest. In the morning, we'll have something to eat and go. Just being able to see more than a couple of hundred feet in front of us should make things seem a little more normal."

"What do you want to do about where to sleep?"

"I don't want to pitch the tent. We might have to leave in a hurry. Clear off the seats and put Ellie on one, Maggie on the other, and Tommy and Emily on the floor. You and Kate will have to tilt the front seats back and sleep there. Angel and I will take turns keeping watch. Put this on the console." He handed her the .45.

When everyone was settled, he and Angel took the AR-15 and the shotgun and found a place where they could see reasonably in most directions without too much moving around. Angel quietly said, "Let me stand guard first. My shoulder hurts too much to sleep right now anyway."

"OK. I'm sorry we never put anything stronger than ibuprofen in the first aid kit. Wake me in about two hours. Say about five." He paused. "I hate to say it, but I think tomorrow could be even worse."

"God, I hope not. This has been hairy enough. If Kate hadn't—"

"I know. I hope she doesn't have nightmares. Hell, I hope *I* don't. Anyway, keep your eyes peeled." He curled up on the ground on top of a sleeping bag and, after tossing and turning for a few minutes reliving the evening's events, sleep finally overcame him.

Angel spent the next two hours in the darkness almost ceaselessly peering in all directions, trying to detect a movement or light that might signal an unfriendly presence. Every fifteen minutes or so he quietly moved to a different position around the vehicles so as to better see different areas. His shoulder throbbed, but was tolerable. The time passed slowly in his controlled anxiety, and he was glad when he checked his watch and it finally read five A.M. He began to walk over to wake Tom, whose senses detected the sound and startled him awake before Angel got to him.

"It's okay, Mr. Warner," whispered Angel. "Everything's cool."

Tom glanced at his watch in the emerging pre-dawn light. "Thanks, Angel. Good job. Try and catch a little shut eye, but we're gonna get going soon, I think."

Angel lay down on the bag, still warm from Tom's previous occupancy, and was soon sound asleep. Tom stretched and tried to shake off the stiffness and a headache from his interrupted nap on the hard ground. He thought back over the last twelve hours, and shook his head. He didn't know if they had been foolhardy to leave their home, but he did know that at least to this point they had been remarkably lucky just to be sleeping here peacefully. Two people were dead by their hands, and he supposed that he should report it to the police. But the circumstances seemed to excuse the burden of normal procedure. He decided they would report it after the family was safely settled at Eagle's.

That mental hurdle having been dealt with, he felt more relaxed. He wanted to get the map, but it was in the van and opening the door would turn on the dome light and he didn't want to disturb the others. He was pretty sure they were only an hour or so from Reno, but it did no good to over-analyze the unknown. He glanced at his watch again. He'd let them sleep until seven; then they'd get going again.

Chapter 20

> *"Of all the tyrannies, a tyranny sincerely exercised for the good of its victims may be the most oppressive. It may be better to live under robber barons than under omnipotent moral busybodies. The robber baron's cruelty may sometimes sleep, his cupidity may at some point be satiated; but those who torment us for our own good will torment us without end, for they do so with the approval of their own conscience."*
> —C. S. Lewis (1898-1963)

The country hadn't waited for the President to speak. The surprising announcement out of Washington, D.C. about the government's financial status, usually somewhat erroneously interpreted to mean that certain entitlement payments to the poor and the elderly would probably be delayed, had the same effect as throwing a match onto a tinder-dry field. Congressional telephones, email addresses, and fax lines were flooded with messages of desperation—and of outrage. In many states, the emotions broke loose and violence erupted. In Alabama, Governor Scio immediately sent the already-alerted National Guard into the worst areas, but this merely served to fan the flames, creating pitched battles between citizens and Guard units. In Florida, AARP received almost as many complaints as did government agencies. In California, Governor Schwarzenegger pleaded for patience, and called a special session of the legislature. None of it helped.

Saturday – July 31

It was fully light when Tom began to roust everyone from their fitful slumbers. Laurel had a few moments of complete disorientation until her memory of the previous night sobered her thoughts. She got up and then awakened the others. She brought out the juice, milk, cereal and donuts, and everyone seemed hungry. That's a good sign, she thought. The kids were fairly quiet, but even that wasn't too unusual for an early morning.

Tom and Angel examined the vehicles before they loaded up, but beyond the obvious cosmetics of dents and dings from shotgun pellets and collisions with hillsides, they could perceive little else. Tom had Laurel drive the truck with Kate in the middle, and Angel. Ellie climbed into the front passenger seat of the van while Tom took the wheel, and they drove back down the gravel road toward the highway. Traffic was still surprisingly sparse as they turned onto the blacktop and headed north.

Tom turned the radio on and found a station. *"...just a little over an hour ago. Congressional reaction has been mixed, but generally favorable. Senator Halsey Brownsville, the Senate Majority Leader, seemed to admit in his initial interview that Congress was somewhat surprised by the announcement, but said he would give the President his full support. Senator Morton Packwood of Idaho blasted President Dillard, stating that the Administration, quote, 'has thrown out over two hundred years of constitutional rule and come down as heavily-handed on the American people as any tin-pot dictator in Podunkia,' unquote. Sources at the White House stated that the Pentagon is on notice that the military may be needed, even though they are seldom used for domestic operations.*

"To repeat the top story: At nine o'clock Eastern time this morning, six A.M. local time, President Dillard made the following announcement:

'Effective immediately, I am declaring that a state of emergency exists in these United States. The governors of all fifty states are hereby directed to activate any and all state National Guard units under their command to enforce any and all measures necessary to restore lawful order.

'This extreme measure is being forced upon us by the treasonous actions of significant factions in the country who have illegally and intentionally attempted to bring this great nation to financial ruin through their selfish greed, and who have consequently threatened the well-being of millions of honest, hard-working Americans, senior citizens and the poor.

'Under the authority granted by Executive Order 14896, the "Assignment of Emergency Preparedness Responsibilities," the following provisions are hereby placed into effect:

    1. All persons must remain within the city limits of their residence, unless verifiably traveling to or from their place of employment, for medical treatment, or on official government business.

2. *Any person suspected of any illegal activity may be detained as necessary.*

3. *All firearms must be surrendered to the local police, who are hereby authorized to obtain lists of registered firearm owners from all retail and other sources.*

4. *Assemblies of more than 10 non-related persons must first obtain permission from the local or regional FEMA director.*

5. *The hoarding of food is prohibited.*

6. *All electrical power and transportation fuels will be distributed only under the direction of the Secretary of Energy.*

7. *Persons violating the provisions of this Executive Order may be arrested and held as necessary.*

'These provisions will remain in effect until further notice. Additions, suspensions, and modifications to the provisions of this measure will be made as necessary and as possible. All Americans can join me in abhorring the attitudes of those irresponsible and unpatriotic radicals who have made these actions the only alternative. With your patience and perseverance, we shall deal with these domestic fiscal terrorists and restore our peace, our principles, and our prosperity.'"

The radio announcer then continued, *"Although the President requested the state governors to call upon their National Guards as necessary, the Executive Order stops short of declaring martial law, or ordering US military forces to keep the peace. In the meantime..."*

"What does that mean, Dad?" said Ellie, looking at her father.

"It means that the Constitution and Bill of Rights just got chucked in the dumpster, because the stupid President and the stupid Congress don't want to admit they finally ran out of money. And now everybody's mad at everybody else, and they're all fighting about it—"

"Tom!" Laurel's voice sounded tinny over the walkie-talkie.

Tom grabbed his unit from the dashboard tray. "Right here," he replied, looking into his outside rearview mirror. The truck had not kept pace and, while he had been pre-occupied with the radio announcement, had fallen far behind. "What's the matter?"

"The truck's got a pretty bad shimmy when we go more than about forty."

"The alignment must have been knocked off kilter last night. I guess I'm not surprised."

"What do you want to do?" asked his wife.

"I don't know. Go slower, I guess. I don't want to abandon it if we don't absolutely have to. It's like a pack mule. What's the best you can do?"

"Forty's about it. Any more than that really gets it going."

"All right. Let's just keep it there. Maybe someone in Reno can look at it."

"Okay." A brief click ended the mild static as Tom put down the walkie-talkie. He looked in the mirror at the back seat. "Tommy?"

"Yeah, Dad?" The boy seemed to have lost his anxiety of the previous night.

"You are absolutely the *best* for bringing these walkie-talkies. They have been our best friends ever since we left yesterday."

Tommy smiled, and looked triumphantly at Maggie and Emily. Not even a national calamity could diminish the value of scoring points in front of your sisters.

Tom shook his head. *What else is going to go wrong?* he thought. His original plan to dash from LA to Washington in less than twenty-four hours was a pipe dream. It would take forever at forty. *What next?* he mused. *I'm not sure I want to know.*

It was just after eight-thirty when they hit the outskirts of Reno, the self-proclaimed *"Biggest Little City in the West."* The highway turned into a regular six-lane freeway, so they kept to the slow lane as other vehicles went careening by. They had just passed a big Barnes and Noble distribution center when a sign on another big building suddenly came into view: *WinCo Foods. Open 24 Hours.* He grabbed the walkie-talkie, keyed the mike button and quickly said, "Follow me!" before peeling off the freeway at the next exit. Both vehicles slowed as they came down the off-ramp, then turned left through the underpass and looped back down South Virginia Street to the huge supermarket. The parking lot was lightly occupied. They parked in a vacant area away from the main entrance, and got out.

"I don't know if you guys were listening to the radio—"

"We caught it, Mr. Warner," said Angel. "Are we going to be able to keep going?"

"We're certainly going to try," said Tom firmly. "But, since it may not be *business as usual* anymore, I think we should try to stock up on food and other supplies. This place looks to be open, and who knows what else will be later on? Angel, you and Ellie stay here and guard the cars. The rest of you can come in with Mom and me." He held up his walkie-talkie and said, "Ellie, get yours out of the truck and hold on to it. Holler if anybody even looks at you."

An efficient thirty minutes later they emerged with two full carts of food, other essentials, another large cooler, and a variety of auto supplies. They had bought much more than ought to have been necessary for the remaining trip, but they were learning fast to take no chances. After packing it mostly into boxes and coolers under the truck canopy, they loaded the bodies and rolled out of the parking lot. Just as they crossed back under the freeway and were about to head up the northbound on-ramp, Tom spied a gas station another block up, and headed up to it. As they turned between the islands, they saw a man fiddling with one of the pumps. They stopped, and Tom got out and saw that the fellow was putting a padlock on the old style pump.

"Are you open for business? Tom asked.

"Well, as a matter of fact, I just got a call from my boss that we had to shut down, 'cause the frickin' President said we couldn't sell our own gas." The pony-tailed attendant, about thirty, with a black Misfits tee shirt, jeans, and well-worn cowboy boots, did not appear to hold his nation's leader in very high esteem.

"I don't suppose you'd care to make us your last customer?" Tom said hopefully.

The man looked in the van at all the kids, then noticed the broken headlight and shot-scarred windshield. "You guys having a bad day, or are you just bad drivers?"

"You have no idea," said Tom grimly. He took a chance, and briefly related their adventures of the previous day and night.

The man thought for a moment, then said, "I reckon it's pretty lucky you all showed up here just before I got that call. Otherwise, you'd be plain outta luck. Regular unleaded?" And he turned to unlock the pump.

Tom exclaimed, "You're a prince! I don't suppose you know where I could get a quick alignment on the truck, do you?"

"You might try Les Schwab. Go back under the freeway and turn right on South Virginia. It's about a quarter mile on the left."

"Thanks."

When they had made sure that both the van, truck, and spare cans were completely topped off, they paid for the gas, and Tom pulled out an extra fifty to give the man.

"Nah," the attendant said. "It's cool. Besides, I think you guys are going to need it more than me."

Tom stuck out his hand and shook the other man's with heartfelt gratitude. "Thanks," he said with feeling. "I really mean it." Laurel and Ellie each gave the man hugs, and he blushed under his deep tan.

"Later, dudes."

They got into their vehicles and everybody waved liked old friends. *"Screw the feds!"* was the last thing they heard as they pulled out of the station.

They found the Les Schwab Tire dealership with no problem. Before they had even turned off their engines, a white-shirted young mechanic with a buzz-cut trotted up to their car. Tom explained the problem, and was surprised when they were able to pull the truck right into the alignment bay. A few minutes later, another mechanic, whose shirt proclaimed his name to be "Tyson" informed Tom that a key linkage rod was bent, and they would need to order a part in order to fix it. Tom explained that they were traveling and couldn't wait.

"Hmmm. Okay, sit tight for a sec." And Tyson disappeared back into the shop. About twenty minutes later, he returned, and said, smiling, "I couldn't fix it right, but it I persuaded it to be better. A little creative elbow grease. It's the best I can do."

Tom thanked him, paid the bill in the office, and once more they were under way. They retraced their route back to the freeway, and drove up the on-ramp back onto US 395. As the speedometer hit 60, Tom grabbed the walkie-talkie. "How's it feel?"

"It's shaking pretty good again," said Laurel.

"All right, can you handle fifty-five?" He began slowing.

A minute later, the call came back. "Tom?"

"Yeah, babe."

"It seems fine up to about fifty-seven or -eight."

"Okay, that's still better than it was. I'll try to keep it at about 55, and we'll see if it holds."

They headed up the freeway, feeling pretty good again. The Atlantis Hotel/Casino loomed up off to the left and they passed the Reno International Airport on the right. At the Hilton, next to the freeway, the parking lot was fairly full.

"Nothing slows the gamblers down," Tom remarked to Ellie. "Bad weather, bad luck, or even bad politics—they just keep right on going, hoping to hit a lucky streak."

"Maybe we're on one now," said Ellie.

"I hope so, El."

The Warners cruised up the road, thankful that it bypassed the congested downtown area and comfortably making fifty-five miles an hour without the truck protesting. Highway 395 headed north out of Reno, then curved west back toward California. After studying the map while they had waited at Les Schwab, he had explained his plan to the others. "We'll stay on 395 up to Alturas, then head over to Klamath Falls in Oregon. We could stay on 395 up through the east side of Oregon, but I think that might be *too* isolated, especially if we have any more vehicle trouble. Besides, it would be a lot longer. If we take 97 up the middle, we still avoid the big cities; it's mostly farm areas, and they aren't likely to be in too much of a tizzy just yet." No one else had had any better ideas.

They welcomed the relatively empty roads, and hoped the next 800 miles were easier than the first 500. They crossed back into California at a tourist trap called Bordertown, and a few minutes later were surprised, around a curve, by the sudden appearance of a highway inspection station. Tom had never much minded these stops travelers made for agricultural inspections when entering California from another state, but a moment of panic swept over him as he realized they had no excuse to offer for violating an Executive Order of the President of the United States during a national crisis, not to mention the arsenal of firearms they were carrying. As close as they were to the station, they had no choice but to continue up to the entrance. "Quick, Tommy, shove those ammo cans under the seat, and pile some stuff on the gun sleeves." He grabbed the walkie-talkie, and told Angel to do the same in the truck. Tommy busied himself for a few moments in the back of the van, and had just refastened his seatbelt when they pulled under the roofed area. "Emily, start arguing about something with Tommy!" His tone did not allow for questions.

Tom rolled down his window, and managed a smile. "Hi."

"Howdy," said the middle aged, uniformed man. "Where you folks comin' from?"

"We're from LA, and are headed to my wife's brother's for a little vacation. That's my wife in the Toyota behind us."

The inspector glanced into the van's interior and saw the two young children gesturing and talking loudly. "Looks like a long trip," he said with sympathy.

"You have *no* idea," Tom said for the second time that morning.

"Well, I hate to say this, but you picked the wrong time for a vacation."

"What do you mean?"

"You have to turn around and go home, wherever that is, and probably hope you don't get caught."

"What are you talking about?" exclaimed Tom, feigning surprise.

"Haven't you heard?" The man was almost incredulous. "No travel is allowed."

"NO TRAVEL? WHO SAYS?" said Tom, in desperation.

"The President hisself."

"But that can't be! He can't do that!"

"Well, it seems that presidents can do just about anything they want these days. At any rate, that's what he did. A national emergency, he calls it."

"But people are expecting us," Tom protested, as an unwanted, but unavoidable solution became clear. "Everything was fine when we left yesterday." *At least in the morning,* he thought to himself. "They'll be worried. I could probably call them and let them know what's happening, but my cell phone isn't charged. Do you have a phone?"

The man considered the request. It was against normal procedures to allow anyone into the guard's small office but, on the other hand, this was hardly a normal time. "Well, I guess. Sure. Come on over to the hut."

As Tom started to get out of the van, Ellie whispered anxiously, "What are we going to do, Dad?"

"Punt," he said quietly. He paused, and then made his decision. He stuck his head and shoulders back into the van and told her, "Tell Angel to grab the duct tape and join me. Pronto!"

"But, what—"

"Call Angel!" He picked up the 9mm Sig and slid it carefully into his back pocket. When he glanced at his daughter, she was wide-eyed. "Do it! NOW!" Startled, she reached for the walkie-talkie. Tom turned and left, walking as slowly as he could across the two empty lanes over to the guard hut.

Ellie must have overcome her fear, for Tom had just entered the hut when Angel materialized behind him. When the guard got to the counter, he picked up the phone handset and turned to hand it to Tom. Tom, however, was pointing a very menacing Sig Sauer at the man.

"I'm sorry, but we're not turning back." Tom's voice was strong, but grim. "Things are very bad where we came from and I'm going to save my family. We won't hurt you, but I can't let you make things worse for us." He looked around the small hut, then at Angel. "Bring the chair over here near the wall."

Angel complied as the man looked on apprehensively, fearing his fate. "Sit down on it," commanded Tom. The man hesitated, then walked the few steps over and sat looking back and forth from Tom to Angel.

"Make him secure," Tom told Angel simply.

Angel looked at Tom, then at the roll of duct tape in his hand, nodded, and started pulling the end of the tape free. Using multiple wraps, he taped the man's forearms and wrists to the arms of the chair, his legs and calves similarly to the legs of the chair, and then several wraps around his upper body and the back of the chair. Tom lowered, then pocketed the handgun. When Angel looked like he had designs on gagging the man, Tom stopped him. "No," was all he said. "Go get about eight or ten feet of rope."

As Angel left, Tom spoke to the hapless inspector. "I'm sorry. We don't want anything but to get to our family in Missoula. I know you're just doing your job. But I'm just doing mine. And, frankly, I've had a lousy day."

Angel returned with some quarter-inch nylon line. Tom took it, and then, holding the line in his teeth, wrestled the chair up against the wall near an exposed vertical pipe. He lashed the chair to the pipe, out of direct sight through the outside door, and away from the counter and the phone.

"I'm sorry," Tom said for the third time. "I'm sure someone will come along soon. I can't make you not tell anyone about us, but if you have any kids yourself, I'll bet you'll understand."

"Thanks for not gagging me," was all the man said.

Tom didn't reply. He just nodded at Angel and walked out. As they headed for their respective vehicles, Angel looked at Tom and said, "Missoula?"

"Just in case they want to look for us, I guess." He shrugged. "It's not as though I've done this sort of thing before." Further discussion seemed pointless. Tom climbed into the van, turned the key in the ignition, put it in gear, and slowly accelerated.

The walkie-talkie crackled, and Laurel's voice asked uneasily, "Tom, wha… what did you do?"

"We just strapped him to a chair," Tom said into his handset, staring ahead. "He's okay. It's air conditioned in there. He'll be fine." His tone did not invite further inquiry.

"Is there going to be trouble over this?" said Laurel.

Crap! I don't know, he thought. "Maybe. I dunno," he admitted.

"Couldn't you just have shown him the letter from Senator Hornbrook?"

Tom closed both his eyes as his entire face grimaced. "Oh, for God's sake! I didn't even think of that. That might have saved the whole Rambo act. God, I'm stupid, sometimes! That's exactly why Eagle got it for me." He shook his head. "What an idiot! Well, too late now."

"So now what?"

"We just keep driving. Keep your eyes open. And let me know if there's any problem with the truck. Keep an eye on the gauges, too. Talk to you in a bit."

Tom looked at his watch. It was a little after eleven. He reached over and grabbed the map. Glancing back and forth between the map and the road, he saw that Susanville was the next city of any size, maybe an hour. Since they didn't really need to stop there and he wanted to put as many miles as possible between them and the inspection station, they would continue straight on another ninety-some miles to Alturas, in the very northeast corner of California. If they could get there, they'd leave 395 and cut across to Klamath Falls in southern Oregon. They'd be harder to find, just in case anyone was looking; at least it wasn't the way to *Missoula*. And if they picked up any gas at all up there, they'd be home free.

He put the map down, and settled in his seat, scanning the road ahead, then the scenery to each side of the road. He saw no dangers, just a dry, sage-filled valley, with isolated homesteads farming dirt, and skinny horses grazing on dry weeds. Although it didn't look very inviting, he had to admit that compared to living in the metropolitan mayhem of LA, maybe these people were smarter than he was.

They kept up a steady pace, even as they rolled passed "Roque's Burger Barn" over the combined protestations of Tommy, Emily, Maggie, and Ellie. The surrounding terrain turned progressively rockier. A sign by the road indicated that the hills to the east were called the Skedaddle Mountains. *We're trying to,* thought Tom, *we're trying to!*

About an hour later, they came to Likely, another small farming town. "Hey Dad!" cried Ellie. "Look at the sign!"

Tom saw the community billboard, which proclaimed, *Welcome to Likely, Gateway to the Warner Mountains.* "Hey, whadaya know?" he said. "Our very own mountains."

"Pretty neat," said Emily.

As they drove into Alturas about twenty minutes later, Tom began looking for gas stations. He still had well over half a tank, but if they could top off here, they'd have enough, with the gas cans, to get all the way to Eagle's. But two of the stations were closed completely, and at the last one they were told that they could only sell to locals because of the President's announcements. Tom didn't press. The man let them use the rest rooms, then gave them directions to a small park in the center of town, where they all got out to stretch their legs, and have lunch.

Tom had not really wanted to stop, but felt they had to unwind a bit. He hoped the law enforcement types were busy enough not to get too excited about a bound up, but unhurt, agriculture inspector. He shook his head again, thinking of his oversight, then forgot it. He'd keep the Senator's letter handy from now on, however, in case anyone bothered them again about traveling. Everyone was in good spirits, in spite of the morning's excitement. Ellie and Kate, contrary to their usual exclusionary practice, ate with their three younger siblings, as Angel spun the tale of the hut, making it sound more like a movie than a potentially disastrous run-in with the law.

Tom and Laurel ate at another table. It was hard to believe that it was only yesterday evening that this whole adventure had begun; it seemed like a week at least. Once again, Tom laid out the map—actually, two maps this time, adding one for Oregon. "Okay, we're here," he said to Laurel, pointing to Alturas. "Klamath Falls is here. I still think that going that way makes the most sense, and I don't have anything else to go on, so we're just going to do it. Say goodbye to 395."

"I'm not so sure I'll miss it anyway," said Laurel. "I don't feel like we *drove* it; I feel like we *survived* it."

"I know what you mean," nodded Tom. "Anyway, from here we just follow this little bitty red line to here," he said, pointing again, "and then up this way on 139 into Oregon. It looks reasonably straight, so it should be easy enough. Knock on wood. We're just about halfway right now. If we can drive straight through and have no problems, ha ha, it'll take probably eleven or twelve hours. Let's see," he said, looking at his watch. "That would put us there well after midnight. We could do it, but I just don't know what we're going to find. We can try calling Eagle later. Maybe he'll know more."

"Do we have enough gas?"

"No, not quite. But we don't need much more," he said, sounding more confident that he really was. He looked around the small town park, complete with playground swings and merry-go-round. The sun was hot, but under the shade of the trees, it was almost overwhelmingly relaxing. "Well, it's awfully tempting to stay right here, but we better get going." He stood up and stretched. He walked over toward the other table. "Okay, gang, pack it up. We're outta here."

"But Daddy, I want to go play on the swings," protested Emily.

"I know, honey, but we have long way to go still. Tomorrow, we'll be at Uncle Eagle's, and there'll be lots of time to play."

"Will, I be able to ride one of his horses again?" she asked hopefully.

"I'm sure he'll find one for you. Let's go."

They packed up the lunch stuff, put it in the truck, and climbed into the cars. "Can I ride in the truck for a while?" asked Tommy.

"No, just—" Tom paused. "Okay, sure. Kate, you can ride with us."

"Daaad!" she whined.

"Can it, Annie Oakley. I need you 'riding shotgun' with me."

"Oh, *fine*!"

***

The journey from Alturas began as easy as hoped. They proceeded west along Highway 299 for fifteen or twenty minutes, then turned right and headed north again on 139. The road was smooth, their vehicles well-behaved, and there were no incidents. They made good time and by 3:30 in the afternoon had crossed the border into Oregon. Leaving California felt like they'd climbed Everest.

Not long after they entered the fertile agricultural Klamath River basin, they came over a rise and suddenly found a roadblock barring their passage. "Uh-oh," Tom said. "It *was* too good to be true. Kate, Ellie, pay attention." He grabbed the walkie-talkie, and keyed the mike. "Trouble, Laurel! Stay back a ways, and be prepared to back up in a hurry. Tell Angel to keep a pistol handy." There were no turnouts, and the road wasn't wide enough to consider a quick U-turn. Again he had no choice but to bring the vehicle to a stop, and hope for the best.

The vehicles involved in the barricade were not law enforcement cars, but merely a collection of pickup trucks. There were three men visible in front of the trucks, two on the left side of the road, and the other opposite. Two of the men were armed, each with a rifle or shotgun tucked under one arm, but lazily pointed at the ground.

All three men watched the approach of the white van carefully. When it stopped, one of the two on the left detached himself from his conversation and walked in an unhurried manner toward Tom's side of the van. He was a clean-shaven man in denim overalls, a plain red tee shirt, and green John Deere baseball cap, and did not carry a visible firearm. Tom rolled down his window with his left hand, and felt for his Sig-Sauer with his right.

"Howdy," began the man, who appeared to be in his mid-sixties. He was a big man—not fat, but barrel-chested—with arms and hands that looked like they had seen a lot of work. His face was deeply tanned and lined, and although he was smiling, his manner and movement gave the distinct impression that he was not to be thought of lightly. "I'm sorry folks, but the highway is closed just ahead a bit, and I'm afraid I'm going to have to ask you to turn around and find another route to your destination."

"What seems to be the trouble?" ventured Tom, warily.

"No trouble, really, but as I hope you know the President has declared a state of emergency and has placed a lot of restrictions on the utilization and distribution of a lot of resources, including, possibly, food stuffs. As a matter of fact, I hate to mention it, but you folks are in serious violation of his first order, which was to ban all but official emergency travel and, by crossing the state line, you're damn near felons!"

"Well, just put it on the list for us. God, after the last twenty-four hours, pissing off the President is just about the least problem we've had," Tom said fervently.

"I'm truly sorry about that, but we've all got problems. And, unfortunately, you being here is adding to ours."

"Look, we don't want anything, but just to get through Oregon. We don't even need to stop. We're just trying to get up to Washington where we can ride out this thing for a while. And if we have to backtrack, then gasoline is going to be a major problem for us."

"Sorry, can't help you. Transportation fuels are restricted, too. Life's tough all over. First the feds took all our water, and now they want our pitiful harvests as well. And we have all decided to tell 'em to go to hell. So no one comes in, and no one just 'gets through.' You all are just gonna have to do a U-eee, and try something else." His features were hardening, and his posture more erect, as though to make himself even more imposing.

"Look," Tom repeated, "we don't—"

"What part of 'NO' did you fail to comprehend?" the man said more loudly. His companions were now also standing with both hands holding their weapons diagonally across their chests.

This time, Tom remembered the letter Eagle had given him. Originally, he hadn't known quite what to do with it. But after the incident at the agricultural inspection station, he had stuck it in the van's glove box where it would be most convenient. "Hey, you don't like the feds, right?" he asked, almost desperately.

"You got that right, pal."

"Well, look, you know who Washington's Senator Hornbrook is? I mean, no one's fought the President and his bunch more than he has. Right?"

"Yep, he's one of the good guys, at least in my book. I even know a guy who works for him."

"Me, too! My wife's brother works for him, and the Senator gave us this letter to try and make it easier for us to convince people like you that we should be left alone."

"Let me see that." He took the letter from Tom's extended hand and skimmed over it. "Hmmm. I don't know. Like I said, he *is* one of the only decent politicians I know of, but…"

Just then, Emily whined. "Daddy, can't we go? I want to get to Uncle Eagle's and get out of this car!"

"Just hold on for a sec," Tom said, impatiently.

The man looked up suddenly. "Did she say Uncle Eagle? That wouldn't be Eagle McCall by any chance, would it?"

Tom was startled, but immediately said, "It sure is, mister. He's my brother-in-law, and my old college roommate. He works for the Senator. We're headed to his place."

"Well, shit, why didn't you say so?" the man said, breaking into a huge grin. "I know Eagle. Hell, I've even been to his little spread. He calls it his *place* 'cause it's embarrassingly puny to be called a ranch. Anyway, a couple of his neighbors are my nephews, and I go visit them once or twice a year, since their mom passed on—she was my sister. And a few years ago Eagle came to Klamath Falls on behalf of the Senator to get our side of the water dispute."

An enormous wave of relief passed over Tom. He knew a dangerous moment had past. "Hey, let me introduce you to Eagle's sister," he said, opening the van's door and jumping out. "My name's Tom, Tom Warner." He stuck out his hand, which was enveloped by the larger man's beefy paw.

"Mine's Ankeny Hill. Don't ask. My friends call me Kenny." Tom waved excitedly back to the truck, which Laurel had stopped about fifty yards behind them. She put the Toyota in gear, and edged forward. Tom and the man approached, and she got out, having observed the sudden change in attitude with amazement.

"Laurel, this is Kenny Hill. His nephews live near Eagle. He knows him!"

"Pleased to meet you, ma'am. Your husband here was just about to get me mad, before he told me where you all were headed."

"He frequently has that effect on people," she said smiling. She also sensed they'd just had a major stroke of good fortune. "I suppose it's appropriate to say something like, 'Gee, small world.'"

Hill laughed. It was more like a sonic boom. "Well, little lady, you can tell your husband here that he's damn lucky he married you. Actually, if you don't mind my saying so," he said with a twinkle in his eye, "to these old eyes I'd say just about any man would be damn lucky to be married to you."

Laurel blushed, but did not have a chance to respond before the big man continued, this time without the humor in his voice. He looked at Tom. "But it's a different kind of luck you're having today, Mr. Warner. I was serious about the sad state of affairs around here. There *is* a lot of anger in this region, stemming from our long-running water rights battle with the government, and with this latest turn of events, we've simply had it."

"I can imagine," said Tom.

"We've sorta taken charge of affairs here, and we're telling the government and anybody else who butts in to just butt the hell out. So we ain't letting no one in, 'til we get things sorta sorted out. But I'm of a mind to make an exception for you folks, cause your wife's pretty, and 'cause I know Eagle well enough that if I don't be nice, he'll come down to beat my sorry ass." The sonic boom sounded again. "Course, he wouldn't be able to, but I'd truly hate to have to bust him up." Another boom erupted.

He continued, "Tell you what. It's nearly four, and getting perilously close to my supper time. You're better than five hundred miles from where you're headed, and unless you're a little nutso, I don't think you oughta try and push through all the way today—at least I hope you weren't thinking of it. 'Cause chances are you're gonna run into a few other areas like this that aren't taking too kindly to outsiders. And as California cityfolk, you all might just as well paint targets on the side of your rigs. So why don't you just come on with me for now, and I'll persuade the missus to throw an extra cow in the oven. The young 'uns can stretch their legs, and you can tell me all about what's going on in LA. I'll call Eagle and tell him we're holding you hostage, and in the morning, you can get on your way bright and early."

Tom was not believing their luck. "Mr. Hill, that's very generous. If you don't think—"

"Shit, boy, the missus would be mighty disappointed if'n I tell her I let you drive off with out stopping. She's mighty fond of McCall, too."

"Well, what can I say? Sure! We'd really appreciate your hospitality."

Mr. Hill turned and went to talk to the other two men for a few minutes, then he turned his head and shouted over his right shoulder. Two other figures materialized out from behind the bushes, jumped the roadside culvert, ambled up to the first trio, and joined the conversation. When Hill returned, he told Tom, "Everything's all set here. You can follow my rig on in. Let's go. I'm getting hungry."

Hill climbed into an old, battered, faded red Ford pickup which formed part of the front line of the barricade, and jockeyed back and forth a couple of times until he was aimed down the road. By the time he was ready, one of the other men had backed another truck off to the side of the road, out of the way so that Hill, and the Warners, could get by.

Hill led them down Highway 139. After about half a mile, they crossed some railroad tracks, then pulled off onto a dirt road, which they followed a few hundred yards before turning into a driveway of an impressive two-story home that looked only slightly out of place in front of a variety of large and small barns and sheds of various vintages. The drive curved around and they all came to a stop in front of a short set of steps leading up onto the front porch. The weary group got out, and Hill directed them toward the door.

"Don't you even think of coming in that way, you big oaf!" came a loud, female voice through the front screen door. Then the door opened, and out stepped a heavyset woman with frizzy white hair, wearing blue jeans and a large red blouse only slightly shorter than a muumuu. Her face was round and her eyes peered out mischievously over puffy pink cheeks. "These nice-looking people are welcome to come in, but you take your lard-ass around to the back door like I told you 'bout a million times." Her voice boomed nearly as much as her husband's. "I swear, that man's heart is as big as a barn, but sometimes he's just dumber than a post."

Tom and Laurel glanced at each other with smiles. It was incongruous to think of the man who had been so intimidating at the roadblock rendered as meek as a lamb by this farm wife. They both instantly liked her. Introductions were made all around, and they learned her name was Maxine. She said, "Actually, supper's about an hour yet, but I've got some lemonade if you feel a mite parched. There're some swings out back if your kids would like to go play a bit. Our grand kids haven't quite worn them out yet."

Emily, Tommy, and Maggie went out through the back door and disappeared, glad to have a chance to run around. After enjoying glasses of iced lemonade, Kate, Ellie, and Angel also walked out to look around. Kenny Hill came in—through the back door where he shed his boots—and lumbered up the stairs, while Tom and Laurel sank into comfortable, overstuffed arm chairs in the living room and allowed the tension to slowly seep out of them. They shared a feeling of disbelief that arose from the suddenness of the change in their circumstances. They savored it.

When Hill came back downstairs, he spied Tom sitting in the chair sipping a glass of lemonade. He yelled toward the kitchen, "Hell's fire, woman. From the looks of this man's beat up rigs, I 'spect he needs to pacify his psyche, not his sweet tooth. Bring him a beer, for chrissakes!" His sonic boom laughter launched again. "And since he like to beat me up for stopping him, I 'spect *I* need one, too!" He laughed again. Tom looked over at Laurel, who was obviously enjoying the show. Growing up in this household must have been an adventure.

After a while, Maxine called everyone to the table. They all gathered around a huge dining table and enjoyed a fine, friendly, relaxed meal. As he chowed down, Tom thought he couldn't have ordered a better meal, and said so. Hill said, "You got it, boy. Just look at me—forty-two years of these meals, and fit as a fiddle."

"A bass fiddle," said Maxine.

"Stifle yerself, Edith," said Hill. He gestured at Laurel, "You need to stick around here for a while and learn from the master," he said pointing at his wife. "Then you'll be able to fatten up this little feller you're married to."

"Oh, I like him pretty well just the way he is," Laurel replied.

"What's the matter with kids these days," he mocked. Then he turned serious. "Tom, why don't you give me an idea how your van and truck came to look like survivors from a demolition derby?"

Tom spent the next twenty minutes describing the roller coaster of events of the past twenty-four hours. He probably went into far more detail than was necessary, but much of the story-telling was simply to convince himself that it had all really happened. When he had finished by telling of his emotions when they had come upon the Klamath roadblock, Hill nodded, then excused himself and went out through the kitchen. They could hear him calling to someone out back, and after he came back inside a few minutes later, they heard him talking on the telephone. It was fifteen minutes before he resumed his place at the table.

"I took the liberty of sending one of my hands off in your little truck. I know someone who's a whiz bang mechanic and he's gonna fix your shimmy. If'n he don't got the parts, then a buddy of his got a wreckin' yard down the road a piece. They'll find something to patch you up. By morning you'll be ready for the Indy 500."

"Mr. Hill—," began Tom.

"Kenny."

"Sorry. Kenny, all this is *way* more than we have the right to ask of you. We're forever in your debt."

"Nonsense. This is how people used to treat each other. Even strangers, in better days. Before the government tried to be everybody's best friend. And half-killed us in the process."

"Just the same, I hope sometime we'll be able to repay you."

"You need to tell the Senator that there ain't nothing more basic than food, and if'n he's grown fond of it over the years, he might just want to get his cohorts there in Dee-Cee to think about laying off the Soviet heavy-handed stuff." And with that, he dismissed their indebtedness. "Now, what are your plans from here? I hate to say it, but I hear tell that Portland's kinda uneasy." And he briefly described some news reports he'd had of civil unrest in many urban areas around the country, a mere twenty-four hours since the precipitating events. "Portland and Seattle are just the same. And soon as they all discover that it ain't gonna get better in the city right away, then people'll start flooding into the countryside. That's another reason we've taken the steps we've taken here. I reckon none of this is too surprising to you, since you came up the back way from LA."

"You're right. We heard of a lot of problems in LA and the Central Valley. I figured we'd probably stay on 97 clear up into Washington before crossing the mountains to get out toward the peninsula."

"Yeah, you'll be wanting Highway 12 out of Yakima. That's probably your best route, all right," Hill agreed. "You're still going to have to cross I-5 at some point and, like I said before, the yahoos rattling around between Portland and Seattle could be a little nutso."

"Well, we're just going to have to face that when we get to it."

About an hour later, their Toyota truck reappeared. The man who brought it back parked it next to the van, got out with a bag, then busied himself in front of the van. After just a few minutes, the van's shattered headlight had been replaced. Then he walked up to the back door and knocked. When Kenny opened it, the man said, "Truck's fixed, Mr. Hill. Got the light, too. And full tanks and cans all 'round."

"Good job, George," said the big man.

George departed off to the barn, and Hill went back inside. "You're rigs are all fixed and fueled and ready to go, Tom. What say we give old Eagle a holler and let him know where you are, Laurel?"

"Thanks, Kenny. I don't even know if he's on this coast, but I sure hope so." He showed her the phone in the kitchen, and she called her brother. The phone must have rung six or eight times before it was answered. *"McCall,"* she heard.

"Eagle! Thank God. It's Laurel!"

"Hey, sis. What's new?" he answered, nonchalantly.

"Nothing besides getting shot at, run off the road, and attacked by a madman," she replied, equally easily.

"I assume you mean by someone other than Tom."

"Yes, you idiot." She gave him a brief summary, concluding with their surprising meeting of Ankeny Hill and his wife.

"Good grief. What are the odds?"

"God, Eagle, we were so lucky." He could hear her voice quiver.

"How are you *really* doing, Laurel?"

"I'm okay, now. Last night just seemed so unreal, and when I saw that roadblock this afternoon, I was close to panic. I thought we were done for. But I think we're going to be good now. Kenny got our truck and van fixed, and filled our tanks. He's like an angel from heaven."

"God's got some ugly angels," smirked McCall.

"Not to us, so you just shush."

"Is Tom there? I need to talk to him for a minute, to give him some directions."

"Okay, hold on. See you tomorrow, I hope."

"You bet. Now go get Tom."

She put down the phone, and went to find Tom. He was in the living room, talking with Hill. Everyone else had disappeared.

***

After Hill had left Laurel to call her brother, he had Maxine take everyone out to pick berries in the garden, then he sat down with Tom. "I called the sheriff a little while ago and spoke to him about the little problem you had last night. Dilbert's his name. Even wears glasses like the cartoon guy—don't look much like a sheriff. But he's a good guy. We play poker together sometimes, and he always beats me. I figger it's cheaper than having the law mad at you. Anyway, he's going to check into it and let me know what he finds out. When I explained where you were headed, and whose elbows you would be rubbin', and that you'd all be available to make a statement later if needed, he didn't have any problem in letting you continue on your way—off the record, of course, since officially travel ain't allowed. After you get settled in, have McCall put you in touch with the sheriff up there and have him call Sheriff Dilbert. He's going to do some checking with the Nevada police. He doesn't figure there'll be any trouble from it."

"Thank God," said Tom, with feeling. "Kenny, I can't thank you enough. It all happened so fast. There was no choice, but I've been pretty worried about it. It's not your average vacation experience. We were very lucky."

"It sounds like it was preparedness, not luck. Your daughter okay?"

"I think so. We spoke about it a little bit. If we get through tomorrow in good shape, I'll have a good long talk with her."

"Take her along to talk to the sheriff, too. It'll do her a world of good to hear herself exonerated by someone official."

"That's a good idea."

"Now, tomorrow," Hill said, moving on to a new topic, "you'll find our little Klamath cocoon extends up to about Beaver Marsh, then past that there shouldn't be any problem for a while. The dumb yuppies in Bend don't know shit about what's going on in the world. They'll behave until they run out of croissants. Past Madras, and probably all the way to the Columbia, I hear tell of some action like ours here. I don't know anything about what's going on in Washington. You could get roadblocked again, but I'll give you a note from our Klamath basin combine. There should be a little reciprocal sympathy in the rural areas. And along with the letter from your Senator Hornbrook—and a little luck—you'll be at Eagle's in no time."

Just then, Laurel walked in from the kitchen. "Tom, Eagle's on the phone. He wants to talk with you." Tom rose, stopped to silently shake Hill's hand, then left the room as his wife sat down in his chair.

When he picked up the phone, he said, "Hey, Beret."

"Tom, I'm glad everything's okay."

"Yeah, a little worse for wear, but our luck here has made up for it all."

"It's incredible," said Eagle. "Kenny's real people. Wait until you meet his nephews, Red and Boomer. They're classics. Oversized bookends, and not the sharpest knives in the drawer, but good to have on your side."

"If they're at all like their uncle, it'll be my pleasure."

"Okay, now look. Things are getting a little tense. I don't know what you've heard on the radio, but there's almost a war going on. Dillard and his ilk have successfully sold the idea over the years that every bad thing that happens in the country is the fault of the greedy rich, and that only government can fix things. So now that the government itself is a shambles, it's real class warfare, with the emphasis on *war*."

"Well, that's what you predicted. In spite of our adventures, I'm glad we didn't try to go up through central California."

The Hornbrook Prophecy

"Nope, you never would have made it. But you aren't in the clear yet. Laurel told me Kenny thinks you'll be fine, but you never know. Taking the route he mentioned is best, but you could still have some problems in Yakima—a lot of poverty there—and maybe even before then. Highway 97 goes right across the Yakima Indian Reservation. I don't know their mood right now. If you do get stopped around there, it probably won't help you to wave the Senator's letter in their faces. He's had me meet with a number of tribes a lot in the past, trying to seek ways for them to help themselves solve some of their own economic and social problems. Some of the tribes have not been too pleased. The best thing in your favor is that they may not have organized themselves very well about these latest developments just yet."

"God, I hope not. It's hard to circle the wagons with only two."

"Relax. Besides, Laurel's a Blackfoot—half, anyway. You can always convince them you're headed back to *her* reservation. Anyway, when you get to Yakima, call me again. That's about 180 miles from here, and I'll plan on greasing the wheels on this side of the mountains in time for your arrival." He did not share any details, and Tom knew better than to ask him what he meant.

"We'll be fine," said Tom, hoping he was right.

"You'd better be. I've got the shop all cleared away for ping pong, and I'd sorely miss being able to whip your butt."

"In your dreams." Tom smiled. "See you tomorrow."

"Beer's cold. Take care. I mean it." The phone clicked off.

As Tom hung up the phone, he found everyone being swept through the back door by Kenny who got the displaced family to enjoy a madcap game of whiffle ball outside in the warm summer evening. No one kept score, and no one cared. The energy level was high, the emotions light, and the intentions realized. When at last the gathering darkness—and exhaustion by some—made continuation impossible, they went inside for ice cream and then were sorted out into various sleeping accommodations, where they lapsed gratefully and peacefully into slumber.

Chapter 21

"Our calamities will be heightened by reflecting that we furnish the means by which we suffer."
—Thomas Paine (1737-1809)

Sunday – August 1

When Tom's wristwatch alarm sounded at five the following morning, it took several moments before the strangeness of the dark surroundings gave way to comprehension. He rolled over, put his arm around Laurel, and kissed the nape of her neck, then gently ran his hand up and down her spine until she stirred and rolled onto her back. He propped his head up on one hand, and said, "Gooooooooood Morning, Klamath Faaaaaaalls."

Laurel struggled to shake the fuzzies out of her own brain, then pulled the sheets up snugly under her chin. "I've changed my mind. I think I'll just stay here. Ummm. It just feels too good." She rolled onto her side again, facing away from her husband.

"Fat chance, wench!" Tom flung the sheet toward the foot of the bed and smacked his hand on her buttock. "Stay here, and you'll turn into Maxine."

"That's fine, she's nice."

"Have it your way," he said, and started to pull up the hem of her nightgown.

"Fat chance, yourself, letch," she echoed, and pushed herself into a sitting position as her feet slipped over the edge of the bed and planted on the floor. She sat for a moment rubbing her eyes, then rose and padded off to the bathroom down the hall.

Tom smiled to himself, then lay on the bed for a few minutes, thinking about the day ahead. Finally, he rolled out of bed and gathered his clothes. By the time he reached the bathroom, Laurel was emerging from the shower. He playfully feinted toward her, but she scurried out of the way, then left him to consider his two-day old beard.

Laurel got dressed, then pried the others out of their beds and herded them zombie-like in appropriate directions. Maxine was already downstairs, and the sounds and smells coming from the kitchen made the early morning more familiar and enticing. By six o'clock, all were bathed, clothed, fed, packed, and ready to leave.

Finally, they gathered their bags, went out the front door, and descended the steps from the porch to the waiting vehicles. Tommy, Maggie, and Emily climbed in the back of the van again, and Ellie joined them, tired of the cramped confines of having three persons in the small pickup. Kate jumped in the front seat. Angel headed for the Toyota.

The goodbyes were surprisingly emotional. Tom stuck out his hand toward Hill and said, "Kenny, you'll never know how much this meant to all of us. You've been like an oasis in the desert."

Tom's hand nearly disappeared when the big man grasped it. Hill's laughter boomed out once again as he pumped his arm. "We're peas in a pod, kid. It's just that my pod's bigger'n yours." His laugh boomed again.

Laurel embraced Maxine, then tried to hug Hill. Her arms couldn't even reach around his shoulders. "Now, Tom, you best take good care of this pretty lady, 'cause I don't think you'd be much of a match against both me and Eagle."

Tom and Laurel got in their vehicles, and Hill came up to Tom's van window and handed him an envelope and a bag which clinked like glass when handled. "This here's a letter of good will from our Klamath co-op. It might help you if you run into any more roadblocks by other stupid farmers like us. And the bag might help persuade others—actually, you can give one of them bottles to our gang up on the north end of the basin when you see them. 'S'been a pleasure, Tom. Stop by anytime."

"We're in your debt."

And with that, the engines were started and the small procession looped around the circular drive and down the road. Once they reached US 97, they turned right and headed through the city of Klamath Falls. As they reached the outskirts north of town, Tom saw that the speed limit was 55, but he nudged the van up to 60. "Kate, ask Mom about the shimmy." Kate picked up the walkie-talkie and made the inquiry. Everything was fine, so far.

Tom felt pretty good. They had a nice early start, the vehicles were whole again, and they had *gas*—more than enough now. If they could just keep peeling the miles off…

***

The road was straight and smooth. They let the speedometer creep up to 65, and the truck did not complain. About an hour north of Klamath Falls, they passed Diamond Lake Junction. Tom realized they were not far from Beaver Marsh, which was where Hill had said to expect another roadblock, but facing the other direction. He decreased speed to 55 again, and more carefully scanned the road ahead as they went. They passed through the small collection of buildings called Beaver Marsh at about 40, and did not accelerate once they passed. Sure enough, about two miles later, they saw a blockade.

Tom took the walkie-talkie from Kate, who'd been holding it like a delicate treasure. "Heads up, Laurel. It's show time."

The men at the roadblock looked mildly surprised to be approached from behind, and as they turned, Tom could see their rifles—in their hands, but held casually. He took a deep breath and pulled right up to them.

"Howdy, gents."

"Who the hell are you?" one asked suspiciously.

"Friends of Kenny Hill," said Tom with a smile. He gave him Hill's letter, which the man read, then handed back. "Okay. If Kenny's says you're mint, that's good enough for me. It said you're gonna get that Senator Hornbrook to help us. That true?"

"I really don't know. But I do know that he knows you guys have been getting screwed. But right now I guess he's kind of got a lot on his plate."

"Well, if he wants food on that plate, he and his friends back east better wise up."

Tom reached into the bag and pulled out one of the bottles. "Kenny also said his good friend, Jim Beam, wanted to help you guys relax after your shift here."

The man smiled widely. "Any friend of Hill's a friend of mine. Have a nice trip."

Tom pushed the van back up to 65, and Laurel kept pace easily. By eight-thirty, they were in Bend, slowing only as much as necessary to accommodate the speed limit signs. Tom didn't want to attract any attention, and he didn't want to get off the highway to see if the yuppies, as Hill had said, were out of croissants.

A half-hour later they had passed through Redmond and were approaching Madras when they encountered another roadblock. This one, however, consisted of a single old pickup manned by a lone, unenthusiastic man in his mid-twenties chewing on a wood matchstick. Tom hardly had begun to explain their need to pass, and hadn't even pulled out Hill's letter, when the young man lackadaisically waved them on by. Tom didn't wait for an invitation and they squirted around the end of the truck in the opposite lane without looking back.

After that, nobody bothered them. They got through Madras and in the wide open stretches beyond they let their speed creep up to 70, slowing only where turns required it. The terrain was arid and mostly flat, boring almost, except for the stark contrast of the snow-capped, volcanic Cascade peaks to the west. They continued through the nothingness of a barely-rolling landscape which featured only an occasional outpost of humanity. Passing through another "blink-and-it's-gone" town, they saw the local high school sporting a proud sign, *"State Champions, 1989/1994."* It didn't say of what they had been champions.

Finally, they wound down through a small canyon and found themselves overlooking the Columbia River Gorge. Tom looked at the dashboard, and then his watch. They had covered about 280 miles already, and it was barely eleven. Halfway. He checked the gas gauge—plenty for now. He thought they could go a while longer before they used their cans.

They didn't stop and they weren't asked to. As they crossed the overpass above Interstate 84, Tom noticed there was hardly any traffic. That few would be heading west into Portland he could understand, but not why no one was trying to get out. The authorities must have clamped down pretty hard.

They eased across the bridge over the wide river, and started to wind their way up the steep north bank. Taking advantage of the relatively mild "climate," he decided this would be a good spot for a break. There was a nice spot overlooking the river, so he veered off the road and down a sloped grade into the park.

When they had stopped, everyone jumped out and groaned while stretching out their various stiff limbs and blood-deprived backsides. The females attacked the rest rooms with a vengeance, while Tom, Angel, and Tommy pulled bags and coolers out of the back of the truck. Once the girls had returned they set about fixing a simple lunch before resuming their journey north.

***

Laurel was driving the truck with Angel, the latter's left shoulder still rendering him unfit as a driver. Everyone else was in the van. They climbed steadily up the grade out of the Gorge until they reached Satus Pass, then began a gradual down grade. They were now on the Yakima Indian Reservation so, while they kept their eyes busy, they sped up to 75.

As it turned out, their speed was their ally. They were better than halfway across the reservation when they suddenly came upon a barricade in the road. It was, however, nothing more than a couple of highway sandwich board type folding signs, the kind with the flashing caution light affixed to the top. Tom saw them, one in the middle of each lane, but no bodies on the road that he could see. He made a quick decision, told Ellie to call Angel and tell them to keep going, and veered to the middle of the road, streaking between the two signs.

He saw some men about the same time as they saw him, but by the time they could react, both vehicles had sped by them, leaving them shaking their fists in their rearview mirrors. One of them loosed a load of buckshot at them, but it was much too late for a scattergun.

Tom wouldn't have wanted to admit it, but he had an adrenaline rush going that gave him a feeling of exhilaration. He looked at the speedometer, which read 90, and mentally cautioned himself not to start feeling invulnerable. He eased up on the accelerator and let the speed bleed off until they were back to a more manageable 75. He heard Angel's voice come over the walkie-talkie.

"Way to go, Mr. Warner!"

Tom took the mike. "Sorry, I got a little carried away there. But it didn't look like much of a risk. How's the truck?"

"Smooth as silk, all the way." Tom heard Laurel say something in the background, then her voice came over.

"Not quite, Tom. The temperature gauge is really high. I'm afraid it's overheating."

"Okay, we'll slow down to sixty and see what happens. If it doesn't drop real quick, let me know."

Two minutes later, Laurel called again. "It's still high, and not dropping."

Crap! "All right, I'm going to find a place to pull over." A dirt road branched off to the right about a quarter of a mile later. Tom pulled the van off the highway, and cranked the steering around enough so they were pointed at the highway again. Laurel eased in behind him, and as he got out he could see steam coming out through the grill of the truck.

"Don't turn it off!" he said quickly. "Pop the hood." He unlatched the hood release and propped it open. The overflow reservoir was empty, and the steam was blowing out through a small hole in the front of the radiator. He opened the top of the reservoir and had Angel drain melted ice water out of the cooler into an empty two-liter pop bottle, which he then added to the reservoir. Most of it disappeared into the radiator. "That will have to do. Damn! I can't believe we didn't bring extra water containers. Well, if we can limp into the next town, we'll get some there."

He peered down the front of the radiator. "I think we must have caught a shotgun pellet the other night when they ran us off the road. A bullet would have left a bigger hole, unless it hit something and caused some shrapnel fragments. Whatever it was, it probably lodged tight and sealed itself until we pushed it too far. When it got hot enough it just popped it out like a cork." He went to the back of the van and rummaged through his toolbox until he cried out in triumph.

"Ah HA! Just the ticket." He held up something that looked like an ice pick with a wire attached. "This continuity tester should do the trick." He threaded the tool through the grill and inserted the tip into the steam leak, working it back and forth a little until it seemed completely jammed. Then he looped the wire around a piece of the grill and used the alligator clip on the end of the wire to fasten it to itself. "Okay, let's get out of here!"

Everyone got back in and they lurched back up onto the asphalt. The jerry-rigged plug held and twenty minutes later they were in the city of Toppenish, where they bought some five-gallon jugs and filled them with water. Unfortunately it was Sunday, and they could not find an auto parts dealer open. Tom had wanted to buy some Stop-Leak which he had hoped would help seal the circuit tester probe into the hole. They would just have to keep checking it every so often.

Tom had nothing against Toppenish, or even the reservation and its inhabitants for that matter; he just wanted to keep moving. He had no way of knowing if the travel restrictions were widely enforced. His only concern was reaching Eagle's, which meant keep moving, lest he find greater barriers to his progress than he had encountered so far. Yakima, just another 20 miles, was actually the only remaining city of any significant size in their path. The population was only about 60,000, but it was the center of a major agricultural region, and if the government was tempted to regulate the distribution of foods during the state of emergency, then their control of the roads was probable.

They checked their gasoline levels, having come over 350 miles so far today. The van had under half a tank, but the truck was nearly empty. *That was stupid*, Tom thought. *How could I have forgotten that the truck only had half the capacity? That could have been trouble. Oh, well.* No stations were open—once again they thanked their lucky stars for the assistance they had received from the Hills. Using their cans, they filled the van completely, but only put five gallons in the truck. Tom was worried about the radiator, and if they had a major problem they might have to abandon it. Better to have to keep adding gas than to have to leave a full tank behind.

After they finished with the gasoline, Angel put the cans away, and came over to Tom as everyone was getting in the cars. "Mr. Warner, I was looking at the map earlier, and I think we should go *around* Yakima. We could take this road here," he said, pointing at the map, "and might have a clearer shot."

"You must be clairvoyant, Angel," said Tom. "I'm worried also about the major highways through there. They very well could be closed. There are probably even better routes, but only the locals would know them. So, what the heck. Let's give your idea a go."

Tom led the way as they traveled up the road a couple of miles, then climbed the on-ramp and eased onto a nearly empty interstate 82. Tom felt exposed, and was glad they wouldn't be on the highway for long. Laurel followed behind in the truck, with one eye on the temperature gauge. Less than fifteen minutes later, they exited the freeway at Union Gap, managed to find enough signs to weave their way around the back roads, and somehow discovered themselves intersecting US Highway 12 about twelve or thirteen miles north and west of Yakima. Tom was ecstatic, but cautious. With luck it was only about three hours all the way to Eagle's. With luck.

***

Laurel called her brother shortly after they hit US 12. Eagle was happy to hear from her, but sounded reserved. "There doesn't seem to be much action on I-5. They've pretty much got people bottled up in the cities, so you shouldn't have much trouble. But call me after you're over the pass and back in cell range. I'll probably try to meet up with you. Look for me right where 12 intersects the freeway. There's a little restaurant there called *Spiffy's*. If I'm not there, don't sweat it, but call me anyway." He told her to be careful. "I've heard of a little trouble around Morton. That's on this side of the pass. I'm not sure what's going on, but those people are fit to be tied when it comes to city people. Their economy went in the tub after the spotted owl thing, and I think

The Hornbrook Prophecy

they probably would have boarded up the whole town if Mt. St. Helens hadn't blown up right next door and created a draw for tourists. It's a really pretty little town, but it's had hard times not of its own making. Anyway, be careful," he repeated.

"Okay, big brother, we promise," she said. "God, I'll be glad when this is over."

"I'm afraid we're a long way from having this over."

"Maybe. See you soon, Eagle."

"Bye, sis."

There was still no telling how easy the rest of the journey was going to be, but one thing was certain—no doubt this was far and away the most scenic part of their entire trip. They were on US 12 heading west, climbing the east side of the Cascades, traveling through a rocky canyon alongside the Tieton River. It was after two now, and on certain turns of the road, the sun filtered through the trees and reflected off the cascading water like ten thousand sparklers. Presently, the stark rocky canyon gave way to forested slopes as they gained altitude, and the hillside dropped away from the road more precipitously.

It had been hot down on the flats, and the heat chased them up the slope for a while. The Toyota seemed fine for the first thirty or so miles out of Yakima, then the needle started to move up, even as the ambient temperature finally began falling.

"Tom," came Laurel's voice over the walkie-talkie, "it's getting hot again."

"Okay," was the only reply. The road was so narrow there was no place immediately to pull over. About a half mile up the road, Tom spied a turnout, and he pulled in. As he got out, he could see that the truck was steaming far more than it had been the first time. By the time he had gotten the hood open, Angel had already pulled out the water jugs.

"Damn!" exclaimed Tom. "We lost the plug. Crap!" The water and steam were spurting out of the hole in front. Tom headed for the toolbox, but after rummaging around through every corner, he could not find a suitable alternative for the continuity tester. He grabbed a Philips head screwdriver and a hammer, figuring to pound the point into the existing hole, but the shaft of the screwdriver was too short to reach through the grill.

"I'll fix that," said Angel. Five minutes later, he had dismantled the entire grill and removed it. Tom then took the Philips, put a layer of duct tape over the end, and with a few solid whacks drove the tip through the radiator wall and wedged it into the core. The duct tape around the shaft helped form a better seal. The steam leak had been greatly reduced, although not completely eliminated.

"If that holds, it should be good enough. But there're still another ten or fifteen miles to the summit. Get a towel and let's add as much water as we can." A few minutes later, they stashed the jugs, and got in. "Okay, if we can just get to the summit, we can coast for fifty miles. Here's hoping."

As they pulled out of the turnout, Laurel hit a good-sized pothole at the edge of the lane. It jarred their teeth. It also jarred the screwdriver, and the tip slipped out of the core, leaving the tool to be held only by the friction of the taped shaft in the outer wall of the radiator.

As they gained altitude, the air temperature continued to drop, but only slightly on the clear, warm summer day. The road, however, deteriorated, showing the effects of many harsh winter snows and freezes. Potholes were numerous and it was impossible to miss them all. They had only gone about five miles when the screwdriver was finally shaken completely free of the radiator. It rattled down through the braces of the frame, dropped to the road, and passed beneath the truck unseen.

Within moments, enough water had escaped the larger hole the screwdriver had made to send the needle up again. Angel noticed it first. He first caught a hint of steam escaping the hood when they slowed for a turn, and immediately glanced over at the temperature gauge.

"Mrs. Warner!" he cried. "It's really hot! Pull over!" He grabbed the walkie-talkie and called the van. "Trouble, sir! We're hot! We're going to stop."

Laurel spotted a small gravel road and turned into it. As she was decelerating, steam suddenly started pouring out from under the hood, and as she came to a stop, the engine died. Angel grabbed the towel and got out as Laurel pulled the hood release. Angel managed to find and flip the latch in front relatively easily, as the grill had been removed. Steam now escaped the engine in multiple directions.

Just then the van drove into the gravel road and stopped. Several doors opened and everyone got out, Tom to head for the truck, and the others just glad for the chance to get out. Tom took one look under the hood and pronounced the Toyota dead. "I can't tell if it's just blown the head gasket or if there's an actual crack in the block from the overheating. But it doesn't matter. We can't fix it either way." He lowered the hood. "Let's get everything rearranged in the van, and then we'll transfer what we can from the truck."

With only a couple of hours of traveling remaining, hopefully, comfort was secondary. They packed all they could in the rooftop carrier, then under the seats, and then beside the seats. They crammed some in the rear of the van and the rest ended up on their laps.

They emptied the last of the gas out of the cans into the van's tank. "Ready for some good news, Tom?" said Laurel.

"Sure, what?"

"The truck was almost empty anyway. You put in just enough."

"Yeah, that's us," he grunted. "Kissed by Lady Luck."

They were set to discard the six, now-empty gas cans, but Tom decided not to. "No telling if they might be valuable later," he said.

Ellie protested, "But, Dad, there's no place for them. Not even on our laps."

"Not to worry." He pulled a short length of cord out of the camping box, and loosely tied the cans—and the empty water jugs—together by their handles, and hoisted the mass of them up onto the roof of the van, and tied them to the back of the cargo carrier. Then, producing the roll of duct tape, he strapped it all down as best as possible to keep them from bouncing around in the wind.

The remaining items, whether trash or judged non-essential, were gathered and put in the back of the truck. With Laurel at the wheel, Tom, Angel, and Tommy pushed the truck far enough down the dirt road to get it around the first curve and out of sight. Then they locked it, thanked it for its years of service, and headed back to the others. "Who knows," Tom said, "maybe we can come back and get it in a few days."

"Probably not," said Laurel.

"Probably not," agreed Tom.

A few short minutes later, they passed by the deserted White Pass winter ski area and then were over the summit. "Home stretch, everyone," remarked Tom with optimism. The tendency to be subdued after the loss of the Toyota, which had been a part of their family almost as long as they had been a family, was overshadowed by the need to make adjustments to the newly-cramped interior of the van, now carrying eight people and all their worldly possessions. Tom had asked Angel to ride up front, after Laurel had relayed the cautionary note from Eagle about possible trouble as they descended out of the mountains. Angel obliged, bringing a small bag up with him. Tom knew Angel's shoulder was painful, but he had come to value the young man's instincts. Laurel, Kate, and Emily sat on the middle seat, and Ellie, Maggie, and Tommy were in the rear.

Not long after they had crossed the summit, they rounded a corner and were awestruck by the sudden appearance of the majestic slopes of Mount Rainier, the tallest and most dominating feature of the Washington state landscape. For a few moments Tom found himself gawking like a tourist at the magnificent scenery.

After a few miles, the twisting and turning of the road began to ease and as they lost altitude rapidly they found the road smooth, dry, and straightening out. The terrain was a complete contrast to the east side of the summit. The heavily-forested, lush slopes of the west side of the Cascade Mountains benefited from annual precipitation totals of up to 80 inches, with average snowfalls of as much as 15 feet or more. The combination of volcanic peaks, beautiful lakes, rivers, and timbered mountains made the Cascades a stunning visual experience.

As the road ran down through the valley of the Cowlitz River, they had no trouble picking the pace up to 65 miles an hour for the most part. They passed through several small mill towns, and Tom was just about to answer a question Emily asked about the checkerboard bare patches on the mountainside, when the outside rearview mirror on Angel's side suddenly exploded with a loud crack and a shower of glass fragments.

Tom's arms reflexively jerked the car to the left at the surprise, and then he fought to keep the van from swerving out of control and off the road. He heard another impact above his head, probably on the cargo carrier, and realized they were under fire—from where and by whom he had no idea, but he screamed for everybody to get down. He quickly scanned the road ahead and saw nothing. He didn't want to stop if they had passed the attackers, but he didn't want to continue if he was headed toward them.

There were several hard thuds and the sound of glass breaking at the back of the van. Tom looked in his own outside mirror and saw a pickup truck racing up behind them, with someone standing up, apparently in the truck bed behind the cab, and aiming a rifle at them.

"SHIT!" he yelled at nobody in particular. "They're right behind us. Angel, point something at them and try to make them back off!" Several more shots hit the back of the van as the two vehicles careened down the road at almost 80 miles an hour. It was like a corny scene from a low-budget hillbilly movie, but it was terrifying. *Thank God the back is full of sleeping bags and camping gear,* he thought. *We can take the fire without getting hurt. Camping gear! Oh, my God! If they hit a propane bottle, it's all over!*

Angel had other ideas. "I'm not gonna just *point*," he muttered to himself. He reached into his bag and pulled out the Calico with the 50-round beehive magazine. He rolled down the window, reversed his position as best he could, stuck the gun out, and winced in pain at the awkward movement of his dislocated shoulder. He bit off a cry, then aimed the gun back toward the trailing truck. He pulled the trigger, but nothing happened. He hadn't chambered a round, and he hadn't wound the magazine spring tight. Quickly he did both, and repeated his firing effort. A single round fired, but he had no idea where it went. It was nearly impossible trying to aim. It wasn't like the movies—you couldn't just fire over your shoulder and automatically shoot out the tires.

He said, "To hell with this!" and started pulling the trigger as fast as the semi-auto would let him. He knew he was spraying bullets all over the landscape, but hoped it would get their attention.

"My God!" cried Tom. "Look!"

Angel stopped firing as he saw the truck swerve first toward the shoulder, then veer sharply back across the road before hitting the ditch, bouncing up, and slamming into a fifty-foot tall Douglas Fir. No flips, no explosions, no bodies flying in slow motion like in the movies. Just the sudden movement and then, *WHAM!*—the truck impacted the huge tree and swallowed its own bumper.

Tom didn't go back to see if anybody needed help; indeed, he didn't even slow down. The van virtually screamed past the main street leading into Morton, and while they neither saw, nor came upon, any other associates of the attackers, Tom was not going to give someone an opportunity to come looking for them. After another ten minutes had passed, he began to feel easier.

The immediate danger past, most of the kids were talking excitedly, except Emily, who was being comforted by Laurel. Tommy said he couldn't wait to go back to school after summer so he could tell all his friends, and could Dad please not fix the van until he showed everyone?

Tom saw that Angel was sitting very quietly after rolling his window back up after the attack. Tom had no idea if Angel had actually hit anyone, but either way, there was no question that he had caused the truck to crash. "You had no choice," said Tom softly, trying to read the young man's thoughts.

"I don't know. Maybe I *should* have just pointed the gun at them like you said."

"Angel, you *did*, and they didn't stop. We have propane in the back. That could've been the end of us."

"Yeah, I know. I'll be okay." Kate unbuckled her seatbelt, leaned forward and put her arms around Angel's neck. She said nothing, but it wasn't really necessary. They had each faced a life-or-death situation where they were forced to do something exceedingly repugnant, and while loved ones had been saved by their actions, it seemed small consolation. They shared an unwelcome bond.

Fifteen minutes later the van sped through Mossyrock, across the causeway on Mayfield Lake, and was nearing the intersection with Interstate 5. When they spied the *Spiffy's* restaurant that her brother had mentioned, Laurel cried, "Oh no. I forgot to call Eagle." No sooner had she said that, than Tom braked and turned into the restaurant parking lot adjacent to Fast Eddie's Gas Station. They saw no sign of Eagle. The gas station was closed and deserted, and while there were two vehicles outside the restaurant, the sign indicated it was closed.

They parked next to the other cars, and Tom couldn't keep anyone inside. The doors burst open and everyone poured out like the end of a harrowing carnival ride. However, seeing no sign of life inside, Tom was about to make them all squeeze back into the van when the restaurant door pushed open, and a man emerged with a cup of coffee in one hand, and a plate with a huge slice of sour cream apple pie in the other. "Man, their pie is the absolute best!" said Eagle. "Hi, guys! How was the drive?"

Laurel didn't know whether to throw her arms around him or kick him in the shins. But after all they'd been through the last three days, her relief at seeing him at last won out, and she literally jumped into his arms. "Oh, Eagle," she wept. "I'm so glad to see you."

Struggling to keep the pie on the plate, Eagle almost fell over backward when she hugged him. Almost simultaneously, he was mobbed by his nieces and nephew. Finally, the clutch loosened, and Eagle emerged still holding his pie and coffee. He put the cup down on the planter next to the van and took Tom's hand and gripped it firmly. Then, as he looked at the starred windshield and scarred paint on the van's hood, he took a big bite of pie and began to circle around the perimeter of the van, noting in particular the dozen or more bullet holes in the rear doors, those in the rooftop carrier and gas cans, and the shattered outside mirror. When he reached the front of the van again, he noted an unfamiliar face. He reached out and said, "Hi, I don't believe I know you. I'm Eagle McCall."

"Angel St. Paul, sir," was the reply as they shook hands.

McCall noted Angel holding his left arm oddly, and Ellie standing next to him with her chest wrapped tightly. He turned to Tom and Laurel. "Judging from the looks of your van here, and the battering of your passengers, I think you ought to consider driving lessons."

Tom and Laurel did not seem particularly amused, and McCall read them correctly. "I assume it was pretty rough," he said quietly. "We'll talk later, but I'd like to get us all home, before the North Powder Union guys forget who I am." He didn't elaborate. "Hey, where's the truck? I thought you were bringing it."

"It's somewhere the other side of White Pass. A bad case of heat stroke, brought on by lead poisoning," said Tom. "We'll follow you."

"Tommy, Maggie, why don't you come ride with your favorite Uncle Eagle?" said McCall, looking at Tom, who nodded. The youngsters wasted no time running around and jumping in the big, forest green Ford Bronco four-by-four. "Tom, we'll be passing a checkpoint of sorts in about twenty minutes or so. I'll explain later. But don't worry. They're friends. And they're expecting me back, along with you and the gang."

Tom nodded, trusting his old roommate. Everyone else got settled back into the van, and the two vehicles headed out of the parking lot, turned first left onto the road for a hundred yards or so, and then right down the sloped on-ramp onto the Interstate. A quarter-hour later, they left the freeway for a smaller two-lane highway. They sped down the road for about ten minutes, and as they came to a narrow bridge on the near side of a small collection of houses and a general store, they were stopped by a flagger with a large, red, hand-held 'STOP' sign in front of the bridge. Tom, in the van behind Eagle, slowed to a stop and saw his brother-in-law lean out the window and speak to the man. After a moment or two the man laughed hard, shook McCall's hand, and stepped back. Thinking of their encounters with blockades near Klamath Falls, Tom was relieved when the man moved out of the way and he saw the Bronco accelerate. As Tom approached the bridge, the man waved him across with a smile.

He spent another forty minutes or so following his brother-in-law, negotiating various small highways and rural roads through agricultural farmland and river valleys, until finally the Bronco slowed and turned into a long, looping gravel drive, past a wire-fenced green pasture, and stopped in front of McCall's well-kept gray and white rambler with a large garage and separate, workshop adjacent.

Tom and his weary passengers got out of the van, and they could not quite believe that they had actually made it all the way at last. It was almost seven in the evening, but the Northwest summer sun was still bright in the sky. The surrounding hills, trees, pastures, and lawns were almost brilliant in their greens, and the horses grazing in the front pasture made the whole scene pastoral. McCall led them through the front breezeway door and into the back yard overlooking the back pasture, beyond which lay the alder-lined banks of the east fork of the Postas River. Had Tom not been here several times previously it would have seemed nearly surreal in contrast to the metropolitan unrest of the Los Angeles area they had fled just two days before.

McCall had evidently called ahead on the way, as Tom saw smoke rising from the barbeque on the backyard deck. A pretty, pony-tailed woman, wearing blue jeans, a white Portland State University tee shirt and white sneakers, was basting marinade on steaks with one hand, and flipping some hamburgers with the other. She put down the brush and spatula when she saw the new faces, and came down the short stairway to the group.

McCall began, "Okay, everyone, I'd like you to meet the maid. This is—," and stopped as a barbeque mitt smacked him across the back of the head. "She does that a lot, so be careful about turning your back on her."

"Hi, guys," the woman said as she smiled and held out her arms toward Laurel and then hugged Tom. "I'm so glad you made it finally."

"It's SO good to see you again, Sunny," said Laurel. "I thought we'd *never* make it!"

"Just a drive in the country," smiled Tom.

"Yeah, right," said Angel, who then introduced himself to Sunny. "You're a Congresswoman, right?"

"For now," she nodded. "I'm not so sure I like it in the 'other' Washington."

"Angel said he always wanted to see the Northwest," Tom added. "We just tried to make it fun for him."

A few minutes later they were sitting at the tables on the deck, enjoying the meal and the security of their new surroundings. Later, the kids disappeared into the family room to watch a video, and Tom, Laurel, McCall, and Sunny sought the quieter living room and had some brandy while Tom recounted the adventures of the past forty-eight hours. Only occasionally did McCall or Sunny interrupt to ask a question, as Tom spun a remarkable tale of shootings, roadblocks, crashes, "hostage" taking, and high speed chases. Sunny sucked in her breath when Tom described the scene in the desert when Kate had saved the family, and McCall just shook his head in amazement when he heard of the escape from the Morton attackers.

Laurel had to fight back some tears when she wondered out loud when they would be able to return to their home, or if it would even be in one piece. "I guess the bright side," she said, wistfully, "is that it wasn't much of a house, so maybe no one will bother it."

"I don't think even the Senator could tell you what's going to happen next. He's not overly optimistic right now, and clear thinking seems to be in short supply in D.C. He sent me out here to take care of some local issues, and may very well be joining us in the next couple of days—the airlines are apparently still flying, although there's a lot of confusion over the legality of surface transportation when you get where you're going. I think a lot, maybe even most, people are ignoring at least some of the restrictions.

"I can think of an agricultural highway inspector who probably wishes he had," said Laurel, looking at her husband.

Tom smiled and said to Eagle, "It's been interesting."

"I'm sure. Like I said, who knows what's gonna happen at this point. But," added McCall cheerfully, "in the meantime we've got plenty of space here for you, and plenty of things to do to enjoy yourselves for a change."

They all toasted that idea.

Chapter 22

"So long as the people do not care to exercise their freedom, those who wish to tyrannize will do so."
—*Voltairine de Cleyre (1866-1912)*

Monday, August 2

The forested green hills surrounding the small river valley that McCall called home were already bathed in cheerful sunlight when Tom awoke, roused himself out of bed in Eagle's guest room, dressed quickly in blue jeans and a long-sleeved tee, slipped on his sneakers, and found his way out down the hall, through the family room filled with sleeping bags and hidden forms, and into the kitchen. The sun was so brilliant, streaming in through the south and east corner windows and reflecting off the white cabinetry, that Tom felt like he should be wearing sunglasses. He greeted Sunny and Laurel who were already up and busying themselves fixing breakfast for the crowd, then saw Eagle through the window and went out through the utility room into the breezeway.

"Hey, Beret," said Tom, the screen door banging closed noisily behind him.

"Good morning, Sleeping Beauty," said his host. "You haven't missed anything. Sunny was up out of the den even before I got up; Laurel came out about a half-hour later. Our job seems to be to stay out of their way."

Tom glanced guiltily at his wristwatch. It was only nine, but it seemed like he'd been asleep for a day. The last couple of days had taken a lot out of him. Nonetheless, he felt refreshed just having arrived in one piece. The first thing he noticed, standing outside in the backyard overlooking the pasture by the river, was how incredibly quiet it was. No cars, no sirens, no horns, no city noise of any kind—just a few birds chirping, and the barest rustling of the alder leaves in the gentle morning breeze. The air was chilly, in spite of the bright Northwest summer sun.

"It didn't register right away yesterday when you mentioned it, but I meant to ask you. Who or what is the North Powder Union?" asked Tom.

"Well, this isn't exactly your run-of-the-mill suburb. Most of the people out here are pretty independent types; you know, they're used to taking care of themselves. They hunt, they fish, they have vegetable gardens. A lot of them used to work in the woods, in the timber industry, until the damn spotted owl and other environmental fairy tales cut the legs out from under a lot of their jobs. There's a huge proportion of families that have two, three, maybe four generations all in the area. It's real Americana. Some Peyton Place kind of nonsense, but these are real people, hard-working types, who have put up with a lot over their lives. At any rate, while they may not have a lot, they tend to be pretty protective of it. Not a lot of city lovers out here. They like their peace and quiet."

"And the Union?" asked Tom again.

"Well, some folks are a bit more protective than others," explained McCall. "And a bunch of them over the years sort of began to get together and talk about mutual interests. That evolved into the North Powder Union. It's not really a militia group; more of a plan ahead group. Until this week they've never done much more than talk."

"Where'd they get the name?"

"Oh, I think a lot of them hunt with muzzleloaders. You know, black powder rifles."

"Okay, I get it. So what's different this week?"

"Well, suddenly their paranoia seems real. They're prepared to take care of themselves, but they're afraid—apparently with good reason, from what I'm seeing and hearing—of the cities getting out of hand with the problems going on right now. So the Union decided among themselves to sort of seal off this area and keep outsiders on the outside. Right now, it's mostly like the flag station yesterday that we went through. They're just being inquisitive so far, more or less pretending like they're helping carry out the President's directives about limiting travel. The sheriff and state patrol don't condone it officially, but it's taking some of the load off them so they're just looking the other way."

"Surely they don't expect a flagger to stop many determined people," scoffed Tom.

"Not at all. But he's the only guy you actually saw," McCall said. "His job is to talk to people, ask them about their business, but actually to let every one through."

"So what good is he?"

"He has a friend out of sight just over the bridge. They both have cell phones, and if either one of them reports a problem, they have friends about three miles down the road who are prepared to deal with it. They tell me that they can completely seal off this entire county in about fifteen minutes if there was a real threat."

"I won't ask how. We've had the radio on a lot, but we really don't have a clear picture about what's going on everywhere. Is it bad?" asked Tom.

"Bad, and getting worse, I think," replied McCall. "The cities in particular are ill-prepared for interruptions in normal routines. It creates runs on the grocery stores and gas stations and so on. Right now there's a fair amount of rioting going on around the country. The thing is it's really only the federal government that's having financial problems. State and local governments haven't been affected yet, although they'll soon start to feel the loss of federal funding. Most businesses are still okay, especially since a lot of them have stopped sending in tax payments. Utilities are still operating. But the feds are a major player in the economy and, more importantly, in the lives of a lot of folks. So even just the *appearance* of problems has been enough to trigger the chaos that's going on. Most people are doing fine, but if the unrest interrupts business even further as a result, then it will cause more shortages. Things will get even worse. And if that happens, a lot of people will flee the cities, like you did, and head for the countryside. So the North Powder Union aims to keep that from being a problem *here*."

"Then I guess we're lucky to be on the inside, so to speak," concluded Tom.

"Well, I hope so."

"So what now?"

"Relax. I'll introduce you to those neighbors you haven't already met when you've been up here before. And you're welcome to come along while I attend to some chores around about for the Senator." He didn't define what 'chores' meant. "I won't lie to you, Tom. This is going to be an interesting ride, but not a fun one. Nothing like this has ever happened to the government before, and not only is there going to be a lot of fallout, but it's not going to be easy to fix, let alone get things back to normal again."

"In other words, I shouldn't get too anxious about getting home any time soon?" said an obviously worried Tom, pursing his lips.

The Hornbrook Prophecy

"Hey, relax," soothed his friend. "You're gonna like it here! You remember? *The fire's always hot and the beer's always cold*," repeating his favorite approach to life in the Pacific Northwest.

"Yeah, yeah."

Chapter 23

> *"The State is not armed with superior wit or honesty,*
> *but with superior physical strength. I was not born to*
> *be forced. I will breathe after my own fashion.*
> *Let us see who is strongest."*
> —Henry David Thoreau, *Civil Disobedience* (1849)

Saturday – August 7

The shoe salesman was tired. And afraid. The fighting in many Alabama cities, including here in Mobile, had raged for an entire week. The National Guard unit he commanded had sustained some casualties, although they were not serious. Nothing the authorities did seemed to make any difference.

Right now he had a major confrontation growing on the north side of Mobile between Black youths on one side and police and his Guard unit on the other. A white television news van was parked down a side street behind the National Guard deployment, and cameras had been capturing the mayhem.

Just as he thought all hell was about to break loose, a black Lincoln limo with darkened windows drove right into the thick of it, parking in the middle of the intersection between the two ragged lines of combatants, and briefly taking a few rounds of small arms fire to the exterior. Then it stopped. Neither side knew at first quite what was going on. After the car had been there about twenty seconds, unmoving in the ensuing quiet, the front passenger door opened and out stepped a well-dressed Black man. A moment later, the driver's door opened and another man emerged.

The latter immediately began walking toward the crowd of black youths at the forefront of the protestors. The first man headed toward the cluster of the National Guard vehicles. When he reached the shoe salesman commander, he said, simply. "Captain, take your men and leave the area. There will be no further trouble here."

"Look, buster," said the Guard leader, "I don't think you know how lucky you are to be standing here after that stupid stunt you just pulled, but in case you haven't noticed, these people have been tearing up these businesses, looting, burning, and terrifying citizens and we're here to stop them."

"Captain, take your men and leave the area," repeated the Black man evenly. "There will be no further trouble here."

"Who do you think you are?" said the incredulous officer. "Get the hell out of here, or I'll have you arrested!"

"Captain, I'm sure you learned the importance of situational awareness in your summer and weekend training programs. Please realize that you are currently a good fifteen feet from the nearest vehicle and forty feet from the nearest building. And if you look up on top of the three stores across the street and in the third floor windows of that building directly behind you, you will see a total of four armed and angry men with sniper rifles. I wouldn't want to have to tell them that you decided not to take my advice." The captain's eyes darted from one building to another, and he was unable not to spin around to look behind him.

"This is not your neighborhood," continued the man before him. "Again, I strongly urge you to return to your own, and we will take care this matter."

"I can't just *leave!*" protested the officer.

"Of course you can, my friend. Do you hear any gunfire? Do you see any projectiles in the air? Do you see anyone running around? There will be no further trouble here."

The uniformed man considered the situation. Short of leveling the entire neighborhood, there was probably no realistic way to put an end to the violence without a major war, and if this guy had a way to calm things down and he didn't try it, it would be worse for everybody. *For chrissakes*, he thought, *I'm a salesman, not George Patton!*

"Okay, maybe we can try it your way, but I gotta call my commanding officer first."

"Very well, but time is short before bad things get even worse."

The salesman turned to walk away, when the man cried, "Stop!" The man froze. "I'm afraid my friends up above will get very nervous if you leave my side. They're very protective. Perhaps you best have your radio come to you."

Five minutes later a compromise was reached, and the National Guard units pulled back an initial two blocks. The Black man spoke a last time to the shoe salesman. "My friend, you have acted courageously in recognizing the potential for greater harm and the opportunity for resolution. I thank you. I shall remember your good sense." He shook the commander's hand and then walked back across the intersection, past his car, to the crowd of Blacks who had been talking to his driver and watching from the distance. As he walked, the news van moved closer, then discharged two persons, one with a camera, the other with just a microphone. Having tipped the news station himself that there was going to be a "development" here, the man was not surprised by the presence of the news crew.

When he reached the crowd, the Black who had taken charge began, "The army has accepted our terms for now." There were several shouts of approval. "So, how are the good citizens here?" His driver introduced several of the unofficial leaders of the group, many of whom were holding firearms. Then the well-dressed man addressed the crowd. "I know that you are angry—so am I. I know that you feel deceived—so do I. I know that you are worried about how you are going to have enough money to eat and to pay your rent, because the government has cut off your money. I am also worried, but it is not about whether dinner will be on time. No, I am worried because when the White man shouts, you all jump! I am worried because one hundred and fifty years after slavery supposedly ended, you still cannot feed yourselves if your White master decides not to! I am worried because when you feel that you have been wronged your reaction is to burn the stores where you shop and the businesses where you work, and the very neighborhoods where you live!"

"Why shouldn't we!" yelled an angry voice. "They aren't any good anyway!"

"Those are fine words," said another, "but the truth is we can't eat words! Why should we listen to you?"

"You all know my friend here. You all know who I am—and I'm honored and humbled that you do," said the negotiator, with feeling. "You also know that we always stand behind our word. And you must believe me when I say to you that *this*, this trouble, is not going to help you. I *know* this. I have been there. I have been in your very shoes. I have been assaulted, and I have fought back. I have been jailed for it—and I have learned from it." The crowd was quieter now, and nobody paid any attention to the news crew, which was happily but quietly capturing the entire exchange. "There is a way to fix this, to help you, to help our neighborhoods and cities. What I'm going to ask you, you must take at face value, at least for the present. You must trust me for now. If I let you down, I will accept responsibility, but I am asking you to let me help achieve a permanent solution. It will just take a little time."

"What do we do today, or tomorrow, in the meantime?" said a older Black woman.

"Go home. Put your guns away. Take care of your children. Don't overreact. There's no reason to panic for now. There's plenty of time to work out solutions. Let's not give others the satisfaction of seeing us destroy ourselves. Go home. As soon as we can—within a few days, I'm sure, a week at the most—we will be back to see you with some answers."

There were some general, but subdued conversations, and a few more questions, which he answered as encouragingly as he could. Finally, with a few more handshakes, and pats on the back, he and his companion were able to leave. They walked back across the huge intersection, and the driver climbed into the Lincoln, while he made another trip down the street to where the National Guard troops were holding. "Captain," he said, when the Guard commander came up to meet him, "the people are going home and, as I indicated to you before, there will be no further trouble here."

"Mister, I assume you must be someone they respect, and I'm sorry I don't know you, but thanks."

"My name is Perry Robbs."

"Holy smokes, not—"

"Yes. Now, I know you and your superiors must have some concerns about bringing to justice those responsible for the damages here and the injuries to your men," said Robbs.

"Honestly, I don't know. I would think that would be up to the police. The Guard was charged with restoring order."

"Which has now been accomplished," said Robbs. "But to make this a substantial and lasting restoration of order it has to be mutually meaningful. They are withdrawing to their homes, thus removing the threat to you and your troops. Now you must withdraw to your own, and remove the threat to them and their families."

"I have to call my boss, and he'll have to call his boss, but I'm sure it'll happen."

"Then I would reiterate what I said to you before: I shall remember your good sense."

***

The evening news carried the entire story of the intervention in Mobile by Robbs and Pendleton and the immediate cessation of violence that resulted.

The complete details included that virtually every other sizable focus of unrest across the state also evaporated within two hours of the turn of events in the state's major Gulf Coast port city. There was no official explanation for this, but most of the speculation that evening was based on reports by various media sources and their contacts that each location was visited by unidentified men who somehow managed to get the rioters to cease fire and pull back from any threatening posture. Because of this the on-site National Guard commanders in each location issued cease fire orders and had their troops pull back partially so as to demonstrate a less hostile demeanor. Further investigation discovered that the recommendation for such Guard reaction had originated with a Guard captain in Mobile who, it was reported, normally worked in a shoe store.

At a news conference the following morning, the Governor expressed his pleasure that the rioters finally heeded his pleas and warnings. Across town, at a larger press gathering, Perry Robbs was the center of attention.

"Mr. Robbs! Mr. Robbs! Thank you," said a reporter he pointed to. "Didn't it seem foolhardy to drive into the middle of what has been described as a gunfight, and then get out of the car to walk through the crossfire?"

"Ma'am, the only foolhardy actions lately have been those of the federal government with their irresponsible fiscal management; the reprehensible abuse of public trust by the managing editor of the *Independent*, and the criminal, yes, *criminal* behavior of Governor Scio."

"What are you going to do now, Mr. Robbs?"

"What *I* do can hardly be of major interest to your readers and listeners. But *they*, on the other hand, should be asking *you* why you, in the wake of the outrageous lies and fabrications of the phony news stories which you all so eagerly presented about the Hopes program, are not demanding the convening of a grand jury to investigate the very obvious criminal conspiracy to defame, defraud, and destroy the hopes and dreams of the people of this state by Jefferson Scio and Biggs Wasco!"

***

On Monday, August 16, Scio and Wasco were indicted by the Montgomery grand jury. Scio was reduced to tears and tried to plea bargain in return for testifying against Wasco. But as prosecutors felt their case was strong enough and that the people of Alabama deserved to have a full trial, they declined to offer any plea arrangement whatsoever. Wasco was belligerent and outraged, and declared to the press not only that he was completely innocent, but that his lawyers had assured him that the case was sure to be thrown out of court for insufficient evidence.

Less than a week after the indictment was handed down, the "witness" from the Montgomery sports bar was killed in a Saturday night tavern knife fight. The assailant was never identified. Three days after that, the man Jordan Stowell had spoken to about an alleged meeting between the Lieutenant Governor and a corporate officer in a Birmingham restaurant died in an automobile accident after swerving off a road into a swampy bog. There was no evidence to suggest the incident was the result of foul play. The following day, authorities admitted that with the loss of these two key witnesses, the case against Biggs Wasco was irreversibly damaged. His lawyers demanded the case be dismissed. They were successful.

Four days later, Biggs Wasco was found in his Mobile penthouse, dead from a single .22-caliber bullet behind the left ear. No incriminating evidence was found to indicate the responsible assassin. Rufus Pendleton was interrogated at length, but regretted that he was unable to shed any light on the matter. He personally had been in Huntsville with Perry Robbs that evening, and there were plenty of witnesses willing to support that assertion.

Chapter 24

"Every government is a scoundrel. In its dealings with its own people it not only steals and wastes their property and plays a brutal and witless game with their natural rights, but regularly gambles with their very lives."
—H. L. Mencken, 1928

Thursday – August 26

Over the past three and a half weeks, Sebastian Fellsmere's predictions about the nation's problems had proved accurate. As transportation was disrupted by the federal dictates and fuel restrictions, many consumer products soon came to be in scarce supply. Even as Alabama quieted, more and more cities across the country fell victim to various degrees of civil unrest, and more and more people began to leave those areas in search of safety, despite travel restrictions. Neither Congress nor the President had any immediate solutions to the shortfalls in the Treasury. The stock market had continued to fall as investors cashed out or went looking worldwide for better deals while they could. Tax revenues fell even further. The nation's leaders and the nation's media—both without any constructive ideas—began to resort to a favorite pastime: The blame game. Everybody blamed everyone else. And while name-calling was rampant, it was expected. It wasn't until the President's televised address nearly two weeks after the first historic announcements of the country's fiscal impasse that the words themselves led to problems.

"My fellow Americans," began President Dillard, dressed in a dark gray suit and sitting formally at his desk in the Oval Office of the White House, apparently attempting to create the most authoritative impression he could, "it is truly distressing to have to come before you this evening, near the end of what I know has been another difficult week for most all of you, to inform you that in spite of all my best efforts, I have been unable to persuade Congress to adopt the measures necessary to solve this terrible crisis.

"Never before in the long and illustrious history of our nation has your government been unable to meet the full and entire demand of its financial obligations, the very obligations which you, its citizens, have demanded over the years. And while many might say, 'Good! No government to bother us,' what would they have us say to the millions of senior citizens who depend monthly upon their Social Security checks? What would they have us say to the millions of poor who have been denied the opportunities over the years to help themselves? What would they have us say to the children who may need medical care or school lunches just so they can make it through the day?

"Many of you have called or written, asking simple questions. Questions like 'Why is this happening?' Or, 'Aren't we the richest country in the world?' 'What is the cause of this?' And, finally, 'Whose fault is this?' The simple answer is that while we once were the most productive, wealthiest nation on earth, greed has destroyed us. But it's not the greed of the many, it's the greed of the few. Like the treasonous TEA Party and its founder, Mr. Shadwell, who feel that they can live in this great land, with all its blessings and benefits and not pay a single penny of tax to help it remain great.

"Our nation has been beset by numerous egregious blows to our economic well-being, largely as a result of corporate excess and a narrow-minded profit mentality. Your government has spared no effort to provide financial support and assistance through a myriad of economic avenues in attempts to redirect and restore our financial vitality. And yet these corporate giants, under the transparent guise of compassion for their own exploited workers and indignant outrage at their own plight, see only an opportunistic chance to line their pockets and the pockets of their shareholders by reneging on their responsibility to pay for the services of their governments under whose protection and benevolence they have enjoyed the sheltered environment of the marketplace in which to conduct their business at home and around the world.

"The citizens of this great America, and even the citizens of nearly all nations around the globe, have come to expect that when all else fails, they can depend on the United States government to help them. Now that government has failed them.

"Let me point out, however, that it's not everyone in government who has acted irresponsibly. Many dedicated Congressmen and Senators have worked very hard to see that all citizens are assured of living their lives with dignity. But a few influential ones have labored long and hard to undermine the efforts of the others. One Senator in particular has made a career out of serving as a roadblock to the nation's progress. One Senator in particular has worked so diabolically that although he was unable to engineer the defeat of the landmark American Employment and Financial Freedom Act, passed successfully earlier this year, he is directly responsible for encouraging wealthy individuals, and groups like the TEA Party, to criminally ignore the law and illegally refuse to pay their taxes. The result, of course, has been that your government has been denied the funds you have demanded that it collect in order to provide the necessary services that you deservedly require and are entitled to expect.

"That one Senator is Mr. Henley Hornbrook, who by now must be a complete disgrace to the fine people of the great state of Washington.

"It is utterly unprecedented for a President to tell Americans, as I am about to tell you, that it is vital that they act now to help restore the integrity of their government. But these are unprecedented times. Every one of you who is a constituent of these obstructionist Senators and Congressmen, such as the shameful Mr. Hornbrook, must immediately take steps to remove or recall them from office. Your legislatures know that a sound and strong United States Treasury is imperative for their own states' economic survival, and they will undoubtedly give you guidance and help expedite the procedures for such recall movements.

"I have worked these last few months like I have never worked before, to try and solve the great problems we face in our country. Now I need your help. Together we can restore common sense, responsibility, and accountability to our government that will enable us to solve our difficulties and regain our position and reputation as the greatest nation in the history of mankind.

"Thank you all, and may God Bless America."

***

Henley Hornbrook was at his D.C. home with some of his colleagues when the President's speech was aired.

"Good God!" exclaimed Lew Weiser.

"Well now," said Henley Hornbrook, mildly. "Isn't it always nice to hear your own name on TV?"

"That was positively criminally irresponsible," growled an outraged Morton Packwood. "Has that man no shame whatsoever?"

"You hardly have to ask that question," sneered Weiser.

"Oh, Henley," said Loren McClintock, "I simply can't believe that even a louse like Dillard would stoop so low."

Just then the telephone rang on the lamp table next to Hornbrook. The LED flashed for line two for which only a select few people had the number. He leaned across the arm of the chair and picked up the handset. "Yes?"

"Senator? It's Elma. I have Senator Brownsville on the line. He called here looking for you. Would you like me to patch him through?"

"Oh, sure. Why not?" He covered the mouthpiece, and said, "Brownsville," to the others in the room. "Senator!" he began as he heard the Pennsylvanian's voice come on the line. "What have I done to deserve the personal attentions of both the President and the esteemed Senate Majority Leader on the same evening?"

"Henley, I'm terribly sorry," said Brownsville. "You did not deserve that at all. He's like a lot of people who get stumped and just lash out at the nearest target."

"A lot of people don't get to lash out on national prime time television."

"Yes, well, he is being a bit difficult about things."

"Sometimes being difficult can be an asset. Being ignorant and utterly without a clue as to how to mend this mess is unforgivable in a President."

"Yes, of course. I'm sure you know that the courts have ruled some time ago that holders of federal elective office cannot be recalled."

"Do you really think that's important? At this point I personally don't give a damn."

"Well, anyway, several of us will be meeting with him over the weekend, and hopefully we'll be able to put together an emergency package with some of the biggest banks, the Fed and maybe even the IMF, to provide some short term relief while we restructure our debt and issue some new government securities to cover the temporary shortfalls."

"Oh, for heaven's sakes," protested Hornbrook. "You're living in a dream world, just like Dillard. First of all, the International Monetary Fund is mostly *our* money to begin with, and it's a drop in the bucket compared to our problems. Second, our default here has dropped our credit worthiness to zero, not to mention that we're already in so far over our heads that we can't even imagine where the top is. Nobody is going to loan us a dime. Besides, interest rates have skyrocketed worldwide because a lot of other countries are beginning to suffer the same dilemma, mostly because of us. And if you try now to pay your bills with a lot of new rubber checks and phony greenbacks, the inflation will eat us alive, including whatever private reserves there may be left. Dillard had the chance earlier, but he didn't take it. Now it's too late."

"But—"

"No buts this time, Senator. You can't solve this problem with the same smoke-and-mirrors bullshit that we've been pulling for the past seventy-five years. The capital's gone. Up and left the building. Either flown the coop to other markets or just shriveled up and pulled back like your wienie in an ice bath. Now, I'm sure you'll have a splendid little meeting after which you can posture and wring your hands in front of the cameras and spin your little stories. I regret I won't be watching. You never cared much about what I think, so I think I'll go home and go fishing. That is, if I don't get lynched first by the President's legions of admirers."

Hornbrook hung up the phone without saying goodbye. As soon as the handset hit the cradle, it rang again, and he picked it up in anger. "What do you want now!" he said heatedly, thinking it was Brownsville again.

"Whoa, Senator, it's McCall."

"Oh, I'm sorry, Eagle. What's the good word out West?"

"Well, I hate to say it, but the natives are restless. It seems the President tapped into an exposed nerve and some of the vocal militants up Seattle way are echoing his words, and calling for action."

"Wow, that's pretty fast. Thanks for the update. Keep me posted." He put the phone down and said to the others, "Dillard's hit a nerve, and people are developing a new focus for their anger. I think it's us—or at least me."

There was some general head shaking, but Weiser responded first, rising from his chair. "I'll get us a flight. Like you said, you're probably wasting your time here, and people will think your first duty will be to come home and help your constituents, even if you can't do anything directly."

"Are you sure that's a good idea, if everyone's so angry?" asked a concerned Loren McClintock.

"Yes, Lew's right. I need to go talk to people and get things calmed down. We probably all should. First available, Lew. How are the airlines doing?"

"There's really not much problem. I don't think even a nutball like Dillard would dare cut aviation fuels to the airlines. I also have been led to believe that a lot of federal workers, including the TSA people are, in fact, still getting paid. So while the government isn't issuing other checks, it's not like the entire nation has shut down. Fortunately, we're not like a lot of countries where there is no private sector. As a matter of fact, the worst thing that could happen to the government right now is for everyone else to discover they don't need them except to break up fights."

"Good. No time like the present, then."

***

Henley Hornbrook, Loren McClintock, and Lewiston Weiser flew together on the 11:45 redeye United Airlines flight out of Dulles, through the darkness over the troubled country, to Portland, Oregon. For Hornbrook and his chief-of-staff who would be accompanying him to his home, it only added about thirty minutes to the driving time compared to coming into Seattle, and they could still travel together with Loren.

To their surprise they were met in the baggage claim area by Eagle McCall, who had been given the heads up by Elma McCleary about their return to the state. "I was glad to hear Elma say that you were flying to Portland," said McCall on the drive up Interstate 5 after they parted company with Senator McClintock, "because we'll be able to get home without attracting any attention. Freddie up at your Seattle office has already reported a number of minor incidents and threatening-type phone calls."

"What kind of incidents?" asked Weiser.

"A bunch of protesters stormed into the office within about thirty minutes of Dillard's address, demanding to see the Senator, and then busting up the place a bit before they left. Freddie called the cops, and they put an officer there and downstairs near the elevator. There were some picketers on the street outside about an hour later, but they behaved."

"Well, protesters and picketers are nothing new in politics," said Hornbrook.

"I don't think this will be routine before it's all over," warned McCall.

"What else happened?"

"One of the phone calls Freddie got was clearly menacing, talking about retribution and paying you back for your betrayal. That sort of stuff."

"Bastards," said Weiser.

"I'll bet Freddie was a bit freaked."

"Nah, she sounded fine," McCall assured them. "She was more worried because it sounded like they might come after you at home. So that's the real reason I came to get you. Some of our neighbors are taking some precautions on your behalf."

"McCall, what the hell are you up to?"

"Relax, Senator, no rough stuff. But it doesn't hurt to err on the side of safety."

"Hmmm. What a sorry state of affairs."

"Don't worry, everything's under control. Gene's got your place opened up for you and the entire area's solidly behind you."

"You've been a busy boy, haven't you?"

"I don't like surprises. But you need to know what it's like in the real world. Tomorrow I think you should talk to my brother-in-law, Tom Warner. He and his family drove up here from LA after it all first hit the fan, and it was a real nightmare: Gunfights, car chases, blockades. And they tied up a guy and left him in his highway inspection hut because he told them to turn around and go home. All with a car full of kids. They're staying at my place. Sunny's here, too, right now, and she's been pretty active also, calling and visiting a lot of people in her own district."

"Great. That will be really helpful. How about if Lew and I come over to your house after breakfast?"

Lew glanced at his watch. "Mid-morning all right?"

"Sure," said McCall. "I can use my beauty sleep, too."

An hour or so later, the Senator and chief aide slumping slightly as they snoozed, McCall guided Hornbrook's white Suburban through the gated entrance to the former game farm and glided to a smooth stop in front of the Senator's well-illuminated home. After McCall roused them from their temporary slumber, they brought their bags inside, and thanked McCall who then said his good-nights and climbed into his Bronco for the four-mile run to his own home. The hour being so late, Weiser headed straight for the guest bedroom he had used on previous occasions. A few minutes later, Hornbrook crawled gratefully into his old, but deeply comfortable bed and, in the brief moment before sleep found him, reflected that Dorothy was right: *There's no place like home.*

He had no idea how much the next few days would challenge that.

CHAPTER 25

> *"I have a feeling that at any time about three million Americans can be had for any militant reaction against law, decency, the Constitution, the Supreme Court, compassion, and the rule of reason."*
> —John Kenneth Galbraith (1908-2006)

Friday – August 27

The morning Senator Hornbrook returned from Washington, D.C. began innocently enough. Hornbrook arose after a brief but gratefully restful sleep, and shared a leisurely breakfast with Lew Weiser and Eugene Springfield, the retired next door neighbor and friend who had for many years acted as caretaker for his home. Gene lived with his brother Hugo, who had moved in with him after they had both become widowers. They had been in the Postas Valley longer than anyone else around and were fiercely proud of the Valley's favorite son, Senator Hornbrook. As they worked on the omelets, muffins, and juice that Henley had rustled up, Gene gave them his own evaluation of the news and mood in Western Washington. As always, there were enormous differences between the Puget Sound metropolitan areas of Pierce, King, and Snohomish counties, and the rural areas which constituted the rest of the state. Lots of protesters were on the city streets, posturing for the cameras and giving inflammatory soundbites for the news programs. So far, said Gene, there had been plenty of the usual "blame the rich" kinds of demonstrations, but no central focus.

"I gotta be honest, though," he added, "the 11:00 news last night did begin to carry interviews with some of these nuts who started mentioning your name, blaming you for a lot of their problems. It's really stupid, but these days a lot of people *are* stupid."

"Okay, let's just play it safe. I want to talk to people out here—that's why we came out—but we'll keep it low key. I'm not looking for publicity for this trip anyway. I just want to hear what the people are thinking. Take some ordinary precautions. Right now, I'm going over to McCall's. Lew, his number's on the kitchen speed dial if you need me." He got up from the table, and about five minutes later was negotiating the hills and turns heading up McCall's road.

***

"Hi, Mister," said a brightly smiling young girl standing next to the car when Hornbrook opened the door to climb out. "Who're you?"

"I'm Senator Hornbrook, young lady. And what's your name?"

"I'm Emily. Pleased to meet you," the youngest Warner added, sticking out her small hand to greet the stranger. "I'll go get my Mom." And she whirled around, ran up on the porch and disappeared into the house.

"MOM!" Hornbrook could hear her call out. "There's a Cen-tar out front!"

"A Centaur?" He heard an older, muffled voice answer. "This should be interesting."

Moments later Sunny Turner stepped outside. "Aw, heck. It's not a centaur after all. Hi, Henley. Welcome home."

"Hello, Sunny. It's always great to be back, isn't it?"

"And how. Whatever happens with this mess, I think I'm probably through."

"I know what you mean, but don't give up yet. We'll need clear thinkers like you before it's all over."

"Thanks, but will it? Be over soon, I mean?"

"Honestly, Sunny, you know as much as I do about what's going on there. But, no, it's far from over. Dillard's gone off the edge, and Brownsville's still carrying his hat. The prospects aren't all that hot."

"Well, Centaur," she said, smiling, "come on in and meet the rest of the gang." There were three or four young bodies of various sizes scattered about the family room evidently absorbed in a video game being played on the television. Sunny led Hornbrook on a serpentine path around them and into the kitchen, where two adults were cleaning up the breakfast dishes. Henley glanced through the French door into the dining/living room and saw McCall pacing back and forth by the sliding patio door, talking on the telephone. Seeing the motion out of the corner of his eye, McCall glanced up, saw the Senator, and gave a brief wave of acknowledgement.

Sunny introduced the Senator to Tom and Laurel Warner. "I understand you had an interesting trip up from California recently," began Hornbrook.

"You have no idea," replied Laurel, who with a grin glanced at Tom, who smiled at the line that was becoming their patented understatement of the year.

"I sure want to thank you, Senator," interjected Tom, "for your letter of safe conduct. It came in very handy a couple of times."

"Please call me Henley. And that really was McCall's idea. Sometimes his thinking is way ahead of mine. Anyway, I very much want to hear the details as soon as we can sit down and talk. Perhaps this evening."

"Oh, it's no big thing. We just left our jobs, abandoned our home and almost all our possessions, and subjected our children to ambushes and gunfights all over the West."

"Yes, we *really* have to talk."

Just then McCall came into the kitchen. "Good morning, Senator."

"Morning, McCall. Talking to your bookie?"

"Yeah, sure. Actually, it was Freddie again. Evidently, Lincoln Burbank is up to his old tricks."

"Who's he?" asked Laurel.

Hornbrook answered, "He's a rather militant activist up in Seattle. He got his start about ten years ago, stirring up trouble during some WTO meetings. Burbank was actually a homeless advocate at the time, was identified in the thick of the violence, and only managed to avoid prosecution because the police seemed to be just as guilty and nobody wanted to drag the whole ugly affair through the courts."

"And since then," continued McCall, "he's become more vocal, more militant, just generally more obnoxious."

"So what's the latest?" asked Hornbrook.

"He's using Dillard's statements last night to stir up the mob, so to speak. Right now he's holding a rally near the Pike Place Market downtown, and the word is the crowd is getting bigger and angrier. I told Freddie to go ahead and close the office, just to be on the safe side."

"Good. There's almost no purpose in being there anyway right now, so there's no point in being vulnerable. Did she follow procedures?"

"Natch. She and the others did a full sweep, and all classified, constituent, or other important papers are protected."

"Thanks, McCall. You've trained them well."

"A stint in a Middle East embassy tends to teach you things. But she and one of the other staffers are going over to the rally to just sort of hang around to see if anything comes of it."

"Okay, I hope she's got the sense to stay out of the way."

A beat up old pickup truck and a relatively late model Ford Explorer appeared in front of the house, and several people got out. McCall said, "Good, everyone's here. Senator, you said you wanted to speak to some of the neighbors."

"Right. Thanks, McCall. Is there someplace...?"

"Sure, we'll go in the living room there. Come on, Tom, I'll introduce you, too." McCall led the way outside to greet the visitors. The pickup disgorged two mountain-sized men. Each of the bearded giants was dressed in jeans supported by dirty orange suspenders with the faded Stihl logos just visible through the oil stains. Their jeans sported the shortened and torn hems favored by generations of timber fallers. Their tee shirts—one red, one green—barely contained their bulging chests and massive shoulders. Their appearance rendered them a strange and imposing hybrid of Paul Bunyan and TweedleDee/TweedleDum, indistinguishable except for their hair color. As Hornbrook felt his hand disappear into the immense paw of the first he reached, McCall said, "You remember the Hills?"

"Sure. How are you, Boomer? Red."

"Tom?" asked McCall. "I'd like you to meet Kenny Hill's nephews. This pile of rocks," he said, indicating the red-bearded one nearest his brother-in-law, "is Red Hill." McCall paused while they shook hands, "And this is Boomer. Guys, this is Tom Warner, Laurel's husband."

"Howdy, Tom," said Red.

"Hey," said Boomer, the baritone syllable giving brief but obvious evidence as to the origination of his nickname.

"A pleasure," said Tom, flexing his own hand after the two greetings. "Gee, I'd never have guessed you were related to your uncle," he added in jest. "He was a big help to us a couple of days ago."

The Hornbrook Prophecy

Hornbrook turned his attention to the SUV's passengers next, as McCall introduced his neighbors from across the road, Clark and Bertha Terwiliger, and two men from down the road, Webster Johnson and Otis Orchards.

"Clark retired from the phone company; he was a lineman," McCall began. "Web here started as a choker-setter in the woods, and now is in management for Weyerhauser. Otis has the tree farm down the road beyond the boat launch, as well as about 180 acres he puts in corn or peas." After Tom and the Senator had greeted them, they all went inside, crossed the entry, and settled in the comfortable chairs and sofas of the living room. Sunny and Laurel joined them. After Hornbrook had talked about the latest developments in the "other" Washington, the others were invited to give their own individual views.

"Bertha and I are probably the most affected in this group," began Clark, "because we get Social Security and Medicare. But we're in no dire straits since we still have the phone company retirement and some personal savings. Frankly, we pretty much eat year round out of our own garden, with canning and all. I expect a lot of retired folks aren't as well off. Just keeping the lights on may be a problem for some if they don't get their checks on time."

"I'll tell you what," interjected Web Johnson, "I'm fifty, so I've got a ways to go before I can hang it up. Our local economy's been in the dump out here for twenty-five years, all because of some goddamn spotted owl, and a bunch of other trumped-up reasons the environmentalists came up with for not cutting trees."

"I know, Web," empathized Hornbrook. He glanced up as McCall jumped up and left the room to answer the phone.

"Well, it's just stupid!" Johnson went on.

"I'm not here to debate that. But let's focus on how this breakdown is going to affect you or your job or what you think could be done to help."

"Well, I can sure as hell live without government help. But the whole economy would be given a shot in the arm if the timberlands were opened up. Look, out here, in the northwest, a good Doug fir or hemlock is harvestable in about thirty-five years. Forty, tops. Even if you allowed a good margin for error, you could still cut two percent of the timber annually and have easily sustainable growth. Christ! You'd think these environmentalist nuts who are so hell bent on recycling would jump all over the ultimate in renewable resources." Hornbrook shifted, about to try to refocus the discussion on the immediate problem, but Johnson gestured and said, "I know, I know. Keep to the point. Okay, here it is. Our whole state could get by without the feds if we didn't have to send so much of our money to them to start with, and if we could sell the resources that we have just rotting on the mountainsides. We know how to do it responsibly, so that they will last forever. We just have to be allowed."

"You'd be surprised to know I've been bribed by the President himself, not that long ago, with an offer to do just that."

"So why didn't you take it?"

"The price was too high at the time. How's the farming community, Mr. Orchards?"

Otis Orchards was in his early sixties but looked fit and trim. "We won't sell many Christmas trees this year, I expect. Most of our stock is Noble firs that go back east; some even go to Europe, especially Germany. But shipping's an unknown right now, and it's getting late to start looking for other markets. As for the feds, well, 'round here I don't know anyone who's involved in subsidy programs or whatnot, so that's not really a major problem. Again, getting the crops to market may be a problem. We just don't know. Most of my stuff stays pretty local. Frankly, though, my biggest fear—and of most of the other farmers here 'bout—is having a bunch of city folk come blasting through like a herd of locusts if their supermarkets run out of stuff."

"Otis," intoned Boomer, "I don't think it's called a 'herd' of locusts."

"Oh, for crying out loud!" was Orchards' retort. Red laughed and slapped his brother on the back.

"Otis may not be far off the mark," announced McCall who had come back into the room a few moments before. "That was Freddie again. Burbank's on the move. They commandeered a bunch of city buses and were supposed to be heading for Olympia. She said they were talking about storming the Capitol to get the attention of the legislature and the Governor."

"The legislature's not even in session," said Sunny, "but I suppose they'll be happy as long as they get some TV coverage."

"Frankly, Senator," added a concerned looking McCall, "I wouldn't put it past Burbank to come knocking on your front door."

"I can't see that even Lincoln Burbank would be that dopey. It accomplishes nothing to tar and feather me. His followers gain no money, no food, no security. Nothing."

"Except his being the one man in America who finally delivers what the President called for."

Hornbrook considered the situation. "I still don't think so. He's got a lot more to gain by chasing the Governor up a tree. The legislature would give him the key to the state vault before they'd stand up to a mob like that."

"I hope you're right, Senator," concluded McCall. And he left the room again.

Hornbrook and the others continued their discussions for some time. McCall wandered in and out of the room over the next hour, and when he wasn't on the phone he was never more than two steps from where he left it sitting on the counter. When it rang next, he grabbed it and punched the "Talk" button before the first ring had finished. He listened a few moments, asked a couple of short questions, and hung up. Without hesitation, he walked into the living room. Sunny and Tom Warner were in one corner with the Hill brothers, while Laurel, Orchards, the Terwiligers, and Web Johnson were speaking with Hornbrook.

"Senator."

McCall's voice and tone had also caused everyone to stop and look up. Hornbrook broke off his discussion with Web Johnson, saw the expression on McCalls's face and said, "Yes, McCall. What's up?"

"I just talked with Freddie again. When she reported that Burbank and his gathering had grabbed the buses and taken off, I had her hustle back to her car and try to catch up to them to see what was up. As you know, she's got one of your U.S. Senate passes so she's okay to drive around. When she hit Olympia, she got off at the downtown exit and headed for the Capitol plaza, which had been their announced destination. But the buses weren't there. That's when she called. She's lost them entirely."

"Maybe they went somewhere else altogether."

"Senator, I think we need to consider the possibility that they never intended to make a fuss in Olympia, that they never intended to even stop there," said McCall, beginning to adopt a "game face" that he had not worn since his service in the Army.

"So where else would they have gone?" asked Sunny, getting a chill down her spine just looking at him and sensing his answer.

"Sir, I think they're headed here," replied McCall. "I called the NPU outpost, which was stopping traffic at the 101 split. They hadn't seen or heard anything yet, but are shutting down the highway until we know more."

"How are they doing that?" asked Tom.

"They dropped trees across the road from both sides. They can clear them away easily enough, but if Burbank shot through Olympia on his way here, that'll stop 'em and we'll know it in a couple of minutes."

The Senator was silent for a moment. He wasn't afraid to acknowledge that he was out of his depth for something like this. "McCall, this is obviously a concern, not just for me, but for everyone around here. What do you suggest we do?"

Just then the phone rang again. McCall answered, listening closely, a frown creeping onto his brow. "Right. Thanks." He turned back toward the Senator. "That was the NPU outpost. They haven't seen any buses or other big groups. They said everything's pretty quiet."

"So where the hell did Burbank go?" said Hornbrook.

"Right now, sir, I obviously can't answer that. But I'd like your permission to initiate some precautionary measures." McCall didn't specify what he meant.

"If you think it's necessary."

McCall left the room, nodding at Red, Boomer, and Tom, who followed him out.

"Hey, Mom!" came a voice from the family room. "Come here, quick!"

Laurel rushed out of the living room and had her attention directed to the television, where there was a breaking news report about a series of robberies at sporting goods and gun stores in Olympia. Laurel immediately called out to Hornbrook and the others. They all watched a summary by the on-scene reporter,

"To recap, we first had four Sound Transit buses evidently hijacked from their service routes in downtown Seattle allegedly by a large group of people who had been attending a Lincoln Burbank rally. We have reports that some of the hijackers brandished knives or pistols, but we have no confirmation of that. We also have no confirmation as to whether Burbank himself was involved or whether he is with the buses at this time. The buses then got on I-5 southbound and headed toward Olympia. Witnesses in Seattle reported hearing that the group was going to go to the Capitol and/or Governor's Mansion, but the group has not been seen in this city as of yet. As a matter of fact, no one seems to know the current whereabouts of the buses.

"There is also breaking news right now about armed robberies that have occurred at three local stores where firearms are sold—a Big 5 in West Olympia, Gart Sports in Lacey, and Big Tony's Guns in downtown Olympia. We have no evidence as to whether the perpetrators in these robberies were working together,

but the timing seems like too big a coincidence to be otherwise. An exact accounting is not yet available, but at all three locations, the robbers took pistols, rifles, and shotguns of various makes and models, as well as ammunition. Each of the robberies—from entry to exit—lasted less than three or four minutes, indicating that those responsible planned the entire attack in advance. By the time the police were summoned to the scenes the robbers had departed. There were apparently two getaway vehicles used at each location, including a minivan or full size van, and license plate numbers of the getaway vehicles were noted by store employees at two of the locations. The identified vehicles have already been found, abandoned. No doubt the perpetrators had other vehicles waiting for them.

"Finally, although the buses that were hijacked were supposed to be heading for Olympia, and the robberies occurred about the time the buses were to have arrived in the Capitol, there is no evidence as yet that the two incidents were related in any way. Back to you, Linda."

"So where the hell is Burbank now?" asked Hornbrook.

As if in response to his question, the female television anchor said,

"Thank you, Charles. The police have just told us that the buses went straight on through Olympia and headed south on Interstate 5. The state patrol closed and blockaded I-5 on the north side of Centralia and have set out spiked tire strips in order to stop the buses. It's only a twenty-minute trip to Centralia, but as of this moment—which is about twenty-four minutes after the buses are thought to have left Olympia—they have not arrived or been seen in or near Centralia.

And that's all the details we have right now. Bill?"

"Okay, now I'm really confused," said the Senator. "But I don't like it. What on earth are they up to?"

"No good, and that's for sure," offered Otis Orchards. "A bunch of nuts swiping buses and running around shouting slogans is one thing, but if they've got anything to do with a bunch of gun thieves, then we've got quite another."

They were still discussing the events, when McCall and Tom Warner came back into the house. Hornbrook quickly filled them in on the developments related on the TV report. "Well, that certainly changes the equation," said Tom.

"True," agreed McCall, "but the steps we've taken so far are still the right first steps. Red and Boomer are part of the North Powder Union, and they are putting the NPU plan for county isolation into readiness."

"Fill me in," said Hornbrook.

"Okay. There are less than a dozen roads of significance leading into the county. The first stage is dropping trees across the roads at key points. Long ago they identified the best suited trees at each choke point. Each of those will soon be wearing some explosive PrimaCord around the trunk, cleverly positioned so that when detonated it will drop the tree in a pre-determined direction. And all the trees at any given site are wired in parallel to a central trigger so that, when required, a single, out-of-view operator can drop all the trees simultaneously. I don't care what you're driving, you can't ram through a pile of 18-inch logs very quickly. The trees can be cut away, but it buys time in case long-term or permanent closure is required."

"Sounds good."

"That's the beginning. They've also sent out over thirty observers to strategic lookout locations around the county, where the highways can be observed at a distance, or where there are important logging roads that could give access to knowledgeable intruders. Those routes aren't ready to quick fire but progress over such roads is comparatively slow enough to allow other appropriate reaction in a timely manner."

"Is that it?" said Hornbrook, marveling at the efficient organization of the group.

"For now. The next stage is alerting a network of people throughout the area who can get the word out about an imminent threat. Let me clarify something about the NPU. These guys don't play war games, or want to overthrow the government, or anything like that. They are just concerned about being able to keep things under control in this area in case of a serious natural or social disaster, at least if the police were unable to, and it's obvious in many places around the country that the authorities have indeed been unable to control the civil unrest. This is the first time they've ever actually taken any action of any kind, but they feel they're ready to."

"Well, for God's sakes, I hope this is all just an exercise for them."

There was no further news forthcoming for the rest of the day about the whereabouts of the Burbank mob, as they were being referred to locally, for want of a better description. They apparently vanished before reaching Centralia. There was lots of speculation, but little official action to resolve the mystery.

The Terwiligers, Web Johnson, and Otis Orchards all left to meet with other neighbors and take care of matters at their homes. The Hills did not reappear that day. Senator Hornbrook went back to his home to see what news

Lew Weiser might have from D.C. and to talk about it all over dinner with Gene and Hugo Springfield.

Laurel Warner had an uneasy feeling she couldn't shake. She and Tom spent a quiet, serious evening talking with her brother and Sunny about the bizarre events of the day involving Lincoln Burbank and the vanishing buses. They speculated about their behavior, their whereabouts, and their intentions. Laurel was thinking only about the potential threat to her children's safety. She could not help thinking that it was horribly ironic that they might have fled one menace only to be caught up in a greater one. Sunny was unusually silent, apparently caught in her own thoughts and perhaps sharing Laurel's maternal fear of family dangers.

Tom and Eagle settled into a quiet private discussion, broken only when Eagle dashed into another room to grab a road or topographical map; sometimes he wrote on the maps or made other drawings to explain an idea. Later, they went out to the shop for a while. It was nearly midnight when they turned out the lights and the household finally fell silent.

Chapter 26

> *"Righteous ends, once justified, absolve of guilt the most violent means."*
> —Robert Ardrey (1908-1980)

Saturday – August 28

The image of a huge Chinook salmon breaking the surface of the fog-shrouded river and thrashing to break free of the hook lodged in its mouth ought to have brought a satisfied smile to McCall's face, but instead he frowned, because something was wrong. Something was out of place, and he fought to understand the mystery. It was the noise! It shouldn't be noisy! It was early morning, dawn's weak light struggling to lift the reluctant veil of night, foggy, a light mist over the river, and yet there was a cacophony of overwhelming and increasing discordance that pounded into his head and paralyzed his brain. Then, in the midst of an anguished convulsion six inches above the water, the fish froze in place, the scenery fragmented, and the pieces dissolved as the noise coalesced into an incessant ringing sound.

The jarring of the telephone finally penetrated the deep sleep that McCall had been enjoying. He lurched to his left and by the time he had grabbed the phone and brought it to his ear his feet were hitting the carpet. He said, "McCall."

"McCall? It's Boomer. We've got trouble—big trouble. The Burbank mob is inside our perimeter!" McCall listened for a few minutes while Boomer told him what they had just discovered, then he hung up and punched the speed dial for the Senator's home. After six frustrating rings, Hornbrook answered the phone, sounding a bit groggy.

"Senator! There's a problem. Burbank's on his way."

"I guess you were right all along. Are your NPU friends closing the roads?"

"That's the problem. They're already inside. They evidently holed up in the Skookumchuk Forest after leaving Olympia. This has evidently been in the works for a while—it's not just a bunch of rally goers deciding to take action. Look, Senator, all this begs the issue here."

"Which is?"

"There's no reason for them to be out in this rural area other than looking for *you*. And I don't think they've gone to all this trouble just to request a lunch meeting."

"What are you saying, McCall?"

"I think you're in danger, sir."

"You implied that yesterday."

"Yes, sir, and I'm even more convinced now. They've gone to extraordinary lengths to hide their movements and get where they are, and there's no other rational explanation. Boomer just told me that his guys discovered them when Burbank's outfit came storming past their observation post. The NPU didn't try to stop them because they said these guys jumped out of the pickups they were in and were all carrying weapons. A number of shots were fired, but our guys escaped without harm. I don't think it's a mystery any longer who robbed the gun stores yesterday. And I don't think we should dismiss the obvious."

"All right, McCall. What do you suggest?"

"We have to play it safe. Your home and the surrounding area is too open, with too many access routes, and too hard to protect or defend if it comes to any sort of confrontation. You need to round up Lew, and the Springfields, and anyone else nearby who might get caught being in the wrong place at the wrong time and get them all over here. In my little valley, there's only one road in, the river is a good defense on our flank, and we can command the high ground around us. In short, Senator, it's time to pull back inside the castle walls."

"I suppose you're right."

"I hope I'm wrong."

"Okay," agreed Hornbrook finally. "I'll get started, but first I'm going to call the Governor and request some National Guard assistance."

"Time is of the essence, sir. I'll send Clark Terwiliger over with his pickup to collect you and your essentials." He hung up without saying goodbye, and next made calls to the Terwiligers', to Web Johnson, and to Otis Orchards. Then he lurched over to the closet, dressed quickly in his BDUs and boots, and went to wake Tom. After getting a quick summary, Tom leapt out of bed. McCall went over a few more ideas and then left the room.

Within a few minutes the ranch house was a beehive of activity. After a quick trip out to the shop with McCall, Tom reappeared in the kitchen with a few backpacks, and gathered Sunny, Laurel, Ellie, Kate, Tommy, and Angel around. "Okay, guys, recess is over. Here we go again." He gave them a rundown on the morning's developments, assuming the businesslike efficiency that had served him so well in numerous hospital emergencies. "Uncle Eagle doesn't know exactly what we're up against, so primarily we're going to make ourselves scarce. I've got our walkie-talkies here, and another pair from Eagle. They're all set to the same channel so keep them on and keep them with you if you're away from the house. We're not going to wage war; we're going to stay out of the way. Our job will mostly be to act as lookouts and observers, but the people around here are going to defend their homes. Tommy?"

"Yes, Dad," said the wide-eyed boy.

"Take these," Tom said, giving him a backpack with a pair of binoculars and one of the walkie-talkies, "and get on down the road to the Johnson's. Callie's going to take you on her horse up to the hilltop above the road up on Quiet Creek Hill." Since the Warners arrived several weeks earlier, Tommy had gotten to know the neighbor's daughter who was just a year younger and an avid 4-H rider. McCall let the Johnsons use his pastures to graze their two horses. "Tie the horse below the ridge, but nearby, and find a good place to hide up there where you can see the road. Just keep an eye out and call in anytime you see people moving—"

"Wait just a cotton-pickin' minute!" cried Laurel. "Are you crazy? We just spent three days dodging bullets and lunatics. And now you want to send these CHILDREN out on a dangerous mission like they're soldiers? I don't THINK so!"

"Mom—!" Tommy began to protest.

"Be quiet!"

As Sunny, remembering her own losses, moved over and put her arm around Laurel's shoulders, Eagle looked at the tears welling up in his sister's eyes. "I know, Laurel," he began in as comforting a tone as he could muster. "I know they're not soldiers. But Callie knows these hills as well as any grownup. Probably better. They don't have to do anything except stay out of sight, watch and call in on the walkie-talkie."

Seeing Laurel forming another protest on her lips, Tom quickly added, "And we're going to need all the adults for the heavy lifting." His jaw tensed as he added firmly, "I-will-not-let-harm-come-to-them."

Sunny found her voice. "Laurel, you know I've known the losses you fear. Old or young, it doesn't matter. It's terrible. But I swore I'd never feel helpless again. And if crazies are coming after us and our loved ones then, by God, we must stop them. We can *all* help."

"But—" she said, almost weak with worry.

"They'll be safe," Tom said with firmness in his voice. And then he resumed giving his directions. "Everyone needs to wear some of this tied around your arm." He reached in the bag and pulled out a roll of bright orange vinyl contractor's tape. Laurel grabbed it, worry having switched to anger, and started to cut it into two-foot lengths, as Tom added, "This will help you see who the good guys are. All the NPU guys are wearing it. So, Tommy, if somebody you don't recognize starts to get too close to you, just keep pulling back to other spots along the ridge. Ellie?"

"Yes?"

"I want you and Angel to get up on top of that ridge across the river and do the same thing. Work your way along it until you reach that tall hill above Foggy Ranch. You can take Uncle Eagle's ATV. It's been clear cut there, so you'll have a good view. Just stay out of sight." He gave them another backpack with another set of binoculars and a walkie-talkie. Angel grabbed the bag and, noting its weight, looked inside to find the Calico with both magazines. He looked up and saw Tom looking directly at him. Angel nodded his head slightly. Tom continued, "Laurel, give Tommy and Ellie water bottles and some food to take. Nobody's had breakfast and I don't know how long this may last." Laurel glared at him, but complied. "Kate?"

"Here, Dad," said his second daughter, standing behind his right shoulder.

"You get this walkie-talkie. We don't have enough radios for everyone around here, so you're going to be our courier. Get over and ask Mrs. Terwiliger if you can borrow their quad. Call me if there's a problem. Now, everyone, if there's an emergency and we need to get out of here, go straight up the road and through the trees past the end of the pavement to Old Bridge Park. We'll all meet there."

***

When Lincoln Burbank had stolen the city transit buses and headed south, estimates put his manpower strength at close to two hundred. Based on some subsequent police reports made available to the Senator, McCall assumed that a high percentage of them were now armed. The transit buses had been abandoned in favor of pickup and flatbed trucks, and an old blue school bus that someone had hot-wired and taken from a church south of Olympia. They had hidden in the Skookumchuk Forest at a pre-arranged location where others were waiting with food, drink, and other supplies. One of the locals who had set up the camp originally had known some of the back roads that made access to the forest easy. The summer weather had cooperated and the blankets they had were more than sufficient for the night. The northwest sky stayed light until after 10 pm, and then many of the group lit small campfires and stayed up most of the rest of the night. Burbank himself went from group to group, keeping their emotions channeled in his direction, outraged over their treatment at the hands of leaders like Henley Hornbrook. By the time dawn broke, the group was convinced that retribution would be theirs only if they showed the world they were not to be ignored, made Hornbrook pay for his legislative sins and, in doing so, earn the respect and gratitude of President Dillard.

Lincoln Burbank's goal was to make a citizen's arrest of Senator Hornbrook and parade him through the poorer Seattle and Tacoma neighborhoods, before accepting his "resignation." He figured the rally, the hijacking of the city buses, and their mysterious disappearance would lend a certain mystique to his persona, and enlarge what he envisioned as his legend, so that upon his triumphant return with Hornbrook, his standing in the community would be unquestioned and truly influential. He had known nothing of the gun store robberies by some of his more radical followers until after their arrival in the campground. He applauded their courage and initiative, but chided them for raising the stakes unnecessarily. Nonetheless, he ultimately figured that the appearance of a large and armed force of street refugees would intimidate a "suit" like Hornbrook into submission. He even began to think of himself as leading an impromptu liberation army in a form of popular rebellion that would end up in the history books.

Burbank had not known of the existence of the North Powder Union, or of their resolve not to allow lawless brigands to destroy their property or threaten their families. However, the two sleepy NPU members at the observation post would have been taken by complete surprise had not one of them had gotten up to respond to a extreme sense of urinary urgency and heard the mob coming up the road. Their only option was to grab their phone and hightail it as rifle shots chased them into the woods. Once they realized they were not being pursued, they dialed their area coordinator, Red Hill, and related their story.

The Hornbrook Prophecy

The sudden appearance of the Burbank mob, not at their doorstep but already within their home borders, shook the NPU's confidence, but they reacted quickly. After he hung up the phone, Red talked quickly with his brother and then they both set about passing along the alarm, setting in motion procedures to alert those certain key persons, places, and resources they had prioritized in advance for protection. Every NPU member knew they were not to initiate any gunfire or other offensive action without being under direct threat and without having been fired upon. The initial gunshots fired had defined the nature of and the intentions of the mob, and everyone was warned about this serious development. The mob was armed and therefore dangerous. Before the day was out, people on both sides were likely to get hurt.

The next encounter between the NPU and the Burbank mob occurred at the bridge on the highway leading into Postas. The mob had returned to the major road after exiting the forest. A dozen or so NPU members had been summoned to reinforce the four men already on duty there, and they had all hunkered down, waiting behind some concrete bumpers just over the bridge. One of the men, a logging road builder for Port Blakely Tree Farms, positioned his dump truck and its pup to block both westbound lanes; a cable median fence would keep anyone from crossing to the other lanes.

When Burbank arrived, he ordered the group to stop short of the bridge, and got out to address the men he spotted crouching behind the barricade across the bridge. "My name is Lincoln Burbank," he shouted, "and I have been directed by the President of the United States to meet with Senator Henley Hornbrook. You must let us pass!"

"I don't care if you are *Abraham* Lincoln, buster," replied one of the NPU men. "You ain't coming this way without showing me something a little more official. And then you can come through alone—your hired thugs ain't getting through here no matter what!"

The man who'd been driving Burbank's truck got out, pulling his stolen semi-automatic shotgun with him. "Is this official enough for you!" he yelled, and then he brought the gun to bear and started pulling the trigger. The tremendous explosion from the shotgun reverberated through the canyon, shattering the early morning quiet, and catching both sides by surprise. Others standing in the pickup bed above him opened fire across the bridge, and soon they were joined by a multitude of others.

The sudden and sustained fury of the fusillade made it impossible for the NPU men to do anything but cower down even lower behind their cover. A couple of them curled on the ground, covering their ears. After a few moments the others realized they had to return fire just to slow the onslaught down enough to let them escape. They made a quick plan. On a signal by one of the leaders when there was a lessening of incoming fire, they sat up and quickly aimed their own rifles and shotguns, firing off three or four rounds each in succession as they had been coached, conserving ammunition but laying down an effective blanket of fire.

The very first shot by the NPU had passed less than a half of an inch from the side of Lincoln Burbank's head, and would have missed everything had not his ear stuck out at a congenitally-odd angle. As the bullet ripped through the thin flesh, blood erupted from it, and the pain and shock of it dropped Burbank like a brick. He started screaming as though he'd been mortally wounded, and it caused those around him to break off their gunfire and stare toward their fallen leader. Another man lying on his back attracted virtually no attention from his compatriots, perhaps because he made no noise at all, two .30-06 bullets having made parallel paths through his chest.

In the unexpected break, the NPU men ran crouched over into the cover of the trees. One of them had parked on the small frontage road next to the highway, and they all piled into the back of the truck as he jumped in the cab, got it started, and did a quick 180-degree turn around before gunning it the four miles back toward town.

Burbank's wound was attended to easily and, with his head wrapped in gauze, the ferocious sneer that was now occupying his face made him a frightening figure. "Do you not see what I've been telling you all along?" he shouted at his followers. "We ask to have a meeting, and they try to kill us! No! Not try—they already HAVE killed one of us!" It was a convenient rearrangement of the facts, but it suited the mood of those present. "They don't want to just starve us and give us no means to clothe and house us! They want us eradicated! Stepped on like so many diseased cockroaches! *WELL, NOT ANYMORE! TODAY WE TAKE CHARGE! TODAY WE MAKE THEM PAY!*"

The crowd was now truly a mob. It did not take too much time to maneuver around the nose of the dump truck out onto the shoulder of the highway and pass by with their own vehicles. Soon they were careening down the highway again. A few minutes later, they left the highway, turning north toward the mountains and following a narrow, chip-sealed, two-lane road alongside the Postas River, heading for the address they had for Hornbrook's home. They did not notice a man in hunter's camouflage clothing sitting casually on a rock just inside the tree line about fifty yards from the corner of the highway-road intersection, nor did they notice as he picked up his cell phone as they passed.

***

The NPU observer's phone call to the Union's headquarters—in fact, a taxidermy store south of town—triggered several actions. Because he reported that the mob-army was heading up the Postas Valley without splitting up, the Hills were called immediately and given estimates on the mob's strength. Second, for the same reason, reinforcements were called for from other areas of the county where they had been prepared to defend other potential targets.

Boomer immediately called McCall with a summary of the bridge siege. McCall thought quickly. Burbank's strength was as great as had been estimated—easily two hundred—and as well-armed. McCall and his neighbors were outnumbered by nearly ten to one. They had to keep the mob-army from spreading out; if it broke up into smaller groups their own defenses would be spread too thin. McCall had to keep it concentrated, which meant bringing them up his own road which was in a narrow river valley and which, aside from a few small pastures offered no other access besides driving up the road or walking up the river. If Burbank knew enough to head up the Postas Valley, he must know where the Senator lived. McCall had to give Burbank a reason to head up McCall's road instead, but it would be dangerous. *Oh, well*, he thought.

The next problem was how to stop them when they *did* come up the road. Most of the people in the mob might be angry, but deep down they were just people with problems. Or so he hoped. So that meant no lethal force, if at all possible. Instead, McCall had to gamble that they were mostly just ordinary people with relatively few reactionary zealots. And ordinary people would normally come to their senses if they realized what they were doing wasn't worth the risk. These people had to have the sense knocked back into them. *Maybe <u>scared</u> back into them*, he thought. *Hmmm.* Then he smiled.

***

McCall, Tom, Web Johnson, Clark Terwiliger, and the Hill brothers gathered in McCall's shop. They had a topographical map of their small valley spread out on the table saw, as he explained his surprising idea for repelling the attack.

"What we need is to frighten them enough to turn around and run."

"And how are we supposed to do that?" asked the skeptical Web.

"Simple. We'll use a bunch of small, homemade bombs!" The surprise was complete, but when McCall explained what he had in mind, some taut grins appeared and heads began nodding in agreement.

"That's amazing!" said Tom. "I had no idea you could make napalm that easily."

"Well, it's not exactly napalm, and it won't have the same high explosive nature, but that's good—we don't want to pile up casualties. We know they lost a man in the exchange at the bridge, but we can defend that as justifiable because they fired on our guys first. We'd have a harder time explaining away an outright ambush. All we want is to spread a little fear and this should do it. Fire exploding and raining down on your head tends to do that."

Boomer asked, "So how's this gonna work?"

"We have to do it right here," said McCall, pointing at a spot on the map, "because it's the narrowest part of the valley. The hillsides are steep and the rocks in the river right through there are harder to negotiate with the water so low. So they'll pretty much be forced to keep to the road. If we're up on the high ground, we'll be in position to stop them."

Johnson protested. "Jesus, McCall, you're going to let them waltz almost all the way up the road unmolested, and then hope that this stuff works! What if it doesn't? My house is the first one here, just around the bend from where you want to do this. If this fails, my place is toast. And the rest of you are not that much further. Why not try something further down the valley, so if they get through it and keep coming we've still got some room to fight?"

"No, Web," said Red Hill. "McCall's right. We can't fight them toe-to-toe. There's too many of them. We'd get creamed. This makes sense. We'll take a chance. If it works, great! If it doesn't, then we just retreat to the woods."

"And if they destroy our homes?"

Red calmly replied, "Better than being dead."

Boomer asked McCall again, "So how's this gonna work? How are we going to deliver these bombs on target from a safe distance? You sure as hell can't throw them far enough to hit more than the closest part of the road, even from the top of the bluff."

Tom Warner answered that, "Mortars!"

Boomer looked up at him and raised an eyebrow. "Mortars? I'll bet even McCall doesn't know how to cook *those* up in a hurry."

"Actually, he does," said Tom, matter-of-factly. "We used to have water balloon wars in college. We used to launch the balloons at the frats using giant slingshots made out of six-foot lengths of surgical tubing tied to a rag or something for the pocket of the sling."

"What did you use for the fork of the slingshot?" asked Boomer.

"Nothing! We just had two guys spread their feet fore-and-aft, and hold the tubing with straight arms. Then another guy put the balloon in the sling, stretched it back, and let her rip!"

"That's absurd. Even if the balloons don't dissolve from this stuff in them, I'd be willing to bet the acceleration when you let go would so fast that the balloons would burst even before they left the sling."

"Funny you mention that, Web," said McCall. "They actually did exactly that. We had to limit our pull to prevent premature 'detonation.' But that's not a problem for what we have in mind. We're going to put the stuff in glass containers. I originally thought of just chucking them off the bluff, but as Boomer pointed out, we wouldn't have much range. Tom's mortar idea solves that little detail. And glass containers are even more impressive when they hit something. All we have to do is rig some kind of fuse."

"Hey!" exclaimed Tom. "I think I've got the answer to that, too. Last year when we were up here for Fourth of July, Tommy got a bunch of fireworks at that tribal reservation south of here. Remember? You can't buy fireworks in LA, so it was a real treat for us. But some of that stuff was pretty powerful, like M80s or something. When we found out, I wouldn't let Tommy use them. As far as I know, he left the whole bag here."

"Geez, Tom, I haven't seen them."

"Hang on." And Tom ran out of the shop. A few minutes later, he was back with a plastic sack full of little round firecrackers. "I called him on the radio. He had stashed them on a shelf in the garage. If we get this going fast enough, we can take some practice shots and figure out how long the fuses ought to be. They don't have to be too accurate. Air bursts would be even more effective than impacts, I would think, and the timing is easier."

"Perfect," said McCall. "Now all we need is tubing."

"I've got enough for two," said Red, without explaining further. He left.

Clark offered, "I don't have any surgical tubing, but we've got a pile of old bicycles at our place from the kids, and grandkids. The tire tubes ought to work just as well. And Bertha's got a huge stockpile of canning jars that should do the trick for the vessels. Pints, quarts, and smaller ones, like for jam."

"All right, you and Web go get that stuff. Boomer, we need time! The Senator and I will give them a reason to come up our road, but you need to delay their progress until things are ready here. Remember, we want them to keep coming, just not too fast. So nothing major; after the Senator and I pull our retreat routine, just drop enough trees to slow them up, and to keep them from stringing out. We want them kept in a group. But we need a good hour. Maybe more. And one more thing: I don't want them getting past that the bend before Web's house. Not a foot. Drop the whole hillside down if you have to, Boomer."

"Got it!" Boomer left in a lumbering trot.

"Roomie?" said McCall, turning to Tom. "You missed your calling. But you're going to have to handle things here for a while. I've got to get down the road and lure them up this way. I'll be back in time to help you with the stuff."

"Here's hoping," said Tom.

"Yeah."

***

McCall and Hornbrook tore down the road as fast as they could in McCall's Bronco. Ellie had radioed that the mob-army was in sight, not too far away from where McCall's road split off from the main road leading to the Senator's ranch.

"I must say, McCall, I can't remember the last time I was staked out as bear bait," said Hornbrook. He would have been much more worried had it not been for his complete faith in his special assistant.

"Just remember, when I say 'Go' you gotta go!" McCall reminded the Senator. "Jump in the truck and we'll scram. I have some NPU guys who will make them keep their heads down long enough for us to get around the first bend in the road."

"Okay."

"Did you get hold of the Governor?"

"Yes. He claimed to be worried about Burbank and his mob, but said he couldn't send any Guard units out to help because they were now under overall command of Dillard and the military."

"Even if he could it will take some time either way, and I think things will be over and done with here in a couple of hours, tops." His radio crackled, and he held it up and keyed the mike. "McCall here."

"Uncle Eagle?" the voice was faint and broken with static. The walkie-talkies were supposed to be good up to two miles, and they were probably pushing that limit where they were.

"Yes, go ahead."

The Hornbrook Prophecy

"It's me, Ellie. Me and Angel are up on the . . . above Foggy Ranch. We can see your Bronco on . . . now. We . . . also see a whole . . . trucks. . . bus . . . just the other side of the . . . launch."

"Okay, keep your eyes open, especially if any of them split off and head up the main road. Then they'll be on your side of the river and you'll really need to be careful."

"Was that one of your nieces?" asked the Senator.

"Yes, sir, Tom's eldest. She's with a friend of theirs who came up with them. I'm sorry you didn't get a chance to talk to Tom about their adventure. But Angel, the kid she's with up there, was a big help, and had to shoot up a truck that was chasing them even though he had a dislocated shoulder from an earlier ambush."

"My God," exclaimed Hornbrook, "they've been through a lot, haven't they?"

"Yes, sir, and right now I don't think I did them any favors by getting them to leave LA. Okay, here we go." They rounded the curve and found themselves at the intersection with the road up to Hornbrook's house. There were three men with orange armbands who, upon identifying McCall, stepped out from behind some trees. McCall did a quick U-turn and parked in the middle of his road, halfway between the intersection and the first curve. He and Hornbrook got out, leaving their doors open and the engine running. McCall instructed the Senator to stand near the rear of the car but within a step of cover behind it. Then he trotted over to the NPU men.

"Hi, guys! Fun and games is about to start, so listen carefully. I need a tree down here, across the road between the intersection and the Bronco. Then I need three or four more down across the other road up from the intersection. And we're about to get company, so I need it quick!"

"We're on it," said one of the men. Two of them grabbed chain saws and trotted across the intersection. Five minutes later, the main road was completely blocked, and the men came back. Just then the first truck of the mob-army came rolling up over a small hill leading a convoy which was close behind. One of the men with the saws quickly went to work on a large hemlock jutting out at the top of the embankment over the road, and let it crash down just before Burbank's truck pulled up. McCall quickly instructed the men to throw their saws into the back of his Bronco and take their rifles and find a place where they could hide but provide cover for them if he signaled, which he would do by dropping his truce flag.

"Way ahead of you, Mr. McCall. We've got our own truck up there already, on one of the road spurs off the C-line. We have a clear view from there, and can take off right up C-line if we have to. The men quickly scampered up the hill to a small outcropping of rocks, leaving McCall and the Senator to welcome the oncoming horde. McCall grabbed a white towel off the seat and started to wave it back and forth over his head.

***

Seeing both roads blocked, Burbank's convoy had to come to a quick halt. Afraid of a possible ambush, he instructed one of his lieutenants to jump out and carefully scout the scene. The man quickly spotted the white flag waving fifty yards up the road the other side of another fallen tree on the small side road. He turned back to Burbank. "Mr. Burbank, I think somebody wants to talk. I don't see but two guys next to a single truck."

Burbank was acutely conscious of the pounding pain on the left side of his head, but he got cautiously out of the pickup and walked up to the tree where he could see the man with the flag. He nodded at his aide, who then shouted, "WHAT THE HELL DO YOU WANT?"

The man on the driver's side of the vehicle stopped waving the flag, and shouted back, "I HEAR YOU WANT TO TALK TO SENATOR HORNBROOK!"

"MAYBE SO! WHO ARE YOU?"

"I'M NOT IMPORTANT, BUT THE SENATOR IS RIGHT HERE IF YOU'D LIKE TO TALK!"

That was when Burbank noticed the other man standing at the rear corner of the SUV, and realized that it was Hornbrook himself. *Goddamn! There he is,* he thought. *He's come right to his own funeral!* Burbank stepped out into view and spoke out, "HORNBROOK, YOU—." He broke off abruptly as his own shouts seemed to make his head explode and he grabbed it in pain. Then, as it subsided, he heard another voice call out.

"WHAT'S THE MATTER, BURBANK? CUT YOURSELF SHAVING?" said Hornbrook, seeing the familiar figure with his head bandaged, and unable to contain his contempt for this would-be terrorist.

"GOD DAMN YOU, HORNBROOK!" shouted Burbank, ignoring the pain in his growing rage. "YOU ARE THE CAUSE OF ALL THIS!"

"OH, DON'T BE AN IDIOT, BURBANK."

"SCREW YOU!" And just as the aspiring avenger for the poor turned to call his new army into action, McCall pulled his white towel down and threw it on the ground, yelling at Hornbrook, *"GO! GO! GO!"*

The NPU men up on the hill immediately opened fire at the mob, aiming harmlessly over their heads but causing everyone on Burbank's side of the felled trees to duck down instinctively. The delay it caused was more than enough time for McCall to gun the Bronco up the road, around the curve, and out of sight. Just as soon as McCall had disappeared, the NPU ceased fire, and withdrew far enough up the road to join the Hills and their crew.

Burbank's rage was barely contained, but his language wasn't, and he unleashed a long string of profanities. Eventually he calmed down enough to make himself understood. His first order sent several men in a truck back into town, where they sought out a store where chain saws were sold, and stole several of them at gun point. Upon their return, Burbank directed the chain saws to cut away the solitary tree so they could chase after Hornbrook. As his orders were being carried out, his longtime assistant, a man named Frank, took him aside and said, "Lincoln, Hornbrook lives up *this* way," he said, indicating the main road. "That was almost like he was daring us to come after him. We should think twice about following him, 'cause we don't know what's up there."

"I don't give a shit what's up there! *HE'S* up there! And we're *gonna* get him."

"At least let me send some of the men up the other side of the river just in case it's a trick."

The man made sense, even through Burbank's anger. "All right, take twenty or thirty for it."

"I'll just send ten. They won't make as much noise or be seen as easily."

"Fine. But we're ready to go." Burbank got back in his own truck while the aide took off to select his own group. The chain saws cleared away the main road sufficiently to pass, and the two groups split off on separate paths.

High up on the ridge above Foggy Ranch, the split had gone unobserved by Ellie and Angel because, while their vantage point had given them view of most of the lower stretch of her uncle's road, they could not see the intersection itself.

***

McCall's ranch was a madhouse. He had returned with the Senator from their encounter with Burbank and found that most of the small valley's residents had gathered to see what needed to be done. There were several tri- or quad-ATV's out front; even a few saddled horses were munching grass on the front lawn.

McCall had first shown Tom and Clark Terwiliger how to make the explosives he had in mind. "It's pretty simple. Just take one of these big buckets, here, fill it about half full with gasoline, then take this stuff," he said, pulling out the contents of a bunch of boxes he had thrown down out of the loft in the shop, "and break it up into pieces and dissolve it in the gas. Just add enough to make it kind of thickened, like gravy. That's it."

"Wow!" exclaimed a surprised Tom. "Simple as pie."

"But for God's sake, no smoking!"

"Duh!"

Soon, Tom and Clark were directing a group of people working feverishly on the concoction which they were planning to launch at the horde now making its way up the four miles between the turn off and their homes. Red and Boomer Hill were coordinating the efforts to slow the army's progress, buying time for the others to finish their preparations. Kate had gotten the Terwiliger's ATV and a small tow cart, filled the cart with glass canning jars and their lids from Bertha and a couple of her other neighbors, and then hurried back home. Once there, the jars were taken to Tom and Clark while Sunny and Laurel took the lids and directed another group of workers whose collective job it was to punch a hole in each lid from the under side, and thread the firecracker fuse through it so that when the lid was on the jar, only the fuse protruded. Earlier, Tom and Clark had rounded up Red Hill's surgical tubing and cut up the tubes from several of the bicycles at Terwiliger's, and fashioned them into four giant slingshots. Using canning jars filled with water, they tested their range and found they could lob the "shells" nearly a hundred yards—from the bluffs above the road, that would be be far enough. They timed the flights, tested some of the firecrackers and then tried to adjust the fuse lengths to coincide with the duration of flight. It was crude at best.

Tom and Clark took the batches of their "mortar mix" and half poured, half scooped it into the jars. They tested one mortar and, somewhat to their surprise and certainly to their relief, the concoction actually burst into flame. After the successful test firing, they quickly set about assembling the rest. When a bunch of lids were ready they were fitted to the jars and loaded into boxes of a dozen each. By the time they ran out of materials to make the mix, they had made up just under a hundred mortar shells. Just as they loaded the last dozen jars into a box, a voice called out from Tom's waist. Lifting the walkie-talkie off his belt, Tom keyed the mike and said, "Go ahead."

"Dad," came the young voice, "it's Tommy."

"What is it, Tom?"

"A big bunch of people in trucks just passed right below us."

"Where are you exactly?"

"Right on top of the hill between the river and road where it goes up over the hill."

McCall heard the exchange, and took the radio from Tom. "Tommy, this is Uncle Eagle. Listen to me. Turn your radio volume down real low, so you can't hear it from even two feet away. And you stay there until they've gone completely by you and are out of sight again. You can't move without them seeing you. So just stay down low and keep out of sight. Okay? You understand me?"

"Sure, Uncle Eagle," was the confident reply.

"Where's your horse?"

"Tied up across the road. We came over here because we could see further down the road."

"Okay. Don't worry about the horse. Even if those people see it and mess with it. Okay? I mean it. Stay out of sight! These aren't nice people."

"All right." This time the reply was quieter.

"When they've all gone by, wait ten more minutes, then sneak back and get on your horse and take the D-line logging road back up to the hill above Callie's house. She'll know the way. Be careful!"

"Okay."

McCall gave the radio back to Tom. "Burbank's getting pretty close. We've got to get into position." They loaded all eight dozen filled jars into the ATV cart, piled on the slingshots, threw in some extra firecrackers, and then McCall called everyone together.

"I need four mortar teams. Each team needs two holders, one loader, one launcher, and a couple of guys with rifles." Eventually four groups were picked, one each headed by McCall, Tom, and Red and Boomer Hill, who had just returned from their road-blocking efforts. Web Johnson had decided he wanted to be at his house. He was afraid that an ambush with flaming gasoline could produce unwanted side-effects. He had a 5.5-horsepower Honda water pump down by the riverbank that could suck 220 gallons per minute out of the river and pump it through a buried 2-inch pipe to an outlet near his house. It wasn't legal to take river water without a permit, but he had installed the system for fire emergencies. He figured this could end up being one.

When the teams were assembled, McCall continued. "Each team gets two dozen rounds. We're going up on the high ridge just down river from Web Johnson's house. It's too steep for them to climb from the road very easily, and it gives us a good, elevated firing position. I want two teams near each end of the ridge above the bend in the road. That should give us good cross-firing angles, even if it's all from the same side of the road. It will make our force seem larger than it really is. We don't have many rounds, so you'll have to get a feel in a hurry for distance, angle, length of pull back on the sling, and so on. Maybe you should practice with some fist-sized rocks when you first get in place.

"When you see my first shot explode, you can commence your own firing. I want each team to fire their rounds about every thirty seconds, which will make for a total of eight rounds per minute between us. Hopefully we can coordinate so there aren't big clumps and lulls in firing. In between, the riflemen can make them keep their heads down, but unless our people are at risk, I don't want any people shot—just hit trucks and stuff. They have to feel outgunned, and surrounded. We can only keep this up for ten or fifteen minutes, but I can tell you, when artillery is raining down on you, ten or fifteen minutes is an absolute eternity. They should turn tail and run before then. But if we finish too quickly—before they retreat—then we've lost the game."

McCall gave other instructions to the rest of the group regarding emergency evacuation if their efforts failed to stop the mob-army. The plan was simple: Everyone should jump in a car and take off up the logging roads and make their way out. Some, like the Warners, were going to rendezvous first at Old Bridge Park. Sunny and Laurel would take a car right now and contact all the other neighbors not already at McCall's, helping anybody who wouldn't be able to get out without assistance. "Don't be a hero," McCall told everyone. "Your home isn't worth your life, and if they get by us, then you'll be hopelessly outnumbered. The Senator will have the radio and we'll call him if you need to scram. Just be ready to. Okay, any questions?"

There were none. Some people were mad, some were frightened, some were just confused. But there was no more time to do anything else.

"Okay, let's get going."

Each of the four teams had one or two ATVs to help carry their equipment. Some of the men rode horses, and the rest just scrambled up the hill behind Terwiliger's house to reach the nearest spur that branched off the logging road leading to the designated ridge. A pickup truck had been parked at the end of the spur and those who had walked up the hill jumped in to ride the rest of the way. Ten minutes later, the teams were in position, the napalm-like rounds distributed, the slingshots set up, and the riflemen set. They were just starting to take some practice shots when the point truck of the mob-army came around a curve and into view.

***

The lead truck stopped as they broke out of the trees into a narrow clearing at the base of a fairly steep bluff that appeared to be eighty or ninety feet high to their left. The river was immediately to the right of the road. On the other side of the river the hillside was also high and steep. The clearing itself was perhaps two hundred yards long and about fifty yards wide at its widest. The driver got out, looked around for a moment, then signaled to the rest of the vehicles behind them to stay put. He then got back in the truck and drove forward across the open area. When he reached the other side they came upon a huge pile of fallen trees, perhaps twenty or twenty-five of them in all. He did a quick turnaround and drove back to the others. Lincoln Burbank got out of his truck and approached him.

"What's it look like?" asked the leader of the mob-army.

"Just the same as the rest of the way up. No sign of anyone. The only difference is they got a little carried away with their stupid tree chopping. The next pile's a bit bigger than before."

"They're getting desperate," scoffed Burbank. "We're coming through, and a bunch of trees ain't gonna stop us. Let's get on with it so we can get going." He turned and signaled the trucks behind him and then led the procession up the road. When they reached the trees, they got the chainsaws out and went to work. Realizing it would take the better part of an hour to cut through and clear the tree roadblock, most of the rest of the people piled out of the trucks and the bus and milled around. Some pitched rocks in the river for fun.

***

The fuses on the M80s were short, so the timing had to be near-perfect. McCall stretched the tubing back, cradling the jar in the sling as the two holders strained against the load, and as he reached the necessary length he paused, and another man leaned in with a cigarette lighter and lit the fuse. McCall immediately released the sling to launch the first mortar. Instead, the angle of the cloth sling was just off enough in the manner in which it was tied to the tubing that the sudden acceleration dumped the jar right at his feet as the sling shot forward and fired a pocket full of nothing. "Shit!" exclaimed

McCall, and he instantly lunged for the jar, and yanked the fuse barehanded out of the M80.

McCall set the jar aside, accepted another from the lighter, and restarted the launch process, making an adjustment in the placement of the jar in the cloth. Once again the sling was pulled back, the fuse lit, and the mortar released. The entire team watched as the jar sailed out in a graceful low arch before dropping down toward the crowded road. The jar impacted just beyond the road, glancing off a log and shattering harmlessly on the ground without exploding, the sound muffled by tall grass. A couple of men standing idly near the edge of the road heard the sound behind them and turned around, but saw nothing out of the ordinary, and the event passed otherwise without notice.

"Either the fuse was blown out, or it was too long," said McCall.

"It better not have been blown out, or none of these are likely to work," said Boomer Hill, who was commanding the other south ridge mortar team next to McCall's. "Try taking off a half-inch and try it again. Here!" He handed a pair of wire cutters to McCall, who took them and snipped off the fuse of another mortar. He was about to reload the sling, when he paused.

"We're going to have to gamble. We won't have time to cut them all if it works, so let's cut one box each. We'll launch those at the closest part of the road, and launch the other box with the original fuses further down the road. We'll just have to hope for the best."

He quickly modified the fuses in the first box, handed the dykes back to Boomer, who did the same to one of his boxes, then sent one of the riflemen with the tool along to the two teams at the north end of the ridge with instructions on changing the fuses and firing methods.

They waited a long five minutes, praying that the tree cutting below was going slowly. Finally, McCall received a wave from Tom who was with the other two teams. All was set. The loading process was begun again, and this time Boomer was working in tandem—if McCall's shot worked, his would be ready to go. Boomer nodded at McCall, who finished the pull. The fuse was lit once more, and McCall released the mortar. Again the jar shot out into the air, and then swooped down toward the unsuspecting group below.

The teams on the ridge were almost as surprised as the hoard on the road when the M80 exploded about twenty feet above the ground, shattering the jar, and igniting the jellied gasoline mix. The makeshift napalm landed on a bare spot on the road, hitting neither vehicle nor person, but it had the desired effect. A few women in the mob screamed, everybody dropped to the ground, and heads swiveled in every direction trying to determine the source of this sudden threat.

A few seconds later another jar exploded and showered an empty pickup truck with flaming napalm. Coats, paper bags, and other debris in the pickup bed ignited and began to burn rapidly. Within a few moments, there were new explosions of noise and flames beginning to erupt along the entire length of the road through the clearing. Simultaneously, rifle fire from the ridge began to create new havoc, as the snipers targeted truck windows and headlights to create the noisiest and most visual commotion and destruction they could.

As the mortars rained down every few seconds, their launchers gained experience and the effects became more devastating. Vehicles were burning, fires were erupting in the brush near the road, and several people were splattered with enough drops of flaming goo to create panic among the entire mob-army. One round passed cleanly through the driver's window of the old blue bus, bouncing off the seat cushion as the firecracker went off filling the front of the bus with burning gasoline and setting off new fires on the two front rows of seats. Several people who had been playing cards near the back of the bus jumped up in alarm, tried unsuccessfully to open the rear escape door, and ended up crawling out of the windows and falling headlong to the ground.

Lincoln Burbank had been watching the chain saw crews clearing away the trees blocking the road when the mayhem erupted behind him. He spun around and watched as his people were sent in near hysteria in every direction as they sought cover and protection from the fire raining down from places unseen and unknown. As he started to run back toward the scene, a mortar exploded just to his right, the surprise of it knocking him to the ground. His head started hurting again and he realized the bandages had caught fire. Rolling up onto his knees, he jerked the gauze wrapping off his head, pulling the clotted blood from his ear and starting the bleeding all over again. One of his men who had been with him up by the trees ran up to him, ripped off his own tee shirt and held it to the side of his leader's head.

Preoccupied momentarily with his own predicament, Burbank failed to realize that his people were beginning to flee the area, heading back down the road they'd just traveled up from town. By the time he regained his feet, his "army" was in full retreat, and most of them had also abandoned their weapons. A couple of undamaged trucks were trying to make U-turns, and people were jumping in the back of them, hoping to get out faster. A mortar round hit right on the hood ornament of one of the trucks, but did no damage and failed to stop its escape.

Burbank tried to rally those men closest to him to stop the panic and try to fight back, but a few more mortars seemed to target his own immediate vicinity, and the exodus down the road accelerated. A horn sounded behind him and he turned to find Frank waving at him from his truck. As it pulled up alongside, the door was flung open, and Burbank, hesitating only a moment, jumped inside. The truck tore down the road, as the driver leaned on the horn to scatter those on foot who were running down the road.

Scarcely twelve minutes had passed since the first mortar exploded, and the entire clearing had been relinquished by the mob in defeat. Boomer Hill let out an awesome explosion of sound that echoed across the valley, and the other members of the mortar teams joined in the cheering and hand-slapping. McCall surveyed the scene below and saw no stragglers or bodies. Unless someone had been caught in one of the burning vehicles, his goal of no serious casualties appeared to have been realized. He took the walkie-talkie and quickly called Senator Hornbrook.

"We did it, Senator!" cried an exuberant McCall. "They've tucked their tails and are heading back to their holes as fast as they can."

"Thank God!" exclaimed a much relieved Hornbrook, turning and giving a big thumbs up to those gathered around who responded with cheers. "You've really earned your keep today, McCall."

"Thanks, Senator. But we've got another problem on our hands and now we need the help of everyone else. We've got a zillion fires going in the brush down here, and it's going to be a major calamity if we don't get on it. Tell Clark to send a couple of tractors, and maybe his old loader down here, along with all the chain saws he can muster. They'll need to finish opening up the road first."

"Will do. But I'll have to get them to calm down here first. You'd think it was VE day or something." The valley's residents who had been waiting for news while listening to the sound of distant explosions and gun fire, were all jumping up and down or hugging each other. Hornbrook was able to find Clark Terwiliger and explain the remaining problem. The older man nodded his understanding and grabbed several other men who left with him.

When the sound of a single gunshot reverberated up through the valley, the celebration abruptly came to a halt. More gunshots sounded in quick succession. Up on the ridge, McCall instinctively dropped to a crouch, and yelled for everyone else to get down as well, aware that they were silhouetted against the sky from some angles. His walkie-talkie crackled and Tommy's voice said, "Dad, Uncle Eagle? Are you there?"

McCall clicked the talk button and answered, "Go ahead, Tommy."

"Ellie and Angel are on the other hill over there, and it looks like some men are trying to get them!"

McCall grabbed a rifle from the man standing next to him, and used the telescopic sight to scan the top of the hills across the valley. It wasn't until his third pass back and forth that he spotted movement, and realized it was his niece and her friend, scrambling over the slash left from the recent clear-cutting of the hill. Then he spotted eight or ten men climbing up toward them. In an instant he realized that some of Burbank's mob must have gone up the other side of the river for some reason, and they must have seen the two. If they reached the two kids, they would have valuable hostages. McCall didn't like the scenario.

Tom was frantically trying to call to them on the radio, but there was no answer. "Eagle, we have to do something!"

***

Ellie and Angel had witnessed the mortar attack on the mob army, although from their vantage point they couldn't see most of the explosions because of the trees along the river. But there was no mistaking the effectiveness of the effort when they saw people and trucks heading back down the road, and heard the distant screaming and yelling. Angel had leapt up from behind the tree stump where they were hiding and pulled Ellie to her feet to join him in a jubilant hug.

"It worked," cried Ellie. "They're leaving!"

"I don't know how Mr. McCall and your dad came up with those things, but, boy, that was cool!"

Angel felt a tearing pain through his left shoulder before he heard the gunshot. He was knocked over by the force of the blow, dropping the walkie-talkie in the process. Ellie screamed when she saw the blood flowing down his arm, and she fell to her knees next to him. Angel was writhing, and Ellie started crying.

In spite of his pain, Angel cried out to her, "Ellie! See if you can see anybody!"

She turned and tried to look around the tree stump to see who was shooting at them. After a moment, she spied several heads weaving and bobbing as they climbed up the hillside toward them.

"Angel!" she cried, "a bunch of men are coming up HERE!"

"Who? Where did they come from?"

"I don't know! They must be part of the mob, but I don't know how they found us clear over here!"

"We have to get out of here!"

"What about your arm?"

"We have to get away!" he repeated. "I'll manage," he added but almost immediately cried, "*God, it hurts!*" He remembered the backpack. "Look in the bag! Find something to use as a bandage."

She complied, and quickly pulled a shirt out of the backpack, wrapping it around the wound as tight as she could. Then sucked in her breath when she saw him reach into the bag and pull out the Calico pistol.

"Angel! Don't! We can't shoot it out like some movie!"

"Don't worry. I just want them to duck while we get out of here. You carry the bag. Now, get ready. Where are they?" She told him where to look and he peered around the stump until he spotted them only about a hundred yards away. *Damn!* He wound the magazine spring, and pulled back the slide awkwardly with his right hand to chamber the first round. Then he propped the gun up on the tree stump so that he wouldn't have to hold it with his recently dislocated and now wounded left arm. Aiming for the ground in front of the approaching men, he opened fire with at least twenty rounds from the 9mm gun. The gun jumped with each shot, but he really didn't care where the rounds went. He fired until he saw no sign of movement at all, then yelled, "LET"S GO!"

The two ran along the back of the hilltop out of sight of their unknown attackers. Angel kept looking over his shoulder, hoping no one would appear until they were off the clear-cut site and into the dense underbrush of the heavy woods beyond. If they could get there, it was only another fifty yards to the logging road where they'd left the ATV. The ground was cluttered with broken branches from the logging operation, and had not yet been gathered into the huge slash piles that normally were burned to help clean the area of debris. They both tripped and stumbled repeatedly, Angel grunting with the pain each time, but they made the edge of the woods without being fired upon.

"Angel, stop!" said a breathless Ellie. "I have to rest!"

"Me, too!" he grimaced through his teeth. "Get behind a tree and stay out of sight." He turned and waited to see if the men would appear. He figured they would make for the same stump where they had seen Ellie and him, because otherwise they wouldn't necessarily know which direction they had fled. Sure enough, a minute or two later he sighted a couple of cautiously moving heads. When the first man reached the stump, he scanned the clear cut for a moment, then turned quickly, bent down, and picked something off the ground. The man first held it to his ear, then in front of his mouth, and Angel realized it was the walkie-talkie he had been holding when he had been shot. He must have dropped it when he fell.

***

"Who's there?" came a gravelly sound over the walkie-talkie.

"Who's this?" said a frowning Tom and the sound of the unfamiliar voice.

"Just an angry hunter. My game's just been shootin' back at me."

"LEAVE THEM ALONE! THEY'RE JUST KIDS, AND YOU FIRED FIRST!"

"I think they might be useful," the voice said menacingly.

"HARM THEM AND YOU'RE DEAD!" screamed Tom into the radio. He spun around toward McCall and pleaded, "*Eagle!*"

Next to Eagle, Red had arrived with one of the riflemen from his team. "Leave that to us. We'll keep them busy," Red offered. "Kent here is damn good."

McCall said, "That's at least a thousand yards."

"I know," said the man, quietly. "But, if you'll pardon the expression, I'll give it a shot." He sat down behind a small log, rested his rifle barrel on it, and looked through the enormous scope on top of his gun. After what seemed an eternity, he fired a shot, worked the bolt rapidly, fired another, then another, then another.

***

Angel heard first the shots from across the valley, then the cry of one of the men who was chasing them, now just over fifty yards behind. The man fell to the ground, holding his knee. Angel could see at least half a dozen of their pursuers, and although they all dropped suddenly when the other man was hit, Angel still had a clean line of sight to them. So he lifted his pistol again, re-tensioned the spring crank on the magazine, aimed, and pulled the trigger five times as fast as he could. He paused for a moment, then fired five more, and kept repeating the sequence until he had exhausted the 50-round magazine. He then detached it quickly, and reached into the backpack for the other, larger magazine.

It was not needed. Caught in a crossfire from two uncertain locations, the small group of attackers had cowered under the rapid fire, then took advantage of the lull while Angel was changing clips, and made their retreat over the hill and out of sight back toward the road intersection, half-carrying, half-dragging their wounded cohort.

Angel wanted to give chase, and make sure they didn't change their minds, but the pain in his left shoulder persuaded him otherwise. His right hand holding the pistol dropped to his side, and he turned to Ellie and said, "I think it's okay now. I think they're gone."

Ellie rushed to him to embrace him in a bear hug, releasing him immediately when he winced out loud in pain. "Oh, Angel, I'm sorry. I was so frightened."

"It's okay," he repeated. "Let's get the ATV and go home. But you'd better drive."

***

Across the valley, Tom and the others had been jubilant when Kent Westland had hit one of the men from such a distance, and then ecstatic when they saw the rest retreating with the wounded man. Only Kent was downcast. "I can't believe it. I was aiming at his other leg," he said with a half-grin. They waited a few minutes to make sure there would be no further danger there, then McCall sent the riflemen to follow the mob to make sure they kept retreating down the road. The rest of them gathered their equipment and loaded the ATV cart. Of the original eight dozen mortar rounds they had but three rounds remaining—they had come that close to not stopping the mob-army.

They traveled back to the spur road, then descended down the hill behind the Terwiligers' house, and were met with a boisterous celebration. Laurel and Sunny hit the arms of Tom and McCall at a dead run, almost simultaneously, and the scene was repeated by numerous other couples. There were demands for details, and somebody stepped forward and said their video camera was ready now, and could they please do it all over again? Lots of laughter followed, and the crowd was in no hurry to disperse. About thirty minutes later, the tractors and loader came lumbering up the road having successfully put out the fires started by the mortar attack. Even the irascible Web Johnson appeared happy. The celebration was renewed when Tommy and Callie rode into the gathering on her horse, having successfully eluded detection by the mob-army when it passed them both ways.

The Hornbrook Prophecy

The raucous mood dampened when Ellie and Angel appeared. Ellie cried out to her mother for help. When Laurel and Sunny saw Angel's bloody shoulder, they rushed over, calling out to anyone for a doctor as they did their best to attend to the young man. As Tom came over, he was muted by a devastatingly angry look from his wife. She had feared such harm and he had ignored her. It was going to be cold in the valley for some time, he knew.

Boomer Hill pulled up in his pickup to whisk Angel, with both Sunny and Laurel in attendance, off to the hospital in town, taking a back way on the logging roads to avoid overtaking the Burbank mob.

Everybody was concerned about Angel's wound, but relieved to realize he was the only casualty of what became known locally as the Slingshot War.

***

Henley Hornbrook was enjoying the celebration in the valley after the defeat of Lincoln Burbank's mob-army when a Washington state National Guard helicopter captured everyone's attention. Appearing suddenly from over the hills to the east, it landed in the pasture behind McCall's house. Everyone was surprised to see the Governor himself step down out of the craft and make his way toward the joyous gathering.

"Well, Governor, welcome to our little corner of the state," Hornbrook began. "You missed all the fun."

"I'm sorry I couldn't respond sooner," said the Governor sincerely. "I couldn't get any help from Dillard so I finally released two Guard units myself to see what was going on out here. Evidently, on the way they met up with a sorry-looking crowd heading toward town from this direction. It's seems like we've located Mr. Burbank finally, and he is at present attempting to explain his borrowing of Seattle city buses. And when he finishes that, he can carry right on with another explanation of how he and his group came to be in possession of weapons that have been tentatively identified as some of the stolen merchandise from the Olympia gun store robberies yesterday."

"Do tell," said Hornbrook.

"I should mention that he was complaining that his group was illegally and outrageously attacked without cause or warning while they were attempting to explore options for relocating inner city people to the countryside."

Hornbrook laughed. "Well, gee, tell them we're sorry, and see if they'd like to come back for a BBQ."

"Speaking of which, I spotted a lot of smoke down the valley not too far from here."

"Sort of a late Fourth of July party," the Senator explained. Then he set the record straight. "Governor, those people are damn lucky they weren't all killed. I believe my friends here showed remarkable and commendable restraint in the face of overwhelming odds and a clear and present danger to their lives and property."

"I know. And, again, I'm sorry we could not get here sooner. I'm glad it ended without serious injuries. By the way, we may have been late, but I think the Guard may have prevented more bloodshed. Evidently we arrived just ahead of a bunch of other locals who were well armed and must have heard you were under siege."

"Ah, reinforcements were on their way. Well, that's another story. Sometimes it's best we don't always know everything our constituents are up to, Governor. Would you like a beer? You look like you could use a break, too."

"I'd give my eye teeth to kick back right now," said the Governor, with feeling. "But there's trouble all over. I've got to get going. I'm glad everything's okay here." They shook hands, and the Governor climbed back into the Huey and after a few moments the copter lifted off and disappeared down the valley.

Lewiston Weiser appeared at Hornbrook's side. When Henley saw him, he repeated the Governor's words. "There's still trouble all over, Lew. Something's got to be done. We can't go on this way, and Dillard's clueless."

Weiser said the unthinkable. "Maybe we should roll our own, Henley."

Hornbrook, initially taken aback, considered the words, then simply replied, "I wonder." He turned and they slowly walked across the pasture back to McCall's house. "Get us on a flight, Lew. McCall, too." His chief-of-staff didn't have to ask to where.

Chapter 27

> *"The natural progress of things is for liberty to yield and government to gain ground."*
> —Thomas Jefferson

Sunday – August 29

The scene in the Oval Office would have been almost comical had it not been so serious an occasion. President Dillard was pacing back and forth furiously while Florence yelled at him on and off from halfway across the room. A wildly-gesturing Vice President Branford was in a heated conversation with Halsey Brownsville and Sullivan Veradale near the fireplace. Brownsville glanced over at Dillard and thought he looked more like a chicken running around with its head cut off than the leader of the Free World. Decisions Brownsville had made over the years were generally rooted in certain philosophical values and convictions. Dillard's decision-making process, the Majority Leader knew, generally relied mostly on public opinion polls. This time, though, polls were useless and the President appeared to be rudderless.

The lead story on most of the Saturday evening news programs had been about a battle between a renegade mob and the residents of a small rural valley that included the Washington state home of United States Senator Henley Hornbrook. Hornbrook, the reporters and anchors pointed out, had been the subject of prime time finger-pointing by the President, and Dillard was taking a lot of heat for accusing the Senator of causing the nation's problems. Combined with the fact that some sectors of the country were mired in near Depression-like economic conditions, were suffering widespread civil unrest and the entire nation was saddled with a dysfunctional central government, the negative press seemed to be taking a serious toll on the President's psyche.

"Winston!" said Florence, commanding her husband's attention. "Would you listen to Sheldon for a minute?"

"Fine!" said an exasperated Dillard. "What?"

"There's no use kidding ourselves," began the Vice President. "What's important is that we need to restore law and order long enough to put the economy back on its feet."

"Yeah, sure, smart guy," sneered the President. "Like that's a revelation?"

"Don't piss me off, Dillard," snapped Branford, his own patience wearing thin as well. "You don't have a whole lot of friends right now."

Florence interjected, "*Listen* to him, Win. He's got some ideas."

"Okay! Okay! What are they?"

"First is order. The National Guard's not cuttin' it. We need to send in the military, and shut down the rough stuff for good."

Speaker of the House Veradale objected, "You can't do that!"

"Sure he can. Lots of Presidents have."

"Legally, sure," said Veradale, "but it'll be like lighting a powder keg if you send in the army."

"Tough shit," said the Vice-SOB. "People will have to learn we're not going to put up with a bunch of destructive tantrums."

"Sheldon's right," said Florence.

"Shut up, Flo, and let him talk," said Dillard.

"All right. Next, you can't control people who don't know where they're getting their next meal from. So we also have to expand our emergency powers to take over the distribution and rationing of the nation's food supply. Starting right at the farms. That might seem a bit Soviet, but the big boys who control the agricultural industry are not about to threaten their usual flow of subsidies and everything else. They'll play ball."

Dillard just nodded.

"Finally, it's a big mistake to let these assholes like Shadwell stand up and say they're not going to pay taxes anymore," Branford was nearly growling now. "Round up all those guys and throw 'em in the slammer. Confiscate their assets just like under the forfeiture laws for drug dealers, and they'll fold like a house of cards."

Brownsville had heard enough. As big a proponent of big government as he had been over the years, he knew there were some lines you simply couldn't cross and still call yourself the land of the free. There were appropriate laws to follow regarding tax evasion; sending in the military wasn't included. "Wait a minute. You're sending in the army and marines into our own cities, taking over the farming industry, and starting a round-up and imprisonment of a whole new group of citizens. What's next? Gulags and a KGB?"

"Don't be ridiculous," said Florence. "The country's in deep shit, and the people will accept a little inconvenience just to get their security back."

"All right, enough!" said the President, finally taking charge of the discussion. He pressed a button on his phone. His secretary responded immediately, grabbing her note pad and coming into the Oval Office. "Set up a meeting here at two with Transportation, Commerce, Treasury, and Agriculture. And I want the Defense Secretary and the JCS Chairman over here immediately. That's all for now." His secretary finished her quick notations, and left the room.

***

When Secretary of Defense Lane Herrick and the Chairman of the Joint Chiefs of Staff, General Canby Hubbard, were shown into the room, there was still a spirited discussion going on. General Hubbard, making his usual instant assessment and evaluation of his surroundings, observed that the President, First Lady/Senator, and the Veep were pressing home arguments against the Congressional leaders.

"Good morning, Mr. Secretary, General Hubbard," said Dillard, directing his remarks to the newcomers. He went over to the Presidential desk, picked up a piece of paper, glanced at it, and sat down. "Gentlemen, we are in a crisis situation. Our nation's cities are paralyzed and the people are in desperate need of help. Our first need is to restore law and order. The governors and their National Guards seem unable to contain the unrest, so I want you to have on my desk, within twenty-four hours, comprehensive plans for the military to do so. I want this crap 100 percent shut down! You will have authorization to utilize any resources under your command. Any questions?"

The abruptness and brevity of the remarks left the two men momentarily silent. Secretary Herrick, formerly a Fortune 500 CEO but a political appointee nonetheless, asked a single question. "*Any* resources?"

"Yes," was the President's short reply.

General Hubbard sighed, and looked over at Majority Leader Brownsville, who was hanging his head as if suddenly exhausted, and Speaker Veradale, who was staring across the room and shaking his head slowly back and forth as if in disbelief. The General had been a no-nonsense leader all his military life, but he'd always had a tough time with orders that ignored reality. Not long after being appointed as Chairman of the JCS, he had attended a White House reception for a foreign dignitary and had overheard the President remark that, in their formal mess dress uniforms, admirals and generals looked like *"nothing more than fancy bellhops, but not as useful."* He'd had little respect for his Commander-in-Chief since.

Hubbard said, "Sir, with all due respect, the men and women of the military have not been insulated from the events of the past several months, and emotions are running high. I would have reason to believe that ordering our forces into their own cities at this time, possibly to fire upon their own fellow citizens, is going to meet a great deal of resistance from a large percentage of the officers and men."

"I'm giving you an order, goddammit," said an angry President. "We have a state of emergency, and I don't give a rat's ass if it bothers you or them. Disobeying a direct order is mutiny, is it not, General?"

Hubbard was beginning to share Veradale's disbelief. The President of the United States was ordering him to initiate full-blown martial law like some two-bit banana belt dictator. But a good military man doesn't easily reveal his position. "Yes, sir, I understand," he ventured. "I'll study the options."

"Study, my ass!" said Branford. "He said do it, so do it!"

"Yes, sir," was all that Hubbard replied.

"All right, then," said the President, getting up from his desk. "That's it for now. Thank you all for coming. Oh, Lane, stay for a moment, will you?"

Brownsville, Veradale, and General Hubbard soon found themselves out in the corridor, and they left the West Wing in silence. The General's car was waiting for him and the other two accepted the offer of a ride back to their respective offices.

"Sully," began Brownsville, "this is crazy! What's happening?"

Speaker Veradale was still shaking his head, as if it wouldn't stop. "I'm afraid this will only make things worse. General, what's your take?"

"Sirs, it's inappropriate for the military to question its orders," he said tentatively, not wanting to reveal too much of his true feelings.

"Bullshit!" barked Veradale. "You're talking about constitutional chain of command; we're talking about constitutional destruction!"

"What you say right now won't leave this car, General," interjected Brownsville. "You have a respected record of service to your country, and we'd like to know what your personal opinion is."

Hubbard hesitated a moment. "They're making a huge mistake, sirs. My people are going to have a major problem with carrying out such orders if they are issued. A single incident in South Central LA may be one thing, but we're talking coast-to-coast martial law."

"We understand," said Brownsville, looking at Veradale who nodded in agreement. "Look, General, we believe the President may be on the verge of precipitating a catastrophic constitutional crisis, and if the shit hits the fan there's no telling where it may land. All we're asking for now is to drag your feet as much as you can while we try to see if there's any way to head this off. Can we rely on your cooperation?

"I can't promise anything, sirs, except that the decisions I make and the contingencies I plan for will be those that are most likely to support my oath to defend the Constitution and the nation against all enemies both foreign and domestic. I will resign my office and commission before I violate that oath."

"That, General, gives me more peace of mind than anything else I've heard for weeks."

"We can't ask for any more," added Veradale.

Chapter 28

"In periods where there is no leadership, society stands still. Progress occurs when courageous, skillful leaders seize the opportunity to change things for the better."
—Harry S. Truman

Monday – August 30

The day after Biggs Wasco was murdered, Jefferson Scio released a statement that he was resigning his office, effective immediately, citing reasons of personal health. Elgin LaGrange was now the Governor of Alabama. At the news conference accompanying the swearing-in ceremony, he made a startling announcement of his own. "Ladies and Gentlemen of the press, and citizens of Alabama, I have spent all my life in this great state, and have been exceedingly fortunate to have enjoyed a certain degree of success which has too often been denied to others. It was to expand these opportunities that I worked to help develop the *Hopes* program, and I would like nothing more than to see its continued and growing success. That was the primary reason I decided to run for Governor, and to give the people of Alabama a real *choice* in the November election. Now, it seems, I've screwed it all up."

The press in attendance appeared confused, but he proceeded. "Yes, I won the primary election in June and was to oppose Jefferson Scio. But with his resignation I have become Governor *without* an election, and there is no opponent for November. The voters will still have no choice come election day. Normally, the procedure would be for the former candidate's party to name a new standard bearer, but this would mean that your choice would be made by a few men in one of those famous smoke-filled rooms. I think the citizens of Alabama, in light of these unforeseen and unprecedented events of the last few weeks, ought to have the opportunity to once again field their own candidates. Therefore, tomorrow I will go before the legislature and request that they provide the necessary legislative arrangements to hold, in one month, on Tuesday, September 28, a second, special primary election. The filing period will extend for the balance of this week. This special election will permit any candidate from any party to run and the top two vote getters will automatically advance to the general election in November."

There was a outbreak of commotion, and questions were shouted at him from several directions. He held up both hands to ask for silence.

"Please, let me finish. I feel strongly about Alabama's future, but I am a single voice. It's time for our state to think about its future and its direction. I want there to be a full debate not just between two candidates, but in every home, in every business, in every place that our fine citizens meet. Don't let fate and the courts decide your choice. Let's have a *real* election! And then let's get this state moving forward!"

CHAPTER 29

> *"If you are a member of Congress and one of your constituents who doesn't know anything, and does not want to go into the bother of learning something, and has no money, and no employment, and can't earn a living, comes besieging you for help…you take him to…Washington, the grand old benevolent Asylum for the Helpless."*
> —Mark Twain

Tuesday – August 31

Few citizens were being spared by the nationwide economic calamity. There was a growing perception that the lack of progress towards some form of resolution might be less on account of the severity of the circumstances than it was because those in power actually *desired* the suffering to continue, as if for penance for the sin of being unappreciative.

Suspicions leaked out of the White House that the President was about to expand the use of his Emergency Powers. The leaks, by the infamous "unnamed senior White House official" also included remarks that the President was beginning to feel that Congress itself might be inadvertently or unnecessarily preventing the restoration of order and normal national functioning, and that greater use of Executive Orders might be necessary to, according to one such quote, *"expedite the initiation of productive solutions to our country's problems, and that the President stood ready to take whatever steps were necessary to protect the interests of all Americans."* Rumors were running unbridled.

The Senate floor resembled the Oval Office of two days before, thought Halsey Brownsville, only on a grander scale. Confusion. Turmoil. Anger. Nothing substantive was being accomplished.

"Mr. President!" said Henley Hornbrook, looking toward the presiding officer for the day, Milton Freewater. Hornbrook had flown back to D.C. the day before.

The Hornbrook Prophecy

"The Chair recognizes Senator Hornbrook," said Freewater, gravely.

"May I address my colleagues a final time?"

"I said you had the floor," snapped Freewater. Patience was in short supply in Washington, D.C. these days. Then the New York Senator did a mental double-take. "Wait a minute. What do you mean 'a final time?'"

The Senators grew silent as they awaited Hornbrook's first public comments since the attack on him and his neighbors.

"I'm not sure there's much left for me to say or do here, but I cannot leave without comment." He paused for several moments, and you could have heard a pin drop as he collected his thoughts. "It is hardly an honor to stand before this august body on such an inauspicious occasion. Here we are, the grandest deliberative body in the history of governments, gathered not in a celebration of democratic ideals, but in the shadow of an egocentric idiot and under a very real threat of armed interruption unheard of since the days of King George III. What makes it truly amazing is that most of you have no idea just how unique a place in history you have carved for yourselves.

"Man has spent every day since he was thrown out of the Garden of Eden attempting to create the perfect society. We've tried kingdoms and empires, theocracies and democracies. We've submitted to dictators, despots, and warlords. We've anointed kings and caesars, pharaohs and presidents. We tried monarchy—it failed. We tried oligarchy—it failed. We tried feudalism—it failed. We tried fascism—it failed. We tried communism—it failed. They *all* failed.

"Although democracy had been tried before, our founding fathers took advantage of the evolution of political thought to craft what they felt was the right balance of governing authority and individual rights. But they had no idea how fatally flawed was their new social experiment. But one of their contemporaries made the most important prediction ever about the nature of democracies. As a matter of fact, I think it is such an insightful and accurate forecast about the future of America, that I consider it to be nothing less than a *prophecy*.

"A Scottish jurist and historian, Sir Alexander Tytler, is credited with saying more than 200 years ago, '*A democracy cannot survive as a permanent form of government. It can last only until its citizens discover that they can vote themselves largesse from the public treasury. From that moment on, the majority will vote for the candidates promising the greatest benefits from the public purse, with the result that a democracy will always collapse from loose fiscal policies, always followed by a dictatorship.*'

"Sir Alexander's prophecy, it seems, was a simple paradox: Mankind, in democracies, attempts to pursue freedom by traveling a path that inevitably leads back to bondage."

The Senate chamber was still, and he went on. "You have all, collectively, succeeded in one of the most time-honored pursuits of ambitious men. You have all gained power over others. Though in the past such success was the result of superior arms, or treachery, or simply genetics, yours is unique because the people you rule actually *gave* such power to you—via the voting booth. And as much as you crave such power *before* you are elected, once you have it you are relentless in its wielding.

"Why? Because once elected you catch the worst disease of mankind. Economist Frederick Hayak called it the *Fatal Conceit*. Having power is more addictive than the strongest narcotic, and rare is the junkie who can kick the habit. Once infected your head swells, your common sense withers, your morals are abandoned, and you lose your perspective on the real world."

Some of the Senators shifted in their seats, and a few started to complain out loud at his characterization. But he ignored them, raising his voice. "And you'll do anything…*ANYTHING!*" Hornbrook pounded the desk in his anger, the sound echoing around the room and startling many around him, "…to keep it or get more. Fifty percent plus one is all it takes. Get more votes than anybody else and you're in the game. The secret to getting it and keeping it, of course, is no secret at all. Not anymore. Just promise people that you can make their lives better. Don't just stand around letting people live their own lives as they see fit. If they're rich, help them get richer. If they're poor, give them what they want and make somebody else pay for it. Set one group against another, and then step in to save the day. Complicate every aspect of daily life by creating rules and regulations for everything, and make it so confusing that people are forced to come to you for help."

The verbal objections became louder and more numerous. Freewater banged his gavel several times. "The Senate is reminded that, like it or not, Mr. Hornbrook has the floor."

Hornbrook didn't bother to thank him. Instead, he felt his building passion urging himself onward. "It used to be that America was the land of opportunity. See a need and fill it, and the risks you take will be rewarded. But an America that is *too* successful doesn't need *politicians*. So we gradually began to penalize success. It used to be that the harder somebody worked, the more they gained; now the harder they work the greater the compulsory burden that we place on them.

The Hornbrook Prophecy

"Today, the only real success stories are the politicians. Incumbents are reelected at rates of as high as 98 percent. There isn't an entrepreneur alive who wouldn't want a guarantee like that. Old Abe Lincoln used to say, '*You can fool some of the people all of the time, and all of the people some of the time, but you can't fool all of the people all of the time.*' But we have discovered a useful corollary: '*You can fool some of the people all of the time, and all of the people some of the time, and, by golly, that's good enough!*'"

Halsey Brownsville rose and demanded indignantly, "WOULD the Senator yield?"

"No! You can do your grandstanding when I'm done. Now, sit down!" Hornbrook's tone was so uncharacteristically angry for a man who had for years been the most controlled voice of reason on Capitol Hill that Brownsville shrank back into his seat without a word.

"It's time for you all to admit the truth. The underlying assumption for your entire concept of government is that all your constituents are STUPID! They're so stupid that they can't possibly make decisions for themselves and their families about their own lives. Only YOU can help them. This is the fatal conceit. YOU are not stupid. You are wise and benevolent legislators. You are the all-powerful and munificent Oz! You demonized success, and told those who were not successful that they were victims.

"Let me tell you a little joke I heard once: A monkey walks into a tavern and jumps up on a barstool, waves at the bartender, and asks, '*Do you have any bananas?*' The bartender replied, '*No.*' '*Do you have any bananas?*' asked the monkey again. '*No!*' repeated the bartender. '*Do you have any bananas?*' the monkey inquired once more. '*NO!*' yelled the bartender, and he added '*And if you ask me again, I'll nail your lips to the counter!*' '*Okay,*' said the monkey, who hopped down off the stool and disappeared into the crowd. But instead of leaving, the monkey ran down to the other end of the bar, climbed up on a stool and called to the bartender, '*Do you have any nails?*' '*No,*' said the bartender. '*Good,*' said the monkey. '*Do you have any bananas?*'

This time there were a number of chuckles on the Senate floor and even more up in the gallery, as many of those in attendance had become used to jokes from their government. But most of the Senators were fairly subdued, knowing where this anecdote was going to lead. Hornbrook continued on.

"Both the people AND the government often take turns acting like that monkey, trying again and again to either get something they want or to do something they shouldn't, hoping that if they try enough, the other side will get tired of listening to it and give in or at least make it sound like it was *their* idea instead. A number of years ago in my own state, the people repeatedly voted down proposals to build a new sports stadium for the pro baseball or football teams. So the legislature became the monkey: '*Do you want a new stadium?'* they asked the people. '*No.*' voted the people. '*Do you want a new stadium?*' the legislature asked again later. '*No,*' voted the people again. '*Do you want a new stadium?*' '*NO!*' said the people, who added, '*and if you ask us again, we'll vote you out of office!*' So the representatives slinked backed to their office, got together, and figured out how to get what they wanted. '*Is this an election year?*" they asked themselves. '*No? Do you want a new stadium?*' Except they didn't even ask the people this time. They just cooked up new taxes and fees and built TWO new stadiums for a couple of rich owners. Of course, you'd all respond by saying that you only do what your constituents ask of you. But you know even that's not true. Remember when our own colleague, Senator Jay Rockefeller of West Virginia exclaimed, '*We're going to push through universal health care regardless of the views of the American people!*" Are citizens still supposed to believe that we actually represent them?"

The chuckling had stopped. The murmuring re-commenced, but nobody interrupted.

"You stopped listening to reason a long time ago. You haven't been honest with your voters, either. You haven't told them the harm you've done by trampling their rights. You haven't told them the truth about what has happened to the legacy of our forefathers which you inherited on their behalf. So now they have found out on their own. They trusted you to safeguard the country's legacy and you have bankrupted it. Yes! You have made the United States of America—the last, best hope of mankind—intellectually, morally, and constitutionally bankrupt.

You made America *intellectually* bankrupt by persuading the people that the only means to increase prosperity and ease the pain of poverty was by redistributing income and eroding private property rights rather than by generating real economic growth and security. You made America *morally* bankrupt by not telling people that in a truly free society, they are entitled to only what *they* earn, not to what *others* earn, by destroying the family and religious values that once were the backbone of a flourishing civil society, and by replacing compassion with compulsion.

"In addition, you made the country *constitutionally* bankrupt. Because our Constitution is what sets us apart from every other social experiment in human history, this is perhaps the cruelest blow of all. You created a welfare state that has no basis in the Constitution written by our founding fathers. And when I say *welfare* I'm not just talking about poor people on food stamps and Medicaid. Certainly when you give someone cash or other benefits for which they didn't work, you are taking the fruits of labor from someone who has worked for it. But there are many forms of welfare. When you give one group a tax cut, all you do is shift the burden to someone else who must pay. When you let one group shelter income, you must turn around and extract the taxes from others who have no such shelters. When you require that someone be paid more than the market would pay otherwise, you raise the cost of the product or service without raising the productivity. When you pay a farmer to plow under his crop, you force prices artificially higher, creating surpluses which benefit no one. When you keep prices artificially low, you create shortages. When you impose a tariff to protect one group, you raise the prices for others, which decreases their standard of living. When you bloat the budget with pork barrel projects in one community, you do so at the expense of every other community. When you artificially inflate the economy with money you do not have, you force prices to rise, which robs honest working people of their buying power. Indeed, when you gave, without constitutional authority, all those trillions of bailout dollars to mismanaged, inefficient, and irresponsible private entities you passed along a truly hideous burden of debt to generations yet unborn. These are all welfare wolves in different sheeps' clothing. And you care NOT about the sheep!"

Hornbrook paused momentarily, but nobody sought to interrupt, perhaps because they felt their carefully crafted veneer of "sacrifice" and public "service" was being too painfully peeled away to withstand. He continued. "When the Declaration of Independence says that *all men are created equal* it does not mean that we should all *be* equal, or that we are all equal in our abilities and possessions. It only means that we all have the equal rights to pursue our happiness in whatever manner we choose, providing only that we respect the equal rights of others. There is no legal guarantee that if we cannot obtain such happiness then we are allowed to forcibly deprive others of their property in order to obtain it. Nowhere does following the will of the people give you leave to abandon the law. When you changed the role of the federal government from one of protecting the rights, persons, and property of *all*, you broke your oath to uphold the Constitution!

"And having intellectually, morally, and constitutionally bankrupted the nation, you have successfully brought us to the state in which we find ourselves today. *Financially bankrupt* as well! We are all to blame! We do not come to Washington just to do our part and then return home after a couple of years to live with our children in a better place. No, we find it far more satisfying to perpetuate the problems so we can *stay* in Washington. Year after year after year after year. No more is having the power of elected office the means to an end. It *is* the end. Unfettered, unrestricted, uncontrolled. Power.

"For years, the people have been trying to tell us we're *wrong*. And we would not listen. It reminds me of the famous Allegory of the Cave, a parable from *Plato's Republic*. For those of you who spend too much time reading public opinion polls, or who have always considered the classics of Western thought to be something written by Louis L'Amour, let me familiarize you with this. Just remember Plato was writing this over 2500 years ago.

"In the Allegory, Plato has Socrates telling a story of a people who are imprisoned in a cave where they can see nothing for all their lives except shadows on a wall made by a strong light from behind them to which they are unable to turn because of the chains binding them. The shadows are of many different things held up by others, but neither the true objects nor the holders are ever seen. And when a prisoner escapes and finds his way to sunlight, at first he cannot see as the light of truth is so strong. And then when he can see, he does not believe it, as it is so much at odds with the only version of the truth he had ever known. Finally, when he comes to realize how wrong he was, and how wrong were the 'truths' in the Cave, he tries to go back and explain to others how the world really is. Naturally, no one believes him and he is ridiculed, and if they could, they would have killed him to keep from destroying their illusion.

"Well, my *esteemed* colleagues. The Cave of the 21st century is Congress, along with the people who have put trust in you. And even though you are the shadow makers you have been in the Cave so long you have no idea what life is like out in the real world. But, in the last months, the people who have been there with you have had to escape because of your foolishness, and because you kept them in the dark so long, they are suffering in the harsh light of truth, even as I speak. They are now realizing how wrong your illusions are, and how you have deceived them with shadows—or smoke and mirrors, if you prefer. And yet even while they try today to convince you to see the light yourselves, you sit here clinging to your chains of financial deception and constitutional dishonesty."

The Majority Leader once again felt it was his duty to object. "Mr. President! Would you remind Senator Hornbrook—"

Hornbrook fired back quickly. "I need to be reminded of nothing! Except, perhaps, of one last little story. And I do believe, in the light of developments around the nation, that you are going to want to pay attention to this one."

Brownsville, frustrated by events beyond his vast experiences, glared first at Hornbrook and then at Freewater. When the latter shrugged his shoulders, Brownsville sighed and simply sat down.

The Hornbrook Prophecy

Hornbrook didn't hesitate. "I once read a swashbuckler by Rafael Sabatini. In it, the sixteenth or seventeenth century hero is testifying for his life in a serious legal proceeding and, being the hero, he is naturally overly self-assured and contemptuous of the fools he is forced to suffer. But at one point, the prosecutor admonishes him by saying something to the effect, '*Do not assume, sir, that your head is so firmly fastened to your shoulders that it cannot be separated!*' Well, I'm not so sure I don't hear someone sharpening the local guillotine outside the walls of Congress. I can't tell, though, if it's Dillard trying to keep you from the light, or the people who are giving up trying to make you see it.

"The Constitution doesn't say much about how to join the Union. It's completely mute on how to leave. But Jefferson spelled it out pretty clearly for King George, and while a lot of his points are valid once again today, the mechanisms are unclear. We began a war, in 1776, to separate from one union, and eighty-five years later we fought another to keep the new Union together. Today my admonition to you is, *Do not assume, sirs, that the states are so firmly attached to Washington that they cannot leave it!*

"Look outside your Cave! That is the harsh light of truth there right now! You have broken the laws, you have broken the faith, and you are perilously close to breaking the bond—that sacred and historic bond that has united these states in a revolutionary and extraordinary experiment in humanity for nearly two hundred and thirty-five years.

"How unique is that place in history you have carved for yourselves? History will not honor you like the fifty-six men who penned their names to the bottom of the Declaration of Independence. Instead, you will be remembered with disgust, probably with anger, and perhaps even with some sorrow. I knew a nun once who told me that she and her missionary sisters went where they were needed but not wanted, and left when they were wanted but not needed. You, however, have led the American people to a point where they are saying '*We don't __want__ you and we don't __need__ you!*' And *that* will be *your* legacy.

"I will leave you now. It is obvious that the capacity for righting the ship has eluded you, and I am going to return home to help my friends and neighbors consider their options. Their government has failed them. Their leaders have betrayed them. I doubt they will suffer quietly much longer."

And with that, Henley Hornbrook turned and walked out, leaving the Senate chamber in absolute silence.

Chapter 30

"Stroke of the pen. Law of the land. Kinda cool."
—Paul Begala, Clinton aide, on Executive Orders

Wednesday – September 1

While Henley Hornbrook was having a quiet lunch with Lew Weiser and the Springfield brothers, the small television in the kitchen was tuned into the Broadcast Systems News channel more out of habit than any desire to stay abreast of current news developments. But there are certain words that can penetrate consciousness no matter how it might otherwise be occupied.

"We interrupt this program to bring you the following breaking news story. Now, from BSN headquarters in Washington, D.C. here's Garrison Dumfries."

"Oh, what now?" said Hugo.

"Shhh!" said his brother.

"Good afternoon, America, I'm Garrison Dumfries. A few minutes ago, the White House announced that four new executive orders had been issued by President Winston Dillard, to deal with security and economic issues currently facing the nation. The first of these, Executive Order 14901, states that 'Units and members of the Armed Forces of the United States and Federal law enforcement officers will be used to suppress violence and restore law and order in and about any of the fifty states, wherever such violence shall exist.' This order was issued after President Dillard had first issued Proclamation 7288, commanding 'all persons engaged in acts of violence and disorder to cease and desist therefrom, and to disperse and retire peaceably forewith.'"

"Can he do that?" asked Hugo.

"Sure," answered Lew. "There are lots of instances in our history where army troops have been used for civil violence. The last time was during the Rodney King riots in Los Angeles back in the early '90s."

"Wait, there's more!" said Hornbrook.

The Hornbrook Prophecy

"*The justifications for this type of Executive Order can be found in the Code of Federal Regulations, 32 CFR 501, and in Chapter 10, Section 332 of the United States Code, which states, in part, 'Whenever ...unlawful obstructions... or rebellion against the authority of the United States, make it impractical to enforce the laws of the United States in any State or Territory ...(the President) may call into Federal service such of the militia of any State, and use such of the armed forces, as he considers necessary to enforce those laws or to suppress the rebellion.' This power is particularly broad, as the U.S. Supreme Court has stated that a Chief Executive may act unilaterally both in deciding whether an insurrection is in effect, and how much force is necessary to address it.*

"*Congressional leaders have reacted with unusual opposition to the President. Both Majority Leader Halsey Brownsville and House Speaker Sullivan Veradale objected to the decision by the White House to call in the military.*"

"Big deal," mused Hornbrook.

"*The use of federal armed forces in domestic applications was sharply curtailed, after multiple abuses by state and local officials during Reconstruction after the Civil War, by the Posse Comitatus Act in 1878, which stated that, quote, 'From and after the passage of this act it shall not be lawful to employ any part of the Army of the United States as a posse comitatus, or otherwise, for the purpose of executing the laws, except in such cases and under such circumstances as such employment of said force may be expressly authorized by the Constitution or by act of Congress.' Unquote. However, no federal statutes appear to specifically define martial law, and, in practice, the word 'Constitution' has prevented the Posse Comitatus Act from substantially limiting presidential application at will, and he may apply it even in the face of objections from the states.*" Dumfries paused, and looked at the camera with concern. "*Next, Executive Order 14902 directed that all food resources, farms, and farm equipment are to be placed under the direction and management of the Secretary of Agriculture...*"

"What!"

"*...in an apparent effort to see that foodstuffs are distributed—maybe even rationed—in a manner designed to ease citizens' immediate concerns about their basic needs.*"

"Can he do *that*?" asked Gene this time.

As if in response to Springfield's question, the news anchor continued,

"*The Supreme Court has ruled in the past that, quote, 'Whether the President, in fulfilling his duties as Commander-in-Chief suppressing an insurrection, has met with such armed hostile resistance, and a civil war of such alarming proportions as will compel him to accord to them the character of belligerents, is a question to* be decided BY HIM, and this Court must be governed by the decisions and acts of the political department of the Government to which this power was entrusted.' Unquote. In other words, The President has the power to determine what degree of force the crisis demands.

"This is a particularly important determination, as in essence the highest judicial body in the nation has decided that the President can, under certain extreme conditions, command virtually dictatorial power, and that the President has the power, under the circumstances that he can individually deem imperative, to suspend constitutional protections to any and all belligerents he names in any area he deems to be suffering insurrection."

"I think the other shoe is about to drop," ventured Lew.

"It was apparently with these circumstances in mind that the President issued the following press release in conjunction with the remaining two Executive Orders: 'Because the unbiased integrity of any electoral process cannot be guaranteed under circumstances of widespread civil unrest, I have issued Executive Order 14903, which will suspend the upcoming Congressional elections for six months. This order may be shortened or extended depending on the duration of the unrest.'"

"Oh, my God," said Hornbrook.

"The President then declared, and again I quote, 'The decision to defend the integrity and security of all Americans against the unrestrained lawlessness which currently exists in the majority of major cities throughout the United States made necessary the utilization of all of the government's resources, including the armed forces. Unfortunately, although it has been unable to create any other means by which to accomplish this vitally important restoration of law and order, and has been otherwise unable to suggest any viable alternatives to the decisions that I made after close consultation with the Vice President, Congress has vigorously opposed these decisions. Such opposition and obstruction to the President and Commander-in-Chief, under a state of emergency such as currently exists in the nation, must be seen as being no different from a refusal of duty in time of war. Such insubordination threatens the very existence of our democracy, and cannot be tolerated. Therefore, in order to assure appropriate and undivided application of our emergency national policies, I have issued Executive Order 14904, suspending all funding of the operation of the legislative branch of the federal government for the same duration specified under the provisions of Executive Order 14903, and directed the Capitol Police, with the aid of any necessary units of the armed forces, to deny any members of Congress access to any public offices or buildings for the duration of the emergency. When I was inaugurated as your President, I took an oath to preserve, protect, and defend the Constitution of the United States. I regret that Congress has not joined me in upholding their own pledges, but I want *to assure all Americans that your nation will survive, and that Vice President Branford and I are determined to work tirelessly to accomplish these noble goals. Thank you.' Unquote."*

When Dumfries had finished reading the press release, he looked perplexed momentarily, touched his earphone briefly, then looked at the camera, and continued,

"Although it is a frequent political event to dissolve legislatures like Parliament in Great Britain, there is no precedent for such action in the United States. Congressional leaders issued only a single, terse response, and I quote, 'The American people have done nothing to deserve the destruction of their democratic rights to representation and the upending of over two hundred years of freedom and progress. We will respond appropriately in the very near future.' Unquote."

"Holy shit," exclaimed Gene. "He's kicked Congress out of the Capitol?"

"Yes, definitely a new chapter for US History classes," added Lew.

Henley Hornbrook said nothing, but he was thinking of Sir Alexander.

***

The prophecy had been right.

Robert Wickes

Part Three

To Secure These Rights…

"We hold these truths to be self-evident, that all men are created equal, that they are endowed by their Creator with certain unalienable Rights, that among these are Life, Liberty and the pursuit of Happiness. That to secure these rights, Governments are instituted among Men, deriving their just powers from the consent of the governed, That whenever any Form of Government becomes destructive of these ends, it is the Right of the People to alter or to abolish it, and to institute new Government, laying its foundation on such principles and organizing its powers in such form, as to them shall seem most likely to effect their Safety and Happiness."
—Declaration of Independence, July 4, 1776

The Hornbrook Prophecy

Robert Wickes

CHAPTER 31

"When a long train of abuses and usurpations, pursuing invariably the same Object evinces a design to reduce them under absolute Despotism, it is their right, it is their duty, to throw off such Government, and to provide new Guards for their future security."
—The Declaration of Independence (1776)

In the summer of 1776, fifty-six men affixed their signatures to the most daring document ever written. The Declaration of Independence stated simply, yet eloquently, the fundamental precepts about the nature of man, exhaustively itemized the grievances those signers had with a government and a king who ignored those basic principles, and proclaimed for all the world to hear that it was time to eradicate the wrongs and establish a new relationship between those who seek to rule and those who consent to be governed.

The men who signed this unprecedented document were not wild-eyed zealots. Some were lawyers or jurists; others were merchants; some were farmers or plantation owners. There was a teacher, a musician, and a printer. But they all signed knowing the risks of their actions. They were well-spoken men of position and education. Most had financial security, but they all prized their liberty even more, proclaiming,

"For the support of this declaration, with a firm reliance on the protection of the Divine Providence, we mutually pledge to each other, our lives, our fortunes, and our sacred honor."

And indeed the consequences extended far beyond that historic July 4th occasion. During the War for Independence which followed, many had their homes and property destroyed or looted; several were captured and imprisoned by the British; some lost family members. But perhaps the attitude of the signers could best be represented by the first, John Hancock. Contemptuous of unreasoned authority, and knowing that the British had already placed a bounty on the heads of several of the leading colonists, including his own, he signed the Declaration with an oversized flourish, stating "The British ministry can read *that* name without spectacles; let them *double* their reward!"

Thursday – September 2

Henley Hornbrook had returned home after what he was certain was his final speech before the Senate, and had listened in dismay to the announcements of the latest Executive Orders. Now he stood on the exposed rounded cobblestone of the river bed, in the afternoon shade of the grove of gray-barked alders along the bank behind him, and watched various leaves and twigs bobbing and drifting along in the eddies as his aging black, bobbed Australian shepherd waded noisily through the shallows.

The rivers in western Washington act like yo-yos, their levels surging up and down with often-startling rapidity, reflecting the whims of the frequently rain-laden weather. The east fork of the Postas River was no different. Serving a relatively small watershed area, it could rise suddenly with a few inches of rain, and had been known to reach well above flood stage in as little as twenty-four hours. On the other hand, as soon as the rains lessened or stopped, the level quickly dropped back to normal, more often than not leaving behind a tangled gaggle of logs and other river debris on the banks and sandbars.

It had not rained significantly in several weeks, and the late summer river level was very low. The gentle riffles and quiet pools near the banks reflected the coming autumn changes. The alder tree leaves were beginning to tint with yellow and the vine maples drooped their delicate blends of orange and red over the water.

A thousand thoughts clamored as one for Hornbrook's consciousness, and he failed to notice the rustling of the tall, lush grasses and the noisy parting of branches as other footsteps approached him on the uneven ground. Only when a cool bottle brushed against his arm did he notice the outstretched arm, and he half-turned his head to acknowledge his longtime friend. Silently taking the beer, he took a long pull, and let the bitter brew slide easily down his throat.

His thoughts slowed and sorted themselves and, as he watched a lone duck come round the bend and dart upstream barely above the water, he asked, "Lew, what is it about the concept of governments that drives men to bother with them? I mean, with the establishment of any form of authority, the individual—by design—is forced to surrender some degree of his own individual sovereignty. True?"

"True," agreed his friend. "But don't forget only a tiny number of the governments that have existed over the centuries have been the result of the voluntary granting of that authority. Most of the time, it's merely the biggest bully on the block who takes charge and forces everyone to play by whatever rules he makes up."

"OK. Granted. So if we turn back the clock a couple of hundred years to our colonial days, we find Paine, and Jefferson, and Adams and all the rest chafing badly under the rule of King George and very much wanting to make up their own rules. Yes?"

"Of course. So we all learned in grammar school."

"Why?"

"Why what?"

"Why did they want to make up their own rules? Why were they willing to risk their homes, their property, their businesses, and even their lives just to turn around and form yet another monstrous authority to govern their lives?"

"Well, of course, the answer is that they didn't intend to create a monster."

"That's true. They embraced their concepts of liberty and freedom, but they still assumed that government was a necessary evil."

"And they assumed that a government formed by virtuous people with virtuous intent would, in kind, be virtuous."

Hornbrook pondered the water currents for a moment. "Lew, we've got a monumental mess on our hands."

"That's a wonderful understatement, Henley," replied Weiser.

Hornbrook looked down, scanning the rocks with a practiced eye, then bent over and picked up a smooth, flat stone lying by his right foot. He brushed it off, moved it about in his hand until it nestled comfortably in the curve of his forefinger and thumb. Stepping forward, he leaned over and with a quick flick of his arm and wrist, sent the stone skipping effortlessly across the water. Then he straightened, took a deep breath and let it out slowly, regretting perhaps the long-past simplicity of childhood, when throwing rocks into any available body of water was a mindless yet satisfying endeavor. "Lew, let's get the others together. Here. Say in an hour. Did you ever talk to the sheriff about Tom Warner?"

"Yes," said Weiser. "There's no problem. Tom gave a report to the sheriff not long after they got up here. I called him, too, and just heard back. The victims in the carjacking attempt had records, the car they had with them was stolen, and their prints were all over a home near Sacramento where two security guards were shot and killed earlier that night. The Warners did everyone a favor. The Morton ambush was some idiots who had been harassing other cars, too. They evidently meant no real harm, but the sheriff said that Tom was justified in returning fire. It was just a tragic outcome of a senseless prank."

"Make sure you let Tom know."

"I will. And nobody seemed to know anything about a hog-tied agricultural inspector, so I didn't press on it."

"Probably just as well, I imagine."

***

Senator Hornbrook walked through the doorway from the kitchen into the large dining room/living room area of his home, and gazed about at the various friends and colleagues that Lew Weiser had called and invited over. Senators McClintock and Packwood had arrived the night before for some brainstorming. Most of those present were veterans of the Slingshot War. Weiser was talking quietly with Tom Warner next to the sofa where Laurel and Sunny Turner were also in quiet conference. Conspicuous by his absence was Eagle McCall.

Hornbrook asked for attention, and in short order the conversations died out and heads and bodies turned toward him.

"The last few months have been a period unlike any in our nation's history," Hornbrook began. "Two hundred years ago we chafed under rule from afar, but we've never witnessed the self-destructive throes like what we, even here in our quiet little corner of the country, have experienced recently. I don't believe there are many in our nation now who would question that changes must be made. And the question, therefore, becomes what will be the nature of those changes?"

He looked around the room at the quiet but interested faces. "Earlier I asked Lew here why the hell, if they were so unhappy with living under one government, did our founding fathers want to rush to form another? Would anybody like to venture an opinion?"

"Well," began Sunny, "if you don't make at least some rules then you have total anarchy."

"And is that bad?"

"Sure it is," she replied. "In the absence of some kinds of guidelines, I suspect that human nature would make things get kinda ugly. The seven deadly sins, and all that. I think we all just had a taste of that kind of orderless vacuum."

"Okay. Let's assume Sunny's right. What would happen?" posed Hornbrook.

Mort Packwood, whose mood, which never could have been described as cheery and had only become even more sour by the events of the last few months, ventured, "Let's cut the bullshit, Henley. What you're asking is why the hell do we need government, and the answer is that, in the best possible world, we don't. Everybody could just do their own thing, and be just fine. The problem is that this is far from the best possible world."

Loren McClintock, as serious as Packwood, offered, "Mort's right. We are all believers in the concept of the inalienable rights of individuals to do, as Mort put it, 'their own thing.'"

"So what are you really asking, Hornbrook?" asked the older senator.

"Okay, let's get down to it," smiled Henley. "Our beloved Founding Fathers first gave us a historically-unique Declaration of Independence, which inspired a great war for self-determination, and then they wrote a Constitution, which has been held in reverence in the name of liberty by half the world for more than two centuries. And yet here we are, a nationwide, dysfunctional rubble heap. They had a great idea, and now it's screwed!"

He paused, looking around the room again. "I suppose what I am really challenging you to do is tell me how *you* would have changed things, if you had the chance, to prevent what has happened to us from happening to us! If we assume that freedom is preferable to bondage, and since any sort of organization implies that people must give up at least some of their own autonomy to a central authority of some kind, the question remains why should anyone be willing to be less free, less in control of their own destiny, and more subject to the will of others?"

Tom spoke up, saying, "Sunny answered that. Some sort of central authority is an efficient way of protecting ourselves from aggressors. I think that's pretty much what Jefferson meant in the Declaration when he said we have certain rights and that it is, ah, ah…"

"to 'secure these rights'?"

"Yeah, 'to secure these rights' that we form governments. Right?"

"Exactly."

"So the most basic purpose of a government is just to protect those rights so that we don't have to spend all our time looking over our shoulder and sleeping with one eye open so that no one slits our throat or steals our beans."

"Well put, Tom," joined in McClintock. "And it's not only efficient, meaning it takes a relatively small number of people to protect the others, it's also damn convenient, freeing everyone else to *pursue their happiness*, if you will."

"All right, then," said Hornbrook. "So what did Jefferson mean by so-called 'inalienable rights'?"

"He was reflecting John Locke's ideas about natural rights as he wrote in *Two Treatises on Government* back in the late 1600s," said Packwood.

"What do you mean by 'natural' rights?" asked Clark Terwiliger.

Hornbrook explained, "Locke theorized that when man lived in a state of nature, prior to the formation or organization of governments, he had certain rights, rights that were his by virtue of his human existence and which were not—and could not—be either diminished nor enhanced by others."

"But Henley," complained Packwood, "the argument against Locke's theories is that man *never* really existed in a pure state of nature. And that every person is subject to the laws of the nation in which he is born."

"That may be true on both accounts," conceded Hornbrook, "but the arguments are irrelevant. Just because an individual never actually existed in a state of nature does not mean that he is not possessed of those same certain natural rights as he would have had, had he indeed, actually existed in the hypothetical state of nature. The circumstances or whereabouts of his creation do not affect his entitlement to those rights! The Declaration, of course, states that these rights are derived from our Creator—God, if you will. But the concept of natural rights does not absolutely depend on a belief in God. The essential concept is that such rights, unlike so-called rights to a job or healthcare, are not granted by any early ruler or body and therefore cannot be taken away. No one else is obligated to give up anything in order for you to have them."

"So what does all that mean?" inquired a somewhat confused Bertha Terwiliger.

Hornbrook took a deep breath before continuing. "The natural rights that Locke and Jefferson and others like them were talking about were fundamental ideas that a person, *any* person, was entitled to his own life and the freedom to live it has he wished, so long as he did not infringe on the equal rights of other persons to live their own lives as *they* wished. Inherent in such natural rights was the right to the ownership of property, because without the right to property a person could not be guaranteed the right to be secure in his own life. And one of the forms that property rights takes is that a person is said to have 'property' in his own body, and therefore is entitled to the ownership of the fruits of his own labor."

"You mean any kind of labor?" asked Laurel.

"The original concept of property ownership was that when a man mixed his own labor with the land, then he was said to own the land and whatever the land produced as a result of his labor. In other words, the land had no intrinsic value until it was physically worked by man, who then owned it and its produce. Of course, that was true only for land that was not being *worked* by someone else already."

"All right, then, Senator Hornbrook," began Web Johnson, "what if I'm not a farmer? What if I can't plow the land?"

"That's the perfect question to ask. Man's history is one of attempting to raise his standard of living, and if you have to spend all your time growing your food, you'll always live a primitive life. So as civilizations grew, there was an ever-increasing division of labor, which allowed greater efficiency and greater productivity per worker. With time, man developed monetary units to make more convenient the exchanges between different types of laborers. Not only farmers produce things. No matter what you do, even if you don't build something entirely yourself, when you add your labor to the overall effort, you create something of value. If you work an assembly line, you contribute to the completion of the particular product, and therefore a certain proportion of the value of the product belongs to you. To make things convenient, the owner of the plant where you work gives you money and sometimes other benefits in exchange for your share of the value of the product. Then he can turn around and sell the product as a complete entity.

"Okay, Senator," said Web, "I understand that. But how come my 'fruit' keeps shrinking?"

"Well, Web, that is indeed the crux of the matter. For if you have a natural, or *inalienable*, right to life and property—even if it's in the form of your paycheck—then you also have the right not to have that property taken from you without your consent. Remember, we said the philosophy of natural rights is the right to live your life as you see fit so long as you don't infringe on the same rights that everyone else has, too. So if someone—or some government—takes your property without your consent, they have violated your rights."

"But don't we give our consent when we form a government?" asked Clark.

"Yes, but with specific limits. The Declaration of Independence stated that all people have certain rights and the reason we consent to form a government is not to *get* those rights, but to protect those rights. Our ancestors professed the idea that a government has no rights itself—it has only *power*. And it should have only the power that it is granted by its citizens solely for the purpose of enabling it to keep them secure in their person and their property."

"But there *is* a cost," argued Clark. "The government has to tax the people in order to have the means to protect those rights, doesn't it? And there are bound to be people who feel like the government's taxing them too much no matter how little they're paying."

Hornbrook agreed. "Yes, of course, Clark. There is a price to pay for that security. But the trouble in this country began when the government began charging people for more than their basic rights' protection. In other words, you can't really complain about the relatively small cost involved in those government services related to protect your rights, because that's the only real justification for government in the first place. However, when the government begins to tax people to pay for other kinds of services, then it begins to cross the line of infringement. That's when complaints become justified."

"But what about when the people vote to allow those services?" asked Kent Westland.

"That, of course, is the big question. Is that not the nature of a democracy? And is not a democracy—even a republic like ours—based on the will of the majority?"

"I guess so, that's the way it's always been."

"It's certainly the way it's been for a long time, but it's not the way it was supposed to be. If we all have individual rights, what happens when we disagree with the majority? Do we forfeit our rights? How do we protect the rights of minorities? And by minorities, I mean anyone who is voting on the side with less than 50 percent on any issue. What protects the minority?"

"The law?" asked Laurel.

"Sure, but *what* laws. Majority votes create laws, too. What determines if a law is really proper? Is there any limit to the power of government to interfere in our lives?"

"The Constitution," said Tom, decisively.

"Yes!" said Hornbrook, pounding a fist into the palm of his other hand. "The Constitution is the limit we placed on our government when we formed it to secure our rights. And the success we have had as a nation is because we let the law rule the men, rather than let the men rule the law. It's only been in the last several decades that we found ways to pretend that new powers of the government were allowed by the Constitution. We rationalized new powers and new laws every year even when they not only had nothing to do with securing our rights, but actually forcibly compelled us to give up our rights, and our property. We gave more and more power, and more and more control over our lives, to the government. And too often that power is misapplied, misinterpreted, or just abused. The Constitution was crafted to specify and precisely define the limits of the power we gave the government. When we ignored those limits we ran risks. When we trampled the Constitution, we abandoned the security of our rights. And what we have now is the result."

"So what now, Henley?" asked Loren McClintock softly.

"Yes," sighed Hornbrook. "What now?"

"Maybe it's time to roll our own, Senator," said Tom Warner, quietly.

"Come again?" said Henley Hornbrook, remembering Lew's identical words.

Tom hesitated, then dove in. "They always say, 'If it ain't broke, don't fix it,' and 'Mend it, don't end it' but the way I see it our government IS broken, and it isn't worth fixing because even if they figure a way out of this mess they'll just go back to doing business as usual. So maybe it's time to do what Jefferson, and Madison, and the Adamses, and all the others did—maybe it's time to say goodbye and start all over, at least out here in the Northwest to start."

There was a momentary pause until the words sank in, and then everybody was talking at once.

"Amen!" said Boomer.

"Yeah!" agreed Red.

The tumult continued for several minutes until the Senator was able to get everyone settled down again. "Please, everybody! Let's not get too excited."

"What did he mean by that?" asked a still-confused Bertha Terwiliger.

"I believe the good Mr. Warner is advocating starting our own country. Isn't that right, Tom?"

"Well, sir, I guess so," said a slightly embarrassed Tom. It now sounded pretty crazy, even to him. "But, it's not—" He stopped.

"Not what, Tom?" said Hornbrook.

"Well, I was going to say it's not like it's never been done before."

"You're right, of course. But consider this: The United States of America was the most extraordinary nation ever established, formed through the efforts of remarkable men with remarkable ideas, and blessed with a fresh slate, a new continent, abundant natural resources, and had two oceans' worth of protection so wide it rarely had to fight a foreign power on its own soil. And yet here we are—in financial ruin, with a maniac at the controls, and under martial law. Why? Where did we go wrong? What was the fatal flaw in this grand experiment? And most importantly, *why do you think you can do better?*"

No one said anything. The Senator's final sentence had been like dousing a fire with cold, sobering water. What might have, in one moment, seemed like a truly exhilarating idea had, in the next, seemed impossible.

"I'm sorry," said Hornbrook. "I didn't mean to sound like a stern father telling you that you can't go out on a date. But it surely must occur to you that today is not like two hundred years ago."

Tom, whose bubble the Senator had burst, now found himself warming to the challenge. "You're right, Senator. It's NOT two hundred years ago. That's actually good, I think. It seems to me that back then the uniqueness of the Founding Fathers' nation building effort was as much a disadvantage as it was their strength."

Hornbrook smiled. *Tom gets it, although he probably doesn't realize it.* "Go ahead, Tom."

"Maybe it would actually be *easier* now," said Tom, "because we don't have to reinvent the wheel. We know what *worked*. We just have to fix the, ah, fatal flaw? I think that's what you called it. Yeah. Just change what made it go bad, and keep the basics."

"Well, just for the sake of argument, let's assume that all of us here, no, let's say that most everybody in our state, or maybe even the whole Northwest, wanted to go along with your idea and just start our own country. But they all agree that it's no use unless we identify that terrible 'fatal flaw.' And how do we identify what *worked*?"

Loren McClintock spoke up. "Well, Henley, we know what *doesn't* work."

"Yes, Loren?"

"Well, another advantage we have in the twenty-first century that they didn't have in the eighteenth is that there have been a bunch of other failed attempts at nation-building in between. Namely socialism and several other forms of totalitarianism."

"So what was it about those systems that doomed *them* to failure?"

"I think it's pretty simple. With socialism and communism and the like, the state is more important that the individual. In this country it was just the opposite."

"Not lately," said the hard-faced Packwood. "But she's basically right."

"Thanks, Mort," said McClintock. "When the state is supreme the individual is subordinated. You don't have any so-called individual rights. The state giveth, and the state taketh away. The system is corrupted from the beginning because those in power make the rules and put up with little in the way of objections."

Hornbrook nodded. "Yep, the idea of equality among the masses gives way to privilege for the few. In the worst-case instances, it gave birth to monsters like Hitler and Stalin and others like them. But even in the most idealistic, theoretical circumstances, there's another killer of progress and growth. What happens when everyone shares equally, no matter what?"

"No one wants to work," said Packwood.

"Right! Why would they? Let's face it, no matter how much you may want us all to be the same, we just aren't. We all have different abilities and different potentials. You can't change that, and you certainly can't legislate it away. All that happens when you try is that you kill the incentives to achieve. If no matter what you do, or how smart you are, or how rare your talent, or how hard you work, you end up with just the same as everyone else, sooner or later you're going to stop trying. When there's no incentive to succeed, when there's no pay-off for taking financial or intellectual risks, then there will be no risk-taking."

"That's it in a nutshell, all right, Henley," said Packwood.

"Other nations have been powerful and wealthy, and had a multitude of natural resources. What made us different, I think, is that we were the first nation where the government was designed to largely leave its citizens alone. And left to our own devices, we took chances, we explored, we became adventurers in every field because of the potential for success. And when our government began to interfere, when the social engineers began to legislate equality, when we began to grant special privileges and reward the non-productive, we took away that potential for success and we lost our incentives.

When we ignored the marketplace, we lost our competitiveness. We lost our advantage and descended into mediocrity."

"And that was our 'fatal flaw'?" asked Tom.

"And that was our 'fatal flaw'," agreed Hornbrook.

"So, Henley," posed Loren. "Can we do better?"

Mort Packwood stood up, needing to move around. "I tell you, Henley, I'm so fed up with things that I've got to admit to being tempted to try it. What do we have to lose?"

Another silence fell upon the room. This time there was a sense of excitement.

"Let me be honest, here, folks. I've given this a lot of thought myself. I've met with a lot of people over the past several weeks, people who represent many facets of our state, in business and other groups. I've also had a lot of conversations with members of Congress and the Senate, besides my friends right here today. And there are a *lot* of them who are inclined to agree with you all. Now," admitted Hornbrook. "I confess that the day the President declared that he was effectively closing Congress, I found myself thinking of contingency plans. One of them was the same action as you are now proposing. I have not discussed it previously, because I am loath to consider it seriously; at the same time, however, any real remedy to this mess is going to have to involve some drastic changes."

"Henley," said Packwood, "if the government fails us or betrays us, are we not obliged to consider change, even if it seems drastic?"

"Yes, you're right. That's something else Jefferson wrote in the Declaration of Independence. But I still think the best-case scenario would be to figure out some means to get the nation to climb back on board the Constitution and eliminate the loopholes that got us in this mess. Personally, I'd hate to be the one who called for an end to the United States of America. Besides, what happened the last time some states tried to 'throw off' the federal government?"

"Civil war," said Tom, grimly.

"Exactly. So are we willing to risk that? What would be our resources to defend our choice? What if the whole state was behind us? Would we fight? Could we?"

"Maybe we could use the National Guard," said Boomer from the far side of the room.

"Sure, maybe," Hornbrook said. "And sure, maybe, we get our heads handed to us. I don't think they'd be capable of standing up to a determined US Army, do you?"

Sunny had a sudden revelation. "Excuse me, Henley. Where's McCall?"

Hornbrook smiled. "On an errand."

"What kind of errand?"

"To get some answers for us," was his reply.

Chapter 32

> *"Our way of living together in America is a strong but delicate fabric. It is made up of many threads. It has been woven over many centuries by the patience and sacrifice of countless liberty-loving men and women."*
> —Wendell Lewis Wilkie (1892-1944)

Friday – September 3

Even the press had loudly applauded the highly unusual proposal by new Governor LaGrande. It played well across the state, and the legislature approved the one-time electoral procedure change by a wide margin, but after an entire week almost no one stepped forward to challenge the likeable new Governor.

Almost.

***

"PERRY ROBBS?" exclaimed Elgin LaGrande.

"Yes, Elgin," said a subdued Athena Weston. "Just before the filing period closed late this afternoon, he submitted his name for the special primary election the legislature approved at your request."

"Well, I know I asked for it," LaGrande said, somewhat bewildered by the news. "Was he the only last minute filer?"

"The only one."

"Then according to the protocol passed by the legislature on Tuesday, there won't actually be a primary election after all. He and I would be the top two vote getters by default, so we'll just automatically go on the November ballot. They set it up that way to save the cost of another election if they could. And that's fine with me. I fully expected a challenge; I just never expected it from out in left field."

"I didn't either, but I guess I'm not surprised." Athena was pensive. "Perry's always been a grandstander, of course, and although he's never been a politician, he's got a pretty good opinion of himself. And now, after his role in stopping the riots, he's gained even more popularity and a boatload of good publicity. That's always fuel for ambition."

"Yeah, it certainly makes a good launch pad for a campaign."

"Do you think he'll have a hard time with bad publicity?"

"Like what?"

"His association with Rufus Pendleton is no secret, and everyone knows the stories about Pendleton and the Black Guard. And Biggs Wasco was obviously assassinated in the same manner as the other Guard murders."

"*Alleged* Guard murders—they never could prove the Black Guard was responsible. And all four of those earlier cases were scumbags, so legal or not, there was never a lot of outrage. And Wasco wasn't a whole lot better. So, if anything, there's a little bit of the folk hero aura around Pendleton. No, I don't think Robbs is carrying any baggage coming into the race."

"Do you think it will *be* a race?"

"I think Perry is very good at stirring emotions in people, and emotions get people to the polls. He has a colorful background, a reputation as a champion for civil rights as well as the poor, a newsmaker, and now, as you said, new credentials as a peacemaker. A lot of people are going to like him as a candidate. I think the next two months will be even more interesting— and challenging—for me than if Scio had been running against me as the incumbent."

"I guess we'll get our first clues in a couple of days."

"Meaning?"

"He's got a press conference scheduled for Monday. It's not like him not to pass up an opportunity to build momentum. After all, today's filing *was* a surprise for everyone, not just us."

"I think that's precisely why he's waiting. He also knows it was a surprise, and by not saying a word for a couple of days, he's creating speculation and building interest. It's a sure way to guarantee widespread coverage in the media, even on a holiday. And that's a great way to kick off a campaign."

"I guess we'll know more then."

"I guess."

Chapter 33

> *"Whenever the legislators endeavor to take away and destroy the property of the People, or to reduce them to slavery under arbitrary power, they put themselves into a state of war with the People, who are thereupon absolved from any further obedience. By this breach of Trust they forfeit the power the People put into their hands for quite contrary ends, and it devolves to the People, who have a Right to resume their original Liberty."*
> —John Locke, 1689

Saturday – September 4

Both Eagle McCall and the Chairman of the Joint Chiefs-of-Staff were dressed in casual attire. The two men shook hands when they met outside the entrance to the small Italian restaurant in the old brick building on King Street. Cate's Bistro, in Old Town Alexandria, attracted a lot of tourists, and the older man had chosen it for that reason. Most of the government types avoided it, in spite of its excellent menu. As they walked past the narrow staircase leading to private rooms upstairs and entered the main dining room, McCall knew that it was a good choice. In the small, packed environment, the noise level was high. The woman at the black baby grand piano in the middle of the room kept up a constant medley of pleasant melodies, and mixed with the clamor of diners struggling to talk to each other over the competition of their neighbors it made a single conversation difficult to hear from more than a few feet away.

After they had been seated at the elegant linen-laid table, the waiter handed them their menus and rattled off the house specialties for the evening. When he departed, after first taking their wine order, they perused the offerings. "Well, General," began McCall, "what's good?"

General Canby L. "Hub" Hubbard replied, "I haven't been here in a long time, Major, but as I recall the *tortellini alla boscaiola* was pretty good."

McCall took his advice, adding a tomato salad with red bell peppers, sweet fresh basil, scallions, extra virgin olive oil, and fresh lemon dressing. Hubbard chose the *Insalata di mozzarella* to begin with, and *Agnolotti di Napoli* in tomato sauce with fresh herbs and garlic. At Hubbard's urging, McCall spent a few minutes recounting the adventure of the Slingshot War against Lincoln Burbank and his mob.

After they were served, Hubbard waited patiently. It was Senator Hornbrook who had contacted him to request this meeting, so the ball was in McCall's court. "General," began McCall a few moments later, "I'd like to thank you again for taking the time to meet with me."

"Major, I'll take most any excuse to get out of the Pentagon these days, and especially away from the White House. Besides, I was intrigued by your boss's request to keep this quiet," Hubbard responded, keeping his voice just loud enough to be heard by McCall. "But in this case, it's my pleasure, both because I always admired your testimony before Congress after Afghanistan, and also because your boss is one of the few people on the Hill I admire."

"The Senator appreciates that. He also appreciates that you're in a very difficult situation right now as Chairman of the JCS, since *your* boss is so, ah, unique."

"Man, there's an understatement." The very un-military response served to relax him. "Okay, so what's on the Senator's mind?"

"General, Senator Hornbrook—and several other of his colleagues in the Northwest, and other areas—are deeply concerned over events, and are not convinced that the Administration will be able to pull this one out of the fire. They feel that right now there are only three possible courses of action. First would be to do nothing, and just let things happen. But at the current rate of deterioration of the economy, they feel it could be years or maybe decades before the country might recover from the damage. Second, they could overthrow the existing government."

The Chairman stopped his fork in mid-air. "You can't be serious!" he exclaimed.

"Oh, don't worry. I mean, it's a serious and real enough alternative all right. But not to them. They discarded it immediately as both illegal and unconscionable."

"And the third?"

"There is a building sentiment out there to bite the bullet and go it alone."

"What do you mean?" said Hubbard reflexively, and then, with sudden understanding, added incredulously, "*Secede?* You *can't!* You *mustn't!*"

"The Senator is struggling to see another way. But he is afraid that something extreme must happen to reverse the present course."

"You can't!" repeated the general, raising his voice. Then realizing he had drawn a few stares from nearby tables, he dropped his tone again. "We are one nation, *indivisible!*" His look steeled. "And a lot of others spilled their blood for it."

"I know that, General. I've been there, too." said McCall. "Senator Hornbrook, you, me, everyone like us, has fought for it also. This is a worst case scenario. But it is a scenario that must be considered, because the current alternative may be impossible to recover from. Things are in a bad way, General Hubbard, as you know. It's our duty to look for answers. Actually, the Senator thinks it could be not so much a formal and irreconcilable separation as a sort of 'leave of absence' from the Union. It would allow currently interested states to make adjustments to their own local and regional governments and economic operations necessary to re-establish their fiscal and social stability, free from federal interference. He believes that such an example could inspire other states to follow their lead until, eventually, the country could be re-united and reconciled sufficiently to restructure the central government."

"So why come to me?" he asked, knowing the answer already.

"Because if any state actually took such action, Dillard would go ballistic and you'd be his very first phone call. He'd want to fight another Civil War."

"And would you fight?"

"No."

"Why not?"

"We don't have the resources to fight, for one thing. And because a new civil war really *would* destroy the country."

"So, again, why come to me if you're not willing to fight over it?"

"Because the Senator wants to know if *you* would!"

"You mean, would I defy the President and not send the military to stop you?"

"Yes, sir."

"He'd replace me with someone who'd support him if I didn't."

"Not if the military stood behind you."

"Defy the President? He's the Commander-in-Chief! That would be unconstitutional."

"So's shutting down Congress. He's a near-dictator right now, but he only has power if the military backs him up."

"This is the damnedest thing I've ever heard in all my days!"

"Yes, sir. But that doesn't change the question. If they go—that is, if they vote formally for self-determination—would the military back the President?"

General Hubbard did not answer for several moments. He picked up his wine glass and emptied it in one swallow, wishing for something stronger. Finally, he said, "I don't know, McCall. You and I were both trained as warriors, and you know that on the battlefield warriors don't have the luxury of thinking about their decisions. But as much as it goes against a lifetime of training for instant decision-making, I can only repeat—I don't know. I am honestly going to have to think about this."

"I understand, sir."

"When does Senator Hornbrook need to know?"

"To be honest, General, the Senator is reluctant to pursue this course of action, because of all of the same sentiments as you've just expressed. However, as I said, there is a fairly strong movement building."

Hubbard thought for a minute. Then he nodded his head, "Give me forty-eight hours. I have others I'd have to talk to."

"He was hoping you'd say that. Here is the Senator's private number at his residence." He handed the general a card. He would welcome your call at any time. And he appreciates your discretion."

"Goddammit, McCall," said the old pilot. "I should've stayed in the cockpit."

"Yes, sir. I understand."

***

The three stern-faced men sat on the plush furniture in front of the unlit marble fireplace. "I've got to tell you," began General Hubbard, "I'm beginning to think I'm caught in some cheesy B-film, slinking about like some unsavory character in the shadowy underworld or something."

"Well, General, I must admit that we are certainly curious about your request to meet with us privately and urgently, in spite of the late hour," replied Halsey Brownsville, handing his guests their drinks in the study of his home. "But there has been so much going on that's out of the ordinary, Sully and I are beginning to expect it."

The Speaker of the House nodded in agreement. "Halsey's right. Having the Chairman of the Joint Chiefs call us for a secret powwow in the middle of the night hardly seems any more bizarre than the rest of it. So why don't you tell us what's on your mind?"

"What would you say if I told you I've been given to believe that some states are contemplating secession?" His short, abrupt statement caught them by surprise, as McCall's had done to him earlier in the evening.

Brownsville reacted first. "Good God!" he exploded. He looked at Veradale, whose jaw had dropped open. "Are you kidding? What have you heard?"

"Only that some prominent legislators have been having discussions in their home states and are being pressured to take such action in preference to, shall we say, death by abuse from Washington, D.C."

Sullivan Veradale found his voice, "I suppose I can't say as I'm too surprised. As extreme as such a move would be, I think the sense of failure across the country is widespread enough to make it almost inevitable that someone would think about it."

"Okay, Hub," said Brownsville. "You definitely got our attention with that little tidbit. Now, let's talk turkey. The Chairman of the JCS doesn't slink around just to report wild rumors. Just who have you spoken to, and how serious are they?"

"I had dinner earlier this evening with a certain Eagle McCall, who is an aide to—"

"Senator Henley Hornbrook!" exclaimed the Majority Leader. "What a surprise."

"I might have known it'd be him," agreed Veradale. "That son of a bitch! He wants to tear the country apart!"

"No," said Brownsville firmly, shaking his head. "I'm afraid we may have left him no other choice. He's warned us and lectured us and pleaded with us not to do what we've done over the years. He even tried to show us how it could be different. And we ignored him—no, worse than ignored, we derided him. The President even publicly blamed him for everything. He had to fight off an armed mob that attacked him and his friends and neighbors. Who could blame him after all this?"

"It's my understanding, sir," said Hubbard, "that Senator Hornbrook himself apparently *doesn't* want to secede, but there's evidently a significant groundswell of support for it." The general then explained, as best he could, what McCall had characterized as a so-called leave of absence. "At any rate, he's afraid that something akin to such a route may be the only course left to them. They see no hope for positive resolution with the current Administration."

"I'll be damned!" said Veradale. "He's like a lot of people out West who have grown to distrust decisions affecting their homes and lives being made by people a continent away."

"It's more than that," said Brownsville. "It's not so much local control as *self*-control that he's always lobbied for. His principles have been unshakeable, and his actions consistent with his philosophies. I've always admired that. And, much as I'd hate to admit it, it could be that he's been right all along." He got up and walked across the room to the window overlooking the city across the Potomac. He could just make out the illuminated Capitol dome, majestic on the night skyline. He stood alone, and silent for several moments then, as a possible solution occurred to him, he quickly turned and walked back to the others.

"General," he said, "I want to thank you for coming to us with this news. It tells me volumes about your feelings on the current situation. It may not feel like it, but I think you've just performed a great service to your country. But as this is no time for misinterpretation, I have a critical question to ask you, your answer must be definite and I must have it tonight."

"Yes, sir?"

"The President has told the police to bar Congress from meeting, and has ordered the military to ensure that his directives are carried out. Is that your intention, General?"

"Sir?"

"If Congress meets in defiance of the President, it will create the most significant Constitutional crisis in the history of our nation. On one side you have the People of the United States and their duly elected representatives in Congress, and on the other is the President and Commander-in-Chief of the Armed Forces. On whose side will you stand, General?"

The General was silent for a full minute. Then he gave them his reply.

The Hornbrook Prophecy

"I see," said Brownsville. "In that case, I have one final request to make of you."

"Yes, sir. What is it?"

"We need a lift."

"When?"

"Tonight."

Chapter 34

"I do not chose to be a common man. It is my right to be uncommon. I seek opportunity to develop whatever talents God gave me, not security. I do not wish to be a kept citizen, humbled and dulled by having the state look after me. I want to take the calculated risk; to dream and to build, to fail and to succeed. I refuse to barter incentive for a dole. I prefer the challenges of life to the guaranteed existence; the thrill of fulfillment to the stale calm of utopia. I will not trade freedom for beneficence nor my dignity for a handout. I will never cower before any earthly master nor bend to any threat. It is my heritage to stand erect, proud and unafraid; to think and act myself, enjoy the benefit of my creations and to face the world boldly and say: 'This, with God's help, I have done.' All this is what it means to be an American."
—Dean Alfange, Immigrant (1952)

Sunday – September 5

Henley Hornbrook heard the doorbell and, knowing that Weiser and the Springfield brothers had gone into town, he finished tying his shoe and strode out of the bedroom, up the hall, and into the small foyer in the front of the house. When he opened the door, you could have knocked him over with a feather.

"Good morning, Henley. God, it really is gorgeous here today," said a smiling Halsey Brownsville, standing next to Sullivan Veradale as he gestured toward the panoramic view of the hills surrounding Hornbrook's home on the former game farm.

Hornbrook recovered from his surprise, and said, "Well, Halsey, Sully, I just never know who's going to show up on my doorstep. Not too long ago it was Lincoln Burbank and a bunch of his friends."

"I saw the reports on that. It was reprehensible and unforgivable for the President to say what he did on national television."

"Not for him. But that's okay. We lived through it and, as you can see, the sun is shining and the gods are happy. So to what do I owe the honor of your visit this morning to the great Northwest?"

"We want to talk to you about the President," was the short reply.

"Now why on earth would you want to spoil a perfectly good day?" sighed Hornbrook. He backed up and waved them in. "I suppose if you've come all this way, it would be inhospitable of me not to hear you out. Perhaps we ought to find someplace other than the doorway to chew on it."

A few minutes later, they were seated on the deck at the rear of the house, enjoying the morning sun. That is, at least Hornbrook, casually attired in jeans, sneakers, and a golf shirt and sipping a tall glass of cranberry juice, was enjoying the morning sun. The other two men looked decidedly less at ease, even though they also wore just slacks and sport shirts. There were no briefcases open, or papers scattered all over, or pens and pencils out, or aides milling about as would characterize a normal meeting between congressional powerhouses, but the stakes were about to be higher than ever.

Brownsville dropped the first bombshell. "We're going to impeach the President on Tuesday."

Hornbrook was in mid-swallow, and his right eyebrow arched in surprise. Then he put his glass down, and looked at the two other men. "Well, there's welcome news. Did you find the keys to the Capitol doors?"

"A minor inconvenience," said Brownsville, dismissively. "We don't need funding to do what needs to be done. It's a slam dunk in our opinion. High crimes, misdemeanors, treason, you name it—he can't just shut the door on democracy and hope that nobody cares. We're notifying all the members of the House and Senate to reconvene for an emergency meeting."

Hornbrook looked at his watch. "You're off to a bright and early start this morning, but aren't *you* on the wrong coast to take care of that sort of business?"

"This whole thing was triggered by a visit late last night by Canby Hubbard," said Brownsville, who this time enjoyed seeing both of Hornbrook's eyebrows climb his forehead. "And he made some fast transportation available to us. He came to us because of his misgivings about the current crisis and the President's actions. Anyway, we left in the wee hours this morning, and will be returning as soon as we leave here and get back to McChord Air Force Base."

"Gee, nobody called *me* about a meeting. Don't you guys love me anymore?" asked Hornbrook sarcastically. "And why the hell are you out here, anyway? You don't need my permission. And if you impeach Dillard you get Branford. That's hardly a step up."

"We're impeaching Branford simultaneously," said the House Speaker, who joined Brownsville watching the renewed eyebrow action.

"Well, congratulations, Sully! That'll make you the new President."

"No, it won't. Since I'm Speaker of the House of Representatives that will impeach both the President and Vice-President, I'm recusing myself from the line of succession to avoid any appearance of being self-serving."

"So that would put the Senate President *pro tempore* in the White House. And that's—"

"The current Pro-Temp isn't up to the challenge. We know it and he knows it—or at least he soon will. We're going to elect a new one before the House begins the impeachment proceeding," interrupted Brownsville.

"So who do are you going to tab? Milt Freewater? I'm sorry, but I don't think you'd be doing the country a favor."

"No."

"Then who?"

"You," said Hornbrook's long-time political adversary, who was rewarded with Hornbrook's most extreme eyebrow action yet.

"You must be joking!" said a flabbergasted Hornbrook, who rose to his feet in his astonishment.

Brownsville also stood up, and took a step toward him. "No, Henley, we're not," he said with feeling. "I've spent my whole career thinking one way. I've always been convinced that it's the government's job to help the people, that it's a national responsibility to help those in need, to make as many opportunities available to as many people as possible to get ahead, and to make things as fair as we can. I still believe that. Yet, in many ways, obviously, you were right, too. Maybe we did go too far. I admit that with the benefit of 20/20 hindsight there probably were many things we did that we really shouldn't have done. We had good intentions, but even if for the best of reasons, we should have stayed within the confines of constitutional intent and not merely rationalized the law to meet our own needs. It's a sobering experience to have to admit one's own mistakes.

"No one ever questioned your dedication and compassion, Halsey."

"Perhaps, but that's not important now," Brownsville continued. "Only the country matters. I don't believe the world would be better off without the United States, but more than that, our own citizens *deserve* better than what we've given them. And now they deserve a leader who values their abilities, not one who merely covets their votes. You're well respected, Henley, inside and outside the Beltway. That's never been more true than it is now. And, whether you know it or not, your little escapade with Burbank's mob got a tremendous amount of media attention, since it occurred right after the President's speech."

"I can't claim any credit for our success in that incident. McCall and our neighbors were the ones responsible for turning back those thugs. Even the kids played more of a role than I did," Hornbrook added honestly.

Brownsville shook his head in an exaggerated manner. "What actually happened is irrelevant. You know how the media works. In this case it's simple—everyone was aghast at what the President said. Burbank was made out to be acting directly because of it, his ruthless mob attacked your peaceful valley, and you and your friends stood up to them valiantly and successfully. It was a movie script played out across the country on the evening news. Whether or not you personally slayed the dragon doesn't matter. You're a hero. And you've always spoken out against the very policies that are now, finally, being blamed for our economic collapse. The people will rally to support you. And what's more Congress will listen to you. At least *this* time. What do you say?"

Hornbrook walked across the deck and leaned against the railing, staring out at the serene view of green pastures, forested hills, and blue skies. Brownsville started to take a step to follow him, but Veradale put a hand on his arm to restrain him. They left Hornbrook alone with his thoughts for several minutes. Finally, taking a deep breath, Henley turned and slowly walked back to rejoin them.

"No."

"What!" exploded Veradale.

"You *have* to," cried Brownsville.

It was Hornbrook's turn to enjoy the facial expressions of the other two men. "Excuse me. What I meant was, no, not unless you agree to support my conditions."

"Good God, Hornbrook," said Brownsville, "you gave me a start. I didn't realize until just now how much I was taking for granted your positive reply."

"Then you accept?" asked Veradale.

"What I said was that I would consider your proposal, but only if you support my conditions."

"I can't imagine having any problem with that," said Brownsville. "What are they?"

He told them.

Neither the Senate Majority Leader nor the Speaker of the House of Representatives had any idea how high their eyebrows rose.

When Lewiston Weiser returned an hour later, he rushed into the house and found Hornbrook in his library, dressed in a suit, and putting some papers in his briefcase.

"Henley! I just got a call from Sunny, and she said she's been asked to return to Washington for an emergency meeting of Congress. Did you get called, too? Why didn't you phone me?"

"Slow down, Lew. You'll blow a fuse."

"So what's this all about?"

"Get some stuff together, we're going back, too. And we've got a lot of work to do before we arrive."

"Work on what? I thought the Chief-of-Staff was supposed to know what's going on?"

"So get yourself a new job," chided his boss, smiling to himself. "Try the White House. I hear the Chief-of-Staff's job there is about to come open."

"Huh?"

CHAPTER 35

> *"New opinions are always suspected, and usually opposed without any other reason but because they are not already common.*
> —John Locke (1632-1704)

Monday – September 6

Over the past several days the airwaves and newsprint, even in Alabama, had been awash with breaking stories, each competing to surpass the previous, of riots, mini-wars, blistering political speeches, executive orders, unprecedented blows to democracy, and now even rumors of new, impending power struggles between the White House and Congress. It would have been understandable, therefore, if the media had chosen to overlook a mere news conference by an attorney, even one as frequently flamboyant as Perry Robbs. But public demand for news information was at a heightened state and, even on a day as traditionally slow as Labor Day, the national news outlets were enjoying all-time high ratings.

Typical for events staged by Robbs, everything was well-orchestrated. A few well-placed telephone calls had resulted in the presence of camera crews from all four major network TV stations, as well as CNN, Fox, and BSN, all lured with the assurance that if they missed his speech, they would never again be taken seriously as a news source. The media, some legislators, and several busloads of residents from the most poverty-stricken neighborhoods of Montgomery were gathered on the steps of the Capitol building waiting for the appearance of Alabama's newest gubernatorial aspirant.

Robbs waited long enough to assure that everyone was present, and that there had been enough time for speculation to rage back and forth about his announcements, but not so long as to foster impatience and restlessness. When he felt the time was right, he nodded to Rufus Pendleton behind the wheel of the big Lincoln, who started the car, eased out of the parking garage, and navigated the two blocks to the front of the Capitol. A huge roar went up from the crowd, recognizing their newest hero, as Robbs stepped out of the car. The crowd parted for him as he climbed the series of steps up to the podium that had been set up in advance. He shook the hands of the many admirers who pushed forward to get closer, but once reaching the speaking area, wasted no time in beginning his address.

"My friends of Alabama," he said, waving to show his appreciation to the crowd, many of whom could not afford to be other than poorly dressed, "I regret that so many of you were forced to take a bus to come here today." No one cared to mention that he had himself provided the buses and arranged to fill them. "I tried to arrange to hold this conference in your own neighborhood, but the truth is that while we managed to attract some of the television networks here to the steps of the Capitol today, none of them wanted to visit for even an hour the run-down, violent, drug-infested streets where you good people have to live every day of your lives!"

The crowd roared out with boos and shouts, and the camera crews and reporters felt decidedly uneasy, not knowing that Robbs had never even broached the subject with their management. No one would know, and no one would check. All that mattered to Robbs at this point was that his words would be received in the proper environment and create the desired effect. He waited for the noise level to subside somewhat, then continued.

"Let me begin by saying that I understand why you may be surprised by my appearance here today as a candidate for Governor, especially considering that I have been working with Elgin LaGrande for several months on the *Hopes* program and have developed the very highest regard for him as a person and a truly caring representative of the people of Alabama." There were a few shouts of agreement, and general polite applause in the crowd. Elgin LaGrande did enjoy great popularity in the state.

"But it should come as no surprise to anyone to hear that the entire nation is changing, and Alabama is going to have to change as well. It's the logical time to examine the state of our state, and to decide what we are going to do and where we are going to go. It's quite possible that it's time to change our entire way of thinking."

"Amen," said a voice in the crowd.

"Many years ago, Martin Luther King, Jr., Ukiah Hilgard, and many other brave crusaders dragged this nation reluctantly and contentiously into a consciousness of civil rights and new hope for Black Americans. But for the past two decades and more, the country has strayed away from these principles of life, liberty, and opportunity and headed down a mean-spirited

The Hornbrook Prophecy

and misguided path, sweeping aside the moderate and progressive minds who opposed it. And, in what has been until lately the richest nation on earth, the gap between the poor and the wealthy has grown larger and larger. Too many have stopped trying to solve common problems with common solutions, and instead are letting fear, anger, ignorance, and apathy divide us again. The many gains of securing health care for the elderly and poor, affirmative action opportunity for minorities, economic aid for the unfortunate have been abandoned to intolerance and self-interest, leaving the disadvantaged to scrounge in the soup kitchens of the inner city." The crowd again yelled out its collective anger and disappointment over their plight.

"FDR's New Deal is now a *No* Deal, at least for Black Americans."

"Yeah, that's right!" exclaimed the crowd.

"Lyndon Johnson's Great Society is now a *Grunt* Society, at least for Black Americans."

"You got it, brother!"

"Newt Gingrich's Contract With America became a Contract *On* America, at least for Black Americans."

"Amen, Perry!"

"Most people in this country believe in human rights. Most people in this country believe in civil rights. Most people believe in family, in privacy, in sharing, and in respect. Most people even believe in government! So why is this nation dedicated to spending billions on bombs and bankers, and not to helping people get enough to eat, get a job, get a home, and get well? Why is this nation not dedicated to hope?"

"WHY?" the crowd replied, as if of but a single voice.

"Because most of the people who have enough to eat, who have a job, who have a home, and who get health care don't really even *think* about the rest of us!"

"NO!"

"What I want to know is just who in the hell *is* looking out for our future? The Republicans call it 'quotas,' the Democrats call it 'goals' and 'timetables,' and what do *I* call it? *Getting screwed!*"

"Right on!"

"The Right calls it 'favoritism'; the Left calls it 'fairness.' And what do I call it? *Getting screwed!*"

"You tell 'em, Perry!"

"One side calls it busing. The other side calls it equal opportunity. What are we really getting?"

"SCREWED!" the crowd shouted as one, beginning to build emotion.

"The Left says we're getting 'public assistance'; the Right says we're getting 'welfare.' What are we really getting?"

"SCREWED!"

"SCREWED!" Robbs agreed. "And why is that? *Because we're letting them!*"

This time the crowd was subdued. They had been expecting more blame-it-on-them rhetoric, and instead their new hero had held up a mirror for them to see themselves. "And why are we letting them?" he continued. "*BECAUSE WE DARE NOT TO IMAGINE THAT IT COULD BE ANY OTHER WAY!*"

He stepped back from the bank of microphones in front of him, looked about the crowd and at the cameras. Then he leaned forward again. "Almost fifty years ago they passed the Civil Rights laws. It was supposed to help us. Almost fifty years ago they started a so-called War on Poverty. It was supposed to help us. Did it?"

"No!" came the replies.

"Where are we today?" he demanded. "A third of our Black men under the age of thirty are either in prison, on probation, or on parole. A *third* of our young Black men!"

"No!"

"Yes! The most likely victims of crime in the entire country are Black teenage males."

"No!"

"Yes! Unemployment for Black males is *twice* as high as for White males."

"No!"

"Yes! Two thirds of our children are born to unmarried women."

"No!"

"Yes! The population is only 12 percent Black, but nearly *forty* percent of families getting welfare are Black."

"NO!"

"Yes! Is this affirmative action?"

"NO!"

"No, indeed. The Constitution of the United States begins with the words, 'We the People...' But did they mean that Blacks were *People*?"

"NO!"

"NO! The Constitution only allowed us to be counted as three-fifths of a White citizen. It didn't want to call us slaves! Today, we are supposed to be free, and yet Blacks on average earn only about *three-fifths* as much as Whites. Are we really *free*?"

"NO!"

"*Should we be free?*"

"YES!"

"*Do you wish to be free?*"

"YES!"

"*Is it right to be free?*"

"YES!"

"You know what? I agree with you. And that's why I'm running for Governor. It is time for innovation, not administration. It is time for development, not maintenance. It is time to promote challenge, not accept the status quo. Blacks in America may no longer be enslaved by plantation owners, but Blacks in America are enslaved to a system of lost hope, lost opportunity, and lost respect. Many of our leaders, and many White liberals talk of monetary restitution for slavery as being the way to help free us from our modern day plight. But while others say that modern Whites can't be held responsible for the slave owners of 100 or 200 or 300 years ago, Dr. King said, '*When millions of people have been cheated for centuries, restitution is a costly process. Inferior education, poor housing, unemployment, inadequate health care— each is a bitter component of the oppression that has been our heritage. Justice so long deferred has accumulated interest and its cost for this society will be substantial in financial as well as human terms.* Now, let me ask you standing here today: Would restitution for centuries-old slavery help you?"

"YES!"

"But do you ever actually expect to see any of those billions and billions it would take to repay us for our suffering?"

"NO!"

"And that is why I say that things must change, and must change now! It is time for true freedom."

The crowd cheered long and loudly. Robbs allowed only a slight smile to flicker across his face, before resuming his stoic stance. Before the cheering had died away, he spoke out again. "Economic freedom, yes! Educational freedom, yes! But most importantly, the freedom of our minds and hearts!"

"Amen, Perry!"

"No more lifetimes of poverty…"

"AMEN!"

"Dependency…"

"AMEN!"

"Disrespect…"

"AMEN!"

"and hopelessness!"

"AMEN!"

"What has been tried has failed!"

"AMEN!"

"It is not just *time* to try something new. It is *essential*. It is *inevitable*! And so to support my bid, I am here today to announce the formation of a new political party. Not a destructive joke like the mean-spirited TEA Party of Richmond Shadwell, but a bold new opportunity for us to seek our goals. The *New Freedom Party* will be dedicated to a goal of complete freedom for our people."

Once again the cheers and shouts were loud and sustained. But Robbs continued to build the fervor. "The New Freedom Party will have a single message, and a single objective." He paused, letting the anticipation and excitement build, and when he sensed the crowd leaning forward, at least figuratively, he dropped the bomb. "And that is the establishment of a new nation. A nation built *by* Blacks. A nation built *for* Blacks."

There was an eerie silence while the people's minds attempted to catch up to their ears, followed by a collective intake of breath as the words registered with dramatic impact. Then there was a sudden burst of shouts and yells by everyone seemingly at once. Robbs didn't wait this time, raising his voice enough to command attention once again.

"A vote for me is a vote for independence! If I am elected, the New Freedom Party will work throughout the state to ensure that within one year a special election will be held to declare *that the State of Alabama has seceded from the United States of America and will be henceforth, and forever, free!*"

This time there was no pause, no delay for mental processing. Most of the crowd began jumping up and down, waving their arms, dancing with each other, and shouting in joy. *Most* of the crowd. Not all. Others, particularly the camera crews, other media, other officials, and virtually every White person present stood stunned, looking back and forth at each other, not knowing whether to laugh, cry, or call the mental ward.

Robbs didn't let up. Gesturing for silence, he said, "Elgin LaGrande is a fine man, a smart and successful businessman, and a concerned leader who will work tirelessly to improve the lives each of you. That is unquestioned, and I am proud to consider him my friend. But, the system he is up against is hundreds of years old, and hundreds of years entrenched in tradition, in oppression, and in bigotry. So no matter how effective, how diligent, how well-intentioned Elgin LaGrande may be, the question is, can we wait *another* hundred years—or even fifty, or ten?"

"NO!"

"Benjamin E. Mays once said *'The tragedy of life does not lie in not reaching your goal, but in having no goal to reach!'* Well, now is the time to say that we finally do have a goal. And in November, you can decide if you want to try and reach that goal. Champions of individual rights as far back as Virginia's Arthur Lee in 1775 stated the *'The right of property is the guardian of every other right, and to deprive the people of this, is in fact to deprive them of their liberty.'* But Blacks in America have never had much opportunity to call anything their own. It's time to have a country to call OUR country!"

Cheering broke out again, and Robbs let it spread without restraint this time. After a minute or two, he stepped forward to the microphones for his final words, and the uproar gradually subsided. "The New Freedom Party does not seek to overthrow a government or sidestep democracy. Just the contrary—I believe if the people are given a real chance to make a real choice, they will vote for *freedom*. And many of you are thinking that there's no way that a majority of people in the Alabama will vote for secession. Right now you are probably correct. But I think there are probably millions of Blacks around the country who would give anything to have the chance to live in their own country."

"Amen, Perry!"

"Now, I certainly know that currently a majority of Alabama voters will not support these ideas that you find so appealing. That's okay. Because November is two months away, and in Alabama you can register to vote up to thirty days before an election. So I say that every Black who ever dreamed of true freedom and their own nation and who is willing to sacrifice certainty for a whole new concept of liberty, ought to consider moving here, becoming residents of Alabama, and joining with us in creating a new future. We are not going to *level* the playing field—we are going to build a whole new one!"

There were more cheers and celebrating. Finally, Robbs held up his hand for one last exhortation. "Dr. King once said, *'Cowardice asks, is it safe? Expediency asks, is it politic? Vanity asks, is it popular? But conscience asks, is it right? There comes a time when one must take the position that is neither safe nor politic nor popular, but he must do it because conscience tells him, IT IS RIGHT!'*"

"Vote for Perry Robbs and you vote for FREEDOM! THANK YOU!" Robbs took a single step back from the podium, waving both arms over his head as the cheers built to a new crescendo. The crowd surged forward, trying to reach Robbs. He allowed himself to be caught up by them, shaking men's hands and hugging women. Print reporters grabbed their cell phones to call their papers, and television anchors retreated to peripheral areas where they could record their instant analyses and interview onlookers.

***

Elgin LaGrande sat stunned, as Athena Weston hit the *Mute* button on the TV remote. "Good God!" he exclaimed finally. "I have to admit that never in my wildest nightmares would I have guessed that a campaign could so dramatically and so quickly become a stage for revolution!"

"I'm sorry, Elgin. Somehow I can't help but feel that I'm partially responsible. After all, I brought him into the *Hopes* program."

"Don't be silly, Athena," said Elgin, rising from his chair. "He merely has seized upon an opportunity created by the national economic collapse to pursue a fantasy. If anyone gave him the microphone, it was ME, with my lame brain notion of creating choice in the general election."

"I guess you have to be careful of what you ask for," said Athena with a smile.

"No kidding!"

"Now what?"

The Hornbrook Prophecy

"First, I'm going to have to respond pretty soon to this. And in one short speech, he's painted me into a box. Either I'm *for* secession or I'm *against* the hopes and dreams of Black Americans."

"And what *are* you for, Elgin?"

He pondered the question carefully. "I'm not for secession, Athena. America has its flaws, God knows. Especially in race relations. But are we to reverse everything we've ever said about the advantages of diversity and multi-culturalism? Are we to ignore all the good that's in America? Are we to become the new bigots of the twenty-first century? I can't do it! The answer *is* to take back control of our own lives, but not by segregating ourselves. It would be an economic and social disaster! I admit it's attractive, and people should have the right to self-determination, but we are so close to making the substantive changes that would reverse the cycle of dependency so many of our people suffer."

"So what are you going to do?"

"I guess I'm going to fight him."

Chapter 36

"There are those, I know, who will reply that the liberation of humanity, the freedom of man and mind, is nothing but a dream... They are right. It is the American dream."
—Archibald MacLeish (1892 -1982)

Tuesday – September 7

"This is an absolutely unprecedented sight." Linn Benton was speaking into her cell phone to her newsroom at WTOP, knowing it was being broadcast live on the air. The night before, she had received a call from a Congressman who had been trying to get a date with her for months. But instead of his usual request, he had told her that everyone in Congress had been contacted and told to meet at a designated place at nine o'clock the next morning. She was excited because the flying rumors seemed to be coming to a point. As soon as she arrived, she called her station manager and won permission to do the live report she was now giving.

"The initiation of an emergency session of Congress is not unheard of, although seldom does it stimulate attendance by *all* the Representatives and Senators. On the other hand, never before have the doors of Congress been effectively shuttered by a President. While most of the nation tried to enjoy the Labor Day weekend that traditionally marks the end of summer, 99 out of 100 Senators and all 435 members of the House scrambled to respond to the calls they received on Sunday evening to return to Washington. None of them knew what might happen when they arrived, but none of them failed to make the effort. I should add that it is only Senator Florence Dillard, also the First Lady, who appears not to be present today.

"Now, for what apparently were security purposes, all 534 evidently gathered first at the Ronald Reagan National Airport, on the banks of the Potomac, where they boarded buses to make their short but historic journey here to the Capitol. When they found this majestic landmark surrounded by

Army and Marine personnel, there was great consternation, but relief quickly flooded over the legislators upon learning that the military presence was on their behalf, ordered by the Chairman of the Joint Chiefs of Staff to guarantee their sessions today would be not only possible, but undisturbed.

"Just a few minutes ago, and in a great show of unity which was, for a change, not just for the cameras, the legislators ascended the steps together, before assembling in their respective chambers.

"None of the legislators were talking at all, but there's much speculation by observers here about just what business Congress will be attempting to conduct today. Most of the rumors are focused on possible impeachment proceedings for President Dillard. I will report back to you just as soon as I can. From the steps of the nation's Capitol, this is Linn Benton, WTOP news."

The House and Senate both convened beginning at 10:00 am, and events began to unfold quickly. The first action of the Senate was accepting the resignation of the President *pro tempore*, an uninspiring party loyalist who was one of the longest-serving members of the upper house. His replacement, Henley Hornbrook of Washington State, was elected by acclamation.

In the House of Representatives, Representative Glenoma Frost, Chairman of the Judiciary Committee, introduced Articles of Impeachment, first for President Winston Dillard, then for Vice-President Sheldon Osborne Branford. The charges included the illegal and unconstitutional suspension of congressional elections, and, by closing Congress, conspiracy to violate the rights of the people to be represented by their duly elected representatives. The vote to impeach was unanimous. There were no party lines when it came to retribution for violating the power of Congress.

By 10:45 AM, the Chief Justice of the Supreme Court, Byron Oakley, had been informed that the President and Vice-President had been impeached, and the case sent to the US Senate, where the Chief Justice would be required to preside over the trial.

At 10:46 AM, the charges were formally presented to the President, at work in the Oval Office and fuming over the non-appearance of the Chairman of the Joint Chiefs of Staff whom he had summoned after learning of the arrival of the Congressional buses at the Capitol steps. Later, several different staff workers who had been in the West Wing at that time would report that Senator Florence Dillard had flown into the President's office minutes later, and slammed the door. Much yelling and commotion was heard to ensue. The Secret Service chose not to interfere.

At 10:50 AM, the charges were delivered to the Vice President at his official residence on the grounds of the United States Naval Observatory. His only comment was, "Son of a bitch!"

At 11:42 AM, Chief Justice Oakley received a single sheet of White House stationery delivered by Presidential Chief-of-Staff Stafford Oswego. The single sentence read, "I hereby submit my resignation as President of the United States, effective immediately." The signature was the familiar flourish of Winston Dillard.

At 11:48 AM, Chief Justice Oakley received a single sheet of Vice Presidential stationery delivered by Branford's chauffeur. The single sentence read, "I hereby resign as Vice President of the United States, effective immediately." The signature was the normal unrecognizable scribble of Sheldon Osborne Branford.

At 12:01 PM, the Chief Justice received a single sheet of stationery from the office of the Speaker of the House of Representatives. It simply stated that because of the conflict of interest represented by his position as leader of the legislative body that had impeached both the President and Vice President, the Speaker would refuse to allow his office to be included in the normal Line of Succession. If his refusal was disallowed, he would submit his resignation as Speaker.

At 12:10 PM, the Chief Justice of the United States issued a formal ruling to Senate Majority Leader Brownsville and House Speaker Sullivan Veradale, to the Secretary of State, to the Chairman of the Joint Chiefs of Staff at the Pentagon, and to the press, stating that due to the resignations of both the President and Vice President, and the inability of the Speaker of the House to assume the duties of the President, that according to the provisions of the Twentieth and Twenty-fifth amendments to the United States Constitution, and the Presidential Succession Act of 1947, the duties and powers of the President would immediately devolve upon the current President *pro tempore* of the Senate. The ruling stated that the new President was to appear as soon as possible to be sworn in.

At 12:25 PM, the Chief Justice received a request from the office of the President *pro tempore* of the Senate that the official swearing-in be held in the House chamber before a joint session of Congress at 8:00 PM Eastern Time.

***

Any producer on Broadway would have loved to have opened to as packed a house as was found in the nation's Capitol that evening. The floor of the House Chamber was crowded with every member of both the House

The Hornbrook Prophecy

of Representatives and the Senate, as well as the Supreme Court and military Chiefs in attendance. The gallery above was jammed with invitation-only guests—wives, favored staff, dignitaries both foreign and domestic, and of course, the media. The events of the past week had caused an enormous change of mood in the District of Columbia. There was the excitement tonight that was associated with any Presidential address, but the wide range of emotions represented everything from exhaustion, to fear, to relief, to anticipation of the unknown. On the rostrum were Speaker of the House Sullivan Veradale and Majority Leader Halsey Brownsville. No one knew quite what to expect.

The assemblage was called to order, the Chaplain of the House offered a short prayer—and on this occasion everyone listened—and then the north door opened and Chief Justice Byron Oakley walked in just ahead of President-designee Henley Hornbrook. The entire gathering quieted in an instant and rose to its feet as the two strode purposefully down the center aisle to the front of the Chamber. There was no music. There were no introductory remarks or speeches. It was an important event, but not a festive one. The two men climbed the few steps and stood behind the speaker's podium and faced each other. As Justice Oakley held the Bible flat, Hornbrook placed his palm atop and repeated the sentence which was stated so simply in the Constitution, but which instantly transformed mere men into globally omnipotent rulers:

> *I do solemnly swear that I will faithfully execute the Office of President of the United States, and will to the best of my ability, preserve, protect and defend the Constitution of the United States*

The Chief Justice shook his hand solemnly, and the Chamber silence was broken with immediate and encompassing applause. As Oakley took a seat, President Henley Hornbrook turned to the microphone, looked out at the audience, raised his hands both to indicate his gratitude and to ask for their attention, and took a deep breath.

Nearly three thousand miles away, Gene Springfield remarked, "Well, whaddya know, I guess we're now in the new Western White House!"

"Shush!" said Hugo. "President Henley's gonna say something." Both with smiles, they looked at their long-time neighbor and friend as he began to address the nation.

"In the long and tumultuous history of mankind, every war, every conflict, every injustice, indeed, every argument can be traced to an attempt by one person or group to *impose* their will on another," President Hornbrook began. "*There is nothing else I will say tonight that is as important as this one simple point*: Every single dispute that has ever arisen—anywhere, anytime—has been because somebody tried to force someone else to do something *their* way. It matters not whether the intentions were good, or whether any given act may benefit some—or even many. It matters only that involuntary imposition and compulsion, in the end, lead to only bad things. Conversely, we know that voluntary association and cooperation lead more often to good things. Therefore, it cannot be too difficult to imagine which path would most likely lead to success and prosperity, even for an entire nation.

"Our forefathers dreamed of, sweated over, and died for a new kind of country with a new concept of liberty, one where each individual could be free to make of his life whatever his capabilities allowed through the efforts of his own labor. Unfortunately, while they feared a government with too much power, they failed to anticipate the myriad means by which those who seek power can usurp it from those who ignore it. While they enumerated powers and defined rights, they failed to make certain the importance of limiting the former and securing the latter. And while they wrote clearly and simply, they failed to understand the incentives for the unscrupulous to obscure, ignore, and refute their original intentions.

"Over the past several decades the Constitutional system established by the Framers has been largely and deliberately ignored, with the result that governments, especially the federal government, have acted virtually without restraint. These unconstrained actions swept aside civil society, replaced them with political decision-making and bureaucratic administration largely unaccountable to the public, and created innumerable economic and social problems. The federal government assumed an unconstitutional, unlimited, and unchallenged role over the economy, over society, and over individuals. The unchecked expansion of government power, at both the federal and state levels, undermined the institutions of civil society and severely weakened the ability of the people to control their own lives.

"And so we became a nation not of opportunity, but a nation of entitlements. We became a nation not of laws, but a nation of lawyers. We became a nation not of individuals seeking life, liberty, and the *pursuit* of happiness, but a nation of special interest groups demanding special treatment, special rights, and the *guarantee* of happiness. We *trusted* our leaders instead of *challenging* them. We relied on the media to define our lives. We voted based on headlines and soundbites instead of more thoroughly educating ourselves on the issues. We lost our ambitions, we destroyed our incentives, we abdicated our obligations of responsibility and accountability, and, in the end, we discarded our common sense. Today our nation lies in economic chaos, besieged with unrest, and our once great civil society has given way to political and financial manipulation. Even as I stand before you this evening, there are states seriously contemplating leaving the union, in no small part because their government has failed them."

The use of the plural, states, caused some obvious surprise, as only Alabama had made the headlines. This would be more grist for the rumor mill.

"Somehow, in spite of all this turmoil, the true strength and determination of a great republic has survived. Today we have witnessed a sudden and dramatic change in leadership of the country, a change made necessary because of this same turmoil and yet, unlike most other nations in history, this change has been orderly, and lawfully followed. Once again the intelligence and foresight of our Founding Fathers has been illustrated."

The audience applauded heartily and stood as one. They had been listening with rapt attention to every word, wanting to signal their support for their new President, but only now finding the opportunity. After the ovation died away, Hornbrook continued.

"I would like to express my personal admiration for the Chairman of the Joint Chiefs of Staff, General Canby Hubbard, and his courage in defying the misguided orders of a single man and standing up instead for the rights of the people to be represented in their government, and making this orderly transition possible." There was another enthusiastic standing ovation by all the members of Congress, as Hornbrook saluted the General sitting in the first row.

"However," Hornbrook continued, "making a change is not the same as solving the problems that have brought us to this point. The task awaiting the nation tomorrow will be still as daunting and difficult as it was yesterday. But we have our resolve, we have our goals, and we have our Constitution, and these will assure our success."

Again, widespread applause interrupted him. Nodding his acknowledgment, Hornbrook continued.

"Our first step is to deal with some procedural and organizational matters. First, I intend to nominate Senator Halsey Brownsville, our current Senate Majority Leader, to fill the vacant office of Vice President." No one in the huge chamber, or the gallery, or even in the vast television audience was more surprised than Brownsville himself, and he struggled not to show it before the cameras he was sure had turned in his direction. The general surprise in the chamber quickly gave way to enthusiastic applause for this unprecedented bipartisan union.

"He is a man of convictions, and I believe no one holds the interests of the nation in higher regard. Together, we are going to work with Congress to make divisive politics a thing of the past. Indeed, we are going to work to make *politics* itself a thing of the past." There was more applause, although no one yet knew what he might mean by it. "My next official act will be to issue an Executive Order nullifying the recent Executive Orders 14901 through 14904. The military will be withdrawn from our cities, our free market system will be restored, the Congressional elections will be held as scheduled in November, and—although it is enormously tempting not to let them loose again," he said with a smile, "Congress is back in business." This was expected, of course, but the announcement was greeted with another standing ovation, as well as cheers and shouts from one side of the Chamber to the other.

Hornbrook turned serious again. "Although a new President's inaugural address normally avoids itemizing specific policies, these are hardly normal times. Because of the tremendous problems we face, it is imperative that we act *now* to restore our national economic health and integrity. To begin, we must undo the damage that has been done, as well as prevent its recurrence. The federal government must be allowed to exercise its proper functions, and therefore we must recover our sources of tax revenues. This, however, can only be accomplished by convincing the taxpayers that we are *deserving* of their support. And this we can only do by demonstrating that we have learned our lessons, will act with responsibility, and will never again abuse their trust." He was interrupted again with cheers and applause from the gallery and another standing ovation on the floor.

"Accordingly, tomorrow I will ask Congress to take the following immediate steps: First, the American Economic and Financial Freedom Act will be rescinded, and there will be an additional *immediate* reduction in pre-AEFFA tax rates and schedules, across the board and for all taxes and tax brackets, of ten percent." There were a few gasps and many mutterings—as well as much applause—in many parts of the Chamber, but Hornbrook ignored them and continued. "This should begin to alleviate the encumbrance on individuals and businesses sufficiently to jumpstart the economy. Much capital has fled the country into safer, less burdensome havens, but I believe it will return in an electronic instant, simply—but only—by making it financially attractive to once again invest in the tremendous economic capability of this country.

"Second, as there will be an initial loss of otherwise normal tax revenue levels, costs will be offset through the systematic, but deliberate elimination of departments, offices, and programs that are completely unrelated to the enumerated constitutional responsibilities of the government. The unemployed across the nation, as well as those federal employees whose jobs will be cut by these closures, will find the private sector in dire need of an infusion of new workers to enable the expansion made possible by the enormous capital retention it will realize because of reduced taxes. Further reductions in tax rates will ultimately follow, as our citizens re-learn their old responsibilities and re-discover the benefits of personal reliance.

"We have created a nation of dependency, and we have all witnessed the suffering which so many endured when the government collapsed. It has been an unprecedented disaster, and it tells us we have no choice but to change. However, it is impossible to do so overnight without more suffering. Therefore, the budgets of ALL federal agencies and departments will be adjusted immediately so that significant financial relief can be made available immediately to those who have been on public assistance and Social Security and who have no other means of support. This aid will be offered on a widespread but temporary basis until the transition is made to a more permanent, more sensible approach to economic viability for all citizens." The applause this time was polite, but cautious.

"Third, because private property ownership is a fundamental underpinning of individual rights, I will ask Congress to establish the provisions for a new Homestead Act. The federal government is the largest landowner in the nation, and it is only right to make much of this land available to the people whose country this really is. With property ownership comes the potential for economic development and self-sufficiency. For those of you who fear an environmental disaster, forget the deceptions of yesterday. Private property owners have an inherent stake in the future value of their land and, on balance, are far better stewards of its resources than governments. Putting more lands back on the tax rolls will also help local and state governments become self-supporting. It will take time to develop the guidelines for an effective new, environmentally-safe lands policy, one that will ensure that such lands will not end up concentrated in the hands of less-concerned conglomerates, but it has the potential to fuel yet even greater economic growth and development.

Looking straight into the camera, Hornbrook earnestly appealed to businesses and workers across the nation. "I implore all Americans to support these efforts, to recognize their responsibilities, and to resume their tax contributions. Together, we *will* return to financial prosperity. It will be difficult, it will require more sacrifice, and it will take time before we turn the corner. Even then, a greater challenge awaits us," he said, pausing only momentarily as he sensed the importance of setting the stage, "—the challenge to prevent a recurrence of this calamity. We must make numerous and substantial alterations in the way we operate our democracy, or we will again fall prey to special interests, unchecked ambitions, and unscrupulous practices."

Hornbrook paused again. It was not a moment for applause. His silence now added emphasis to his words and as the interval grew in length, the obvious discomfort of many on the House floor also became increasingly apparent. And still he waited. Some of those on the House floor unconsciously began to shift in their seats. The new President was assailing "business as usual" but it was *their* business as usual, and they feared what was to come.

Their fears were quickly realized.

"The corrupting influence in political societies is not the *money* that changes hands, but the *power* that those hands wield. And yet the greatest power of all is the power of those who control the money supply of our economy. As great as is the temptation and abuse of the power of elective office, so much greater has been the temptation and abuse of power by the money controllers. Thus I have a fourth point. I will ask Congress to rescind the Federal Reserve Act."

This was a HUGE bombshell and the audience reacted with astonishment. Although Hornbrook could not see Brownsville sitting behind him, he knew his new Vice-President designee again would again be working hard not to appear as surprised as his colleagues. Hornbrook smiled inwardly. He and Lew Weiser had inserted the fourth point only two hours ago.

"Article 1, Section 8 of the Constitution," he continued, "states that Congress shall have the power to coin money and regulate the power thereof. But in 1913, it essentially gave away this power. For nearly one hundred years, the Federal Reserve has controlled the money supply and interest rates so completely that we truly lost our free-market system without which we have no real liberty. Instead of free enterprise, the market system has been distorted by the reality of decidedly non-market influences of non-elected and non-regulated private banking interests combined with politically-motivated government policy-making. It has been this lethal combination that has created the repeated, but entirely artificial economic climates resulting in alternating periods of excess and recession which destroyed rational business decision-making. And we have universally been suffering from it. These are the 'unsound fiscal policies' which undermine modern democracies. We MUST change."

Hornbrook got no more reaction than he expected. Most lawmakers themselves had never questioned the national monetary organizational status quo. Neither did they yet understand the magnitude of the changes he was going to ask of them.

"When power is not carefully and specifically limited, it grows and grows. We must, therefore, return the power in this country not to the politicians, nor even to the *people*, as many might think or wish. No, we must return the power to the *law* that governs us—to the Constitution. And because there has been no limit to the imaginative ways in which the law of the land can be circumvented, we must provide greater safeguards for its integrity. The power of elective office is seductive, and great is the temptation to abuse it. The law has been vulnerable to such abuse, and therefore the law must be changed.

"Our legal system was originally based on English common law, which was the result of hundreds of years of people searching for rational solutions to their everyday problems. At its core are two fundamental principles: First, do not impose upon others, and second, do as you promise to do. This year has vividly and painfully demonstrated what happens when those two fundamental laws are ignored. So I will say it again: When you impose upon others you break one of humanity's most universal laws! And the biggest violator of that law has been the very government that is supposed to protect us."

The House Chamber was very quiet now. Even though they had already heard earth-shattering announcements, the lawmakers knew the *real* boom was about to be lowered. Hornbrook cared not for their feelings. It had to be done, so he continued.

"For too long our Constitution has been under attack. It has been torn, stretched, watered down, reinterpreted, and simply ignored. *No more!* It is the *law*, and the law is the ultimate protection of our Republic. There can no longer be imaginary rationalizations to justify our actions. There can no longer be reading *between* the lines—there can only be the lines themselves. There can be no more 'tortured interpretations' or powers granted by imagined 'shadows and emanations.' There can no longer be the ability or the desire to have the government do everything that we want it to do—there can only be the ability of the government to do that which is necessary to fulfill its specific responsibilities. It has no right—no matter how desirable it may seem—to take from some to give to others, whether they are rich or poor givers, or rich or poor takers. It must protect our rights, protect our lives, protect our property, and preserve the honesty of the marketplace.

"If the government does these few simple things it will be enough." There was widespread applause, but it was more respectful than enthusiastic this time.

"Over the past two decades there have been demands to reform our system, to make it less susceptible to the corrupting influences of money and power. But they have all failed for one simple reason—as long as there was no limit on what the government could do, there would be no limit on the efforts to corrupt it for special interests. Only by limiting its power do we reduce the *demand* for favors. Only by limiting the demand for favors do we reduce the influence of money.

"Removing the *incentive* to corrupt removes the *desire* to corrupt. But that is only half the problem. To completely resolve the temptation by some to achieve power over others, we must also remove the rewards of *having* such power. Accordingly, in the next few days I will submit to Congress a series of amendments designed to restore the purposeful intentions of our Constitution." This surprise pronouncement caused a renewed stirring throughout the Chamber. Constitutional amendments were major nation-shaping changes, and the new President was talking about a whole *series* of them.

"The first will require that every single bill and budget item passed by Congress must locate the specific source of its authority in the Constitution. It will also include provisions for what is commonly known as a 'line-item veto.'" Immediately, there was stirring and mutterings across the floor of the chamber, but Hornbrook pressed on. "This in no way alters the balance of power between the Legislative and Executive branches of the government. It merely gives the President the ability to treat each provision with a given bill as a separate entity. If he vetoes a provision, Congress can still override the veto. BUT!" He paused for emphasis. "Such a measure will go a long way toward preventing abuse of the legislative and budgeting process which leads to excessive spending. No more pork tacked on to unrelated legislation." He smiled, but stated with steel in his voice, "Don't worry about losing the power of pork to enhance your re-election chances. We'll get to that in a moment." Heads swiveled back and forth and brows furrowed all across the room.

"The second will clarify the power of Congress to 'regulate Commerce among the states,' enumerated in Article I, Section 8, paragraph 3, as being limited to ensuring that states do not interfere with the free flow of commerce among them, which was the Framers' original intention. The commerce clause was never meant to justify the vast regulatory structure the government has built, nor the unending accumulation of social and economic policies that today so greatly restrict our economic growth and development.

"The third amendment will be to limit the scope of the words 'general welfare,' from Article I, Section 8, paragraph 1. There is no question that an unbridled interpretation of the welfare clause completely eviscerates the doctrine of enumerated powers, which was the founding principle of the Constitution to begin with. Congress has taken it to mean that it has comprehensive redistributive powers, and more than anything else, this type of interpretation has been the root cause of the financial catastrophe we are suffering this year. *Thou shalt not impose!*"

The Hornbrook Prophecy

There was renewed murmuring throughout the room, and more than a scattering of boos, perhaps a first for an inaugural address. The new President looked up sharply. "Have you forgotten the last months already?" he demanded like a stern headmaster. "Compassion aside, the Constitution simply does not empower the government to take from some and give to others. The welfare clause was meant to imply that the powers that Congress *does* have were to be exercised only for the *general* welfare; that is, for the benefit of *all* citizens. Our abuse of the Constitution led to those financial policies which were the direct cause of our federal breakdown this year. *We have no choice!* We must prevent a recurrence, and to prevent a recurrence we must change. Put aside your petty political posturing! If you cannot, then quit!" And he smacked his hand on the dais for emphasis. The chamber was in shocked silence. "Go out and get a job in the real world. See what it's like to be one of your constituents. We need leaders who can help the nation regain its financial health, not a bunch of pompous fools granting favors and handing out pork like it's from their own private purse."

Hornbrook forced his rising anger down. The boos had signaled to him just how tough it was going to be. Already they wished to return to the Cave. But he went on.

"Thomas Jefferson himself knew what could happen, for he proclaimed, *'In questions of power, then, let no more be heard of confidence in man, but bind him down from mischief by the chains of the Constitution.'* We can better provide economic opportunity for the needy by enabling private enterprise to flourish, expand, and create jobs and prosperity for all."

"The final Constitutional amendment I will propose to Congress is the simplest, but perhaps the most important. It will affect Sections 2 and 3 of Article I, Section 1 of Article II, and also the Twenty-second Amendment. It will declare that *no person, once elected to the Senate, House, or Presidency, may be reelected.*"

There was an immediate uproar across the floor of the House chamber. In one short sentence, the new President had just declared war on the privileges, rewards, and powers of incumbency. It was the ultimate in term limits, and not only was every legislator affected, but so were the venerable and powerful traditions of seniority. There might be no disputing that past practices led to the economic upheavals of the past six months, but the floor reaction here was another clear indicator that those who championed such practices would not give them up easily. Once more, Hornbrook ignored their protestations and went forward, the forcefulness of his voice silencing the protests.

"There will be those who say that this will limit their right to be represented by those they choose, or that experience is essential to effectiveness, or they will give a myriad of other excuses why this cannot happen. But I say, again, it *must* happen! If we are successful in re-emphasizing the limitations on federal powers, there will be little need for those skilled in manipulation and schooled in pork barrel policy. There is a saying that one lawyer in a town will starve, but two lawyers in a town will make a pretty good living. Well, in Washington, D.C. there are more than 75 *thousand* members of the bar—five times the population of the average town in America—and though there are barely 7500 words in the Constitution, every one of those lawyers is finding a way to get rich off them. This must end. Without the need to raise campaign funds for reelection, legislators can spend more time in their own states and districts, being accessible to constituents, not to lobbyists with bags of money. If our elected officials can't hold productive jobs in the real world, they don't have any business running the country. We can also expect them to be considerably more prudent in their lawmaking habits, too, if they know that they will have to turn right around and live themselves under those very same laws.

"These amendments, as well as a couple of other changes intended to safeguard the integrity of the democracy, must be acted upon immediately. *There can be no compromise!*" Hornbrook reached for the glass of water by the lectern and took a short swallow. It felt refreshing to his mouth, dry with the effort and emotion of his task. When he continued, his tone seemed refreshed as well.

"My friends, I am aware that not all of you will agree with these proposals. There will be those who say that if we eliminate tax deductions and other shelters, we will stifle economic growth, destroy the American dream of home ownership, and devastate charities. But the reality is that by lowering everybody's tax burden such deductions will be irrelevant. It will stimulate unparalleled economic growth, and I believe that once they are truly unfettered by the burdens of oppressive taxation, the natural compassion of Americans will flourish as never before. *We must change*.

"There will be those who say it is cruel and mean-spirited to eliminate means-tested social programs. But it must be obvious that these unsustainable and fiscally irresponsible policies have only helped bring financial ruin upon us. I believe that in the protection of individual rights, citizens can be encouraged to exercise charity, but not coercively commanded to do so upon penalty of loss of liberty or property. The entitlement mentality destroys civility. Recipients often become demanding for goods they do not own, and other citizens become angered by frequent abuse of the system, and hardened by the excessive taxation. Government programs and welfare philosophies have consigned millions of Americans to a lifetime of poverty, dependency, disrespect, and hopelessness as permanent wards of the state. *We must change.*

"There will be those who will say that the states and local governments cannot survive without the federal funding they receive for so many programs. Here, the answer is that these programs were never the responsibility of the federal government in the first place. It will be for the states themselves to decide if they wish to continue them. If they need the funding they can rearrange their own tax structures, but at the very least it will mean that a single monopolistic national tax system will be replaced by fifty competing systems, and each state will have to learn to offer improved services—education, social services, roads, and a good business climate—and to provide them more efficiently and more cost-effectively, or people and jobs will move elsewhere. *We must change.*

"There are those who will say that we can never *all* agree on what the government should be doing. They are wrong. The Declaration of Independence shows us that government has an absolute and definite responsibility to *protect* us, for if it does not, there is no justification for its very existence. However, it must have NO ability to impose upon *all* of us any unconstitutional desires or wants of those who merely have enough votes or enough money to demand them.

"There are those who will say that without government, we will have anarchy. But *limited* government is not the same as *no* government. A legitimate government does have legitimate needs for power, especially the power to maintain law and order. Other powers, however, must be limited. *Our country became the greatest in man's history because it let its citizens enjoy their natural rights.* When it ceased to do so, we became no different from the countless failed and underachieving nations that have gone before us. It is up to us to now take the last, great step to unleashing man's full potential. If we protect our individual rights, encourage and safeguard free enterprise, limit the imposition of government, and shield it all with a strong national defense, we will realize that potential. If these changes are not made, we will someday again sink into the same self-serving, unsound financial policies that are the fatal flaw of democracy.

"It is not enough to end the *era* of big government; we must forever avoid the *error* of big government."

As if they were beginning to understand, the floor and gallery rewarded President Hornbrook with a standing ovation and hearty applause at last.

Hornbrook, in turn, knew he must now lay the groundwork for positive acceptance.

"There is no question that today we are beset with crippling problems. What I have outlined for you are my own preliminary answers to these problems. I believe they are vital and necessary and many of these solutions must, and will, begin tomorrow. However, in a democratic republic, the people and their representatives must decide. Therefore, in conjunction with the November congressional elections two months from now, I will use the provisions of Title 3, Chapter 1, Section 19 of the US Code to call for a special election for the offices of President and Vice President. If you believe that the direction I lay before you this evening is proper, then you will have the opportunity to register your support according to the democratic process. If not, I will gladly lay aside the mantle Congress has, for now, entrusted to me." He paused, took another short sip of water, and gazed about the huge room.

"I sat down the other day and read, once again, the entire Declaration of Independence and the Constitution. Every American should. Thomas Jefferson and the framers of the Constitution felt that Government was the natural enemy of man. They were plainly afraid of power, no matter who wielded it.

"As our nation changed, we persuaded ourselves that government could be a force for good. But the power corrupted those of us who held it, and in our efforts to secure our own positions we began to penalize the successful, destroy the incentive to be creative, and crush innovation and enterprise. In the end we nearly lost the *spirit* that once made us great.

"Now it is time to once again promote hard work, not handouts—to rich or poor. It is time to once again encourage success, not reward failure and inefficiency. It is time to once again reinstill responsibility and accountability. It is time to once again take inventory of our freedoms, and safeguard them. It is time to rekindle the *Spirit* of America." He waited as an ovation swept across the chamber.

"The *Spirit of America* is one of freedom and independence, of discovery and innovation, of compassion for others and for our varied ancestry, and a desire to make things better. Yet it glows in each of us only to the extent that we allow it. We can neither give it to, nor demand it of our neighbor. Citizens do not—and need not—share a complete and exhaustive set of goals, values, and beliefs. Our very diversity makes it impossible. Instead, I believe that a successful government should demand consensus on only a few, vital issues, leaving citizens free to exercise their rights through the private, voluntary, non-governmental associations that are civil society. The obligations imposed by government—including taxation and regulation—must be minimal.

The Hornbrook Prophecy

"*There has never been a government that did not assume that its primary responsibility was to govern.* Today, however, we seek to establish a new kind of government, a nation where men must take responsibility for themselves, and be accountable for their own actions. Today we seek to end the era of imposition, coercion, and compulsion. Today we seek to assure that every person will be allowed to benefit from the *real* equal opportunity to enjoy their natural and individual rights, to live their own lives, and pursue their own happiness as they see fit while respecting the equal rights of others, and welcoming government only as an ally to secure these rights, to prevent others from imposing on them, and to guarantee the honesty, integrity, and openness of the free enterprise system.

"When Alexander the Great once asked what he, with all his power, could do for Diogenes, the Greek philosopher answered, *'Stand a little less in my sun.'* Let me assure you, my fellow Americans, that from this day forward, your government is going to stand a little less in *your* sun. May God bless us all."

As he stepped back from the podium, the Chamber erupted in applause and shouts of encouragement. President Hornbrook turned to shake the hands of Chief Justice Oakley, then those of Majority Leader Brownsville, and Speaker Veradale, both of whom nodded solemnly. He then faced forward again to acknowledge the Congressmen and Senators—both allies and opponents—as well as those in the galleries. Finally he turned and walked out of the Chamber, accompanied by a contingent of Secret Service agents.

As he left, he prayed that he could find the courage to face the challenges ahead, and the strength to live up to the trust of the American people.

Robert Wickes

EPILOGUE

Otherwise Free...

> *"A wise and frugal government, which shall restrain men from injuring one another, which shall leave them otherwise free to regulate their own pursuits of industry and improvement, and shall not take from the mouth of labor the bread it has earned. This is the sum of good government."*
> —Thomas Jefferson, *First Inaugural Address*, 1801

In most parts of the country, people attempted to get back to some semblance of normalcy in their lives. The new President's inaugural speech had restored a lot of peace of mind and instilled hope again for the nation. The economic and social measures he had ordered would have the immediate effects for which he had prayed. With the lowered tax and regulatory burdens on business, capital would flow back into Wall Street and, beginning even the day after the President's inaugural speech, many companies announced plans for new investment and expansion. Also the next day, Richmond Shadwell and his TEA Party would endorse the efforts of the new Administration and give their support for the government's new tax structure, publicly and conspicuously announcing the resumption of their normal tax payments, along with back taxes previously withheld.

A new, albeit tenuous, faith in government would enjoy enough of a resurgence that people would respond to the call for responsibility. The need for immediate sacrifice to help bridge the transition to a new kind of economy would be acknowledged, and tax revenues once again flowed to Washington.

President Hornbrook, Vice President-designate Brownsville, and Congressional leaders would quickly juggle budgets extensively in order to provide relief for those poor and elderly who previously had relied entirely on government checks to live. The old system was destined to change, but it couldn't happen overnight, and in the meantime people had to eat.

Henley Hornbrook would resist moving into the White House, wanting to wait until after the November election to see if the country really wanted him as President. The Secret Service, however, would not even entertain the idea of his remaining in his apartment and the security nightmare it would have been. He would know it was an argument he would not win, and would devote his attention instead to refining his plans for a new type of government.

Hornbrook knew that any temporary honeymoon he might enjoy with both Congress and the media would be extremely short-lived once the present sense of relief changed into a realization of the meaning of his words. He had no delusions that his proposed Constitutional amendments would sail unscathed through Congress and the ratification process by the states. The next two months were going to be unlike any in the nation's history. It was not a matter of reaching a political compromise—this time compromise would not be sufficient. The country *had* to take a giant leap of faith that the new path he had charted for them was the only hope. The existing Congress had overwhelmingly supported the American Economic and Financial Freedom Act that had led down the last steps to the social cataclysm the country was still suffering. What were the odds that they could now completely reverse themselves and endorse such a radical departure from the century-old grip and practice of big government?

But if he was right, the overwhelming majority of citizens would rally behind him and demand that Congress do what was necessary. Time would tell. The election in November would certainly be a fun one for the political pundits to cover. Not only was the country going to set its course for the next century, the very organizational integrity of the United States was at stake. Perry Robb's blockbuster announcement of his intention to lead Alabama out of the Union had taken everybody in the country, including Hornbrook, by complete surprise. The President could only shake his head, and reflect on how close he and his friends had come to pursuing the same action. It was the biggest threat to the strength and unity of America since the Civil War. But this time, the new President reflected, there would probably be no armed resistance. As long as a legitimate election upheld the move, his conscience would not let him oppose the principle of self-determination. The government had lost its moral high ground for commanding others. The United States of America had to be united by consent, not by force. He could only hope that the economic growth and expansion promised by his announced policies would convince everyone, including Black Americans, that a better future could be had by all. It's conceivable, he thought, that the debate over his proposed constitutional amendments and the subsequent road to ratification could lead other states to consider leaving the Union. Mississippi and Louisiana could be candidates to follow Robbs' lead. Maybe Georgia, too. And maybe other states for other reasons. He had no way of knowing, yet, what the country was thinking. He merely prayed that it was up to this new trial.

Alabama had a new Chief Executive also, another twist in the story. LaGrande, he recalled. Elgin LaGrande. He had some good ideas on economic development himself, Hornbrook remembered, but was going to have a fight on his hands with that Perry Robbs in their own election battle. *I wonder if Governor LaGrande would like to have a little talk,* thought the new President.

***

Stretched out fully in the comfort of his favorite recliner, alone in the private residence of the Governor's Mansion, Elgin LaGrande contemplated the ceiling. It was ironic, he thought, that Blacks were going to be leading the first attempt to leave the Union since the Union fought the Confederacy in part to set the Black slaves free. He knew that many Blacks, from all over the country, would flood the state to establish residence in time to vote in the November election. LaGrande would be more alarmed if large numbers of Whites soon began talking about moving themselves or, more importantly, their businesses *out* of the state. *Even if I win,* he thought, *the state could suffer more economic damage.* That the *Hopes* program might be derailed seemed almost irrelevant now. Regardless of the outcome of the election, Elgin was willing to bet that the state was going to experience the worst racial tensions since the 60s as a result of Robbs' visionary ambitions. *What was he thinking?* LaGrande thought. *How on earth does he think this will solve everything? Will Blacks really be better off? I suppose it's no different than the suffering Patrick Henry, and Nathan Hale, and Washington, Jefferson, Adams, Revere, and all the rest were willing to risk to gain their own independence. But good God, is there no other way? Has Robbs really thought about what is involved? Monetary system. Defense. Economics. Trade. A legal system. A constitution.*

Elgin's head was swimming. He shook it off, collapsed the recliner foot rest, and gained his feet. He chuckled to himself. Even Henley Hornbrook wasn't going to have to face these kinds of issues in his November election campaign. *I wonder if President Hornbrook would like to have a little talk,* thought LaGrande.

***

The sky was crystal clear and there was a crispness to the air. The leaves were changing color and already starting their fluttering parade to the earth here in the higher altitudes. The elk's massive head came up abruptly from its grazing on the short grass upon the ridge and, as it sought out the source of the sound it had heard, the antlers swung side to side, creating a magnificent silhouette against the deep blue hues of the background sky.

McCall, steadying himself against a tree, peered carefully through the optics at the beautiful animal, lined up the crosshairs just above the shoulder, took a deep breath and held it so as to steady his aim, and then gently pressed the trigger. *Click!* In an instant the elk registered that the sound was foreign, and therefore dangerous, and it bolted off through the trees, over the edge of the small hill, and out of sight.

Lowering the camera, McCall knew that he had captured a great shot. It wasn't quite the same as hunting, but there was a similar sense of accomplishment that came from the pure contest between man and beast, one seeking to capture and the other struggling to survive.

With Henley Hornbrook now in the White House, hunting trips were bound to become rare indeed. He had stolen a few quick days away at his cabin because the new administration would be involved in a lot of planning and strategy sessions related to the nation's recovery. McCall's new role was, as yet, unknown to him, but he suspected his dance card would be filled very shortly. Chances were it would be quite some time before he would be able to escape again.

He lifted the camera high enough to slip the strap from around his neck, put the lens cover on the end of the telephoto lens, and slipped it into his knapsack before turning and heading back to the cabin. When he came into the familiar clearing, he took a quick look around to make sure that the exterior was secure for the winter. He spotted Sunny through the front window, as she moved from the living room to the kitchen. He laid his small pack on the front porch, and moved quietly around to the side of the cabin. Crouching, he climbed up on a small woodpile directly under the window over the kitchen sink. When he heard the sound of dishes clattering in the stainless steel sink, he stood up quickly in front of the window.

Sunny's startled shriek could be heard plainly, even through the well-insulated walls and double-paned window. *"MCCALL! THAT'S IT! I'M GONNA KILL YOU!"*

He laughed so hard, he lost his footing on the small logs, and tumbled backward completely off balance. He crashed to the hard ground on his back just as Sunny flung open the side door and came storming out of the cabin. She saw him helpless from having the wind knocked out of his lungs and took the opportunity to jump astride his chest and start beating on his head with the kitchen hot pad mitt she had in her hand. He was half struggling to catch his breath and still fighting to stop laughing as he half-heartedly tried to fend off Sunny's blows.

"Okay, okay!" he pleaded. "Uncle!"

"Do you want to be buried here?" she exclaimed, "or shall I just leave your body out here for the bears and buzzards?" She was now just sitting on his stomach as he lay recovering with tears of laughter running down from the corners of his eyes.

"Sorry," he gasped, "but there really aren't any vultures around here, and I'd probably give the bears indigestion."

She whapped him on the nose with the mitt, and started to get to her feet, when he grabbed her arm and pulled her down where he could wrap his arms around her and give her a kiss of apology. She resisted only for a second before yielding. After a short time, she straightened up abruptly, and cried, "Oh, no you don't! You're not getting off that easy!" She hit him once more with the kitchen mitt, and stood up, stepping on his stomach as she left.

"Ooff!" he grunted, and started laughing again. As she slammed the door, he rolled to his side, stood up, and groaned with the effort of it. He shook his head in wonder, realizing how much he loved her, and for the first time in his life contemplated a different kind of future.

***

The small flames danced and flickered along the last of the embers in the huge rock fireplace as McCall handed Sunny her wine glass and settled onto the sofa next to her. She leaned comfortably against him as he put his arm around her shoulders. Neither said anything, as they were content to enjoy the quiet and the closeness of each other's company.

The moment to ask her seemed right to McCall. *Maybe a Rose Garden ceremony?* He leaned to his left and placed his glass on the end table by the darkened lamp, and just as he turned toward her, he heard the cell phone. *Damn*! he thought, angrily. Then he said, "What is it with this place? Do they have a camera hidden someplace?"

Sunny laughed and got to her feet. "Fear not," she said solemnly, "I'll get to the bottom of this." She giggled like a schoolgirl, after mimicking his phrase. Padding quickly across the room in her socks, she grabbed her phone, answered, then listened for a few moments before saying good-bye and hanging up. She was returning to the couch when McCall's phone rang, and he dragged himself reluctantly over to the kitchen to answer. When he returned, she said, "You, too?"

"Yeah. First thing in the morning." Tomorrow they would be heading back to Washington, D.C. The amendments had been drafted and would be submitted to Congress for their consideration. He sighed, and she came over to him. He took her in his arms and kissed her deeply. Breaking the kiss at last, he began, "Sunny, I—"

"I know," she said, putting her finger on his lips. "I just don't know what it is about us and this place."

He kissed her again, first on the mouth, and then on the neck below her right ear. "Fear not," he said softly, as his hand slid slowly and smoothly down her spine, "I'll get to the *bottom* of this."

Robert Wickes

Author's Notes and Acknowledgements

I took a somewhat bass-ackwards approach to writing this, my first novel. All completely fictitious figments of my twisted imagination, of course, the cast of players in this story was actually created long before there was a plot—or, for that matter, before the urge for literary creativity had even developed.

As the primary driver on countless road trips as a father of young children, time and miles often passed more easily while distracted from the countless shenanigans in the rear seats of the family minivan. It was on such a trip up Interstate 5, that I saw a sign in northern California proclaiming the names of two small towns to which the next exit would lead. The towns were "Henley" and "Hornbrook." I thought to myself, *Hmmm. Henley Hornbrook. What an interesting name that would be for a character in a book.* Soon I found myself looking at every sign I passed. By the time we reached our destination, the miles also yielded Halsey Brownsville, Winston Dillard, Sunny Turner (shortened from Sunnyside) and several others. A later trip from Seattle to Boise, Idaho, produced such standouts as Eagle McCall, Lewiston Weiser, Ukiah Hilgard, and the North Powder (a river) Union. I created the NPU group just because of the name. Other names, on other trips, were soon added to the list which grew and grew. It became a game. The only rule was that both parts of a name had to appear on the same sign. Some names—like Biggs Wasco (contributed by my brother's family on a joint road trip later), instantly suggested a personality. Sheldon Osborne Branford, derived from the name of three streets on a sign in the Los Angeles area, was added after writing had begun; the "S.O.B." initials were too good to pass up for a political story.

The Hornbrook Prophecy

Now, what to do with an entire phone book of character names? I thought about a disaster novel. But they've all been done—fires, floods, earthquakes, even comets. Then I realized that a disaster not only more likely but truly widespread would be social, not natural. And in modern America, a social disaster would have politics at the root of it. Modern American politics is, as my fighter pilot son would say, a target rich environment. The mischief is inherent, increasing, and infuriating as the Founding Fathers' ideas unravel further with each new Congress.

The stimulus which actually put me in front of the keyboard at last was not just the reading of Sir Alexander's prophecy about the fatal flaw of democracy, but the notion that the heroes would solve the chaos by starting their own country, a scenario the Postas Valley neighbors eventually contemplate. It was tempting to try. But in the end, like Hornbrook, I decided there was too much good in America's history to abandon it entirely. Call me an optimist. All that was necessary was to fix that so-called fatal flaw. As if. Call me crazy.

The first draft of the story was originally written between 2001 and 2003. I would be remiss if I did not acknowledge the invaluable attention it was given by Loni Crass, who was the first to suffer through my very unpolished first manuscript—more than once. Caitlin Werner, Paula Krapf, and Dr. Bob Rich added later editorial expertise. Naturally, like most first time authors, I failed to attract publishing interest. Ultimately, undaunted, I shelved it to work on a second book, an analysis of American politics viewed from Main Street, USA—*The Myth America Pageant: How Government & Politics REALLY Affect the Ordinary Joe*. Its modest success led me to ReaderViews' sterling author advocate, Irene Watson, who in turn led me to Kevin Aguanno and Multi-Media Publications Inc. who ventured to take a chance with Hornbrook et al.

Please note that the TEA Party group and the Tax Equality Act proposed in this story were originally suggested by one Mr. Gus Hellthaler during my Mad World class in 1996 and should not be construed to be associated with the real-life Tea Party political movement which began in 2009. We had it first!

I also need to thank my wife, Liz, for recognizing that the writing process is born of a passion not to be denied and that writers require eternal tolerance.

Finally, I need to thank my father who read an early draft and thereafter was continually prompting me to get it published before it was no longer fiction. My hope is that readers will help prevent that unhappy transition from fantasy to reality from actually happening.

It will be close.

About the Author

Robert Wickes is an optometric physician in private practice for more than three decades. With his wife of 36 years, he has two sons: an aspiring kindergarten teacher and an F22 fighter pilot. He has served his community as a Boy Scout leader, soccer coach, Rotarian, Chamber of Commerce President, and political volunteer. After coordinating a community education program called "It's a Mad, Mad, Mad, Mad World," he wrote *The Myth America Pageant: How Government & Politics REALLY Affect the Ordinary Joe,* an often amusing look at often-confusing national issues and the grand game of politics, blending history, common sense, and controversy in a thought-provoking, convention-challenging analysis for ordinary Americans. His essay, "Saving Private America," was published in *The Sentinel* of the U.S. Army.

His passion is liberty.

Did you like this book?

If you enjoyed this book, you will find more interesting books at
www.CrystalDreamsPublishing.com

Please take the time to let us know how you liked this book. Even short reviews of 2-3 sentences can be helpful and may be used in our marketing materials. If you take the time to post a review for this book on Amazon.com, let us know when the review is posted and you will receive a free audiobook or ebook from our catalog. Simply email the link to the review once it is live on Amazon.com, your name, and your mailing address -- send the email to orders@mmpubs.com with the subject line "Book Review Posted on Amazon."

If you have questions about this book, our customer loyalty program, or our review rewards program, please contact us at info@mmpubs.com.

a division of Multi-Media Publications Inc.

Terror in Manhattan
By Ross L. Barber

Jayne Keener is a young, single all-American girl who, like so many newcomers to the world of Cyberspace, finds herself drawn into the shadowy world of cybersex and adult chat rooms. Following the murder of a suave, mysterious Englishman she has met in a Manhattan bar, Jayne finds herself sucked ever deeper into the subculture of Internet chat rooms.

It is in one such room that she encounters Phillip H. Dreedle; professional hacker, convicted rapist and stalker. Suddenly, Jayne's once sane life is turned on its head, and not even her closest friends are what they seem.

ISBN-10:   1591460404
ISBN-13:   9781591460404
Price: $15.00

Available from Amazon.com or your nearest book retailer. Or, order direct at www.CrystalDreamsPublishing.com

Monkey Pudding: A Vietnam Hero's Story
By J.B. Pozner

Lieutenant Steve Simmons returned home from the Vietnam war to find his wife Jennifer in bed with another man. In an enraged scuffle, Jennifer falls down the stairs to her death. After psychiatric treatment in a VA hospital, Steve relocates in a new state with a new career and tries to put his life back together.

Then he meets Christina, heir to an international manufacturing corporation. Uncovering a plot on her life, Steve hires a detective and sets out to find the conspirators.

The story begins with gritty combat scenes in the jungles of Vietnam. The battles continue back home as Steve's post-war traumas are intensified by one bizarre twist after another. The fast pace continues to the dramatic conclusion where Steve may at last taste victory.

ISBN-10:   1591460077
ISBN-13:   9781591460077
Price: $12.00

Available from Amazon.com or your nearest book retailer. Or, order direct at www.CrystalDreamsPublishing.com

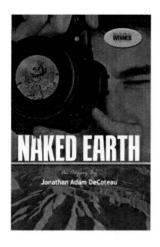

The Naked Earth
By Jonathan A. DeCoteau

Evan "Sindbad" Al-Mohummad specializes in photographing dead bodies for the military in the current Iraq war. Investigating a bizarre double homicide in Basra, he discovers, piece by piece, that the murder is the beginning of a genocide Western governments did nothing to stop.

Underworld warlords place the death mark upon him, impeding his investigation at every turn. Despite their efforts, Sindbad discovers that Basra's gangsters had complicity in the annihilation of his family's ancestral home, Jannah-Ri. Vowing revenge, Sindbad commits a crime against his fellow man so brutal that it costs him his humanity.

Back in America, he must live with his conscience until God leads him on a quest of self-discovery and redemption that will forever change the naked earth of Iraq.

ISBN-10:   1591461227
ISBN-13:   9781591461227
Price: $12.95

Available from Amazon.com or your nearest book retailer. Or, order direct at www.CrystalDreamsPublishing.com.

LaVergne, TN USA
23 May 2010
183621LV00003B/2/P